OTHER BOOKS AND AUDIOBOOKS
BY TRACI HUNTER ABRAMSON

UNDERCURRENTS SERIES

Undercurrents

Ripple Effect

The Deep End

SAINT SQUAD SERIES

Freefall

Lockdown

Crossfire

Backlash

Smoke Screen

Code Word

Lock and Key

Drop Zone

Spotlight

Tripwire

ROYAL SERIES

Royal Target

Royal Secrets

Royal Brides

Royal Heir

GUARDIAN SERIES

Failsafe

Safe House

Sanctuary

On the Run

In Harm's Way

DREAM'S EDGE SERIES

Dancing to Freedom

An Unlikely Pair

STAND-ALONES

Obsession

Deep Cover

Chances Are

Chance for Home

Kept Secrets

Twisted Fate

Proximity

Entangled

Mistaken Reality

A Change of Fortune

from best-selling author

TRACI HUNTER ABRAMSON

AN *Unlikely* PAIR

Covenant Communications, Inc.

Published by Covenant Communications, Inc.
American Fork, Utah

Printed in Mexico
First Printing: June 2021

28 27 26 25 24 23 22 21   10 9 8 7 6 5 4 3 2 1

ISBN: 978-1-52441-704-8

Praise for
TRACI HUNTER ABRAMSON

"A beautifully written romance by Traci Hunter Abramson, *An Unlikely Pair* brings us the story of two very different people coming together and accomplishing great things in the world of ice skating. Enjoy being drawn in by Abramson's aptly titled romance. A thrilling story packed with various aspects of the very different worlds of the main characters—ballet, hockey, and ice skating—all with their own disciplines. The main characters each with their own problems and struggles are brought to life, and we are able to form opinions and feelings toward each one, thanks to the deep and insightful descriptions of their thoughts and feelings. You will enjoy learning about the sacrifice and dedication it takes to be a success in the ice-skating arena. You will also see the great skill, grace, and strength required, and the not-as-much seen darker side of mind games played by competitors. Accompanied by the emotions of upset at the family tragedy and the love aspect in this story, the hopes and desires of the main characters are brought together in what I can only describe as a fabulous story."

—Readers' Favorite five-star review

"Traci Hunter Abramson is a master of her craft, an auto-buy author who never disappoints."

—Sarah M. Eden, *USA Today* best-selling author

"As an admirer of Traci Hunter Abramson's prolific talent, I once asked her how she does it. Her answer blew me away. She said, "I write as I work out on my treadmill." Now, that's devotion. Is it any wonder that this amazing author crafts one award-winning novel after another? Kudos to her as her writing journey continues with yet another awesome series."

—Kathi Oram Peterson, award-winning author of *Treacherous Legacy*

"Heart-stopping action, unexpected plot twists, brave and gallant heroes, warm humor, and sweet romance. It's no wonder readers—especially this one—love everything Traci Hunter Abramson writes. Her books have it all!"

—Sian Ann Bessey, award-winning author of *An Uncommon Earl*

"Traci's books are the perfect recipe: a good dose of suspense, a dash of romance, and a sprinkling of humor blended into a well-written tale sure to keep you turning the pages."

—Paige Edwards, author of *Danger on the Loch*

"Definitely in a league of her own, award-winning, mystery-and-suspense novelist Traci Hunter Abramson has carved out her own niche in the inspirational book market. As a former member of the CIA, her stories have broken molds and garnered praise locally, nationally, and internationally. Her versatility knows no bounds. She can write stories that feature sports and romance or high-stakes action and excitement. Using her vast experience and wealth of knowledge, she writes books that often feature characters involved with the FBI or CIA. Traci's stories give readers a chance to feel up close and personal to her fascinating characters, interesting settings, and riveting plots that will hook them from the first page and hold them on the edge of their seat until the very last."

—Michele Ashman Bell, author of *The Crown of Rosemund*

"When it comes to creating stories that blend suspenseful and romantic notes into symphonies that keep readers riveted—and wanting more—Traci Hunter Abramson is an absolute virtuoso."

—Stephanie Black, award-winning author of the Natalie Marsh Mystery series

For Lynn Gardner
Thank you for your guidance as I started on my writing journey

Acknowledgments

PEOPLE OFTEN ASK ME HOW long it takes me to write a book. This is the first book I ever crafted from beginning to end. It was my learning process of transitioning from a storyteller to a writer. Now, twenty-five years later, it is finally out of the drawer and onto the shelves. My thanks seem inadequate when looking back at the many people who helped me along this journey, but I want to acknowledge those who have supported me from the beginning.

My eternal gratitude goes to Rebecca Cummings, who patiently taught me how to write. Thank you to Lynn Gardner, who was willing to pass along my first manuscripts to her editor at Covenant. Thanks to my many editors who have worked with me over the years, especially Samantha Millburn. You are truly gifted and such a blessing in my life.

I also want to thank Ashley Gebert, Kami Hancock, Laura Combrink, and Annie Petersen for your input on the editorial writing quality committee, as well as Amy Parker and Lauryn Parker for the amazing work you do to get my books out into the world. Thanks to Robby Nichols and the rest of the Covenant family for supporting me throughout my career.

Thanks to my critique partners, Ellie Whitney, Paige Edwards, and Kyla Beecroft, for all your help in polishing this manuscript. And thank you, Sian Bessey, for helping me stay on track.

I also want to thank my family for supporting my dreams, especially my husband, Jon, and my children, Diana, Christina, Lara, Luke, and Gabe.

Finally, thank you to the readers who have encouraged me to continue doing what I love. I appreciate you more than you know.

Chapter ONE

Washington, DC
January 1982

FRIGID AIR, SKATES SCRAPING AGAINST the ice, the scent of stale popcorn. Amaliya Marcell sat in one of the twenty thousand seats of the Cap Centre and laced up her figure skates before she tugged her leg warmers into place and watched while twenty hockey players worked through their last drill.

As soon as they finished, they joined her father at center ice.

The great Robert Marcell. Amaliya still missed watching her father compete, but his transition from player to assistant coach to head coach had allowed her to enjoy her routine of spending time with her dad at work. She could hardly remember a Saturday when the Washington Capitals were home and she hadn't been here with him.

Travis, the goalkeeper, stepped off the ice and gave her a disapproving shake of his head. "You're wearing the wrong skates again."

"You sound like my dad."

"Coach knows what he's talking about," Travis said.

"Maybe for you, but I don't think I'm going to be joining a hockey team anytime soon." Amaliya stepped past him. "Figure skates are more my style these days."

"Too bad. With a bit more practice, maybe you could score on me."

Amaliya's eyebrows lifted. "I scored a goal on you last week."

"That was a lucky shot."

"That's what he always says," her dad said as he joined them.

Amaliya grinned. "Yeah, I know."

"Travis, get some rest. It's the kid's turn to play."

"Kid?" Amaliya stepped onto the ice and twirled to face her dad. "I hate to break it to you, but I'll be an adult next week."

"Don't remind me," Robert groaned.

"Good luck, Coach." Travis started toward the locker room.

"Thanks. I'm going to need it." Robert turned his attention to Amaliya and spoke in French, his preferred language, thanks to his upbringing in Quebec. "Are you going to play a little one-on-one with your old man?"

"Don't you have to check on your players?"

"I can spare a few minutes." He tapped his stick against the ice. "Show me what you've got."

"Okay." Amaliya combined her years of ballet training with growing up on the ice and executed a spin that resembled a pirouette.

"When you skate like that, you look like a ballerina on the ice."

Amaliya laughed. "I am a ballerina on the ice."

"Honey, I hate to break it to you, but most ballerinas can't do that once they put on ice skates."

"If you say so." She skated backward so she could still see her dad. "You're going to let me skate while you're in your meetings, right?"

Robert grabbed an extra hockey stick and held it out. "Play a little hockey with me first, and I might be persuaded."

Amaliya made a quick stop and returned to her father. She took the offering and grinned. "Deal."

Amaliya sorted through the mail on the entryway table until she reached an envelope with her name on it. The San Francisco Ballet. Amaliya read the return address a second time. With a rush of anticipation, she ripped open the envelope. Her fingers tightened on the letter when she read the first paragraph, and a squeak of excitement escaped her. "Mama!"

"I'm in the living room," Katerina called out in Russian.

Amaliya raced from the foyer through the arched doorway and held up the letter. "I got in! They said yes."

"Who?" Katerina asked. "The San Francisco Ballet?"

"Yes." Amaliya did a single pirouette. "I start in two weeks."

"I thought you told them when you auditioned that you can't start until you graduate."

"I did, but they need to fill the position now," Amaliya said. "I can finish school out there. They have a program for high school students."

"Milaya, I'm sorry," her mother began, using the familiar Russian endearment. "You need to wait until you graduate before you join a ballet company."

"But, Mama . . ."

Katerina crossed to her and put both hands on Amaliya's arms. "You are a beautiful dancer, and it is wonderful that they want you to join them, but—"

"Please, Mama." Desperate, she thrust the letter at her mom. "At least read through the information they sent before you decide."

"Fine. I'll read through the information, but I also want to talk to your father about this. I don't think he'll be happy about your leaving early either."

"Just promise you'll think about it."

"I promise."

Amaliya laced her toe shoes, her side of the debate already circling through her mind in multiple languages. Moving across the country to San Francisco wasn't her first choice, but the opportunity to spend her last semester of high school dancing was the culmination of years of hard work and dreams. She'd much prefer that to battling her way through calculus, even if it did mean leaving home early. As a former ballerina, her mother had to understand that this was a rare opportunity.

She padded across the wood floor of the spacious home studio. A barre stretched along one mirrored wall, with two tall windows at the far end of the room spilling in the light glistening off the snow in the yard.

Rather than cross to the barre to stretch, she moved to one of the windows and took in the breathtaking scenery. The gentle slope of her front lawn ended at the George Washington Parkway, the four-lane road the only interruption between her home in Alexandria, Virginia, and the wide bank of the Potomac River.

She should be grateful to have grown up with such abundance and so many opportunities, but right now, all she wanted was to be allowed to grow up.

Restless, she turned and faced the image of her dreams head-on. The photo had graced the wall of the studio for as long as Amaliya could remember: the great Katerina Petrova caught at the apex of a grand jeté.

As a twenty-two-year-old, her mother had captured Canadian and American hearts alike when she had performed *Swan Lake* on a North American tour with the Kirov Ballet. Katerina had given up performing several months before Amaliya was born, but she had passed on her heritage and love of ballet to her daughter. Amaliya had dreamed about following in her mother's ballet shoes for as long as she could remember. If only her mother would let her.

She could imagine it now—the stage, the lights, the dancers, the costumes. Amaliya lifted her hands over her head, twirling as though her movements could make her imaginings a reality.

"You're as graceful as your mother," her dad said in French from the doorway. "Your mom said she'll be down in a minute."

Amaliya's arms dropped, and she faced him. "Have you two talked about San Francisco?"

"You know perfectly well you need to talk to your mother about this before you drag me into the discussion," Robert said.

"Are you talking about me again?" Her mom's voice carried to them.

Her dad's face lit up like it always did when her mom walked into the room. "I was just admiring the grace you passed on to our daughter."

"San Francisco?" Amaliya asked, not willing to let her dad escape the conversation that easily.

"Amaliya, are you sure you don't want to come with us to New York?" her dad asked, changing the subject completely. "You'd only miss two days of school, and we could have an early celebration for your birthday."

Resigned that her father wasn't going to involve himself in the decision, Amaliya shook her head. "Sorry, Papa, but I have a big calculus test tomorrow."

"We'll miss you."

"You're only going to be gone two days," Amaliya said. "You'll be too busy to miss me."

"Never." Robert leaned down and kissed the top of her head.

"Is it okay if Stephanie comes over to study with me tomorrow?"

"As long as Eleanor is home, that's fine," Katerina said, referring to the housekeeper.

"Thanks."

"I need to watch some film," Robert said. "You two have fun."

As soon as he disappeared down the hall, Katerina slid a tape into the cassette player. Switching from French to her native Russian, she asked, "Are you ready to start?"

Amaliya crossed the room and put her hand on the barre. Gathering her courage, she asked, "Have you looked over the information about San Francisco?"

"Amaliya, why are you in such a hurry to grow up?"

"You were already with a ballet company when you were my age," Amaliya pointed out, well aware of her mother's journey from the Leningrad Choreographic School into the Kirov.

"I didn't have a choice," Katerina countered. "You do."

Amaliya jumped on her mother's words. "But I don't have a choice. You aren't giving me one. You and Dad are deciding for me."

Katerina closed the distance between them and gripped Amaliya's arms. "You're only seventeen years old."

"Almost eighteen," Amaliya corrected.

"Almost eighteen," Katerina conceded. "After you graduate from high school, the choice will be yours, but for now, is it too much to ask that you let us enjoy having you home for a little while longer?"

Impatience and frustration bubbled inside Amaliya. She hated when her mom used love, sincerity, and guilt as weapons.

Fighting for calm and reason, Amaliya took a moment before she said, "You defected from the Soviet Union so you could have your freedom. I'm only asking for you to let me have mine too."

Katerina stroked a hand over Amaliya's hair. "I defected because it was the only way I could be with your father," Katerina said. "There will be other auditions after you graduate."

"Will there? You can't know that. My chances of getting in were already slim. If it weren't so competitive, they would let me defer until I graduate, but they aren't letting me." Amaliya fought the surge of anger and clung to the dream that was slipping through her fingers. "I really want this. It's what I've worked for my whole life. You know that."

"I do know that. I also know what it's like to be away from your family and the emotional strain that comes from being part of a ballet company." Katerina gathered Amaliya close. "You're a beautiful dancer. You will have more opportunities. I promise."

Amaliya pulled free. "You're my mother. You have to say that."

"I was a professional ballerina long before I became your mother. Trust me. I know great talent when I see it." Katerina reached out and tucked a tendril of Amaliya's dark hair behind her ear. "You have a great talent."

The sincerity in her mother's voice chased away the worst of Amaliya's despair.

"It may seem like a long time," Katerina continued, "but in a few months, you'll get the chance to follow your dreams."

As much as Amaliya hated the emotional weapons her mother used, she had to admit, they were effective. Amaliya's resistance weakened, but she fought it. "Right now, it feels like it's never going to happen."

"It will. Trust me." Katerina pointed at the photo of her younger self. "One day, your photo will hang beside mine."

Amaliya's heart leapt at the prospect of being anywhere near as good as her mother. She pressed her lips together against her swirling emotions. "Do you really think I can ever be as good as you?"

"Of that, I have no doubt."

Chapter
TWO

KATERINA SLID INTO THE BACK of a taxi cab, eager to get her husband away from the hotel and the loss of tonight.

Robert took the seat beside her and shut the door. "Are you sure you want to go out? We can order room service."

"We're in New York, the same city where I first tasted freedom. We need to enjoy it."

"You're right." Robert stretched his arm across the back of the seat and drew her close. "It's hard to believe how much has changed in the past twenty-odd years."

"Yes, it is. Our baby is going to be eighteen on Sunday. I can't believe it."

"I know. I'm not ready for her to be all grown up." Robert gave his wife's shoulders a squeeze. "It seems like only yesterday that you gave her her first dance lesson."

"And you taught her how to skate." Katerina replayed her last conversation with Amaliya in her mind. A wave of guilt accompanied the memory. "Are we making the right decision?"

"About San Francisco?" Robert asked.

"Yes. Am I being selfish to want to keep her home a little longer?"

"Not any more than I am." Robert leaned down and kissed her temple. "You never had a chance at a normal childhood because of ballet. You've given her the chance to thrive in every area of her life."

"I've tried, but she's right. I had already been dancing professionally for three years when I was her age."

"She'll get the chance. Between you, Linda, and Beth, you know everyone worth knowing in the world of dance," Robert said, referring to her two closest friends. "If she can't get another audition on her own, the three of you will make sure she gets one when the time is right."

Robert's words rang true. Katerina may have walked away from performing almost two decades ago, but she had taught in all the years since then. And Beth and Linda still worked in the world of professional ballet.

"The house will be so empty when she leaves."

"Don't think about that right now. We'll cross that bridge when we get to it." Robert pulled her closer. "Besides, you'll still have me."

A horn honked, followed by the squeal of tires. The taxi driver slammed on his brakes, and headlights flashed through the car window. Metal crunched against metal. Katerina and Robert both jerked forward and impacted the front seat.

Katerina cried out. The car spun around, her world turning with it. Fear shot through her along with an instant litany of prayers. The car came to a jarring stop, and Robert and Katerina skidded across the seat again.

Stunned, Katerina struggled to sit up but couldn't. Her hand reached for her husband's and found a sticky moisture on his skin. In an instant, her concerns of a moment ago faded beneath a new terror: Robert lay bleeding beside her, and she couldn't feel her legs.

Amaliya balanced her calculus book on her lap, a video of *Swan Lake* playing on the television. She read the first sentence again, the words blurring together. Why was it that when her teacher explained it, everything made perfect sense, but as soon as she was alone, the words might as well have been written in Greek? If only she could translate everything from math-speak into simple English, French, or Russian. Was that too much to ask?

Stephanie had canceled; her parents had been unwilling to let her drive on the icy roads. Amaliya could imagine her own parents enforcing the same restriction. The winter storm that had hit the East Coast this afternoon had left the roads an icy mess. She hoped her parents didn't get stuck in New York, or they very well might miss her birthday.

Amaliya glanced at the clock hanging above the mantel. Eleven thirty. Her parents should have called to say good night by now. She gathered her homework and headed for the main hall, surprised that they hadn't followed their usual routine when they were both out of town.

A car pulled into the driveway, the lights flashing on the window over the stairwell. Amaliya stopped on the stairs. Who could be here this time of night? Eleanor had gone to bed over an hour ago. Amaliya had seen her dad on television at his game only a few hours ago, so clearly, her parents were still in New York.

The doorbell rang.

Cautiously, she crossed the entryway. She glanced through the window beside the door, her uneasiness heightening when she noticed a police car parked in her driveway. Had something happened at her dad's game tonight? The Caps were losing five to one at the end of the second period when she turned the game off. Her dad wasn't usually the type to go at the referee, but it wasn't unprecedented.

Amaliya unlocked the door and pulled it open. A female officer stood on the doorstep, wearing a badge, a gun, and a look of compassion.

Confusion and apprehension seeped through Amaliya. She swallowed hard and managed to ask, "Is something wrong, Officer?"

"Are you Amaliya Marcell?"

Dread clawed at her stomach. "Yes."

"Your parents were in a car accident tonight."

"Where? Are they okay?"

"They have been taken to the hospital in New York, but I'm afraid they are both in critical condition."

Amaliya grabbed the doorknob, her knees unsteady. She couldn't have understood the officer correctly. As much as she didn't want to hear the answer, she couldn't stop the question. "Are they going to make it?"

"I'm sorry, but I don't know," the officer said.

"This is a mistake." Amaliya's voice rose, and her heart hammered in her chest. "You must have the wrong house. I just saw my dad on TV a little while ago."

"There's no mistake. I'm sorry."

Critical condition? It couldn't be true. Her parents had been fine when she'd been watching the game tonight.

Ignoring the officer, she let go of the door and staggered to the stairs, where she lowered herself onto a step.

It was a dream, she assured herself. She must have fallen asleep watching TV. Something on the news must have triggered a nightmare. She dropped her head into her hands, the warmth of her fingers pressing against her face.

Her dad was invincible. And her mother was her idol. She couldn't imagine them being hurt so badly . . . or worse. God wouldn't do that to her family.

"Miss Marcell?"

Amaliya spread her fingers and peeked at the door. The police officer was still there. This wasn't a dream. It was a nightmare.

Tyler had to be dreaming. How could his sister do this to him? For more than a decade, they had trained together, competed together, prayed together. Early mornings at the ice rink, afternoons in the gym, followed by more ice time.

"Carolyn, you can't be serious," Tyler said. "You can't really want to give up after all we've been through."

"I'm not giving up. I'm making a change." Carolyn pointed at the ACE bandage on her foot. "We already missed our chance to go to worlds this year because of my ankle."

"That was a freak accident." Tyler fought back the pang of disappointment that still surfaced every time he thought about his sister's ill-timed injury. "The doctor said you should be back on the ice by the end of the week."

"Yes, but getting back on the ice is a lot different from being fully recovered. That could take months."

"We have plenty of time for you to recover. We're still two years from the Olympics."

"Over two years." Carolyn crossed her arms. "Tyler, I'm sorry, but Dan and I don't want to put our lives on hold for that long. We want to start a family. We want to see each other when the sun is up. We want to be able to go on vacation without coordinating with you and the ice rink first."

"If you want to have a family, go ahead. You could have a baby this year, and we would still have time for you to get back in shape for the Olympics," Tyler said, grasping for a solution. "It wouldn't be easy, but it isn't impossible."

"Listen to what you're saying," Carolyn said. "You want me to have a baby and then abandon him or her while we chase *your* dreams."

"I thought they were *our* dreams."

"They were, but my dreams have changed."

The countless hours of training, of nearly succeeding but coming up short flashed through his mind. "Maybe they have, but by changing your dreams, you're taking mine away."

"I'm not taking them away, but there is something else I haven't told you."

"I don't think I can handle any more news from you today."

"Dan had an interview with a company in California."

"You're moving?"

"Nothing is certain yet, but Dan said the interview went well." She put her hand on Tyler's arm. "I know this is a lot to take in, but I'll help you find a new partner. I'll help you train until you do."

"A new partner." Less than two years ago, they had come within a point of qualifying for the Olympics in pairs figure skating. "Do you have any idea how hard it is to find a world-class pairs skater who needs a partner?"

"I'm looking at one right now," Carolyn countered. "You aren't the only person this has ever happened to."

"Yes, but we both know timing is everything."

"Tyler, I love you, but I need to do this."

"I know. I'm sorry." Tyler rubbed his hands over his face. "I'm not trying to be selfish, but I can't imagine finding success with anyone else."

"It will all work out." Carolyn embraced him. "Remember, when God closes a door, He opens a window."

"It's going to have to be a pretty big window."

"Maybe, but I'll help you find it."

Chapter
THREE

AMALIYA COULDN'T SLEEP. SHE COULDN'T eat. She couldn't dance. She could barely breathe.

A weight had crashed over her when the policewoman had announced her parents' accident, and that weight had yet to ease. She doubted she would find her footing again until she could see for herself how they were.

Eleanor had spoken to the police in New York as well as to the hospital. According to the police, her parents had been in the back of a taxi when they'd been struck by a truck that had lost control. The taxi driver had walked away with a few scratches, but both of her parents had several broken bones and internal bleeding.

Details were sketchy, at best, and Amaliya didn't know if the doctors weren't giving Eleanor the facts or if the housekeeper was keeping them from her. Neither of her parents was well enough to speak to her on the phone, and as of yet, they remained in critical condition.

Amaliya paced across her bedroom before returning to sit in the window seat. She needed to hear her parents' voices. She needed to know for herself that they had survived.

The doorbell rang. Amaliya ignored it.

She didn't know how many friends and neighbors had stopped by to offer their sympathy. And she didn't care. Their words couldn't undo the accident or take away the fear that her parents might not ever come home.

Voices sounded in the entryway, followed by footsteps on the stairs. What was Eleanor thinking? Amaliya had told her not to let anyone in.

A knock on her door preceded a familiar voice. "Amaliya?"

Amaliya glanced toward the door as the doorknob turned. Linda Donnelly, her mother's closest friend, poked her head inside.

The compassion on Linda's face brought a new wave of tears to Amaliya's eyes. The need for human contact, for someone who understood, was enough for Amaliya to push to her feet and rush into Linda's outstretched arms.

"Oh, honey. It's going to be okay." Linda gathered her close, both of them clinging to each other as they might after a final curtain call on closing night. "It's going to be okay," Linda said again.

Amaliya sniffled, fighting back the tears. "I didn't know you were in town."

"Miles and I drove down right after we visited your parents in the hospital. We were able to visit your father anyway."

"How is he? How's Mama?"

"Your father is in a lot of pain, but he was able to talk to us for a few minutes. Both of his legs are broken, along with a few ribs, but he's stable." Linda led her to the window seat, and they sat together. "Your mother is still in critical condition. Her back is broken, and she had some internal bleeding."

Amaliya's breath caught. "Is she . . . ? Will she . . . ?"

"I don't know. The doctors operated and think they have the internal bleeding under control." Linda's breath hitched. "We should know more in the next day or two."

The thought of her mother not surviving cut through Amaliya. Not able to fathom such a reality, she focused on the woman in front of her. "Uncle Miles is here too?" Amaliya asked. She knew the aunt and uncle titles her parents gave to Miles and Linda were honorary, but now, with her only family locked away from her in a hospital, Amaliya treasured that connection.

"Miles is bringing in our bags. We plan to stay the night. And we'll take you up to New York to see your parents as soon as they're up for visitors."

Relief swept through her. "Thank you."

Linda stood and motioned to the door. "Eleanor said you haven't eaten anything today. Let's go downstairs and fix some dinner."

"I'm not hungry."

"You need to eat," Linda insisted. "It's either come downstairs with me or deal with your uncle Miles."

Amaliya only debated a minute. Knowing Miles, he would come upstairs, throw her over his shoulder, and carry her to the kitchen. "Fine, but I don't think I can eat."

"Your parents wouldn't want you to starve yourself. Trust me."

"I don't think my parents ever thought something like this could ever happen to them."

"Maybe not, but after our talk with your father, we do have some things we need to discuss." Linda nudged Amaliya toward the door. "Come downstairs, and we can talk about it over dinner."

Tyler shivered as he circled the rink and breathed in the crisp air. The New York City skyline rose above him, the park an oasis in the center of the chaos. The traffic had certainly been chaotic this morning when he and Carolyn had made the hour drive from Connecticut.

He shivered again and tucked his gloved hands inside his coat pockets. He couldn't remember the last time he had skated outside.

"Double axel," Carolyn called out when he approached her.

Tyler complied, transitioning smoothly to skate backward. He watched over his lead shoulder to navigate between the morning skating lessons, waiting until he reached a clear patch of ice before executing the jump. He instinctively looked beside him to compare his landing with his partner's only to remember that was why he was here. He didn't have a partner.

He circled the rink again. A girl who couldn't be more than five did a T-stop, her teacher praising her. The girl's cherubic face broke into a wide grin.

Tyler couldn't help but smile too. It seemed like forever ago when he had been learning to skate at the tender age of three, but the joy wasn't lost on him. Despite the early mornings and the hours of training, he still loved everything about the sport. Not that the guys he graduated from high school with would ever admit figure skating was a sport. Then again, Tyler supposed if he ended up with an Olympic medal hanging around his neck, those guys might reconsider their positions.

Carolyn approached him. "Are you ready? Tammy is here."

Tyler glanced in the direction of the entrance. A teenager with a skating bag over one shoulder approached, her posture erect, her red hair pulled back in a ponytail. A petite woman walked beside her and pointed at Tyler and Carolyn.

"She looks pretty young," Tyler said.

"She's almost sixteen, but she made it to sectionals last year."

"Has she ever skated pairs?"

"No." Carolyn put her hand on Tyler's arm. "Don't worry. She's only one of the people we have on our list."

"Right."

"Promise you'll be open-minded."

"I promise to try."

"Come on. Let's go meet her."

Carolyn skated across the ice, and Tyler tried to muster some enthusiasm for this next chapter in his skating career.

"Six months?" Amaliya stared at Linda and Miles, certain she had misheard them. "My dad is going to be stuck in New York for six months?"

"Yes," Miles said. "For your mother, it will be much longer."

Now she was sure she was hearing things, but at least they were talking as though her mother would still be alive to be part of her future. That alone gave her hope. "Why would Papa need to stay in the hospital so long? Broken legs don't take six months to heal."

"Your father's injuries are significant enough that he's going to need to spend some time in rehab. Your mother will need a good deal of specialized therapy as well." Linda put her hand on Amaliya's arm. "The truth is they're both lucky to be alive."

"Will my mom ever be able to walk again?"

"That's a question for the doctors," Linda said.

"I can't believe this is happening. What am I supposed to do?" Amaliya asked. "I can't imagine staying here in Virginia and not being able to visit them for so long."

"You have three options," Linda said. "The first is stay here and finish your senior year. Second, you can accept the offer from the San Francisco Ballet."

She couldn't be hearing Linda right. Her mother had been adamant she finish high school. The dreams she had fought for dangled in front of her, but Amaliya couldn't summon the energy to grab them. "Mama wanted me to finish high school."

"Yes, your mom did want you to finish. The third option is . . ."

A silent communication passed between Miles and Linda before Miles said, "You can move to Connecticut and live with us."

"Live with you?"

"We know none of these situations is ideal . . ." Linda began.

Amaliya tried to envision all three scenarios Linda and Miles had laid out before her. Stay in Virginia and pretend life was normal while her parents struggled through their recoveries, move to San Francisco like she had originally planned, or leave all her friends behind and move to a new school for the last semester of her senior year. She couldn't imagine dancing right now, nor did she want to live at home without her parents.

"If I move to Connecticut, would I be able to visit my parents in New York?"

"Of course." Linda nodded. "It only takes an hour to get into the city from our house."

"If you move in with us, that would also help your parents' financial situation," Miles added.

"What do you mean?" Amaliya asked.

"Obviously, your dad won't be finishing out the season with the Capitals, and your parents will have a lot of medical bills to deal with. Insurance should cover most of it, but it takes time to work through the red tape." Miles took a sip of water, but Amaliya wasn't sure if he was thirsty or if he was struggling with the difficult subject. "If you aren't here in Virginia, we could rent this house for the next six months or so."

"Rent our house?" Amaliya shook her head. "I don't want strangers living here."

"It wouldn't be a stranger," Miles said. "I talked to the Capitals' management. They're bringing in Will Rowbury to replace your dad for the rest of the season. Your dad's players are struggling right now too. The front office thought it would be an easier transition for the team if they brought in a former player who has coached with your father."

"And you want him to live here?"

"That's right. If he could rent from you through the end of the season, that would allow him to keep his house in New Jersey in case he wants to go back to coaching at Princeton after your dad is well enough to take over his job again."

"Will Dad get well enough to work again?"

"I hope so."

Amaliya closed her eyes against the uncertainty. Everything was changing so fast. First her parents' health. Now her home and school.

A hand squeezed her shoulder.

Amaliya opened her eyes and faced reality.

"I thought we could let Will rent the main level and ask him to leave the upstairs intact," Miles said. "There's the second master suite down here, along with a guest room. Not to mention, your dad's office is already set up for Will to be able to review film."

"It's only him and his wife," Linda added, "so we don't have to worry about kids damaging anything."

Amaliya blew out a breath. "Is my dad okay with this?"

"Yeah, he is. I talked to Will already. He wants to rent the house until the season ends. That will either be through May or mid-June, depending on how far the Caps go in the playoffs," Miles said. "All we're waiting on is a decision from you."

"It sounds like moving in with you is the best choice," Amaliya said.

"We don't want to do anything you're uncomfortable with," Linda said, "but this appears to be the best solution."

"When do we have to leave for Connecticut?"

"We'll leave the day after tomorrow," Miles said. "That will give us tomorrow to get the house ready for Will and to pack what you and your parents will need for the next six months."

A new wave of tears threatened. "I can't believe I'm not going to be living here."

Linda squeezed her shoulder again. "We know it will be an adjustment, but we're here for you."

Amaliya pressed her lips together and nodded. She pushed back from the table. "I guess I'd better start packing."

"Do you need some help?" Linda asked.

"I'm okay for now."

"We're here if you need us," Miles offered.

"I know. Thanks."

Chapter FOUR

SQUEAKING FOOTSTEPS, A BRIGHT LIGHT overhead, unfamiliar voices. Katerina's head pounded, and her mind tried to make sense of it all.

Someone spoke, but through the fog in her brain, she struggled to grasp the meaning of the words.

"Katerina, can you hear me?" a male voice asked.

She understood the words now, but her confusion didn't ease. Where was she? How did she get here? Where was Robert?

Robert! The squeal of tires, the flash of headlights, two vehicles colliding. The images flashed in her mind, and her breath caught. She struggled to open her eyes. "Robert."

"He's okay." The man beside her put a comforting hand on her arm. "Take it easy. You need to stay still."

Katerina tried to turn her head, but she couldn't.

"I'm Dr. Caldwell. You're in the hospital," he said. "Do you remember what happened?"

"Accident."

"That's right." He pulled a small flashlight out of his pocket. "Let me take a look here."

He shone the light in her eyes, aggravating the pain centered there. After he slipped the flashlight into his pocket, he took her hand in his. "Can you squeeze my fingers?"

She did as he asked.

"Good. Now the other hand." He repeated the process. He picked up a pen from the table beside her bed, then flipped up her blanket to expose her feet. "I'm going to check your reflexes," the doctor said, then looked down. "Did you feel that?"

"Feel what?" Katerina tried to see what the doctor was doing, but with her head held in place, she couldn't move.

"What about that?" Dr. Caldwell asked.

Katerina caught a glimpse of movement, and she waited for the doctor to continue his exam. Nothing happened. What was the doctor waiting for? Several seconds passed. More movement. Finally, Dr. Caldwell replaced her blanket over her legs. He straightened, and his eyes met hers. The look of compassion brought with it understanding. Panic bubbled insider her. It couldn't be . . . "I can't feel it. I can't feel anything."

The doctor pocketed the pen and cleared his throat.

"Am I . . . ?" She swallowed hard against the tears that threatened. "Will I be able to walk again?"

"I don't know." Dr. Caldwell stepped closer so she could see him more easily. "Your spinal cord is intact, but I don't know how badly it was damaged. I'd like to perform surgery tomorrow morning to see if we can repair the damage."

"Will the surgery give me my feeling back?"

"I hope so, but there aren't any guarantees."

A tear spilled over. Not prepared to deal with her own reality, she asked, "My husband. How is he?"

"He has multiple broken bones, including both legs. He is recovering down the hall."

"I want to see him."

"I'm sorry, but his leg is in traction, and we can't move you until we're sure doing so won't cause any further damage."

"When?" Her headache intensified, a new panic rising. "When can I see him?"

"Soon. For now, try to rest. I'll be back to check on you later this afternoon."

Katerina tried to nod but couldn't. Instead, she closed her eyes against the possibilities and the pain.

Tyler held an ice pack to his thigh, the cold taking away the worst of the pain. The tryout today with his latest prospective partner had proven his point. Finding a pairs skater who needed a partner was hard enough. Finding one who matched him was nearly impossible.

For three days straight, he and Carolyn had driven into New York City to search for a new partner for him. Eight tryouts, and not one of them was even close to being the right fit.

The contusion on his leg was only one of the minor injuries he had sustained while working with the various skaters. Tyler moved the ice pack to his shoulder.

When the sportscaster came on the news, Tyler stood and turned up the volume. Basketball highlights came first, followed by a story about the New York Jets' injured quarterback.

Tyler straightened when a photograph of him and Carolyn popped up on the right side of the screen.

"We have a new development in the world of pairs figure skating. Sources revealed today that Tyler Linden was in New York this week meeting with a number of skaters. A source close to the Lindens confirmed that Carolyn Carter has announced her retirement. The rush is on for who the lucky lady will be to replace her. As you know, the brother-sister duo placed sixth in the world championships last year and were among the favorites to represent the United States in the Leningrad Olympics in two years."

Carolyn walked in and crossed to the television.

"We were in the news today," Tyler told her as the newscaster continued.

"In other sports news, hockey great Robert Marcell and his wife, Katerina, remain in the hospital in serious condition—"

Carolyn shut off the television.

"Someone confirmed that you're retiring, Do you think Scarlett has been talking to the press?" Tyler said, referring to their coach.

"No. That was me."

"What? Why would you do that?" Tyler asked. "I thought we agreed to wait until we found your replacement."

"Tyler, I'm sorry, but after seeing the best New York had to offer, we need to get the story out so we can cast a wider net."

"So now you want to take applications from skaters no matter where they live?" Tyler raked his fingers through his hair. "We aren't set up to house an extra skater here. Nor would I want to live with my partner."

"You lived with me," Carolyn said. "Besides, my old room is available if someone needs to live here while you train."

"I don't know about this."

Carolyn sat on the couch beside him. "I know this isn't easy, but the right partner is out there. We'll find her eventually. I'm sure of it."

Tyler tried to grab onto some of his sister's optimism. Resigned to the unorthodox method of looking for a new partner, he asked, "Can you do me a favor?"

"What?"

"Can we wait a few days before we set up another tryout?" Tyler moved the ice pack from his shoulder back to his thigh. "I need some time to heal before I go back into the rink for another round."

"Fair enough."

Amaliya sat on her floor and slid books from her bookshelf into the box beside her. *Anna Karenina* in Russian, a French copy of *Giselle*, her high school yearbooks from the past three years, and an eclectic selection of paperbacks in a variety of languages.

She supposed her choice of books was a testament to her multicultural upbringing. She hadn't realized until she was well into elementary school that her friends spoke only one language. In her world, English was rarely spoken unless she and her parents were in public.

Amaliya added a few more books. Lifting the box, she carried it into the hall and set it by her suitcases.

She glanced at the double doors at the end of the hall. Her parents' room. The pressure in her chest tightened, and she blinked against the tears that threatened.

Forcing herself to move forward, she opened the doors and inhaled the familiar scents. Her mom's perfume. Her dad's cologne. The potpourri on the dresser.

She passed through the room and walked into the closet. Even though Linda and Miles had already packed bags for each of her parents, her dad's side of the closet had as many hockey jerseys as anything else, while her mom's side boasted a unique combination of dresses, leotards, and Capitals shirts.

Amaliya selected one of her dad's jerseys to take with her and turned to leave. A cedar box on the closet shelf caught her attention. She reached up to retrieve it and opened the lid, her heart squeezing in her chest. Nestled in tissue paper lay her mother's ballet slippers, the same ones she had with her the day she defected from the Soviet Union.

Tears trickled down Amaliya's cheeks as she fingered the satin toe shoes. Would her mother ever be able to dance again? The realization that Amaliya hadn't packed her own ballet shoes struck her. The day before her parents' accident, she had begged them to let her dance full time. Now she couldn't imagine strapping on a pair of ballet slippers ever again. How could she ever experience the joy and magic of ballet without her mother sharing that world?

Carrying the jersey and the cedar box, Amaliya left her parents' room. She added the last few items to her box of books and carried it downstairs.

Linda and Eleanor stood at the kitchen counter, packing food into a cooler. A pang of longing rose within Amaliya as she considered the housekeeper, who had been with her family since Amaliya's birth; she would remain here while Amaliya moved half a dozen states away.

Miles walked in from the garage. "Are you about ready?" he asked.

"Yeah. The rest of my suitcases are in the hall upstairs."

"Go ahead and put that box in the car. I'll get the rest."

"Thanks." Amaliya walked outside and put the box in the backseat of Miles's car.

Linda followed a moment later, holding the cooler. "Here. Can you squeeze this in the backseat too? I think we're going to need the trunk space for your luggage."

Amaliya took the cooler from her and circled the car so the cooler would be next to her seat.

Miles emerged from the house a moment later carrying a suitcase in each hand and a duffel bag on each shoulder. "I think this is everything. Can you two take a last look around to make sure we didn't forget anything?"

"Sure." Amaliya walked back into the house, nostalgia overcoming her. For the next six months, her home would belong to someone else.

Eleanor looked up when she heard the door and must have understood Amaliya's unspoken turmoil. She closed the distance between them and gathered Amaliya in her arms. "Your house will be exactly as it is now when you come home. I'll take care of everything."

"Thank you, Eleanor."

"Be good for Miles and Linda. They're good people." Eleanor kissed the top of her head. "Give your new school a chance."

"I'll try." Amaliya stepped back. "I'm going to take another look around." She made her way through the living room, stopping when she reached the fireplace. Several photographs graced the mantel, including one of her and her parents at a Capitals game, one of her while dancing *The Nutcracker* last year, and one of her father during his hockey-playing days.

Amaliya took the one of her and her parents and carried it with her to her room. With the exception of her nearly empty closet and the books missing off her shelf, Amaliya's room looked the same as it had before she'd started packing.

She slowly closed the door and headed downstairs. Her footsteps slowed when she reached the dance studio, where she and her mother had shared so many dreams.

Amaliya took one step inside but couldn't go any farther. Her eyes lifted to the photograph of her mother, so agile, so graceful, so not in a wheelchair. Another piece of Amaliya's heart chipped away. Her mom couldn't be paralyzed. She just couldn't.

Grasping for positive thoughts, she closed the door and forced herself to move forward. She carried the photograph with her as she passed back through the living room and headed for the door. Her life was about to change. She hoped she was ready for it.

Chapter
FIVE

Tyler sat across the red vinyl booth from Marie Averett, one of the two skaters he trained with every day. He hoped the impromptu lunch date at the diner would give him a much-needed break from reality. Practicing without a partner wasn't working for him, but he dreaded the auditions his sister had already set up for the end of the week.

"I still can't believe Carolyn announced her retirement." Marie tapped a glossy red fingernail on the plastic-coated menu.

"I haven't been able to wrap my brain around it either. It's hard to imagine skating with someone else."

"Maybe you shouldn't skate with someone else," Marie said. "You're a strong enough skater to switch to singles."

Tyler tried to visualize skating on his own in front of a crowd. "I don't think that would be a good fit for me."

"Why not?"

"Would you suddenly want to switch to pairs skating?"

"Of course not. The skills are completely different, especially for women," Marie said. "I'm already good enough to make it to the top on my own. I don't need a partner to get me there."

"I'm afraid I do."

"Not really. It's not like you can't do a triple, and you have the required elements for competition." Marie put her hand on his. "Besides, it'll be weird for you to skate with someone else while we're dating. You should try skating in the men's competition."

"It wouldn't be the same." How could he explain the joy of timing his moves perfectly to his partner's, of taking two halves and making a whole? "Carolyn's setting up some more auditions. There has to be someone out there who needs a partner."

"I don't know. It's never easy to find someone who is the perfect fit."

A seed of despair settled inside him. "Yeah. I know."

The overwhelming scent of industrial cleaners assaulted Amaliya the moment she walked into the hospital. Miles carried the two suitcases he and Linda had packed for her parents. After a quick stop at the information desk to verify the room numbers, they took the elevator together.

"Let's check on your dad first," Miles said as they stepped off on the correct floor. "He's more likely to be awake."

Amaliya followed him past nurses, doctors, IV stands, and an empty gurney. Fear and dread rose within her as she approached her father's room. Finally, she would see for herself that her father had survived, that he would be okay. She walked inside, stopped, and stared.

Knots tangled in her stomach. Miles and Linda had warned Amaliya about the severity of her parents' injuries, but nothing could have prepared her for the sight before her.

A bandage covered the right side of her father's face, and one leg was suspended at a thirty-degree angle. The other leg lay flat but was also in a cast. His right arm was wrapped with white gauze.

Amaliya absorbed the shock and disbelief that flowed through her as she faced the truth. Her father wasn't leaving anytime soon. Whatever hope she had entertained that Miles and Linda had exaggerated the severity of his condition evaporated. Her father lay broken in the center of the stark-white room.

"Robert?" Miles called his name, and her dad's eyes fluttered open. "We brought someone to see you."

Amaliya forced herself to cross to her dad, keeping her gaze away from the IV in his arm. "Hi, Papa."

"Amaliya." His voice came out in a low whisper. "You're here."

"I'm here." Amaliya took his hand. "I'm so sorry."

"Have you seen your mama?"

"Not yet. We're going to visit her next."

He squeezed her hand. "Tell her I love her."

"I will."

Her dad's eyes fluttered closed, and his hand went limp.

Miles put her dad's suitcase in the corner. "Come on. Let's go check on your mom."

Amaliya's breath backed up in her lungs. That was it? The man who had once dominated the hockey arena was now only capable of fifteen seconds of conversation? She gave his hand another squeeze, placed it gently back on the bed, and blinked against the threatening tears.

"Come on, sweetie." Linda tapped her arm. "We'll come back in a week or two. By then, he should be able to talk with you longer."

Amaliya cast one last glance at her father before she followed Linda into the hall.

"Your mom is this way." Linda motioned back the way they had come.

"Can't the hospital let them be in the same room?" Amaliya asked.

"Once they get out of their specialized care units, they might be permitted to be in the same room, but right now, they both need private rooms and their special care teams until they're stronger," Linda said.

Miles stopped beside the correct room. "I'll wait here so you can make sure it's okay for me to come in."

Linda knocked twice before she pushed the door open and walked inside. Amaliya gathered her courage and followed.

Her eyes widened when she saw her mom. Unlike Robert, Katerina had only a small bandage on her temple but, otherwise, looked completely normal. Well, normal except for the IV running from her arm and the odd contraption on her head that appeared to be keeping her from moving.

"Mama?"

No response.

Amaliya moved to the side of her mother's bed and took her hand. "Mama," she repeated.

Her mother's eyelids fluttered but didn't open.

A doctor entered. Miles followed.

"I'm sorry," the doctor said. "She's still sedated after the last surgery."

"What last surgery?" Amaliya asked.

"We operated again early this morning to try to relieve the pressure on her spinal cord."

"Is she going to be okay?" Amaliya asked. "Is she going to be able to walk again?"

"I hope so, but at this point, we're uncertain."

Tears surfaced, and Amaliya pressed her lips together.

Linda's voice was thick with emotion when she asked, "When will we know if the surgery worked?"

"It could be right away, or it could be another week or two. I'm afraid only time will tell," the doctor said. "We'll keep her spine immobilized as much as possible while she heals. Until she wakes up, we won't know if this procedure was successful."

"What happens now?" Miles asked.

"My expectation is that she will remain in traction for several months, especially if we're able to restore feeling in her lower extremities." His gaze landed on Amaliya. "You're her daughter?"

"Yes."

"Leave your phone number with the nurse. I'll call as soon as I have anything new to share."

Amaliya swallowed hard and forced out her words. "Thank you."

The doctor put his hand on Amaliya's shoulder. "We'll take good care of her."

Amaliya's throat constricted so she couldn't form words, but she nodded. The doctor left, and Amaliya focused on her mother once more. She had to get better. She just had to.

Amaliya awoke in her new room in her new house, unsure what she was supposed to feel. Tomorrow, she would legally be an adult. Her parents were both stuck in hospital beds, someone she barely knew was living in her house in Virginia, and on Monday, she would start at a new school after moving for the first time in her life. Concern for her parents merged with the anticipation of new beginnings.

Her eyes scanned the large attic room, the same guest room she had stayed in every time her family had come to visit the Donnellys. The space was large enough that it could have created two modest-sized rooms rather than one large one, but at one time, this space had doubled as Linda's dance studio. As a result, two tall mirrors lined the far wall, a barre mounted in front of them.

Linda hadn't danced for years, her artistic endeavors now focused on her efforts with the New York Arts Council. Amaliya had hoped Linda's connections would eventually help her gain a spot with the New York City Ballet. Now, Amaliya didn't know what she wanted.

How many times, she wondered, had she and her mother accompanied Linda into the city to attend the ballet? Her father typically opted to stay with Miles, taking advantage of the opportunity to catch up with his longtime friend. The two men had started out as teammates. Shortly after her mother had defected, Miles had retired from competition and taken a coaching job with the Washington Capitals. His first order of business had been to trade for her father.

Robert Marcell had enjoyed a lengthy career before he had replaced Miles as the head coach three years ago.

A glance at the suitcases stacked by the door pushed Amaliya into motion. This was her room now. She kicked off the heavy quilt. The chill in the air prompted her to move quickly to where her suitcase lay.

Amaliya dug out a pair of jeans and a long-sleeved shirt. After changing out of her pajamas, she walked downstairs, where Miles and Linda were sitting at the kitchen table, a plate of bacon and a platter of pancakes between them. The scents wafting up from the platter awakened the appetite she had lost over the past week.

"Oh, you're up. Come eat something." Linda motioned at the spot where a plate and fork had been set for her.

Amaliya slid into the empty seat.

"I thought you would sleep in today." Linda passed her the pancakes.

"The sun is up." Amaliya served herself some breakfast.

"You're like your dad," Miles said. "He was always up at the crack of dawn."

"Or before." Amaliya added syrup to her pancakes.

"Or before," Miles agreed.

"I'm heading into the city in a bit," Linda said. "Would you like to come?"

Amaliya translated Linda's meaning. She was heading to the theater, to the ballet. "Would you be able to drop me off at the hospital?"

"I'm sorry, but I'm taking the train in, and I'll be on the other side of the city," Linda said.

"I'm not sure your folks are up for visiting yet anyway," Miles said. "You saw how they were yesterday."

"I guess I'll stay here."

"You don't want to sit around here by yourself. You can come with me." Miles crunched a piece of bacon.

"Come with you where?"

"The rink."

"Miles coaches a kids' hockey team," Linda said. "They have practice this morning."

"I don't know . . ."

"Grab your skates. We leave in fifteen minutes." Miles finished his last bite of pancakes and pushed back from the table. Before Amaliya could protest, he stood and left the room.

"I guess I'm going to hockey practice."

"I guess you are."

Tyler executed a double lutz-double toe loop combination, concentrating on the position of his top leg during his recovery.

"Almost. It's still a little low." Scarlett approached and moved his leg into the proper position.

Tyler repeated the skill again only to realize what he hadn't done. He hadn't looked. Only a week had passed since Carolyn's announcement, and already, he had gotten out of the habit of checking for his partner's position in relation to his own.

Marie came to a stop beside him. "Are you sure you don't want to try singles?"

"I'm sure," Tyler said instinctively. "Carolyn said she has some new prospective partners lined up. One of them has to work out."

"Marie, I want to see your sit spin," Scarlett interrupted. She turned to Tyler. "You too."

Tyler complied, deliberately waiting for Marie to start her move before following suit.

He practiced one skill after another as Scarlett divided her time between him and the two other skaters she coached in the early-morning session. When practice finally came to an end, Tyler made his way to the bench and sat down to remove his skates. Marie sat beside him.

"I'm heading over to the diner to grab some breakfast," Marie said. "Want to join me?"

"Thanks, but I can't. I promised Hank I would run the Zamboni for him this morning."

"Another time, then."

"Yeah. Sure." Tyler pulled his tennis shoes on. "I'll see you later." He left Marie and headed to the office to store his skates.

He made his way to the Zamboni, letting his thoughts wander as he prepared to clean the ice. He wasn't sure why Marie was pushing the idea of him converting to a singles skater. She'd said it would be weird to see him with someone else, but did she really think he would be better on his own, or did she just not like the idea of him skating with a woman who wasn't his sister? Maybe she was afraid a new partner would shift their on-again, off-again relationship to the permanent off status. Not that their casual dating had ever come close to entering the exclusive category. Regardless of her reasons, Tyler suspected this morning wouldn't be the last time his skating options would come up.

He finished his last sweep with the Zamboni as the first kids arrived for hockey practice. Miles Donnelly walked in, several kids chatting with him as he made his way forward. Tyler's gaze skimmed over the new arrivals until he noticed the brunette following behind the crowd. Her long, dark hair was pulled back into a ponytail, her fair skin radiant. Tyler guessed her to be a couple years younger than him, maybe eighteen or nineteen. She was probably driving her younger brother to practice, but Tyler didn't remember seeing her here before.

She hesitated when she reached the rink, as though she weren't quite sure what to do now that she was here. The oddity that she had a duffel bag with her struck him since the only practices scheduled over the next hour and a half were for the youth hockey league.

Tyler's stomach grumbled. Forcing his attention back to his planned schedule for the day, he headed to the office and retrieved the muffin he had brought from home, then took a bite. Time to kick back while he had the chance. With Carolyn planning to bring another prospective partner to try out after free skate today, he needed all the rest he could get.

Amaliya opened her skate bag, memories flooding through her. She fingered the hockey skates inside, debating whether to wear those or the figure skates she preferred. On the far side of the rink, several boys gathered next to the hockey goal. Beside her, Miles finished lacing up his own skates. He pointed at her bag. "Hockey skates. You can wear those other things during free skate if you want."

"Those other things?"

"Hurry up. Practice starts in two minutes."

Miles's no-nonsense tone cut through the nostalgia and spurred her into action. She retrieved her hockey skates and slipped them on, lacing each one in turn.

As soon as Amaliya stood, Miles stepped onto the ice and joined the boys by the goal. Amaliya followed.

"Okay, boys. Listen up. Amaliya here is going to show you how I want you to do this." Miles turned to Amaliya. "I want you to skate the edge of the rink the way your Dad used to when someone was trying to trap him."

Pushing aside the image of her father lying broken in his hospital bed, Amaliya nodded. She skated the drill her father had taught her when she was a little girl, skating close to the edge of the rink, then stopping and making quick turns to keep the imagined opponent from trapping her against the side.

One by one, the boys repeated the drill, often falling in the spin-outs that Amaliya skated instinctively.

"I remember when your dad taught you this. You couldn't have been more than four or five."

The sweet memory flowed through her. "Afterward, if he couldn't catch me, he would take me out for ice cream."

"He always has had a sweet tooth," Miles said. "Maybe we can sneak some ice cream in to him next time we visit him."

Her mood brightened. "He'd like that."

Over the next hour, Amaliya assisted Miles with various drills and helped teach basic skating technique. It wasn't until the practice ended that she realized she had forgotten why she was in Connecticut. The shock of that fact crashed over her, and she wasn't sure if she should be grateful that she was able to find a sense of normalcy for a moment or concerned that something was wrong with her that she could forget her parents' struggles.

"I've got to look over the schedule with the rink manager this afternoon," Miles said as the boys dispersed to go home with their parents. "Free skate starts in a few minutes. You can skate if you want."

"Maybe I will." She put her hand on his arm. "Thanks for inviting me today."

"Your parents want you to be happy. Don't let their trials get in the way of you living your life."

"Thanks." She swallowed against her rising emotions. "I'll try."

A dozen kids passed the skating office, a sure indication that hockey practice was over. Tyler finished sharpening a pair of skates and shut off the machine.

"Hey, Tyler. Where's Hank?"

Tyler glanced up at Miles standing at the open window of the skate-rental office.

"He's on the Zamboni. Kimberly is running late, so it was either that or skate rentals until she gets here," Tyler said. "He should be done in a few minutes."

"I gather you got stuck with skate rentals."

"Gotta pay for ice time somehow."

"I hear you."

"How are you doing?" Tyler asked. "I haven't seen you around for a few days."

"Linda and I have been out of town." The muscle in his jaw twitched before he added, "Two friends of ours were in a bad car accident."

"I'm so sorry. Are they okay?"

"They're alive, but they're both in pretty bad shape. Katerina can't feel her legs, and Robert has a half dozen broken bones. It'll take some time before either of them will be able to walk again, assuming they can both get to that point."

"That's rough. I take it you're close."

"Yeah. Robert played for me with the Caps, and his wife and Linda are close."

"Do they have any kids?"

"A daughter," Miles said. "She's living with us now. She doesn't have anyone else."

"Well, she's lucky to have you."

"I don't know about that."

The outer door of the rink opened, and the new arrivals spilled inside. Kimberly fought her way through the crowd.

"Looks like your relief is here," Miles said.

"Thank goodness."

Hank approached from the other direction and handed the Zamboni key to Tyler. "Can you put this away?"

"Sure." He put the key on the hook. "Did you need me for anything else, or am I good to go?"

"You're good," Hank said. "Thanks for helping out this morning."

"No problem." Tyler picked up his skate bag and slid the strap over his shoulder. "See you later." He took a step toward the door before he turned to Miles again. "And, Miles, I'm sorry about your friends. I hope they recover soon."

"Thanks. I appreciate that."

Tyler nodded. He was nearly to the door when he remembered he had left his jacket in the office.

Reversing direction, he headed back the other way. Over the loudspeaker, a worker announced free skate, then started the latest Beach Boys song.

Tyler collected his jacket and glanced at the rink. A couple hockey players had already made their way onto the ice. His gaze landed on the brunette he had noticed earlier. He lowered his bag to the ground and stared.

She moved across the ice effortlessly, her posture perfect, her chin level with the ground. Tyler noted her features as she passed him. Blue eyes set in a heart-shaped face, high cheekbones, full lips tinted red.

She made two laps before she smoothly reversed directions and skated backward. Apparently taking advantage of the lack of skaters on the ice, she did a single toe loop before making her way to the center of the rink.

Tyler watched, riveted, while she went through a number of simple spins and jumps. The difficulty wasn't anything beyond what a first- or second-year skater could accomplish, but something about her movements captivated him.

He picked up his skate bag. Maybe he would stay a bit longer. After all, any time on the ice was a good thing.

Chapter
SIX

KATERINA WILLED HERSELF TO FEEL pain, to feel anything that would give her hope that she would walk again. Instead, only a throbbing headache greeted her as she awoke after her surgery.

Though she sensed someone moving nearby, she kept her eyes closed. She focused on sending a signal from her brain to her legs, but nothing happened. Her once-agile body lay limp, lifeless.

She couldn't remember a time when she hadn't danced every day or focused hours every day on keeping her body limber and able to execute the most complex moves with grace and elegance. Even after Amaliya was born, Katerina had followed a rigid routine to maintain the skills she had spent a lifetime mastering.

Amaliya. Her little girl would turn eighteen tomorrow, but the party she and Robert had planned was no longer possible.

Why had she gone with Robert to New York? Had she stayed home, Robert never would have gone out that night, and neither of them would have been in the taxi when the accident had happened. Maybe the accident wouldn't have happened at all if she hadn't been in New York.

Tears leaked from the corners of her eyes. New York had once signified freedom for her, the place where America had saved her from life behind the Iron Curtain, the place where she had stepped into her future with Robert. Was it some cruel twist of fate that the same city had stolen her physical freedom?

The doctor arrived at her bedside, and Katerina forced her eyes open. He conducted the same test he had yesterday and received the same results. She couldn't feel her legs. Even though the doctor said the feeling might not come back for a few days, she couldn't keep the fears from crashing over her. Would she ever be able to walk again?

🦢

A couples skate was announced, and Amaliya made her way to the side of the rink. It wasn't so long ago that she would have looked around for someone to skate with, but today, her eyes remained fixed in front of her. The lights dimmed, and she stepped off the ice. Bypassing a group of ten-year-olds, she found a spot along the railing where she could wait and watch. Across the rink, dozens of kids fidgeted impatiently for their next turn to skate, while only three couples circled the rink beneath the lighted disco ball.

Someone tapped her on the shoulder, and Amaliya turned. *Gorgeous* was her first thought when she took in the guy standing behind her. Dark hair and dark eyes complemented his all-American good looks.

"Do you want to skate?" He offered his hand.

Amaliya barely resisted the urge to look over her shoulder to make sure he wasn't talking to someone else. "Sure." She put her hand in his, and a ripple of attraction pulsed through her.

He led her onto the ice, and they pushed off together.

"I'm Tyler, by the way."

"Amaliya."

He moved smoothly, matching his stride to hers as they rounded the far end of the rink. "I've never seen you here before."

"I just moved here," Amaliya said. "I start school on Monday."

"You're going to the community college?"

"No, I'm still in high school." She caught the surprise on his face, along with a trace of something else. Was that disappointment?

"Transferring mid-year. That's tough," Tyler said. "What grade are you?"

"I'm a senior."

"That's even tougher."

"Some things can't be helped." Eager to divert the conversation away from herself, Amaliya asked, "What about you? Are you in college?"

"No, I'm in training right now. That and working."

"What kind of training?"

"Figure skating," Tyler said. "I don't suppose you know how to dance on the ice, do you?"

"I've never tried."

"But you do dance."

Did she dance? "I used to study ballet."

"I thought so." His hand still holding hers, he skated in front of her and reversed direction. "I can teach you to dance on the ice. Are you up for it?"

"I guess." She instinctively glided, unsure what Tyler expected of her.

"Great." He put his free hand on her waist. "Put your hand on my shoulder."
Amaliya complied.

"Okay, now you're going to push off with your right foot."

Again, Amaliya followed his instructions. They fell into step, Tyler matching her stride for stride.

"You're a natural," Tyler said.

"I don't know about that."

"Trust me." He flashed a grin. "I know what I'm talking about."

"If you say so."

The song came to an end, and Tyler guided her to a stop. A voice came over the loudspeaker for everyone to clear the ice. He released her and put a hand on her back to guide her to the side.

Amaliya noticed the disappointed looks on the kids' faces as they passed. She remembered that impatient feeling well.

"Doesn't it seem cruel to have a couples skate and then the Zamboni right afterward?" Amaliya asked. "Those poor kids are dying to get back on the ice."

"I know, but doing a couples skate first makes it easier to get everyone off the ice quickly," Tyler said. "Kids will do anything they can to extend their time."

"I guess that makes sense." She found an empty bench and sat down. "Do you work here?"

"Yeah. Usually, I work weekdays between practices, but my boss asked me to help out for a bit this morning." He sat beside her.

"Are you supposed to be working now?"

"No. I just thought I'd hang out for a while since I don't do double practices on Saturdays." The Zamboni swept over the ice in front of them. Tyler waved at the driver, an older man wearing a knit cap. As soon as the Zamboni passed, Tyler asked, "How long have you been skating?"

"For as long as I can remember," Amaliya said. "My dad was a hockey player."

"I saw you walking in before hockey practice."

Amaliya pointed at her skates. "I prefer these to hockey skates."

"You've taken lessons?"

"Yeah. That's how I convinced my dad to buy me my first figure skates." Amaliya's heart squeezed in her chest at the memory. "I must have been around eight."

"You still taking lessons?"

"No. I only took them for a summer."

"A few months?" Tyler leaned back as though trying to study her from a new angle. "Seriously?"

"Yeah. I was big into dance, and I didn't have time to do both."

"You're a really good skater."

"Not really." Amaliya shook her head. "I never got past a single axel."

"Want to try for a double?"

"I'm sure that's beyond me."

"A double toe loop, then," he said. "I saw you do a single earlier."

The rumble of a voice over the loudspeaker prompted kids to flood the ice.

"In these crowds? I don't think so."

"Come on." Tyler stood. "Let's go in the center and you can show me what you can do."

"I don't know . . ."

"What do you have to lose?"

Those words echoed through her head. Tyler was right. What did she have to lose? She was still healthy and whole. She pushed to a stand. "Okay, but if you want me to try anything new, you'd better be a good teacher."

"It just so happens that I am a very good teacher."

"Lead the way."

Tyler followed Amaliya into the center of the ice. He couldn't deny his disappointment that she was still in high school. Even though he only turned twenty-one two weeks ago, he doubted her parents would approve of him asking her out.

"What first?" Amaliya asked.

"Show me a simple scratch spin."

"Just spin?" she asked.

"Yeah."

Amaliya complied and raised her hands gracefully above her head. Unlikely possibilities surfaced in his mind. Tyler shook them away. Amaliya wasn't trying out to be his partner, and he didn't have time to train a beginner. She already admitted she didn't even know how to do the basic jumps required for his level of competition. Too bad. Her gracefulness alone would capture both the audience and the judges if she had the skills necessary to compete.

She came to a stop. "What's next?"

"How about a layback?"

"Like this?" She moved into her next spin, arching her back and tilting her head toward the ice.

It was like watching a dancer, a beautiful ballerina who had replaced her ballet slippers with ice skates. Tyler fell into the simple enjoyment of skating for pure pleasure. One by one, they worked through various spins and simple jumps. With each move, she executed the skill with ease and grace. Another couples skate was followed by more time together in the center of the rink.

When the ice cleared for the last skate of the day, Tyler asked, "You ready to try that double toe loop yet?"

"With everyone watching? I don't think so."

After seeing the ease with which she moved on the ice, he couldn't resist pushing. "Come on. Everyone's leaving."

Amaliya hesitated long enough for Tyler to see her desire to try.

That glimmer of interest caused him to try again. "Tell you what. We'll wait until everyone clears out," Tyler said. "My boss won't care if we stay a couple extra minutes, especially if I offer to clean the ice."

"Are you sure?"

"I'm sure." He put his hand on her waist and guided her instinctively around the ice. Taking advantage of having someone to skate with him, he asked, "How about we try single toe loops together?"

"You mean jump at the same time?"

"Yeah." He released her hand. "On the count of three. Ready?"

"You'll help me up if I fall?" Amaliya asked.

"Absolutely."

"Okay. Ready."

Tyler matched his steps to hers and counted them off. "One, two, three."

He glanced at her, adjusting his takeoff to match hers. He executed the simple jump and landed a second after her. The mere fact that he had someone to try to time with brought forward the simple truth that he needed to find a new partner soon.

He took Amaliya's hand again. "See? That wasn't so hard."

"It was also a single, not a double."

"Moving to a double is simply a matter of speed, height, and rotation."

"You sound more like a physics teacher than a figure skater."

"Maybe, but physics teachers have a tendency to make things a lot more complicated than they really are."

The music ended, and the other couples made their way off the ice.

"You ready?"

"I don't think so."

"We'll start with another single, but I want you to concentrate on getting extra height."

"Okay." Amaliya turned and began her approach. She planted her toe pick and launched herself into the air. She completed her turn only to skid and fall as soon as her skate hit the ice.

She rubbed at the back of her leg. "Well, that didn't go the way I planned."

"You got some good height on your jump." Tyler offered her a hand. "It'll be easier when you add the second rotation."

"You still want me to try a double?"

"I do." He saw her skepticism. "I promised to help you up, remember?"

"Thanks a lot."

Amaliya's dry tone brought a smile to Tyler's face. "Come on. Try it for me."

"Fine." Amaliya brushed the ice off her jeans and looked around, apparently checking to see if anyone was watching.

She started again, this time rotating twice. Or almost twice. She landed short, but instead of falling, she caught herself and managed to stay upright.

"Somehow, I don't think that's what it was supposed to look like."

"Not quite, but you're closer than you think."

"Tyler!"

Tyler caught sight of his sister leaning on the barrier.

Amaliya turned toward her as well. "I should get going."

"I guess I should see what my sister wants," Tyler said. "Thanks for skating with me today."

"See you later." She started toward the side.

Afraid he might not see her again, Tyler called after her. "Hey, Amaliya."

"Yeah?"

"If you have time, come skate on Monday night. I'd love to hear how your first day of school went."

"Maybe."

Not sure what to think of her evasive answer, he said, "I hope you can make it." As soon as the words were out of his mouth, he remembered her age. Too bad. She was fun to be around.

Tyler crossed to where Carolyn waited.

"Who was that?" Carolyn asked.

"Amaliya. She's new here." Tyler's eyebrows drew together. "What are you doing here?"

"We have another skater coming to audition today. Remember?"

"Right."

"I promised to help you find a partner," Carolyn reminded him. "It's time we find one."

"I know." Tyler glanced at a tall blonde who was sitting on a nearby bench, lacing up her skates. "Is that her?"

"Yeah. She's supposed to be really good."

Tyler watched Amaliya head for the exit, the dancelike quality evident in her every movement. He forced his attention back to the blonde. "Let's see if she lives up to her reputation."

"I hope she does," Carolyn said. "I don't know about you, but I'd like to have these tryouts behind us."

"Oh, trust me. I'm ready to get past the searching stage and move forward."

Chapter
SEVEN

AMALIYA MOVED DOWN THE HOSPITAL corridor, a potted plant in one hand and a milkshake in the other. Miles and Linda followed her, as did the scent of hamburgers and french fries, a tribute to the impromptu birthday dinner Miles and Linda had picked up on their way to the hospital. It wasn't the birthday dinner she and her parents had planned, but at least they would be able to be together today. Whether they would be awake enough to talk to her was another matter.

For so long, Amaliya had looked forward to her eighteenth birthday. This magical day represented so much: freedom, discovery, the ability to sign on with a ballet company without her parents' permission. Those were her old dreams. Ballet was her past. She didn't know which dreams would take her into the future anymore, dreams beyond seeing her parents walk again.

Voices carried from several of the rooms they passed, evidence that visiting hours were well underway.

Linda shifted the bouquet of flowers she held from one hand to the other. Yellow carnations. Her mom's favorite.

"I'm going to take these to your mom while you and Uncle Miles check on your dad."

"Okay."

Miles gave his wife a quick kiss. "We'll see you in a few minutes."

Amaliya reached her father's room and stepped inside. As soon as she entered, he looked up.

"There's my girl." Robert tried to push himself up higher in the bed. He winced and settled back against his pillow. "How are you?"

"I'm fine." Amaliya took the seat beside him. "The more important question is how are you?"

His gaze swept past her and landed on the food Miles held. "I'll be better if Miles will give me some of those french fries."

The simple request sent a wave of relief through her. Her dad might be broken, but he was still the same person he had been before the accident.

Miles pulled a hamburger and some fries out of the bag and set them on the tray beside her dad's bed.

"We brought you a milkshake too." Amaliya set it beside the food.

"Thanks. How's your mama doing?" Robert asked in French.

"I haven't seen her yet." Fear rose within her. What news would she receive when she got to her mom's room? She glanced at Miles and switched to English. "Aunt Linda is checking on her now."

"This is driving me crazy not being able to see her."

"Have you talked to the nurses about letting the two of you recover in the same room?"

"Yeah, but they don't want to move Katerina for fear they might do more damage to her back, and they don't want me to move because of my leg."

"Maybe you should write Mama a note," Amaliya suggested. "She'd like that."

Her dad's face lit up. "That's not a bad idea."

Amaliya retrieved the pen and pad of paper that lay on the side of her dad's tray. "Here you go. You can write her a note, and I'll take it to her. I want to see if she's awake."

"Thanks." Her dad struggled to find a spot where he could set the paper to write on it. As soon as he finished, he set the pen aside, folded the note in half, and handed it to her. "Give your mama a kiss for me."

"I will."

"Are you okay to find your own way?" Miles asked.

"Yeah. I'll be back in a minute." Amaliya walked down the hall, multiple scenarios rolling through her mind. Would her mom be awake? Had the surgery worked? Could her mom feel her legs?

Amaliya's steps slowed as she approached her mother's room. Her mom's voice inside the room carried to her, and hope took flight.

"Is Amaliya doing okay?" Katerina asked. "I worry about her going to a new school."

"She's doing great," Linda said.

Amaliya walked inside. "Are you talking about me?"

"Milaya." Her mom stretched out her hand. "I'm so sorry your life got turned upside down."

"Don't worry about me." Amaliya closed the distance between them and took her mom's hand. "How are you feeling?"

"Getting a little better every day." Tears welled up in her mom's eyes, and she blinked against them.

Amaliya's throat closed. If her mother was this emotional, did that mean the paralysis was permanent? How many days ago had it been that her mother had been dancing beside her, making every movement seem effortless? Had it really been only a few days? It felt like an eternity. Though she wasn't sure she wanted to face the underlying cause of her mom's tears, she asked, "What did the doctor say? Did the surgery work?"

"I have a little tingling in my legs." A tear spilled over. "It isn't much, but the doctor hopes when the swelling goes down, it will get better."

"There's still hope," Amaliya said.

"Yes, there's still hope."

Amaliya pressed a kiss to her mom's cheek. "That's from Papa." She handed her mom the note she held. "So is this."

Katerina opened it and read the message. She smiled. "This is like when we first met."

"What is?" Amaliya asked.

"Passing notes. Sometimes it was the only way we could talk before I defected." She clutched the note to her chest. "Do you have a pen?"

"I think so." Amaliya fished through her purse until she found one. She handed it over.

Though it took a great deal of effort, her mom scribbled a few words and handed the paper back to her. "Will you give that to your papa?"

"Of course. I'll take it to him right now," Amaliya said. "I love you, Mama."

"I love you too."

Amaliya was nearly to the door when her mom called out. "Amaliya?"

"Yes?"

"Happy birthday."

Amaliya smiled. "Thanks, Mama."

Amaliya sat with Linda across from Amaliya's new school counselor, Miss Thurston, while the older woman punched her fingers on the keys of an electric typewriter. Linda had driven her to school with the promise to have Miles pick her up afterward. If Amaliya had her way, he would be picking her up from the rink instead of the school this afternoon.

Her visit with her parents yesterday had lasted only an hour. As much as she wanted to visit them often, the two-hour round trip to the hospital in New York City had drained her.

The typing stopped. Miss Thurston pulled two pieces of paper out of the typewriter and separated them from the carbon paper that had been between them. "We were able to give you all of the classes you had at your old school."

Amaliya took the paper her counselor offered her and started reading. Calculus first period. Coming to a new school was one thing, but starting her day like that? No thanks. "How many of these classes do I actually need in order to graduate?" Amaliya asked.

"Technically, you only need four: English, US Government, and two electives."

Amaliya scanned her schedule with a new purpose. "In that case, is there a way for me to take the required classes in the morning and get out at lunchtime?"

"Are you sure you want to do that?" Linda asked before Miss Thurston had a chance to answer. "The best way to get to know people is by being in school."

"I'd rather keep things simple," Amaliya said. "I can't even imagine trying to learn calculus right now."

"If calculus is your only concern, we can give you a study period for that one," Miss Thurston suggested.

Amaliya shook her head. "I want to take as little as possible. That way I can try to get a job after school and start saving for college."

Linda gave a subtle nod, and Miss Thurston pulled a thick binder off a shelf above her desk. "Let me see what I can do."

While Miss Thurston jotted down notes on a pad of paper, Linda leaned closer. "Are you sure about this?"

"I'm sure."

"I think I can make it work so you would get out at noon every day," Miss Thurston said. "We can give you psychology, but we still need to add a fourth class. Unfortunately, none of the ones you already had are available in the period you have open."

"What other choices do I have?" Amaliya asked.

"Home ec, PE, chorus, or geology."

"Isn't there anything else?"

"Spanish 3 or French 4, but you would need to meet prerequisites for those."

"I'll take the French."

Miss Thurston's eyebrows drew together, and she looked down at Amaliya's transcript. "I'm sorry, but you don't have any French classes listed here."

"Amaliya didn't take French at school because she already spoke French at home," Linda said.

Some of the wariness on Miss Thurston's face eased but not all. "Speaking and reading are two different things."

Amaliya unzipped her purse and pulled out the book she was currently halfway through. She offered it to Miss Thurston.

"What's this?"

"It's the book I brought to read while we waited to meet with you."

Miss Thurston read the title and flipped the pages to see it was, indeed, written in French. "Okay. We'll give it a try."

"Thank you."

Miss Thurston wrote four passes and handed those and Amaliya's new schedule to her.

"Since all your classes changed, your new teachers won't be expecting you. The passes will give them your information."

"Okay."

They all stood, and Linda gave Amaliya a hug. "Good luck, sweetie. I'll see you when you get home from school."

"Is it okay if I walk over to the rink after school? It's only a couple blocks away, and I thought I might skate for a bit, maybe see if I can get a job there."

"Do you need money to rent skates?"

"No." Amaliya patted her backpack. "I brought mine with me in case it was okay."

"That's fine. I'll tell Miles to pick you up at the rink around four," Linda said. "Call if you want to come home before then."

"Okay."

"I'll show you to your first class." Miss Thurston handed her a map of the school. "This will help you find your way around the rest of the day."

"Thanks."

A bell rang, and Amaliya followed her counselor into the empty hall while Linda made her way to the exit.

They reached her classroom, where a teacher stood in front of the room, instructing the class in French.

"Excuse me, Mrs. Martin," Miss Thurston interrupted. "I have a new student for you."

The petite woman with graying hair gave a slight nod and held her hand out when Amaliya offered the transfer slip to her.

"*Asseyez-vous s'il vous plaît.*"

"*Oui*, madam," Amaliya said to her teacher's request to take a seat. Amaliya noticed the open textbooks on her new classmates' desks as she took a seat in the second row. She asked in French, "Is there a book I can use?"

Mrs. Martin retrieved a book from a shelf and handed it to her.

"*Merci*."

"Someone's showing off for the teacher," a boy in the back row said under his breath but loud enough for everyone in the class to hear.

Several students snickered. Amaliya's cheeks heated.

"Ignore him," the girl beside her said. "He's an idiot."

Amaliya didn't respond, not wanting to draw more attention to herself as the teacher began speaking again.

When the class ended, Amaliya pulled out her schedule and map.

"Do you know where you're going next?" the girl beside her asked.

"English with Mr. Holden. Room 112."

"I'm in that class too. I'll show you the way." She stood and headed for the door. "I'm Sarah, by the way."

"Amaliya."

"That's an unusual name." Sarah's face lit with amusement. "Don't tell me it's French."

"Russian," Amaliya said. "Not French."

Sarah led the way into their second period class. "Come on. There's an empty seat by me."

"Thanks." Amaliya gave her pass to the teacher and settled into the desk beside her first friend in Connecticut. She thought of Tyler and amended that thought. Make that her second friend in Connecticut.

Tyler circled the ice, the footsteps of his latest prospective partner fading as she left the building. He came to a stop at the edge of the rink, where his sister stood on the other side of the rink barrier. "Well, that was a waste of time."

"Sorry. I'm afraid we're getting to the bottom of the barrel." Carolyn leaned on the half wall between them. "Maybe we can look in California near where Dan and I will be living."

"What? You want me to live with newlyweds? No thanks."

"I'm sorry, Tyler. I know everything will work out eventually, but I really thought we would find someone by now."

Tyler tilted his head from one side to the other to stretch his muscles. "Let's take a week off from looking."

"We have another tryout tomorrow. If she doesn't work out, we can take a break for a bit."

"Good. It would be nice to remember what it's like to enjoy skating again."

"You looked like you were having fun on Saturday," Carolyn said.

"Yeah." Tyler thought of Amaliya and the simple joy of teaching her a new skill. "Maybe I should retire, too, and go into teaching."

"Oh no you don't. I'm not going to spend the rest of my life listening to the stories of 'What could have been if I hadn't retired,'" Carolyn said. "We're finding you a new partner."

"Next week."

"Or tomorrow," Carolyn said. "Do you have to work any more today?"

"No. I'm done for the day."

"Maybe you should spend a little time skating before your afternoon practice," Carolyn suggested. "It might help you remember why you spend so much time here."

"Maybe." The door opened, and sunlight spilled inside. To Tyler's surprise, Amaliya walked in. "Hey, Amaliya." He stepped off the ice and crossed to her. "I didn't expect to see you here this early. I thought you'd still be in school."

"I worked out my schedule so I only have to go half days." She glanced around. "Is the manager here? I was wondering if he's hiring."

"He isn't here right now, but I can let him know you stopped by."

"That would be great. Thanks."

Carolyn stepped beside him, and Tyler motioned to her. "This is my sister, Carolyn."

"Nice to meet you," Amaliya said.

"You too." Carolyn glanced at Tyler before speaking to Amaliya again. "You were here Saturday, weren't you?"

"Yeah, I was." Amaliya glanced at the empty rink. "What time does open skate start?"

"Not until five," Tyler said. "We have private practices starting in a little while, and they don't finish up until then."

"Oh."

Tyler heard the disappointment in her voice and noted the bag she carried. "Were you hoping to skate earlier?"

"Yeah. Maybe I'll come back."

"Or you could skate with Tyler now," Carolyn interrupted before Amaliya could retreat.

Amaliya's eyebrows drew together. "But I thought he said—"

"Open skate isn't until five, but Hank is pretty good about letting Tyler take some extra ice time." Carolyn pointed at her bag. "Go put your skates on."

"Are you sure it will be okay?"

"I'm sure."

"Okay. I'll be right back." Amaliya walked over to one of the nearby benches.

Tyler lowered his voice. "What are you doing?"

"Like I said, you need to remember how to enjoy skating again." Carolyn tilted her head toward Amaliya. "She'll give you an excuse to get out there and relax."

Tyler couldn't argue with his sister. He couldn't remember the last time he had enjoyed skating as much as he had on Saturday.

Amaliya finished putting on her skates and walked to them. "Is it really okay for us to skate?"

"Yeah." Tyler led the way onto the ice. "Come on. Let's see if you can land that double toe loop."

Amaliya grimaced. "Maybe I should come back later."

"Come on. I know you can do it."

"Okay. I'll give it a try."

"Great." Tyler pushed off and glided to the center. "Let's see it."

Amaliya did it. She landed a double toe loop. Twice.

"That was great." Tyler skated toward her, a huge grin on his face. "I knew you could do it."

"It only took me twenty times falling first."

"Hey, it took me a lot more times than that."

One eyebrow lifted. "And how old were you?"

"It doesn't matter." Tyler brushed that detail aside and took her hand. "Come on."

"What are we doing?"

"We're going to do it together, side by side."

"Okay." Amaliya followed Tyler's lead, the two of them skating backward, her hand in his.

"Are you ready?" Tyler asked.

"I think so."

He released her hand and counted to three. As they had done with the single toe loops on Saturday, they both launched into their jumps together, but this time, instead of Amaliya falling after her double toe loop, the blade of her skate landed firmly on the ice.

"We did it!" Amaliya said. "Let's do it again."

Tyler took her hand, and they circled the rink again. "Ready?"

"Ready."

They executed their jumps again, and Amaliya surprised herself by landing her double toe loop a fourth time. Out of the corner of her eye, she saw Tyler land his at almost the same time.

Tyler circled to face her. "You're a natural."

"I don't know about that, but I've always loved being on the ice." Excitement rose within her. "What else can you teach me?"

"How about a double salchow?"

"I can try, but it's been a long time since I took skating lessons," Amaliya said. "I'm not sure I remember which jump is which."

"It's not that hard. The only difference in the jumps is what part of the blade you take off from and which foot you land on," Tyler said. "The salchow is the easiest of the jumps that takes off on the edge of your blade."

"It doesn't sound easy."

"Come on. I'll show you." Tyler demonstrated the jump and gave her some pointers on how to convert her single jump into a double.

She attempted a double. As expected, she fell.

"It takes practice." Tyler gave her a hand up.

A few people walked in, and Tyler waved at someone. "It looks like our time is about up."

"Thanks for letting me skate."

"It was my pleasure."

Amaliya followed him across the rink to where Carolyn stood on the other side of the barrier.

"You two looked great out there," Carolyn said.

"Thanks," Amaliya said. "It was a lot of fun."

"Amaliya, do you have to leave now?"

"No. Why?"

"If you want, I can keep working with you on your double salchow," Carolyn said.

"That would be great, but are you sure you don't mind?" Amaliya asked.

"Not at all. Let me grab my skates. I'll be right back."

"What about the manager?" Amaliya asked Tyler. "I don't want you to get in trouble for letting me skate."

"It's not a problem," Tyler insisted. "It looks like he's back from lunch. I'll introduce you while Carolyn gets her skates on."

"Okay." Amaliya followed him off the ice and into the skate-rental office. "Hey, Hank, this is Amaliya."

The older man pushed back from the paper-laden desk in the corner and stood to offer his hand. "Good to meet you, Amaliya."

"Amaliya is interested in working here."

"I don't have any openings right now, but I'll keep you in mind in case something opens up."

"Thanks."

"Carolyn wanted to know if she can work with Amaliya during my practice. Is that okay with you?" Tyler asked.

"As long as Carolyn deals with Scarlett if she complains, I don't mind at all."

"I think Carolyn can handle Scarlett."

"In that case, have fun."

"Thank you." She and Tyler left the office and she asked, "Who's Scarlett?"

"My coach. Sometimes she thinks she owns the private ice time."

"Does she?"

"No, but since she's usually the only one teaching this time of day, sometimes she can be possessive." He put his hand on her arm. "Don't worry. She'll be fine."

"If you're sure."

"I'm sure." He waved at where Carolyn was circling the rink. "Your private instructor awaits."

Amaliya couldn't help but smile. "Thanks. I'll see you later."

"You can count on it."

Chapter
EIGHT

ALL THROUGHOUT PRACTICE, TYLER'S ATTENTION drifted across the rink to Amaliya and Carolyn. Given half a chance to get to know her better, Tyler suspected he would enjoy spending time with her, especially now, while he was dealing with the stress of finding a new partner.

Scarlett called for a water break, and Marie stepped beside him. "Who's that with Carolyn?"

"Just a new girl in town."

"She's pretty."

Recognizing the land mine Marie had thrown in front of him, he kept his comment neutral. "Yeah, I guess." He took a step toward the drinking fountain. "I'm going to get a drink."

Marie followed. "What do you know about her?"

"Not much. Her name's Amaliya, and she just moved here," Tyler said. "That's about all I know." Eager to escape the conversation, he took a drink and crossed to where Scarlett was chatting with Becky, his other training partner. "Scarlett, did Carolyn talk to you about coming to our next round of auditions?"

"She did, but I'm afraid I won't be able to make it. I have to meet with Marie's choreographer," she said. "I'm sorry I haven't been able to help out, but with worlds around the corner, I have to stay focused on helping Marie prepare. If you find anyone worth seriously considering, let me know, and we'll do a second audition."

Tyler bit down his frustration. He hadn't expected his coach to be so hands-off in trying to help him find a new partner. He worked through his individual moves, his frustration rising. When he glanced at Amaliya working with Carolyn, he couldn't help but envy the two of them. They were having fun. He missed that sensation.

The minute his practice ended, he made his way to where Carolyn now stood at the edge of the rink.

"Where's Amaliya?"

"She went to get a drink." Carolyn put both hands on his arms. "I have an idea."

"An idea for what?"

"For your new partner."

"I already told you I need some time before we start searching again."

"Our search is over," Carolyn said. "You should skate with Amaliya."

"Amaliya?" Tyler shook his head at the improbable solution. "You can't be serious. She's not even a competitive skater."

"Not yet, but she could be," Carolyn insisted. "She learns quickly, and she's graceful and athletic."

He couldn't deny Amaliya's grace or her innate ability. After all, not everyone could pick up a double toe loop in such a short period of time, but still . . .

"Tyler, you need a partner. She's the best skater you've been on the ice with since we started this whole tryout thing, and you know it."

"You're right, but she doesn't even have the basics down, not for top-level competition."

"We can teach her the technical aspects of skating, and she clearly has a background in dance. Besides, it isn't like you'd be able to compete in worlds this year anyway. It's only three weeks away."

Tyler tried to picture himself paired with Amaliya in competition. Her elegance on the ice and the grace with which she carried herself couldn't be taught. Their few hours spent skating together already proved she could learn quickly and that she didn't possess the arrogance that prevented so many athletes from improving. Was it possible for Amaliya to improve enough to become a world-class skater? The probability fell into the highly unlikely category.

"Sorry, Carolyn, but there's no way she'd be able to pick everything up fast enough."

"I think you're wrong."

Amaliya skated to them. "Carolyn, thanks again for all your help today. I think I learned more from the two of you than I did in three months of skating lessons when I was a kid."

"I was happy to help." Carolyn glanced at Tyler briefly. "Any chance you're free tomorrow afternoon?"

"I think so. Why?" Amaliya asked.

"We're holding another tryout for a new partner for Tyler. I hoped you might come help us out."

"Partner for what?" Amaliya asked.

Tyler wasn't sure what his sister was up to, but he answered Amaliya's question. "Carolyn may be moving to California with her husband next month, which leaves me without a partner."

"We're pairs figure skaters," Carolyn explained.

"We were anyway, until Carolyn decided to retire," Tyler added.

"What can I do to help?" Amaliya asked.

"Our coach hasn't been the best about helping with the tryouts. I'd love someone else's opinion," Carolyn said. "If you're willing, we can do another lesson afterward."

"I'd love that, but it feels like I'm getting the better end of the bargain."

Carolyn smiled cryptically. "I don't know about that."

Amaliya glanced at her watch. "I'd better get going. My ride should be here. Thanks again for today. I had a lot of fun."

"You're welcome," Carolyn said.

"See you later." Tyler waited until Amaliya left the rink before he asked, "What are you up to?"

"Nothing. I thought it would be nice to have someone else to talk to during your tryout."

"I'm not buying it."

"You don't have to." Carolyn pushed off and started for the side of the rink. "I'll see you tomorrow."

"Yeah. Tomorrow."

Amaliya still wasn't sure what she was doing here. She had followed Carolyn's instructions and put on her skates, even though she wouldn't have anything to do on the ice besides stand beside Carolyn during the tryout.

Tyler and a pretty blonde circled the rink together before coming to a stop beside Carolyn.

"You all warmed up?" Carolyn asked.

"Yeah," Tyler said.

"Let's start simple," Carolyn said. "Tyler, put your arm around Violet's waist and circle the rink for me. Let's see how your strides match."

"Okay." Tyler followed his sister's instructions.

Carolyn counted to three to start them. They pushed off together, but by the third step, their timing was off.

"This isn't a very good start," Carolyn muttered.

"No, it isn't." Amaliya watched the couple's feet. Tyler shortened his stride to match Violet's, but it only took a few steps before they were out of sync again. "I think Violet isn't gliding long enough between strokes."

"She's a little stiff too," Carolyn said.

Amaliya could see it now: the tension in the upper body, the interrupted flow of Violet's movements with each step, the rigid position of her head. "Maybe she's nervous."

"Maybe."

Tyler adjusted several more times to match his partner's stride, but by doing so, he lost the effortless quality he normally exhibited when skating. The couple came to a stop in front of Carolyn again.

The muscle in Tyler's jaw twitched before he asked, "Now what?"

"Amaliya, can you skate with Tyler around the rink? I want to point a couple things out to Violet before we try again."

"Sure." Amaliya switched places with Violet, and Tyler placed his hand on Amaliya's waist. She absorbed the thrill of his touch. "Starting on the right foot?"

"Yes." Tyler counted to three, and they pushed off together.

Unlike with Violet and Tyler, Amaliya noted that with each stride, she and Tyler seemed to become more in tune with each other. They returned to where they'd started.

"Okay, Violet. You and Tyler try this again."

Amaliya switched places with Violet. Though she expected an improvement on the second attempt, if anything, it was worse.

"So much for a demonstration helping," Carolyn said under her breath.

"I hate to say it, but they don't seem very well matched."

"I'm afraid you're right." Carolyn fell silent until Tyler and Violet approached again. "Violet, can you show us your double axel?"

"Sure." Violet pushed off. She circled halfway around the rink, launched herself into the air, completed two and a half rotations, stumbled, and fell.

"Try it again," Carolyn called out.

Violet stood and began again. Another failed attempt, followed by a third. On her fourth try, she landed upright, but her free leg dragged across the ice as she struggled to maintain her balance.

Tyler lowered his voice. "This is a waste of time."

"She's already here," Carolyn whispered. "Let's make it look like it's a real tryout."

Violet approached. "Sorry. I don't normally struggle so much with that one."

"It's okay," Carolyn said. "Let's do some side-by-side spins."

Carolyn called out instructions, and Amaliya couldn't help but analyze the movements of both skaters. Tyler made everything look so easy. With Violet, each movement had an air of deliberation and planning.

After twenty minutes of going through various skills, Carolyn finally said, "Okay, I think that's enough for today. Violet, we appreciate you coming out."

"When do you think you'll be making your decision?"

"I hope in the next day or two," Carolyn said.

Violet offered a forced smile. "Great. Thanks."

Amaliya waited until Violet left before she asked, "Why didn't you just tell her she isn't a good match?"

"It's always easier to make people think you considered them for longer than a few minutes," Carolyn said.

"Yeah, the skating world is pretty small at the upper levels," Tyler added. "If Violet continues to improve, we may cross paths again eventually."

"Since we cut the tryout short with Violet, maybe Amaliya can stand in for a bit," Carolyn said.

"What did you have in mind?" Tyler asked.

"How about some side-by-side spins?" Carolyn suggested. "You need practice timing with someone, and Violet was so far off, you couldn't do it with her."

"Okay. Amaliya, are you up for that?"

"Sure. What do you want to start with?"

"Let's start simple. Scratch spin."

Amaliya glided forward a few yards so she was beside Tyler without being too close. "I'm ready when you are."

"Ready."

Tyler knew what his sister was doing. She had it in her head to turn Amaliya into his partner, and by having him skate with her, she was proving her point. Violet hadn't been one of the better candidates he had auditioned, but like the others, she didn't match his stride or his style. Amaliya matched both. If only her skills were at his level.

Carolyn wiggled her eyebrows at him. "Just for fun, let's do side-by-side double toe loops."

"I'll try," Amaliya said. "No guarantees I won't fall though."

"I have faith in you," Carolyn said.

"You can do it." Tyler took her hand, and they started around the rink together. "Ready?"

"Ready."

Tyler released her and counted to three. He launched into the air, his skate scraping against the ice a second before Amaliya's. He glanced over to see she remained upright. "See? You've got that one."

"Thanks to you and your sister."

They returned to Carolyn. "That was great. Amaliya, do you want to work some more on your double salchow?"

"I'd love to, but are you sure you have the time?"

"Yeah. I usually hang out while Tyler practices. It's nice to feel useful while I recover."

"Recover?"

"I messed up my ankle a little over a week ago. I'm not allowed to do anything with skates on yet, except glide from one place to another."

"That's rough."

"Yeah, but it's been fun living vicariously through you."

Amaliya smiled. "Anything I can do to help."

"I'll leave you to it," Tyler said. "I'd better get to practice."

"Have fun."

Tyler crossed the ice to where Marie and Becky were stretching. Scarlett approached.

"Tyler, how did the tryout go today? Any luck?"

Tyler glanced at Amaliya. Despite his doubts, he said, "I'm not sure yet."

"We need to get a partner sorted out for you as soon as possible."

"I'm well aware."

"Since you're already warmed up, let's go through your jumps," Scarlett said. "I need to work with Marie on her routine for worlds today, so I wanted to have you work with Carolyn."

Though normally he would be annoyed to be pushed aside for the better part of practice, Tyler nodded. "Sounds good."

Scarlett started with Tyler's double lutz, having him repeat it four times while she adjusted his arm position on his landing. His double axel was their next project, followed by his double lutz double toe loop combination.

"Your combination is looking much better," Scarlett said. "Just make sure you get enough extension in your leg on your landing."

A squeal of excitement echoed from across the rink. Tyler turned in time to see Amaliya's face alight with excitement. She rushed to Carolyn and gave her a hug. Tyler shook his head. Surely Amaliya couldn't have already landed a double salchow. She'd only landed her double toe loop for the first time yesterday.

"What next?" Tyler asked.

"Show me your combination one more time. After that, I need to work with Marie."

Tyler complied. After receiving Scarlett's feedback on his latest jumps, he joined Amaliya and Carolyn on the other side of the rink. "What was all the excitement about over here?"

"Amaliya landed a double salchow," Carolyn said.

"Wow. You learned that one fast."

"I have a good teacher."

"Amaliya, why don't you go get a drink? I need to talk to Tyler for a minute."

"Sure. I'll be right back." Amaliya headed for the nearest opening in the rink wall.

"Tyler, you need to skate with Amaliya."

Twin emotions fought within him: resistance and hope. "I don't know."

"Scarlett is working with Marie. Spend the rest of practice with Amaliya and see how it goes."

"You already had me practice with her for a half hour after the tryout."

"I know, but you're being stubborn. You need more proof that the two of you are well matched." Carolyn put her hand on his arm. "I know it's unconventional, but try to open yourself up to the possibilities. You mentioned she used to study ballet, so you know she can pick up the dance side of the sport."

Though his resistance to the idea still ruled, Tyler wavered. "I must be crazy to even consider this."

"Probably, but there's something about her," Carolyn said.

Tyler couldn't deny it. "It's like you're afraid to take your eyes off her because you don't want to miss anything."

"Exactly." Carolyn motioned toward Amaliya, who was heading toward them. "You should talk to her. If it doesn't work out, we can start looking again in a few weeks."

"You're getting ahead of yourself, but I can skate with her for the rest of practice. It'll be nice to have someone to work on timing with."

"Ready to do some more skating with Tyler?" Carolyn asked.

"Sounds good."

Side-by-side jumps, spins, crossovers. Tyler repeated them all. With each passing minute, excitement stirred inside him. As much as he hated to admit his sister was right, he couldn't deny the truth. Amaliya skated beautifully, and their styles matched well.

When their time ended, Carolyn joined them in the center of the ice. "You two look great together."

"Thanks," Amaliya said. "That was a lot of fun."

"Yeah, it was," Tyler agreed.

Carolyn looked pointedly at him, her eyebrows raised expectantly.

A debate waged inside him. He could go back to the endless auditions in the hope of finding a partner, or he could gamble on an unknown. Though doubts plagued him, Tyler forced himself to take a tentative step toward ending his search. "I have a question for you."

"What's that?"

"I wondered if you would be interested in being my new partner."

"Me?" She shook her head. "You're really good, Tyler. Don't you want to find someone who's already at your level?"

"I've tried," Tyler said. "So far, you're the first person I've meshed well with."

"I don't know . . ."

"Amaliya," Carolyn interrupted. "If you weren't worried about not knowing as much as Tyler, would you want to do it?"

"Probably." Amaliya considered for a second. "I love skating, and it's been fun learning new things."

"Then you should skate with him," Carolyn said. "It'll make me feel a lot better if he has a new partner before I leave."

Still uncertain about his sister's crazy idea, Tyler said, "We practice every day from five to seven in the morning and again from one to three."

"That's a lot of practice."

"You don't have to come to the morning practices if you don't want to," Carolyn said.

"I think I'd like to come, actually," Amaliya said. "The more I practice, the better I'll get, right?"

Carolyn laughed. "Tyler, I think you've found yourself a partner."

A new partner. The doubts rushed through him again. What had they done? "Will your parents be okay with this?" Tyler asked, not sure if he wanted her to say yes or no.

Amaliya's smile faded, but she nodded. "I think they will."

"If they are, I'll see you tomorrow at five."

"Sounds good." Amaliya glanced at her watch. "I should get going."

"I'll see you tomorrow," Tyler said.

"Yeah. See you tomorrow."

Amaliya walked into the house, words rolling through her mind. She wanted this. As much as it terrified her that she would never be good enough to skate with Tyler, the idea of pursuing a goal, of finding a productive way to spend her time, allowed a ray of light to penetrate the cloud that had been hanging over her since the accident.

She had nearly blurted out everything when Miles picked her up from the rink, but she suspected she would have better luck if she talked to both Miles and Linda together. But the quick trip to the hardware store with Miles on the way home had taken over an hour, and the suspense was killing her.

"Amaliya, is that you?" Linda called from the kitchen.

"It's me." Amaliya followed the aroma of pork chops and mashed potatoes. "Something smells good."

"It's nothing fancy, but Miles loves it," Linda said. "Where is he, anyway?"

"He said he'd be right in."

The back door opened, and Miles walked in holding a stack of firewood. "Are you talking about me again?"

"Only about your love of pork chops."

"You do make the best." Miles continued through the kitchen and deposited the wood beside the fireplace in the living room.

Linda set aside the spoon she was holding. "How was school?"

"It was okay. The girl who sits next to me in French and English is really nice."

"That's good. I was hoping you would make some new friends." She waved toward the clock on the kitchen wall. "How was ice skating today?"

"Good."

"I forgot to ask yesterday if you applied for a job."

"I talked to the rink manager, but he said they aren't hiring right now."

"That's too bad, but it's probably for the best. It looks like the insurance for the driver who caused your parents' accident is going to pay for the medical bills. That will take a lot of pressure off your parents."

"That's good news."

"It's fabulous news." Linda handed her a bowl of green beans. "Here. Can you put this on the table?"

"Sure."

Miles walked back into the kitchen.

"There's something I wanted to talk to you about," Amaliya began.

"What's that?"

"I met this guy at the rink on Saturday, and we skated together again yesterday and today." Amaliya laced her fingers together to keep them still. "He wants me to skate with him."

"What do you mean skate with him?" Linda scooped the mashed potatoes into a bowl and set them on the table.

"Skate in competitions," Amaliya explained. "He's a pairs skater, but his sister is retiring, so he's looking for a new partner."

"You're talking about Tyler Linden," Miles said.

"You know him?"

"Everyone around here knows Tyler and Carolyn. They placed well at nationals last year," Miles said. "They came in sixth place at worlds."

"Worlds? As in the world championships?" Amaliya asked.

"One and the same."

A new wave of nerves fluttered in her stomach. "Maybe this isn't such a good idea after all."

"I think it's a great idea," Miles said. "You're a beautiful skater, even when you aren't wearing hockey skates."

"And we all know you can dance." Linda set the platter of pork chops beside the mashed potatoes.

Amaliya sat between Miles and Linda. "But if Tyler has already competed at the world championships, he's going to want to skate at that level again."

"Do you like skating?" Linda asked.

"I love it," Amaliya said. "But what if I'm not good enough?"

"You'll never know unless you try." Linda served everyone a pork chop.

"You're plenty good enough," Miles added. "When you put your mind to something, nothing can stop you. You're just like your father."

"And your mother," Linda said, her voice wistful. "This is a chance to take the best of what both of them gave you and see what you can become."

Emotions swelled inside her. Love for her parents, love for ballet and skating. One side of her lips quirked up. "I guess you're right."

"I'll talk to Hank down at the rink and see what we need to do to get you signed up for rink time."

A new thought surfaced. "Is this going to be too expensive?"

"You don't worry about that," Linda said.

"That's right." Miles scooped a large helping of mashed potatoes and a small portion of green beans onto his plate. "You concentrate on learning what you need to know, and let us take care of paying for it."

"You two really are the best."

"Glad you think so," Miles said. "And I'll remind you of that every morning you don't want to haul yourself out of bed."

"Yeah, that's the other thing. Practice is twice a day." Amaliya grimaced. "The first one is at five in the morning."

"Looks like I'll be getting up early for the foreseeable future," Miles said.

"Are you sure you don't mind?"

"I'm sure. The rink is only a couple blocks from the school, so even if I can't pick you up afterward, you can walk."

"Thanks, Miles. Even if you let me borrow a car, since Mom and Dad's accident, I'm still a bit nervous about driving."

"I don't blame you."

Chapter
NINE

TYLER COULDN'T REMEMBER THE LAST time he had experienced this sense of anticipation when going to a regular practice session. But this time, the anticipation came with apprehension as well.

Doubts surfaced several times throughout the night and early morning as he considered the risk he was taking. Finding someone with Olympic potential was an enormous undertaking, even if the basic skills already existed. On the technical side of the sport, he had already taken a step backward. He hoped that step was the first toward many steps forward.

"You know this is crazy, right?" Tyler asked Carolyn as they walked from the car into the rink.

"Yes, but it's the kind of crazy that might work," Carolyn said. "Amaliya learns quickly. I mean, who learns two new jumps in a matter of days?"

"That is unusual."

"I think you'll know within a couple months if she'll max out or if she can get to where you need her to be," Carolyn said.

"A couple months that I could spend with someone who already knows how to skate." Tyler unlocked the door to the rink.

"Amaliya knows how to skate. She'll learn the jumps and figures eventually, and her spins are already beautiful."

"She also has to learn the lifts." Tyler flipped on the lights, the empty rink now illuminated like a beacon. "Trusting a partner isn't always easy."

"Then we should work on that today."

"Go straight to lifts?"

"Nothing fancy, but let's see if she freaks when her skates aren't touching the ice," Carolyn suggested. "If she can't trust a partner, you know you're wasting your time."

"True." Tyler sat and pulled off his shoes. "Of course, that's assuming her parents agree to let her skate. Ice time isn't cheap."

"We'll find out soon enough. If she isn't here in the next fifteen minutes, you'll have your answer."

Scarlett walked in. "Where do we stand on finding a new partner? Have you set up any new tryouts?"

"Actually, we think we found Tyler's new partner," Carolyn said.

"Really?"

"She's coming in this morning." Tyler tugged on his skates.

"I have to work with Marie and Becky for the first hour, but we can do a quick tryout after that," Scarlett said.

"Um . . ."

The door opened, and Becky and Marie walked in.

"Carolyn, you work with Tyler and the new girl until I have time to conduct a proper evaluation." Scarlett turned to Marie and Becky. "Get your music cued up. We're going through short programs this morning."

Tyler tied his skates. "Should I tell her we already offered Amaliya the spot?"

"I wouldn't." Carolyn shook her head. "She's so focused on worlds right now, I'm sure she'll be thrilled to have tryouts behind us."

"Thanks for helping me," Tyler said.

"Hey, I want to see an Olympic medal around your neck almost as much as you do." She opened her bag and pulled out a camera.

"What's that for?"

"I thought I could take some pictures of you and Amaliya today." Carolyn glanced at Scarlett briefly. "Someone needs to document the first practice of the future gold medalists."

"I like your optimism."

The door opened again, and Amaliya walked in. He lowered his voice. "Seems to me that if Scarlett wasn't involved in the tryouts, she shouldn't have a say in my decision."

"I couldn't agree more." Carolyn lifted a hand. "Amaliya, over here."

"Good morning." Amaliya sat beside Tyler. "I hope I'm not late."

"Right on time," Tyler said. "I gather your folks were okay with you skating."

"You could say that." Amaliya put her skates on. "What do we do first?"

"Let's stretch and warm up. Then we're going to start with lifts."

"Lifts?" Both elegant eyebrows lifted. "You aren't planning to throw me across the ice on my first day, are you?"

"Nothing that extreme." The corner of his lips lifted. "We'll save that for the second day."

"I hope you're joking."

"Maybe." Tyler offered his hand. "Come on."

They stretched for several minutes. Then they stepped onto the ice together, and Tyler matched his stride to Amaliya's as they circled the rink twice. They came to a stop beside Carolyn, who had a camera lifted and aimed at them.

She lowered the camera. "Amaliya, let's see how you are with a simple lift."

"What do you want me to do?"

"For now, turn away from Tyler and let him pick you up."

"What should I do with my arms?" Amaliya asked.

Impressed that she would ask such a question, Tyler said, "You can leave them by your side."

"Okay." Amaliya lifted her arms slightly like a ballerina taking a starting position on stage.

"Ready?" Tyler asked.

"Are you going to count it off?"

"Sure. On three." Tyler put his hands on her waist. "One, two, three." Tyler lifted her, surprised when she used her legs to push herself upward. He locked his arms, holding her above him. She arched slightly, as though adjusting her center of gravity to help him balance her weight.

The camera clicked several times.

"Tyler, put her down," Carolyn said.

Tyler lowered Amaliya.

"Now what?" Amaliya asked.

"Let's do it again, but this time face Tyler."

"Okay." Amaliya turned, and Tyler put his hands on her waist again.

"Ready?"

She nodded.

He counted to three and lifted her. Again, Amaliya pushed off to help him elevate her over his head.

When he lowered her back to the ice, Tyler glanced at his sister. "What do you think?"

"I think we should finish your warm-up by having you work on your turns," Carolyn said. "Let's see if we can match your timing."

Doubts melted into excitement, and Tyler nodded his approval. "Sounds perfect."

Amaliya made it through the first hour of practice and only fell twice. The simple lifts were much like dancing ballet. Push with your legs, and trust your partner to do the rest. The spins were more challenging, trying to time her rotation to match Tyler's, but they were better now than when they had started.

When Amaliya allowed herself to focus solely on skating with Tyler and following Carolyn's instructions, she could let herself believe that she could learn the skills necessary to compete. When she let her gaze stray to the other two girls on the ice, her inadequacies became readily apparent. Their jumps were so good, their transitions between elements so smooth.

Amaliya stood beside Tyler as the blonde executed a triple jump of some sort. "I don't know if I'll ever be able to do that."

"Triples aren't common in pairs skating anyway," Tyler said. "Don't worry about what they're doing. They've had a few years' head start on the technical side of things, but you'll get it."

An elegant woman in her forties approached. Her blonde hair was styled perfectly, and she carried with her an air of authority, confidence, and impatience. She stepped beside Carolyn.

"Amaliya, this is our coach, Scarlett."

Amaliya extended her hand. "It's nice to meet you."

"You too." She turned to Carolyn. "I saw you working on the simple lifts. We have some work to do there, but I want to see your jumps."

"Why don't you show Scarlett your double toe loops?" Carolyn suggested.

"Good idea." Tyler took Amaliya's hand.

Nerves fluttered in her stomach as though this one jump might decide her entire future. To her surprise, Tyler led her all the way around the rink.

"I thought we were doing our double toe loops," Amaliya said.

"We are, but you need to relax." Tyler squeezed her hand. "If you fall, I'll help you up, and we'll try again."

Amaliya drew a deep breath. "Okay."

Tyler counted it off, releasing her hand a few strides before they went into their jumps. Amaliya's heart bounced in her chest when she landed and remained upright.

"See? Piece of cake." Tyler led her back to Scarlett.

"Not bad," Scarlett said. "Amaliya, try tightening your arms during your rotation. It will give you a better presentation."

"Do you want us to do it again?" Tyler asked.

"Yes."

They repeated the skill.

"Better." Scarlett nodded her approval. "What else can you show me?"

One by one, Amaliya and Tyler went through the various elements they had worked on over the past hour.

"I think I've seen enough," Scarlett finally said. "It's never easy to work with a new partner, but your strides are well matched. Is she the partner you want?"

Amaliya looked at Tyler expectantly. Would he step away from this partnership before it really began? Or would he gamble that she could learn what she needed to know to compete?

Tyler swallowed hard and spoke with forced confidence. "Yes. She is."

"In that case, Amaliya, we'll see you at practice this afternoon. One o'clock." Scarlett headed toward the other two skaters she had been working with earlier.

Another wave of insecurity crested. "Tyler, I still have so much to learn. Are you sure you want to skate with me?"

"I'm sure." He put his hand on her back. "Come on. I'll introduce you to our training partners."

Amaliya skated with Tyler across the ice.

"Marie, Becky, this is my new partner, Amaliya."

"Hi," Becky said, her voice soft.

Marie gave a subtle nod of acknowledgment. "How long have you been skating?"

"I just started up again," Amaliya said.

Marie's eyebrows lifted, and she turned her attention to Tyler. "Tyler, did you want to get some breakfast this morning?"

"Sorry. I have to work." Tyler put his hand on Amaliya's back again and nudged her toward where they had left their skate bags. "Did you want to leave your skates here today? I can lock them up in the office."

"Actually, that would be great," Amaliya said. "Thanks."

"Thank you," Tyler countered.

"For what?" Amaliya asked.

"For agreeing to be my partner." Tyler sat down and unlaced his skates. Some of the tension Amaliya had sensed in him eased. "I can't tell you how relieved I am to be done evaluating other skaters."

"How many other skaters did you consider?"

"I don't know. I think it was eighteen."

"You held tryouts with eighteen other skaters, and you picked me?" Amaliya asked. "Why?"

"Because none of the others was the right one."

"And you think I am?"

Tyler's eyes met hers. "I really hope you are."

Chapter
TEN

KATERINA CONCENTRATED ON MOVING HER spoon to her mouth without spilling her mashed potatoes. What she wouldn't give to be able to adjust her body into a more comfortable position. But she was alive. Robert was alive. She reminded herself that she needed to be grateful for that.

A knock sounded on her open door.

"Come in."

"I have a new roommate for you." An orderly rolled a bed into the room. The patient's leg hung from a contraption that had been attached to the metal railings of the bed.

Katerina's gaze traveled the length of the long body to the face. "Robert!" She focused on the orderly. "I thought the doctor said we couldn't be in the same room."

"Your husband is very persuasive." The orderly locked the wheels of the bed in place. "I'll leave you two to catch up."

"The doctor has been keeping me up-to-date on your progress," Robert said, switching to French. "I'm so sorry."

"He says there's still a chance . . ." Katerina trailed off. "How are you? The doctor hasn't said much, other than your leg has to stay in traction for a few more weeks."

"I'll have a few new scars, but I'll be okay. I talked to Miles yesterday."

"How is Amaliya doing?"

"She's struggling a bit. She hasn't danced since the accident, but I think she's doing okay."

"Amaliya? Not dance?" Katerina couldn't be hearing Robert correctly. "She must be dancing when no one is around."

"She didn't even bring her ballet slippers to Connecticut. I don't think she wants to dance as long as you aren't able to."

"She can't do that to herself. She's an amazing dancer."

"I know. This has to be so hard for her, starting at a new school, living in a new house."

"I hate that her life has been turned upside down like this." Suddenly cold, Katerina reached down to pull her blanket up higher. When she couldn't reach it, she lifted her knee to bring the blanket closer. "Amaliya should be enjoying her last year of high school, not spending her time worrying about you and me."

"Katerina." Robert stared at her.

"What?"

"You just moved your leg."

"I . . ." Katerina stared down at her legs. The last few seconds replayed in her mind. She concentrated on repeating the movement. Her knee bent. "I moved."

"Try the other one."

Hope bloomed. Katerina straightened her right leg and proceeded to bend her left. "I can move." She put her hands on her thighs. Euphoria poured through her. "I can feel."

"Thank the Lord." Robert spoke the words at full volume. He cast his eyes heavenward before he looked back at her. "I was afraid you'd never . . . I thought . . ."

The moisture in Robert's eyes brought a flood of tears to her own. As hard as she had tried to stay positive, the fear of not walking again, of being a burden on Robert and Amaliya, had always been there. Determination swelled within her now. She could get her life back.

She straightened her left leg again as much to prove she could as to get more comfortable. "I can move." Her voice rose in volume. "I can really move."

A nurse rushed in. She must have misinterpreted their tears because she immediately asked, "What's wrong? What happened?"

"I can move my legs." Katerina spoke the words in French automatically.

"What's wrong?" the nurse asked again. "I don't understand."

"I can move my legs," Katerina repeated in English.

Delight flooded the nurse's expression. "I'll call for the doctor."

"You're causing a stir again." Robert grinned and swiped at his eyes. "And, Katerina, don't worry about Amaliya. I know life isn't what she expected right now, but she's going to do great things, just like her mother."

Tyler walked into the rink to the sound of women's voices, the words spoken in a foreign tongue. He caught a glimpse of Marie's mother and remembered. Marie had come in early today so she could run through her long program without anyone else on the ice.

At the edge of the rink, Marie and her mother spoke in rapid French. Despite living in the United States for over twenty years, Mrs. Averett insisted on speaking to Marie in her native language.

Amaliya walked in behind him. "Are we late?"

"No. Marie came in early to practice her programs. She leaves for the world championships in two weeks. Scarlett had her change a few things in her long program after nationals to increase the difficulty."

"When were nationals?"

"Three weeks ago. Marie placed second."

"Wow. That's impressive," Amaliya said. "I guess you and Carolyn couldn't compete because of her injury."

"Actually, we made it through the short program. We were in first place."

"What happened?"

"She slipped on the sidewalk on our way to practice the next day and sprained her ankle," Tyler said. "It was so swollen she couldn't even get her foot into her skate."

"That's heartbreaking."

"Yeah. She told me a few days later that she was going to retire."

"You've had a tough month."

"A lot of changes, anyway," Tyler said. "Come on. Let's warm up."

They put their skates on and took the ice. "Is Carolyn coming to help again?" Amaliya asked.

"Yeah. She should be here any minute." Tyler took her hand. "Follow my lead."

"What are we doing?" Amaliya asked.

"Let's dance." Tyler reversed direction and put his hand on her waist. He grinned when Amaliya instinctively put her hand on his shoulder.

"How was school today?" Tyler asked.

"It was okay," Amaliya said. "I kind of like getting out at noon."

"You didn't have that at your old school?"

"No." She pressed her lips together. "This move gave me the chance to drop a couple of classes I didn't want anyway."

"Like?"

"Calculus."

"So you're one of those smart kids."

"I don't know about that," Amaliya said. "I am looking forward to graduating though."

"I remember that feeling well." Tyler led her around the rink once and then cut through the center. "Are you ready to start?"

"Sure." They joined Becky and Scarlett at the side of the rink.

"Becky, I want you to work on the first dance sequence in your long program," Scarlett said. "Amaliya and Tyler, let's work on timing your jumps."

"We're ready," Tyler said.

They went through their toe loops and salchows, Scarlett offering critique and suggestions after each one. Tyler had missed this level of coaching and having someone to time with.

"It's getting better," Scarlett said an hour later. "Tyler, you need to get a bit more height in your double salchow so your landing will coincide with Amaliya's."

"I need more height?" Tyler asked, surprised.

She nodded. "Amaliya, I want you to work on speeding up your rotation. You have plenty of height. You just need to learn what to do with it."

"How do I do that?"

"It might help to practice in the dance studio. Do you still study ballet?"

Surprise reflected on Amaliya's face. "How did you know I studied ballet?"

"I can tell by the way you move."

"I only moved here last week, but I have a place at home I can practice."

"Good." Scarlett waved at Carolyn.

Carolyn approached them. "Did you need something?"

"Can you watch their timing?" Scarlett asked.

"Sure."

"Work on their turns, too, especially their sit spins."

"You heard her." Carolyn pointed at the center of the ice.

For the next hour, they did one spin after another, one jump after another.

"I think our time is up." Carolyn pointed at the clock on the wall.

"I don't have to work tonight. Do you need a ride home?" Tyler asked.

"No, thanks. My ride is waiting for me." Amaliya stepped through the opening in the rink barrier. "I'll see you in the morning."

"See you then." Tyler watched her head toward the exit. "I wonder what Miles is doing here. His team doesn't practice on Tuesdays."

Amaliya stopped beside Miles. When they turned to leave together, Tyler's last conversation with Miles played through his mind. His friends' accident. The daughter they had taken in.

One and one slowly equaled two.

"What are you staring at?" Carolyn asked. When he didn't answer, she added, "Is something wrong?"

"I figured out why we'd never seen Amaliya around before."

"Why?"

"Remember how the Donnellys were gone for a few days last week?"

"Yeah. Two of their friends were in a car accident."

"And their friends' daughter moved in with them," Tyler said. "Miles said she didn't have anyone else."

Carolyn glanced at the exit as Miles opened the door and escorted Amaliya outside. "You think Amaliya is the girl who moved in with them?"

"Yeah." Tyler's stomach clenched. He'd finally found someone he wanted to skate with . . . someone who was in the middle of a major life crisis.

"What am I going to do?" Tyler asked. "She has to be going through a lot right now. Both of her parents are in the hospital. She's in a new school. Adding the pressure of training won't be easy."

"I don't think she's looking for easy," Carolyn said.

"You know what I mean. A lot of people with a solid support system behind them can't handle the mental strain of competing at the world level."

"Seems to me Miles Donnelly is giving her what she needs by letting her be here. He was a coach as well as a professional athlete. Who better to give her that kind of support?"

His chest tightened uncomfortably. "Her parents."

"Yes, and I'm sure they'll do what they can from their hospital beds." Carolyn put her hand on his arm. "Be her friend. That's all you can do."

"How do I do that when she doesn't talk about herself?" Tyler asked. "I've made comments about her parents a couple of times, but she has never said anything about their accident."

"The accident was only last week. You said yourself Miles didn't know if her mom was going to be able to walk again. That has to be tough," Carolyn said. "She'll talk to you about it when she's ready."

"I hope you're right."

Chapter
ELEVEN

AMALIYA RUBBED HER GLOVED HANDS together, both to warm them and to try to wake herself up. Though she was normally an early riser, four o'clock was early, even for her.

Beside her, Miles cranked up the car heater and pulled out of the driveway.

"I have a meeting this morning," Miles said. "Are you okay with walking to school?"

"Yeah. I'll be fine." Amaliya tried not to think about the low temperature she would endure while traversing the three blocks. Though she wasn't sure she wanted Miles to agree with her, she added, "If it's too much for you to drive me every day, I can drive myself if you don't mind me borrowing a car."

"Are you kidding? This is like my old hockey days when we used to go in and chase the figure skaters off the ice." Miles grinned. "Good times."

Though she appreciated the humor in his voice, warmth and a sense of gratitude spread through her. She couldn't deny the love and encouragement Miles and Linda had offered her throughout her life but especially since the accident.

Miles rolled the car to a stop in front of the rink. Amaliya couldn't resist leaning over and kissing his cheek. "Thanks."

Surprise illuminated his features. "You have a good day. I'll see you this afternoon."

"Okay." She climbed out of the car and hurried inside, passing the office and approaching the benches where Tyler stood talking to Marie and Becky. Marie noticed her first and shot her a condescending look, then pushed up onto her toes and kissed Tyler's cheek. "I'll see you after practice."

"Yeah. Sure."

Marie moved past Amaliya like a princess who couldn't be bothered to associate with peasants. Becky followed.

"Hi, Amaliya," Becky said.

"Good morning."

Tyler turned to face her as Scarlett approached with Carolyn.

"After you warm up, I want to work on your jumps this morning," Scarlett said. "You two also need to pick music for your programs so we can start on choreography. We can start by adapting your old programs. Carolyn should be able to help with that."

"Sounds good." Tyler led the way onto the ice to warm up and asked Amaliya, "Are you doing anything tonight?"

"Not really."

"Want to get together? We can grab something to eat and talk music."

Even though the offer didn't appear to be anything beyond a simple offer of friendship, Amaliya's pulse quickened. "Yeah, I'd like that."

"Great. I have to work for an hour after practice. Want to meet me around six?"

"Sure. Where do you want to meet?"

"How about Barney's? It's a great little hamburger place on Main Street," Tyler suggested.

"Sounds good."

They circled back to where Scarlett waited.

"Double salchows." Scarlett pointed to the ice. "Let me see them."

"You got it." Tyler took Amaliya's hand, and the familiar tingle worked through her. "Ready?"

"Yeah." Amaliya drew a deep breath. "I think I am."

Tyler sat on the bench between Amaliya and Marie and unlaced his skates.

"Did you hear Charlotte Winters agreed to design my costume for worlds?" Marie asked.

"No, I hadn't heard." Tyler wasn't sure who Charlotte Winters was or why Marie needed yet another new costume. The girl had more skating outfits than anyone he'd ever seen. Amaliya, on the other hand, typically wore a simple leotard, tights, and a ballet skirt to practice in.

"Who's Charlotte Winters?" Amaliya asked.

"Only the best costume designer in the country." Marie rolled her eyes.

"What color is this one going to be?" Becky asked from where she sat across from them.

"Red," Marie said. "I want it to really catch everyone's attention."

Amaliya stood. "I'd better get to school. See you later."

Tyler watched her go, automatically tuning out Becky and Marie's continued discussion about her planned wardrobe. As soon as he had his shoes on, he stood.

Marie stood beside him. "Ready to go?"

"Yeah." Tyler stored his skates and pushed the door open for Marie. When she had suggested going out for breakfast this morning, he'd agreed mostly because he didn't have anything better to do. He wasn't sure what to think about the fact that he was looking forward to his working dinner with Amaliya more than his breakfast date with Marie.

He opened the passenger side door for Marie and waited for her to get in before he circled to the driver's side. He started the car, and Marie droned on about the fashion designer. Maybe it was time to take a break from her again. He really had to learn how to turn her down when she asked him out.

He drove only a block before he noticed a familiar figure on the side of the road. He slowed the car to keep pace with Amaliya, then interrupted Marie's monologue on adornments. "Roll down your window."

"What?"

When Marie didn't comply, Tyler put the car in park and climbed out. "Hey, Amaliya. Do you need a ride?"

"It's only another two blocks."

The wind ripped through them, and Amaliya caught her breath.

"It's freezing out here," Tyler said. "Get in. We'll take you."

"Thanks." Amaliya got into the back seat.

As soon as they were both in the car, Tyler said, "You should have told me you needed a ride."

Amaliya didn't respond. To Tyler's relief, Marie also fell silent.

He pulled up in front of the high school a moment later, the same one he had graduated from three years ago.

"Thanks so much," Amaliya said.

"Any time," Tyler replied.

Amaliya climbed out, clutched her coat tighter around her, and hurried inside.

"Can we go now?" Marie asked.

Not realizing that he had automatically watched Amaliya until she disappeared inside, Tyler put the car in gear.

"You didn't have to do that, you know."

"What?" Tyler asked. "Give Amaliya a ride?"

"Yeah. It was only a few blocks."

"A few blocks is a long way when it's below freezing."

"I guess." Marie shrugged. "You know, Charlotte Winters designs men's costumes too. You should talk to her about doing your next one."

"I don't think I'll have to worry about that for a while."

"I guess that's true," Marie said. "That's what you get for choosing a novice as your partner."

Tyler's jaw clenched. Had he made a mistake? He shook the doubt away. Amaliya might have some skills to learn, but she was far from a beginner.

Amaliya gripped the wheel of Linda's car and concentrated on breathing in and out. Was the temptation of going out with Tyler really worth the risk of driving? The roads were dry, and no one expected bad weather for another day or two. But that didn't take away the pounding in her chest or the dampness of her palms.

Keeping her speed to five miles under the speed limit, she navigated her way out of her new neighborhood and onto the main road that would take her to the hamburger place.

A truck approached from the opposite direction and whizzed past her with enough speed to cause the car to catch in the draft and rattle.

Amaliya's heart pounded, and her grip tightened. She forced herself to breathe. Only another mile. She could do this.

Two minutes later, she pulled into the parking lot and turned off the car. Relief poured through her.

She took a moment before she gathered her purse and climbed out of the car. The scent of hamburgers and french fries carried to her.

Tyler stood when she entered and waved at her from a corner booth.

"Glad you made it." He tapped on the glass-topped table. "The menu is right here. As soon as you decide what you want, I'll go order."

Amaliya looked down. Sure enough, mounted between the table and the glass that covered it was a menu at each seat. "What's good here?"

"Their double bacon cheeseburger is amazing," Tyler said. "And you have to try their french fries."

"That sounds like a lot of food." Amaliya scanned the menu, opting for simplicity. "I think I'll just have a cheeseburger."

"And to drink?"

"Just water."

"One cheeseburger and a glass of water coming up." Tyler slid out of the booth.

"I can get mine." She reached for her purse.

"No, I've got it."

Before she could object, Tyler crossed to the order counter. The door opened again, and Sarah walked in, followed by a guy Amaliya had seen only in pictures until now: Sarah's boyfriend, Kent.

They took their place in line behind Tyler, and Sarah looked around as though searching for an empty table. She spotted Amaliya and said something to her boyfriend. A moment later, she crossed to where Amaliya sat.

"Hey, what are you doing here?" Sarah asked.

"I'm here with my skating partner."

Her eyebrows lifted. "Oh, really?"

"It's not like that," Amaliya said even as her cheeks warmed.

Tyler approached, carrying a tray with their food on it.

"Sarah, this is Tyler Linden," Amaliya said. "Tyler, this is Sarah Jensen. We go to school together."

"Nice to meet you." Tyler slid the food onto the table. "Are you here alone?"

"No, my boyfriend is ordering for us."

"Do you want to join us?" Tyler asked. He waved to encompass the room. "This place is packed."

"Are you sure you don't mind?"

"Not at all." He motioned to the side of the booth opposite Amaliya. "Have a seat."

"Thanks." Sarah sat down.

Tyler touched Amaliya's shoulder so she would slide over. She made room for him, and Tyler slid into the spot beside her. His arm pressed against hers, and her stomach somersaulted, not unlike the first time he had taken her hand.

Kent approached, carrying his and Sarah's food.

"Kent, this is Amaliya and Tyler."

"Amaliya? You must be the girl Sarah's been telling me about."

"Oh yeah?" Amaliya glanced at her friend.

"Nothing bad, I promise." Sarah reached for her hamburger. "I told him how you've been helping me with French."

"You're taking French?" Tyler asked.

"She could teach the class," Sarah answered for her. "Her accent is better than our teacher's."

"I don't know about that," Amaliya said.

Tyler set Amaliya's water and cheeseburger in front of her. "How did you learn to speak French so well?"

Thoughts of the accident surfaced, and she fought against them. "My dad. He's from Quebec."

"I didn't know that." He held out his basket of fries. "Here. Try one."

Amaliya took one and bit into it. "Oh, that is good."

"I have enough to share." Tyler picked up his enormous burger. "Kent, are you still in school?"

"I'm a freshman at NYU."

They fell into easy conversation. Amaliya noted several of her classmates coming and going while they enjoyed their meal, but it wasn't until Tyler finished eating and stretched his arm across the back of the booth that she considered the truth. To anyone who didn't know better, it would look like she was here on a date rather than simply eating with friends.

What would it be like to have a boyfriend again? And would Tyler ever see her as anything beyond his partner?

Chapter
TWELVE

TYLER WALKED INTO THE RINK with a sense of exhilaration. Dinner with Amaliya last night had given him a glimpse of normal life again, something he had missed over the past several months, first because of his intensive training and then because of his search for a new partner.

Even when he went out with Marie, he felt like he was at practice. The girl never talked about anything but skating. Amaliya hadn't mentioned skating once last night, even though the purpose of going out together had been to discuss their music.

Like a breath of fresh air, she walked in, a smile on her face. "Good morning."

"Morning." He helped her take her jacket off.

"Thanks." Amaliya grabbed her jacket from him and set it aside. "I'm sorry we never got around to talking about music last night."

"That's okay," Tyler said. "It was kind of nice not talking about skating for a change."

"What do you mean?"

"I've been focused on making the Olympics for so long that it's not often I get the chance to hang out the way we did last night."

"The Olympics?" Amaliya grabbed his arm, and her eyes widened. "Wait. You think we can make it to the Olympics?"

"That's the plan."

"I'm not good enough for that."

"Not yet, but you will be," Tyler assured her. "Have you given any thought to what music you'd like to skate to?"

"I hate to say it, but other than watching ice skating on television, I don't know much about the competition side of the sport," Amaliya said. "What kind of music do you normally use?"

"If we want to play it safe, we should stick with something traditional."

"Traditional?"

"Yeah, you know, classical, ballet, something along those lines," Tyler said. "We'll need two pieces, one for our short program and another for our long."

Amaliya fell silent for a moment, and a wistful expression appeared on her face.

"Any thoughts?" Tyler prompted.

"What about either Beethoven or Tchaikovsky?"

"That's not narrowing it down much. Any particular piece you like?"

"Beethoven's 'Moonlight Sonata' is beautiful."

Tyler considered the possibility. "I think we can work with that."

"It's hard to believe I wasn't even skating regularly a few weeks ago, and now we're talking about competing on a world stage," Amaliya said. "Do you think we can really get there?"

"We'll find out soon enough."

Amaliya sat between Scarlett and Tyler while Scarlett described the basic short program they would begin learning today. She could hardly believe that only a week ago, she hadn't ever considered becoming a figure skater, and now she was learning her first competitive program. After she and Tyler warmed up, they joined Scarlett by the side of the rink.

"Okay, let's start by going through the required elements," Scarlett said. "Start with side-by-side double axels."

A streak of panic shot through Amaliya. "I'm sorry. I don't know how to do that yet."

"What?" Scarlett looked at Tyler. "What happened to Amaliya being a good match?"

Tyler glided closer to Amaliya. "She's still learning some of the technical aspects of the sport, but she's a beautiful skater."

Scarlett folded her arms. "I'll be honest with you, Tyler. Amaliya moves beautifully, but it's going to be a challenge to get her up to your level if she doesn't already have the required elements."

"She's the partner I want," Tyler said.

"What other skills is she missing?"

"She has all of her doubles except her lutz and axel," Tyler said.

Annoyance rose inside Amaliya. Scarlett could at least acknowledge that she was here too. Instead, she was talking about her as if she were invisible.

"Have Carolyn work with you on her double lutz." Scarlett left them and moved to Marie's side, immediately correcting her body position on one of her spins.

"I guess we're working on your double lutz," Tyler said.

"I guess so."

Amaliya fell. Again. For every other jump, she had been able to convert her singles into doubles with only some minor adjustments. Sure, she'd fallen plenty during the first few tries, but the double lutz had become her nemesis. Not once had she landed it successfully. She didn't want to think about how she would do when she moved on to attempt a double axel.

"I'm never going to get this," she said.

"You will. It takes time." Tyler took her hand and pulled her up. "You've already learned so much faster than I thought possible."

"Apparently, I've hit my plateau."

"Don't get down on yourself," Tyler said.

Carolyn approached from the side of the rink. "Let's work on something else."

"How about figures?" Tyler suggested.

"All I remember about those from my skating lessons was following my teacher around in a figure eight," Amaliya said.

"There's a little more to it than that," Carolyn said. "For each competition, you'll typically be given six designs to practice, and you'll have to perform three. Most are a variation of a figure eight."

"It's basically drawing on the ice with your blade and trying to match the figure to the design you're given."

"Tell me what to do."

"Let's start by having you try to follow a design Tyler creates for you," Carolyn suggested. "Think of it like follow the leader."

Amaliya pretended she was playing the simple childhood game, but following Tyler's tracks was anything but simple. "This is harder than it looks."

"It takes a lot of practice to master them," Carolyn said.

"Let's work on something else." Tyler rolled his shoulders. "How about our camels. Those are always tough to time."

"Good idea," Carolyn said, "but let's work on them as part of your program."

"You want to add the choreography?"

"Yes. No reason to put it off."

For the rest of practice, Tyler and Carolyn taught Amaliya the first part of what had previously been their short program. The lifts were simplified, but by the time their skating session ended, they had the basics down for the first section.

"Great job, you two," Carolyn said.

"Thanks, Carolyn," Amaliya said. "I'll see you later."

Tyler followed Amaliya across the ice. "Oh, I meant to tell you I can give you a ride to school today if you want."

"That would be great, if you don't mind." She stopped at the water fountain and took a drink.

"It's not a problem. I don't have to work today."

"What are you going to do with your free time?"

"Sleep."

"I'm jealous."

"Actually, I'll lift weights first and then sleep," he said. "It'll only be a few months before you graduate, and you'll have that kind of freedom."

A few months until she graduated. By midsummer, her parents could be released from the hospital. Would they be able to return home right away? Would they fully recover? And would she want to go back to Virginia with them? When she left Virginia, she had considered this move temporary, but now that she was skating with Tyler, she didn't know if she would want to leave Connecticut as she'd originally planned.

"What are you thinking?" Tyler asked.

"Just thinking about how much things will change between now and summer."

"Things have already changed a lot over the past week," Tyler said. "It's hard to believe I didn't even know you a couple weeks ago."

"It doesn't seem real."

Ten minutes later, Tyler dropped her off at school, and she was still trying to get a handle on her emotions when she climbed out of his car and collected her book bag. "Thanks for the ride."

"No problem. I'll see you this afternoon."

As she had on Friday night, she let herself step into the illusion of what it would be like to have someone like Tyler interested in her beyond friendship.

She made it to French class, and immediately, Sarah's questions started.

"Why didn't you tell me you were dating your skating partner?"

Several heads turned in their direction.

"Shhh." Amaliya's cheeks warmed.

"Well? Tyler is gorgeous, and he's such a nice guy," Sarah said. "You should have told me you were going out. It's not like he's the type of guy you'd be ashamed of dating."

"We aren't dating."

Sarah's animated expression conveyed her disbelief. "Are you sure about that? You two looked pretty cozy Friday night."

"We spend a lot of time together. That's all."

"Is that all *you* want? Or is that all *he* wants?" Sarah asked.

The bell rang, and Madam Martin began attendance. Sarah's question repeated through Amaliya's mind. If Tyler weren't dating Marie, would Amaliya want to take her friendship with Tyler to the next level? She shook that thought aside.

It didn't matter that she looked forward to spending time with him every day or that her heart always picked up speed when he took her hand. Tyler wasn't interested in her that way, and she didn't want to jeopardize their friendship by letting herself think that would ever change.

Tyler took Amaliya's hand, the naturalness of how it fit in his giving him a comfort he couldn't quite describe. Halfway through practice, Scarlett pulled Amaliya aside for some individual coaching. With a few minutes to himself, Tyler joined his sister at the side of the rink.

Once again, he found himself drawn in by Amaliya's innate grace that had captivated him from the first time he'd seen her on the ice.

Carolyn nudged his arm and lowered her voice. "You like her."

"What? Who?" Tyler turned to face his sister.

"Amaliya." Carolyn hooked her hand around his arm. "Don't think I haven't noticed how you look at her."

"I don't know what you're talking about."

"You've given her a ride to school every day this week, and I haven't seen you go out with Marie since Monday."

"You act like Marie and I are serious," Tyler said. "Besides, it's not easy being around Marie when she's so focused on going to worlds. She tends to forget that I'm staying home."

"I know it isn't easy, but you'll be there next year." Carolyn nodded toward Amaliya. "What about your new partner? Any sparks flying?"

"I'm twenty-one. She's barely eighteen."

"Three years isn't that big of an age difference," Carolyn said. "And you didn't answer my question. Do you like her?"

"It would be hard not to."

"Maybe you should ask her out on a real date."

"What if she isn't interested in me that way?" Tyler asked. "She's got a lot going on in her life right now. I don't want to do anything to throw off the balance, especially while she's still in high school."

"I guess," Carolyn said, "but maybe it would be good for her to know how you feel."

"I'm not sure I know how I feel," Tyler countered. "All of this is as new for me as it is for her."

"What do you mean?"

"Working with a new partner, having you coach us as much as, if not more than Scarlett . . ."

"Taking a back seat to Marie," Carolyn finished for him.

"What do you mean?"

"Whether we want to admit it or not, until my injury, Scarlett gave us the lion's share of her attention at practice. We were her best chance of making it to the Olympics, and both Marie and Becky knew it."

"Marie's her best shot now."

"Today, that's true, but you and Amaliya will get there too," Carolyn said. Tyler's eyes were drawn again to Amaliya. He caught the way Carolyn's eyebrows lifted.

"We're just friends."

Carolyn squeezed his arm. "You keep telling yourself that."

Chapter
THIRTEEN

WORDS ROLLED THROUGH AMALIYA'S HEAD as she approached her mother's hospital room. She couldn't wait to tell her about Tyler and her adventures in skating this week, but she also dreaded sharing her news when her mother still didn't know if she would ever walk again, much less dance.

Linda put her hand on Amaliya's shoulder. "No matter what happens with your mom, she won't want you to stop living your life."

Amazed Linda had ascertained her thoughts so easily, Amaliya nodded. "You're right."

Amaliya led the way into her mother's room, surprised that two beds now occupied the space. Her father lay in the bed on the left side of the room, his leg still suspended in midair by a triangle-shaped contraption. Her mother lay in the other bed, her head immobilized by the funky head gear that encircled her forehead and rested on her shoulders.

"You're both in the same place. How did you manage that?" Amaliya asked.

"I had a little discussion with the nurses," her dad said.

The doctor followed Amaliya, Linda, and Miles into the room. "An argument is more like it."

"My wife and I will heal faster if we're together," Robert said.

"I hope you're right," Dr. Caldwell said.

"How are they doing?" Amaliya asked. "And how much longer will they have to stay here?"

"We won't be releasing them anytime soon."

"Doctor, we don't have to talk about this right now," Katerina said.

Amaliya recognized the evasion and faced it head-on. "Mama, I want to know everything. I want to know if you'll be able to walk again, if you'll be able to dance again, if Papa will be able to coach and play hockey again."

"All of those things are too far in the future for us to answer right now," Dr. Caldwell said.

"Tell me what you do know," Amaliya pressed.

Dr. Caldwell exchanged a look with Katerina. When she waved her hand at Amaliya, he explained the medical challenges both of her parents would face in the coming months. The good news: her mother had regained the feeling in her legs. The bad news: she would have to remain in traction for four months, maybe longer. Her father also faced an extended period of time in bed, but for him, it was his leg that would remain immobilized. Extensive physical therapy would follow and would most likely also be conducted in the hospital.

After Dr. Caldwell finished explaining the current plan, he added, "Like I said, this is all based on what we know at this time. Things can change, and we'll do the best we can to make sure those changes are for the better."

"Thank you," Amaliya said.

"I'll leave you to visit." Dr. Caldwell spoke to her dad. "And, Robert, stop bullying the nurses."

"As long as they let me stay with Katerina, I'll be a model patient."

"Enjoy your visit." Dr. Caldwell disappeared into the hall.

"Sounds like someone is causing trouble," Miles said.

"You know how I feel about hospitals," Robert grumbled. He turned his attention to Amaliya. "Tell us how your first week of school went."

"It was fine. I hope you're okay with it, but I dropped a few classes so I can get out of school at lunchtime."

"Why did you do that?" Katerina asked. "Being in school is the best way to meet people."

"I know, but I thought I could get a job."

"You don't need to work," Robert insisted. "Money will be tighter than we're used to for the next little while, but we'll be okay."

"I'm glad you don't need me to work because I kind of filled my free time with something else."

"What's that?" Robert asked.

"Ice skating."

"Ice skating?" Katerina repeated.

"I met a guy at the skating rink last weekend. He asked me to compete with him as his partner in pairs figure skating."

The words were barely out of her mouth before her dad asked, "What do you know about this guy?"

"You would approve," Miles said. "I've known Tyler since I moved to Connecticut. He works at the rink, and he's one of the top figure skaters in the country."

"I still can't believe he picked me to be his partner." Amaliya sat in the chair between her parents' beds.

"Why wouldn't he pick you?" Robert asked. "You know your way around the ice as well as anyone."

"Figure skating is a little more involved than skating from one side of the rink to the other," Amaliya said.

"If this is what you want to do, I'm sure you'll be amazing," Robert said.

"Is it what you want to do?" Katerina asked. "Less than three weeks ago, you wanted to dance professionally."

"I know, but it doesn't feel right to dance when you—"

Katerina reached out and took Amaliya's hand. "Milaya, whether I walk out of here or roll out of here in a chair, don't let what happened to me or your father keep you from following your dreams."

"Thanks, Mama." Amaliya's eyes moistened, and she blinked against her rising emotions. "I love dance, but it isn't the same without you. I think ice skating is my dream now."

"Then be the best you can."

Amaliya offered a watery smile. "I will."

Amaliya's new routine fell into place so smoothly she could almost pretend her life was normal. Every morning, Miles dropped her off at practice. After practice, she spent the rest of her morning at school, staying long enough to eat lunch with Sarah and do some homework, then it was back to the rink for her afternoon practice. Her parents called once or twice a week to check in, and Sunday afternoons were reserved for visits to the hospital before she started the process all over again.

Marie and Scarlett left for the world championships two days ago, and Becky had apparently decided to take their absence as an opportunity to visit her family. Amaliya didn't have any idea where Becky's family lived, but then again, Becky and Marie hadn't spoken more than a handful of words to her since her arrival at their first practice together.

Amaliya walked into the rink to find Tyler standing in the office, the phone to his ear.

"No, it's not a problem. I'm happy to help," Tyler said to whomever he was talking to.

Amaliya continued past the office to where Carolyn was skating on the ice. Carolyn executed a double axel with an ease and grace that made it look effortless.

"That was amazing," Amaliya said. "I didn't think you were allowed to do jumps yet."

"The doctor cleared me yesterday." Carolyn beamed at her. "I can't tell you how good it feels to do that again."

Amaliya pointed at her foot. "How does it feel?"

"A little stiff but not too bad."

Tyler approached. "Yeah, she got the doctor to clear her just in time to start packing."

"You're really moving?"

Carolyn nodded. "Dan and I leave at the end of next week."

"At least she's waiting until after Scarlett gets back from worlds," Tyler added.

"I have to take advantage of my last chance to boss my baby brother around," Carolyn said. "Speaking of which, you two need to warm up."

"Yes, coach." Humor and a hint of sarcasm laced Tyler's voice, but he complied, stepping onto the ice to start his warm-up.

They spent the rest of practice working on various lifts and jumps, with Carolyn filming them as they integrated moves into their short program. When their practice time ended, Carolyn packed up the video camera.

"You should come over tonight, and we can watch our film," Tyler suggested.

"You want to spend your Friday night at home looking at film?" Amaliya asked skeptically.

"Yeah," Tyler said. "I told Miles I would give you a ride home anyway."

"What?"

"His wife's car broke down, and he had to pick her up from the train station," Tyler said as though they talked about her living situation all the time. "He called right before you got here and asked if I could take you home."

"I didn't realize you knew Miles."

"Everyone around here knows Miles," Tyler said.

Amaliya made her way to a bench to put her shoes on. Tyler sat beside her.

"I should have offered to give you a ride a long time ago. You're right on my way home." He paused and put his hand on her arm. "I'm sorry about your parents' accident. How are they doing?"

"They're both ready to be out of their hospital beds and moving on their own again."

"I can't imagine." Tyler fell silent until they were both ready to go. "What do you say? Want to come over tonight?"

"Sure. I'd like that."

"Great. Then tomorrow, we should get together and watch the world championships. The pairs short program will be on TV."

"That sounds intimidating."

"It's always good to know your competition."

"I suppose you're right." The easy friendship warmed. "I guess I could be persuaded."

"I'll order pizza."

"That's an offer I can't refuse."

Amaliya knocked on the front door of the blue-and-white Victorian home. White gauze curtains framed the window to her left, brightly colored pillows visible on what she assumed was a window seat.

The door swung open, and Tyler's broad shoulders filled the entrance, and the scent of pizza wafted toward her. "Hey, glad you could make it." He waved at Miles, who was still parked in the driveway, and stepped back to let Amaliya in.

After he closed the door, he led her into the empty living room, where a projector was set up facing a white sheet hanging on the wall.

She thought of her dad's office at home and the projector and screen that were permanent fixtures there. She'd never considered what a huge convenience his setup was compared to what she saw before her.

"Are your parents okay with us taking over their living room tonight?"

"They're used to it." Tyler continued through the room to the doorway on the far side. "Come on. Let's eat first. It'll be easier to watch film after it gets dark."

"Sounds good." She followed him into the kitchen, where his parents stood by two pizza boxes lying on the table.

"Mom, Dad, this is Amaliya."

"It's nice to meet you, Mr. and Mrs. Linden." Amaliya shook hands with both of them.

"It's our pleasure," Tyler's mom said. "We've been looking forward to meeting you. Tyler has told us so much about you."

Tyler pulled a chair out and motioned for Amaliya to sit.

"Thanks." Amaliya sat as everyone else settled around the table.

"I'll offer the prayer," Tyler's dad said.

Everyone folded their arms and bowed their heads. Mr. Linden offered a heartfelt prayer of gratitude, not only for the food but also for Amaliya's presence.

After they'd said their amens, they all put some pizza on their plates.

Amaliya expected the usual questions to follow about her parents' conditions, but surprisingly, the conversation centered around Carolyn's impending move and the possibility of snow in the forecast.

"Amaliya, has it been difficult adjusting to the early-morning practices?" Mrs. Linden asked.

"It hasn't been too bad," Amaliya said. "I've always been an early riser. Going outside in the cold has been an adjustment though."

"I'll bet. I imagine it's a lot colder here in Connecticut than what you're used to."

The winter storm the day before her parents' accident filled her mind.

"I hear Virginia gets its share of cold weather," Tyler said.

"Yeah, it does."

Tyler picked up his plate and pushed back from the table. "Amaliya, are you ready to watch film?"

"Yes." She stood. "Thank you for dinner."

"You're welcome," Mrs. Linden said. "Let me know if you want me to make popcorn later. From what Tyler said, you have a few hours of film to go through."

"Thanks, Mom." Tyler took Amaliya's plate and stacked it on his own. He set them in the sink and led Amaliya back to the living room. "Grab a seat. You're about to see the best show in town."

"The best show, huh?" Amaliya couldn't keep the smile from her lips. "I don't think we're there yet."

"Maybe not yet, but we will be."

Tyler leaned back on the couch and barely resisted putting his arm around Amaliya. Last night, they had spent three hours watching film and analyzing every move and how they could improve their timing. Tonight, they would watch the world's best.

The top French pair took the ice amid a chorus of cheers. They began their short program, each jump timed beautifully.

"Wow. They're good."

"They are, but their difficulty probably isn't enough to get them into the top six."

"I can't do half of those elements."

"You haven't learned half of those elements," Tyler corrected.

Amaliya leaned forward. "Think like a judge. Tell me the things they will get marked off for."

"It's not only what will mark them down but also what will help them increase their marks."

"I want to understand it all."

"Okay." Tyler proceeded to critique the couple on the screen. They discussed each set of competitors in turn, analyzing everything from their technique and artistry to their music choices and costumes.

"When we get ready to redo our choreography, I think we need to capitalize on your dance background," Tyler said. "Your dancing is one of our strengths."

"Who normally does your choreography?" Amaliya asked.

"Scarlett and Carolyn did most of the dance side of our routines. I was mostly involved in ordering technical elements." The Soviet couple favored to win glided onto the stage. "This is the couple who will be our biggest competition next year. Popov and Sidrova."

The music started, and the two skaters opened with an intricate dance move followed by side-by-side double axels.

"Wow. They are good."

"And they know it."

They watched in silence.

"Every move. Every spin is perfect," Amaliya said.

"Not perfect, but close," Tyler agreed. "They'll be in first after the short program, and they're even better in the long."

"Wow. Do you think anyone has a chance at beating them?"

"I don't know, but we're going to try."

Popov and Sidrova took their places in front of the cameras, along with their coach as they awaited their scores. The audio picked up their conversation as they spoke in Russian with their coach.

"They agree with you," Amaliya said.

"How do you know that?" Tyler asked.

"Their coach just said they should be in first and that if they don't have any major mistakes, they'll win overall."

Tyler shifted beside her so he was facing her more fully. "You speak Russian?"

"Yeah. My mom is Russian."

"Your mom is Russian," Tyler repeated. "How did she end up in the United States?"

"She defected when she was on tour in New York with the Kirov Ballet." Her voice grew wistful. "She was dancing the lead in *Swan Lake* when she met my father."

"They met in New York?"

"Canada actually. That's where my mom's North American tour started. My dad's hockey team stayed in the same hotel as my mom's ballet troupe."

"Wait." Tyler put his hand on her arm as two and two slowly added together. Miles's trip to DC, the newscast about the accident of the Capitals' coach, Amaliya's last name. "Is Robert Marcell your dad?"

"Yes, he is."

"I didn't realize you came from hockey royalty," Tyler said, curious about how many other significant details she hadn't shared with him yet. "It kind of makes sense though."

"What?"

"Your dad is a skater. Your mom is a ballerina. Combine the two and you get a figure skater."

"I guess that's one way of looking at it."

The scores popped up on the screen, followed by the standings. Sure enough, Popov and Sidrova took a commanding lead.

His conversation with Amaliya replayed in his mind. "You said your mom was dancing *Swan Lake* when she defected?"

"Yes."

"That's what we should use for our long program."

"*Swan Lake*?" Myriad emotions appeared on her face.

"What do you think? We could do it as a tribute to your mom."

Tears threatened, and she blinked against them.

"We don't have to—" Tyler started.

"No, I'd like to." Amaliya put her hand on his. "It would be the perfect way to honor her and the heritage I come from."

"I know you studied ballet. Did you ever dance *Swan Lake*?"

"Not on stage, but my mom taught me her part in our studio at home." Amaliya withdrew her hand and motioned to the TV. "If we're going to be competitive, though, I think we should consider using a professional choreographer."

"That would be great, but good ones don't come cheap."

"I know, but I know of one who might do it for us as a favor."

"Who?"

"Linda, Miles's wife."

"She's a choreographer?"

"She hasn't done it for a long time, but she used to work a lot with the ballet. I know part of that time was doing choreography."

"It's worth asking," Tyler said.

"We have music; we might have a choreographer. It's all starting to feel real."

"Just wait until we're making travel plans to go to Finland next year for worlds."

"Finland? I think I'd like to visit there."

"Then we'll make it happen."

Chapter FOURTEEN

AMALIYA WALKED INTO THE HOUSE to find Linda waiting up for her, Linda's fingers busily using her crochet hook to turn a ball of yarn into an afghan.

"Did you have a good time?"

"I did." Amaliya dropped her purse on the couch and sat across from Linda. "The skaters we watched tonight were so good."

"They would have to be to make it to the world championships."

"It's so strange. One minute, I can't fathom being able to do everything those skaters do so effortlessly, but then the next, Tyler will talk like it's a given that we'll make it to worlds next year, and I let myself believe."

"There's nothing wrong with believing in yourself," Linda said. "You've studied ballet your whole life. You learned to skate almost as soon as you could walk. Putting those two skills together is a perfect recipe for figure skating."

"Tyler said the same thing tonight."

"He's a smart man."

"I do have a favor I want to ask you though."

"What's that?" Linda asked.

"Tyler and I decided to skate to music from *Swan Lake* for our long program. I thought maybe you would help us with the choreography."

"Honey, I would love to help you, but that's not something I'm very good at."

"My mom said you used to do choreography when you were with the ballet."

"That was a lot of years ago, and there's a reason I moved into the administrative side of dance." Linda set her crocheting aside. "How soon would you need this choreography?"

"Tyler wants us to get the basics down sooner rather than later. We already have the basics for our short program."

"Have you already chosen your music for that too?"

"We were thinking about using the 'Moonlight Sonata.'"

"That would suit you well," Linda said. "Tell you what. Let me make a few calls on Monday. I have a couple friends who might be willing to help. Between me and your mom, I think we can find someone who can find some time to work with you."

"That would be great. Thank you."

"It's my pleasure. If you're going to compete in the world championships, you need to be ready."

"You sound like Tyler. When I hear you say that, I almost believe it's going to happen."

"I believe in you. So does Miles, and so do your parents." Linda's expression went soft. "No matter what happens, though, we are all so proud of you."

Amaliya swallowed the lump that formed in her throat. "Thanks, Linda. I wish they could be here to see me now."

"I know, but these next few months will fly by. They'll be out of the hospital and sitting in the stands in no time."

"I look forward to that day."

"We all do."

He'd been looking for her. Tyler hadn't recognized it until Amaliya had walked through his front door and joined the throngs of guests currently filling their living room, but he acknowledged it now.

The going-away party for Carolyn and Dan had started out as a small event with a few close friends but had quickly expanded to include the entire neighborhood and a number of friends from the rink.

Miles and Linda followed Amaliya inside and approached where Tyler stood with Hank.

"Looks like you have quite the crowd here." Miles shook hands with Tyler.

"You should see the kitchen. It's packed."

"Tyler, have you met my wife, Linda?" Miles asked.

"I don't think so." Tyler shook her hand. "It's nice to meet you."

"You too. With as much as these two talk about you, I feel like I already know you."

"I know what you mean."

Miles nudged his wife. "They're both here together. Tell them the news."

Amaliya glanced at Linda. "What news?"

"Remember how you asked me about helping you with your choreography?" Linda asked.

"Yeah," Amaliya said.

"I finally connected with a friend in New York. She agreed to choreograph your new routines."

"That's great. Who is she?" Amaliya asked.

"Beth Williamson. You may remember her. She visited you a few times when you were younger."

A vague image of a tall woman with a New England accent formed in Tyler's mind.

"I think so. Is she the one from Boston?" Amaliya asked.

"Yes, that's her," Linda said. "She's been choreographing in New York for ten years now, but she's taking a month off between productions. She said she'd love the chance to work with you."

Tyler's jaw dropped. "Wait. Is this the same Beth Williamson who choreographed for Marlena Hammond when she won the silver medal?"

"That's right," Linda said. "Beth's with the New York City Ballet now, but she's worked with a few skaters in the past, and she said she was excited for a change of pace."

"You know of her?" Amaliya asked Tyler.

"Yeah. She's a legend in the skating community," Tyler said. "She used to be the most sought-after choreographer in figure skating, but she hasn't done anything with the sport for several years."

"Don't spread it around that she's helping you. She isn't taking on any other new clients."

"This is amazing news," Tyler said. "Thank you."

"Don't thank me yet. She's demanding."

"That's okay. It will be nice to have someone make demands that focus on the artistic side of the sport."

"Miles, you're my witness," Linda said.

"When do we start?" Amaliya asked.

"She'll be here to meet with you a week from Monday," Linda said. "She wants to watch your practices to get a feel for your style. We thought we could all have dinner together that night so you can talk before she goes back to the city."

"That sounds great," Tyler said. "Thank you so much."

"It's my pleasure."

Chapter
FIFTEEN

AMALIYA ENTERED THE ICE RINK with Linda following behind her. "Are you sure Mrs. Williamson said she was coming to our morning practice?"

"That's what she said." Linda looked around the rink. "Looks like we got here first. Will your coach be okay with Beth working with you today?"

"I don't see why not."

The door opened behind them, and Marie breezed inside. She shot her typical condescending look at Amaliya before passing by without a word.

Linda waited until Marie was well past them before asking, "Who's that?"

"Marie Averett."

"She's not very friendly."

"She doesn't think I'm good enough to be here," Amaliya said in a low voice. "She's also dating Tyler, so I don't think she's very happy about him spending time with me."

"She doesn't seem like Tyler's type."

Another gust of cold air blasted toward them when Tyler opened the door and held it open as someone else entered.

"There she is." Linda waved to get Beth's attention. "Thank you so much for coming."

"I'm happy to help."

Linda waited until Tyler approached before she offered introductions. "Beth, you probably remember Amaliya."

"It's been a long time." Beth took Amaliya's hand in hers and held on. "I'm so sorry about your parents' accident. Your mother is one of the most talented dancers I've ever had the privilege to work with."

"Thank you," Amaliya said. "I know she has great respect for you."

"And this is Tyler Linden, Amaliya's partner," Linda said.

"Tyler, it's a pleasure."

"The pleasure is all mine." Tyler shook her hand.

"Where would you like to start?" Linda asked.

"For now, I only want to observe, if that's okay," Beth said.

"Of course," Linda said. "I'm excited to see Amaliya skate. This is my first time at the rink since she started skating with Tyler."

"I'll try not to fall," Amaliya said.

"Just pretend we aren't here," Beth said.

Beth and Linda walked to the far side of the rink, where they could sit on a set of risers. Scarlett approached. "Who's that?"

"My aunt and one of her friends," Amaliya said. "They wanted to watch practice. I hope that's okay."

"As long as you don't make it a habit." Scarlett nodded toward the risers. "I don't like having an audience during practice. Family members have a tendency to interfere."

Amaliya glanced at Tyler. How and when should they tell Scarlett that Beth's sole purpose for being here was to interfere?

Tyler put his hand on Amaliya's back. "Come on. We should get started."

As soon as they were out of earshot, Amaliya lowered her voice. "We need to tell Scarlett what Beth is doing here."

"I know, but Linda said Beth didn't want us to mention who she was to anyone," Tyler said. "We should wait until after we talk to her tonight."

"You're right. I'm not very good at keeping secrets though."

"Are you kidding?" Tyler turned around so he was skating backward in front of her. "You don't give anything away. If you don't want someone to know something, they aren't going to know it."

"That's an exaggeration."

"Maybe, but not by much," Tyler said. "Had I not seen you with Miles when we first started skating together, I probably still wouldn't know about your parents' accident."

"You would have figured it out," Amaliya said. "You're intuitive about things like that."

"My family would disagree with you, especially Carolyn." Tyler reached out a hand. "You ready to show Beth and Linda what we can do?"

She placed her hand in his. "I'm ready to try."

"We should start with—"

"Double toe loops," Scarlett commanded.

"Double toe loops," Tyler repeated.

"That wasn't what you were going to say."

"Are you sure? I'm intuitive, remember?"

"How could I forget?"

Tyler sat beside Amaliya at her kitchen table, Beth and Linda opposite them. The leftover pot roast from dinner had already been put away, and Miles stood a short distance away, washing dishes.

Beth had come to both practices today, the first with Linda and the second alone. Tyler had expected Scarlett to protest Beth's presence, but either she'd been too preoccupied with changing Marie's routine to care, or she hadn't noticed their visitor.

Now, here he was with his partner of only two months, sitting in the presence of one of the greatest choreographers in the country.

"Where does this go?" Miles held up a serving dish.

"Cabinet over the sink," Linda said. "What do you think, Beth? Can you help them?"

"When I found out they planned to use *Swan Lake* for one of their pieces, I had to see for myself," Beth said. "Amaliya, you are every bit as graceful as your mother, and you and Tyler move beautifully together. I already have a few ideas of how we can incorporate the ballet into your routine."

"Should we use *Swan Lake* for our short program or our long?" Tyler asked.

"The music is much more suited to showcase your artistic talent and the creativity inherent in the long program," Beth said. "I also want your input on the order you want your required elements."

"Our coach likes to put the double axels early in the program so we get through those while we're fresh," Tyler said.

"In my opinion, we should do the opposite."

"Why?" Amaliya asked.

"Neither of you has stamina problems. Putting the double axels at the end gives you time to capture the crowd and also showcases your athleticism."

"Isn't that risky? I can't even do a double axel yet," Amaliya said. "If I fall during competition, that's the last impression the judges will have."

"A fall takes off a specific number of points regardless of when it happens," Tyler said.

"Don't worry about a fall. That's the best gift you can give yourself during competition," Beth said. "Just as in ballet, visualize the dance as you practiced, as your best performance, and that is what you will create."

"That sounds like something my mother would say."

"She did say it. Many times."

Tyler instinctively put his hand on Amaliya's and squeezed. "Where do we start with all of this?"

"I'd like a couple weeks to play with some ideas before we meet again," Beth said. "I'd also like you to master a few more lifts so I know how to formulate the transitions between those skills and the dance."

"We've mostly been concentrating on Amaliya's jumps the past few weeks."

"I know the jumps are important, but from the creative side, I need the other pieces as well." She removed her napkin from her lap and set it on the table. "Choreographing a pairs program is more complex than most people realize. It'll take some time to get it right."

"We can't thank you enough for agreeing to help us," Tyler said.

"I'm happy to do it." Beth nodded at Amaliya. "Please understand, though, that I am doing this as a favor for a dear friend's daughter. I'm not taking on new clients, and I don't want this favor to turn into a flood of choreography requests."

"We understand," Tyler said.

"Does your coach know you planned to bring in a choreographer?" Beth asked.

"We talked about it, but Linda asked us not to share your name with anyone yet, so we haven't said anything to her."

"Good. Please keep it that way," Beth said. "I've heard about Scarlett. She'll use any advantage for her athletes, and she's relentless when she sees something she wants."

"How are we going to explain our new routines to her?"

"Tell her the truth. Say a family friend choreographed them for you. Just leave my name out of it."

"You don't want credit for creating our routines?" Tyler asked.

"I'll take the credit once you get to the Olympics. By then, it will be too late for your competitors to ask for my help."

"I love how you assume we'll make it all the way to the Olympics," Amaliya said.

"Oh, honey. You'll make it," Beth said. "You have the Petrova grace and the Marcell power on the ice. Add that to the right partner, and you two are magic waiting to happen."

Tyler's longtime dreams swelled within him. "You are very kind."

"You won't use that word to describe me when I put you through your paces in a few weeks, but what I am is honest," Beth said. "You two have something special."

The affirmation of Tyler's choice of skating partner brought with it new confidence. "Thank you," he said.

"I'm looking forward to working with both of you." Beth reached into her purse, retrieved an envelope, and handed it to Amaliya. "I also have something for you."

"What's this?"

"Tickets. Ironically, the ballet I'm working with right now is *Swan Lake*. It would benefit you both to come see the stage version before we take the ballet to the ice."

Amaliya's eyes misted, and Tyler put his hand on her back to remind her she wasn't alone. "Thank you."

"You're welcome." Beth pushed back from the table. "Linda, thank you for dinner. Tyler and Amaliya, I will be in touch soon."

They all stood, and Linda walked Beth to the door.

"It was nice having someone compliment us for a change," Amaliya said.

"I was thinking the same thing," Tyler said. "I expect we'll get plenty of compliments when Scarlett sees our new program."

"Will she be upset we didn't include her in our plans?"

"It's hard to say," Tyler said. "When I was skating with Carolyn, she wanted to be involved in every decision. Since Carolyn retired, she's been a lot more hands-off."

"You mean since I started."

"No, it was before that," Tyler said. "I hate to say it, but right now, Marie is the favorite child, and we've dropped out of favor."

"Do you think that will ever change?"

"I hope so," Tyler said. "I have to think she wants to see medals hanging around our necks as much as we do."

Chapter
SIXTEEN

TYLER PARKED IN THE RINK parking lot after he dropped Amaliya off at school, relieved to see Scarlett's car was still there and Marie's wasn't.

The success he and Amaliya had shared in mastering required elements over the past couple weeks had given Tyler a plan, but he needed Scarlett's help.

He climbed out of his car as the door to the rink swung open and Scarlett walked outside.

"Scarlett, I was just coming to find you." Tyler crossed to her. "I want to enter regionals this weekend."

"You want to what?" Scarlett shook her head. "Amaliya's not ready."

"She is ready," Tyler countered. "I know she has a few skills she hasn't mastered, but we have basic routines we can use, and it would be good for her to experience competition."

"I don't know, Tyler," Scarlett said. "I'm not in the habit of taking skaters to competition who aren't prepared to win. And regionals? Everyone there is hoping to advance."

"When Carolyn and I started, you used to push us to compete so we would gain the mental toughness needed to survive in this sport," Tyler reminded her. "Amaliya is ready for this next step. And who knows? With any luck, we'll qualify to move forward to sectionals."

"That's ambitious but not very realistic," Scarlett said. "Amaliya isn't even qualified to skate seniors."

"And she won't ever be qualified if she doesn't compete." Suspecting the root of Scarlett's hesitation, he added, "All I need is for you to help me register. Amaliya and I will understand if you need to spend all of your time with Marie and Becky."

"Are you sure about this?"

"I'm sure. I don't want to miss out on this year's competition season if I don't have to."

"Okay." Scarlett opened her coaching bag and riffled through it until she found what she was looking for. She pulled an application out and handed it to Tyler. "Get this filled out, and bring it back to me by this afternoon."

"Okay, thanks." Tyler took the paper from her. "There is one more thing."

"What's that?"

"Can we keep this conversation between us?"

"Why?"

"Marie and Amaliya don't get along well, and I'd prefer to talk to Amaliya about all of this in my own way."

"Be careful, Tyler," Scarlett said. "Pushing someone into competition before they're ready is never a good thing. I'd hate to have this backfire on you."

"She's ready. She may not know it yet, but she's ready."

Amaliya walked out of the high school and breathed in the scent of spring. White and pink blossoms covered the trees, providing a picturesque setting on the path between the high school and the skating rink.

The warmer weather had given her a reason to walk every day, even when Miles or Linda was available to drive her. A breeze tugged at her hair and brought with it a sense of new beginnings.

Her father had finally escaped the prison of his hospital bed and had even managed his first few steps since the accident. If only her mother could join him in taking literal steps forward. According to Dr. Caldwell, she still had another two months in traction.

Seeing her each week, immobilized, Amaliya could hardly believe that in January, she had been studying ballet beside her mother. Now the only ballet she studied was to prepare for her time on the ice.

She reached the rink and went into the bathroom to change into her typical workout clothes: a long-sleeved leotard, tights, and one of her ballet skirts. She really needed to consider buying some real ice-skating outfits, but from listening to Marie and Becky talk, they sounded expensive. Amaliya wasn't sure who was taking on the financial burden of paying for her ice time and coaching fees, but whether it was her parents or the Donnellys, they had already sacrificed enough. She didn't want to ask for anything she could do without.

She emerged from the restroom and went into the office to retrieve her skates. Tyler sat inside with Hank, the recording equipment out on the desk.

"Oh, good. I was hoping you would get here early," Tyler said. "Hank said he would film our programs for us before everyone else shows up."

"Thanks, Hank. That's great."

"Not a problem." Hank leaned down and retrieved Amaliya's skating bag, then held it out. "Here you go. I'll cue your music and get ready while you two warm up."

Amaliya and Tyler put on their skates and warmed up. Then Tyler led her to the middle of the rink.

"You ready?" he asked.

"I've never done this without other skaters on the ice."

"We're way past due for this." Tyler turned to Hank. "No matter what, finish the program. If you fall, get back up and keep going."

"Okay. I'll try."

Hank called from the side. "Ready when you are."

"We're ready."

Hank hit the record button on the camera before he ran back into the office to start the music.

The first notes began, and Amaliya closed her eyes. She and Tyler executed their first dance moves that led into a combined spin. The double axels came next, but Amaliya singled hers. No reason to fall on purpose.

One by one, they moved through each skill. Jumps, spins, throws, lifts. They reached their second-to-last move, the death spiral. Amaliya willed her body to relax, to see this as simply another piece of the dance. Tyler took her hand, performed a back pivot, and before she knew it, her body was extended horizontally and her hair was brushing the ice.

They straightened together, worked through their last dance sequence, and struck their final pose as the notes faded away.

"That was amazing," Hank said from where he once again stood behind the camera.

Tyler blew out a breath. "Well, that was a workout."

Her own pulse rapid, Amaliya nodded. "I'm going to need a little recovery time before we do the long program."

"I'll leave the camera set up," Hank said. "You two let me know when you're ready."

"Okay, we will." Tyler took Amaliya's hand. "Come on. Let's cool down for a minute."

They were halfway around the rink before reality caught up with her. "I didn't fall."

"Neither of us did," Tyler said. "I'd call that a win."

"I didn't do the double axel though."

"That's okay. We can tackle that later." Tyler led her to the side of the rink. "Let's get some water and sit down for a few minutes before we do our long program."

Amaliya glanced at the clock. "Do you think we'll have time before everyone else gets here?"

"I think so. Besides, it's no big deal if they see us," he said. "Marie and Becky are our usual audience."

Amaliya took a drink from the water fountain and moved aside so Tyler could have a turn. "I have a feeling skating in competition will be a lot different from what I'm used to."

"How so?"

"When you're on stage for the ballet, the house lights are dark. You can pretend no one is there." She sat on a bench.

Tyler sat beside her. "Until they applaud."

"Until then," she agreed.

"Then it won't be much different from ice skating after all," Tyler said. "As soon as we pull off our first jump, the audience will be applauding. Trust me."

"I trust you, but that's hard for me to imagine."

"You'll be able to visualize it sooner than you think."

Chapter
SEVENTEEN

TYLER RETRIEVED THE SIMPLE GIFT from the front seat of his car and started up Amaliya's front walk. For the past two days, he had worked nonstop to set everything up for him and Amaliya to compete this weekend. At least, he had done everything except tell Amaliya about his plans. He hoped his efforts weren't about to backfire.

He rang the doorbell, and Miles answered.

"Is everything ready?" Tyler asked.

"We did what you asked, but are you sure about this?" Miles asked. "I don't know how Amaliya is going to react to this kind of surprise."

"Right now, I'm not sure about anything, but I know she's ready to compete," Tyler said.

"That's out of my area of expertise, but every time I see the two of you, I'm amazed at how good you look."

"Thanks." Tyler followed Miles inside.

Amaliya looked up from the couch. "Tyler. What are you doing here?"

"I'm here for your birthday celebration." He held up her present.

"My birthday was three months ago."

"I know, but I heard you didn't get much of a birthday celebration this year."

Linda walked in carrying two long, narrow boxes. "Let's have her open these first."

"You didn't have to get me anything. We already celebrated my birthday."

"A dinner from McDonald's at the hospital hardly counts." Linda laid the first gift on Amaliya's lap. Everyone sat, and Linda motioned to the gift. "Go on. Open it."

Amaliya carefully slipped her finger under the wrapping paper where it was taped on the end. Slowly, she unwrapped it and peeled the paper away to reveal an unmarked, white garment box. Amaliya lifted the lid and pushed back the tissue paper. She gasped. Inside lay a white skating outfit. Amaliya lifted it out of the box. "Linda, this is beautiful. Thank you."

"You're welcome." She handed Amaliya the second box. "Now, the next one."

Amaliya slid her finger under the fold of the wrapping paper, but this time she ripped it without care of saving the paper.

"Oh, wow." She held up the contents of the second box, another skating outfit, this one in pale blue with a sheer skirt. "This is stunning."

"I'm so glad you like them. I was nervous picking them out without you," Linda said.

"Where did you even find these?" Amaliya asked.

"Tyler gave me the name of a store in New York City where his sister used to buy her skating costumes."

Amaliya turned to face Tyler. "Is that why you came over tonight? So you could see what Linda picked out?"

"That and to give you this." Tyler handed Amaliya her gift. "It's not much, but I hope you like it."

"Thank you." Amaliya undid the bow and opened the box. Her face lit up when she saw the pink skate guards. "This is great. I needed new skate guards."

"There's more." Tyler pointed at the envelope nestled in the tissue paper beneath her main gift.

"What is it?" Amaliya opened the envelope. Her eyebrows furrowed together, and she looked up. "A registration form?"

"I entered us in the competition this weekend."

Now her eyes widened. "This weekend? As in this Saturday?"

"Yeah. We leave right after you get out of school tomorrow."

"This weekend," Amaliya repeated.

Tyler put his hand on hers. "You need to stop thinking of yourself as a beginner. You're ready for this."

"This is why you've been pushing so hard to practice our programs all week."

"Yeah."

"Why didn't you just tell me?"

"I didn't want you to stress about it," Tyler said. "I also asked Scarlett not to tell Marie and Becky we're coming. I didn't want Marie to play any of her mind games on you."

"What kind of mind games?" Amaliya asked.

Time to come clean. "Skating is as much mental as it is physical. I hoped that by not giving you a lot of time to worry about competing, it would make it easier to stay relaxed. You're a beautiful skater, and you're ready for this. I want to prove that to you without your nerves getting in the way."

"With as fast as my heart is beating right now, I don't think there's any way I'm not going to fall victim to my nerves," Amaliya said.

Linda reclaimed her seat beside Amaliya. "It's no different than opening night at the ballet. The nerves will be there, but you'll use them to make you better, to help you shine."

Amaliya turned her attention back to Tyler. "You really think I'm ready for this?"

"Yes. We'll do it just like we practiced."

"Okay," Amaliya said. "I guess we're going on a trip this weekend."

Excitement leapt in his chest, and Tyler squeezed her hand. She said yes. Finally, they were moving forward. Finally, he and Amaliya would see how good they could be together.

The crowded parking lot, the van from the local television station, the energy buzzing through the audience. The way Tyler had talked, Amaliya had pictured a small competition where the pressure would be kept to a minimum. He hadn't mentioned that they would be competing in Massachusetts or that the nationally ranked skaters present would draw out the local media.

"There are so many cameras," Amaliya said.

"Ignore them. They're setting up for the short programs," Tyler said. "They won't waste their time on compulsory figures. They aren't enough fun to watch."

Amaliya skipped forward. "You're saying our other programs will be on television?"

"No. They'll focus on Marie and the other nationally ranked skaters."

"You're a nationally ranked skater."

"I was, and eventually, I will be again, but today is all about qualifying. We don't have to win, and I doubt the media will pay any attention to us." Tyler put his hand on her shoulder. "Don't worry. Focus on what we've practiced. That's all you need to think about."

Her stomach curled with nerves. She could do this. Tyler said she could do this. Despite the hammering in her chest, she said, "I'll try."

"Good. We're in the next session. I'll meet you back here after you change."

Amaliya went into the locker room and changed into her skating outfit, her nerves multiplying with every minute that passed. When she and Tyler warmed up together, she tried to pretend they were in their home rink but failed miserably.

When they reached the staging area, Tyler put both hands on her shoulders and waited for her to look at him. "Just like in practice. The judges are looking for precision, grace, and poise. You have all three in spades."

"I hope you're right."

"It's just drawing on the ice with your skates," Tyler reminded her. "You can do this."

Only a few minutes after they finished their warm-ups, their names were called, and they stepped onto the ice. One by one, they worked through the three figures given them. As soon as they finished, Tyler whisked her off the ice and toward the locker rooms.

"Don't you want to wait to see our scores?"

"No. I asked Miles and Linda to write them down for us."

Amaliya stopped. "Why don't you want to see them?"

"Because today isn't about winning and losing. It's about qualifying," Tyler said. "The last thing either of us needs is to get focused on something that doesn't matter."

"Okay. I'm trusting you."

"Good. Let's go get something to eat," Tyler said. "There's a restaurant down the street where we can grab some dinner before we have to come back for our short program."

"How are we going to get there if Miles and Linda are staying here?"

"They're coming with us. They'll be done by the time we finish changing," Tyler said. "I'll meet you back here in a few minutes."

"Okay." Amaliya went into the locker room, a familiar voice carrying to her.

"I don't know why he doesn't drop her," Marie said.

Amaliya absorbed the familiar stab of insult and was tempted to turn and leave. Before she could, Becky and Marie came around the corner.

"Well, speak of the devil." Marie's chin lifted. "We were just talking about how surprised we were that Tyler would bring you here today. I thought he would wait until you were ready." Marie paused and then laughed. "Oh, wait. That's assuming you'll ever be ready."

Beside her, Becky's cheeks flushed like a child caught with her hand in the cookie jar.

Tyler's words repeated through Amaliya's mind. *Skating is as much mental as it is physical. You need to stop thinking of yourself as a beginner.*

Amaliya straightened her shoulders and focused on Becky. "Good luck today, Becky." She gathered her energy and forced herself to take the high road. "You too, Marie."

Without waiting for a response, Amaliya continued farther into the locker room and changed her clothes.

When she found Tyler a few minutes later, he lowered his voice. "Did something happen with Marie?"

"No. Why?"

"I don't know. She looked rattled when I saw her a minute ago."

"I just wished her luck." Amaliya tucked her arm through Tyler's. "Come on. Let's find Miles and Linda so we can eat. I'm starving."

One day blended into the next, and Katerina ached to be able to do anything new. Robert had finally been freed from the bonds of traction a few days ago and could now navigate his way around the room with his wheelchair. Within the next couple weeks, he would start working with a cane. He was moving forward, and she was standing still. Or rather, lying still. She hated it.

"Do you want me to read to you?" Robert asked.

"No." Katerina looked at the clock on the wall. Amaliya was performing in her first skating competition, and Katerina was trapped inside this hospital. Oh, how she wished she could be there for Amaliya. "Do you think she's skated yet?"

"Miles and Linda will call as soon as they can."

"I know, but I hate relying on everyone else to tell us about our daughter." Katerina drummed her fingers on her thigh. "I hoped Beth would stop by to tell me how things went this week."

A knock sounded on the door. "Did someone say my name?"

"Beth, come in." Katerina waved her inside. "How are you? Did you see Amaliya this week?"

"I did." Beth crossed the room and took Katerina's hand. "Your daughter is amazing. Truly."

"She's been skating since she could walk," Robert said with a great deal of pride.

"She doesn't skate. She floats," Beth said. "I can't wait for you to see her. She and her partner are going to do great things. I've already started on the choreography."

"Show me?" Katerina asked.

"Of course."

"Tell me more about this partner of hers," Robert said before the conversation could continue.

"Robert, even you would approve. Tyler is quite the gentleman."

"He'd better be, around my little girl."

"Miles is keeping an eye on her," Beth said. "Tyler and Amaliya are well matched. If they would switch coaches, who knows how far they could go on the world stage."

"What's wrong with their coach?"

"Scarlett is better with singles skaters," Beth said. "I think Tyler and Amaliya would do better with someone who excels in coaching pairs. I don't know if he would be willing, but Gordon Alexander isn't coaching anyone right now."

"Has he coached anyone since his wife died?"

"I don't think so."

"Maybe I'll have to give him a call," Katerina said.

"I'd hold off for a week or two so you can make sure Amaliya and Tyler are willing to make a change, but Gordon would be an excellent fit for them."

"Assuming he'll take my call." Focusing on the positive, she said, "Show me what you've got in the choreography so far."

Beth pulled some pages from her purse. "I think you're going to like it."

Amaliya wasn't ready for this. Even though she and Tyler had stayed out of the rink until it was their turn to warm up, the energy and nerves had been building since Thursday when she'd learned about the competition.

"You ready?" Tyler asked. "We're up next."

"I don't know about this."

Tyler took her by the arms and turned her so she was facing him but not able to see the ice. "Pretend we're back at our rink in Connecticut. We get the ice all to ourselves, and it's our turn to have fun."

"Fun." Amaliya lifted her gaze to meet his. "Fun would be when I'm not shaking."

"Come here." Tyler pulled her into a hug. "I know you can do this. Trust me."

Amaliya soaked in the comfort of the embrace. Tyler believed in her. She needed to believe in herself if for no other reason than to prove he hadn't made a mistake in choosing her as his partner.

When Tyler stepped back, she looked up. "You'll help me up if I fall?"

"I will, but you aren't going to need my help. You'll be great."

"Linden and Marcell," a man at the rink's edge called out.

Tyler took her hand. "Come on. Let's show everyone how amazing we are."

His confidence, delivered with a cocky grin, eased her nerves.

"I'll follow your lead."

"That's all I can ask for." Tyler stepped onto the ice, and Amaliya followed.

They circled once, and the crowd cheered when their names were announced. Or rather, when Tyler's name was announced. No one in the skating world would have a reason to cheer for her.

She and Tyler came to a stop in the center of the rink.

The moment they took their starting positions, their music started. Amaliya closed her eyes for a moment and let the notes sweep through her. Mirroring Tyler, they began their program. Their dance flowed into required elements, each item getting checked off in turn, with one glaring exception: Tyler executed a double axel, but Amaliya only completed a single.

That was planned, Amaliya reminded herself. Tyler pulled her close for their final lift. She held her position over his head and cartwheeled down before her skate connected with the ice. They concluded their routine, the music faded, and the crowd once again came to life.

Tyler held her hand up above their heads before sweeping it down as he bowed and she curtsied. Then his arm came around her waist, and his lips pressed against her temple. The familiar ripple of attraction multiplied.

"You were amazing." Tyler led her across the rink, leaning down to scoop up a bouquet of flowers that had been tossed onto the ice. He handed it to her, and Amaliya clutched the flowers to her chest.

"Are we staying for scores this time?"

"It might be best if we skip them."

"Okay. I'm trusting you on this."

Tyler smiled. "That's always a good decision."

Chapter
EIGHTEEN

HER FIRST COMPETITION AND HER parents weren't here. Amaliya padded across her hotel room and looked out the window. A fresh dusting of snow covered the parking lot. The scrape of shovels against concrete sounded from below, where a boy about her age cleared the hotel sidewalk. In a matter of hours, she and Tyler would be back at the rink for the final portion of the competition. Nerves fluttered in her stomach.

Amaliya had no idea how she and Tyler had done overall, but she couldn't deny that she had enjoyed the applause when they'd completed their short program. The energy of the crowd was different when she was on the ice compared to when she danced. Was it because she could see peoples' faces? Or perhaps the air of competition created that extra buzz of excitement. Had her father experienced the same sensation when he'd played hockey?

She couldn't count the times she had sat with her mom in the Cap Centre and watched her dad play, always delighting when his name had come over the loudspeaker. Yesterday had been the first time the name Marcell had been announced when it was referring to her rather than one of her parents, but they weren't there to hear it.

A wave of nostalgia washed over her. Her mom had been at every performance until yesterday. Her father had made every performance when he'd been in town. Tears surfaced, and she sniffled. When she had begged her mom to let her join the San Francisco Ballet, she'd never considered how empty she would feel when she performed without her parents in the audience.

Adult or not, she still wanted her parents to be part of her world. As wonderful as Miles and Linda had been through all of the weeks of practices, her heart ached knowing her life was moving forward while her mom's and dad's were stuck in idle.

The phone beside the bed rang. Probably Linda making sure she was awake. Amaliya swiped at her tears and cleared her throat before she answered it.

Her heart lifted when her mom's voice came over the line, her words spoken in Russian. "Hi, Milaya. How are you?"

"Nervous. How did you get this number? I didn't think I would get to talk to you this weekend."

"Linda told us where you were staying. Your father and I wanted to wish you luck," Katerina said. "How did you do yesterday?"

"Good, I think. I didn't fall."

"Of course you didn't." Her mom's smile carried in her voice. "You are the epitome of grace."

"Thanks, Mama."

"Good luck today." Before Amaliya could respond, Katerina said, "Here. Your father wants to talk to you."

"I love you."

"Love you too."

A moment later, her father came on. "Did you tear up the ice yesterday?"

Amaliya mentally shifted from Russian to French. Her mood lightened. "Papa, this isn't hockey."

"You know what I mean. How did it go?"

"Tyler was really pleased."

"That's nice, but how did you feel about your performance?"

"Really good. I miss you and Mama though. I wish you could be here."

"We do too, but with or without us, I know you'll do great." Her dad's voice thickened when he added, "Know we're thinking about you."

"Thanks, Papa."

"Call and let us know how everything turns out."

"I will."

Tyler couldn't believe it. He and Amaliya were in second place. Even more unbelievable was that if Amaliya hadn't needed to single her axel, they likely would be in first. While he had insisted on ignoring their scores from the first two sections, Scarlett had been quick to call when the results had posted.

Though tempted to tell Amaliya the good news, he decided against it. This morning, they needed to relax and stay focused on what lay ahead.

He picked up the basket his mother had put together for them, then left his hotel room, walked across the hall, and knocked on Amaliya's door.

She answered a moment later, moisture evident on her eyelashes.

His heart melted. Why had she been crying? And what was he supposed to say to her?

Surprise illuminated her face, and she glanced down at her watch. "I thought we weren't supposed to leave for another hour."

"We aren't, but I brought you something." Tyler lifted the basket into her view. "A little good-luck present."

"You didn't have to do that."

"I didn't. It's from my mom for both of us." He held it out.

She took it and looked at the contents. Apples, bananas, oranges, and some of his mom's blueberry muffins. "This is great. Thank her for me."

"I will." Tyler waved toward the elevator. "Want to come downstairs? There are some tables in the lobby where we can eat breakfast."

"I'd like that. Let me put on my shoes." She handed the basket back to Tyler. "I can trust you with this, right?"

"Of course." She didn't need to know that one of the muffins had already disappeared when he'd wanted a snack last night.

As soon as she returned, they walked down the hall. Acting on instinct, he slipped his arm around her waist. "How are you doing today?"

"It's hard not having my parents here."

"I'm sorry. That can't be easy." Tyler dropped his arm when they reached the elevators. "How are they doing?"

"They called a few minutes ago. They sounded good, but every time I think about my dad fighting to learn how to walk again and my mom stuck in traction, it's hard to think I'm so focused on doing the things they can't." The elevator doors opened, and she stepped inside.

"If they're anything like my parents, I'm sure they're more worried about how you're doing than how they're doing."

"You're right. All Dad could talk about was how I was going to do great today."

"Does that mean you're ready?"

"I think so," she said. "I'll feel a lot better, though, when we're skating to our own program instead of one of your old ones."

"That will happen soon enough."

"How do you think we did yesterday?"

"We did great," Tyler said.

"You know our scores, don't you?"

"Not exactly." Not wanting to put any pressure on her, he said, "If you want, we can wait for our scores after our long program."

"I'd like that." She stepped off the elevator and glanced over her shoulder. "Assuming I don't fall, that is."

"You won't fall." He reached out and took her hand. "Positive thinking."

The figure-skating competition would end in another hour, and Amaliya hadn't seen a single other skater perform. Tyler had insisted that watching others before he and Amaliya competed would cause them to lose focus. She wouldn't mind losing some focus right now. The anticipation was driving her crazy.

She closed her eyes and visualized their routine—each turn, each lift, each move. If she wasn't ready to compete now, she doubted she ever would be.

Tyler touched her arm, breaking her out of her thoughts. "Time to go."

"Is it bad that I'm ready for this to be over?"

"Enjoy today. No pressure."

No pressure. The words repeated in her mind as she followed him into the competition area. A moment later, they were signaled onto the ice.

The crowd had doubled in size from yesterday. How had she not noticed that when they'd warmed up twenty minutes ago?

They took their starting positions, and then their music began. Words Scarlett, Carolyn, and Tyler had spoken over the past months repeated in her head as she performed the new skills she had gained since meeting them. Echoing behind them were her parents' voices. *Ankles straight*, her father always told her. *Feel the music* was her mother's advice.

They reached the halfway point in their program, the moment when she and Tyler separated and came together again for a combined spin. His hand curled around her waist, and the music changed. She stretched one leg behind her and arched back as Tyler held her in place, and then they spun together. Emotions rose within her, a brightness and hope she hadn't experienced in months. As she had yesterday, Amaliya let herself get swept up in the dance, but this time, she let herself feel as she hadn't dared to before.

Side-by-side double toe loops in unison, a pair camel spin, a throw double salchow.

The crowd cheered, breaking through her concentration for the first time. A fish lift, another dance sequence, side-by-side spins, and their final pose.

Tyler took her hand. She curtsied to the crowd as he bowed, but when she straightened her jaw dropped. The entire crowd was on their feet. Applause continued, rumbling through the arena.

Tyler squeezed her hand, a silent signal to curtsy again. She did so, but this time when she and Tyler straightened, he pulled her closer and swept her into his arms.

"That was amazing," he said.

"What just happened?"

"I think we just qualified to compete this season."

"Seriously?"

Tyler nodded. He released her, took her hand, and waved to the crowd. Then he led her toward the exit, scooping up flowers and stuffed animals on their way. By the time they reached the edge of the rink, their arms were full.

"Come on. Let's see how the scores turned out."

Together they climbed onto the small platform where a seating area was situated in front of a television camera. They sat as Scarlett joined them.

The oddity of Scarlett's presence struck Amaliya. She couldn't remember seeing their coach at all until this moment.

"What would be a good score?" Amaliya asked.

"Six is a perfect score. For this competition, we want to be anywhere in the fives," Tyler said.

Tyler took Amaliya's hand and squeezed. In front of the judges, the first set of marks were lifted into view. Five-ones to five-threes, with a four point eight as an outlier.

"Not bad for technical," Scarlett said.

The artistic marks followed, these several points higher.

Applause echoed again.

Tyler hugged Amaliya before he stood and offered his hand. "Come on. Let's go watch the last three couples and see if our scores will hold."

"Will hold what?"

"First place."

Amaliya stopped and stared. "Wait. We're in first place?"

Tyler grinned. "We took first place in compulsory figures and fourth in the short program. If we win the long, we win."

"That isn't possible."

"Oh, it's possible."

They won. Tyler still couldn't wrap his brain around it. He and Carolyn had won this competition twice previously and had placed second twice more, but it had taken them years to reach the podium. How had he and Amaliya succeeded on their first try?

A reporter approached, trailed by a man holding an enormous video camera.

"Hi, I'm Lila Adams with Channel Six news. Can I interview the two of you for a minute?"

Tyler glanced down at Amaliya. She shrugged.

"Sure. Where do you want us?" Tyler asked.

"Right here is fine." The reporter angled the two of them so the rink would be behind them. She lifted her microphone and nodded at her cameraman. "This is Lila Adams with Channel Six News, here with Tyler Linden and Amaliya Marcell, the winners of tonight's pairs figure-skating competition in Boston." She turned toward Tyler. "Tyler, I understand this is your first time competing with your new partner. What was that like?"

"Different, but good," Tyler said. "Amaliya is a beautiful skater, and I'm excited for our future together."

"It was only a few months ago that your sister and former partner announced her retirement. How have you achieved this level of success so quickly?"

"A lot of our success is thanks to my sister, Carolyn Carter," Tyler said.

"Amaliya, would you agree with Tyler?"

"Yes. Carolyn spent a month teaching me many of the elements we used in our program today."

"She also choreographed programs for us before she moved to California," Tyler added.

"Her efforts clearly worked." The reporter faced the camera fully. "You heard it here, folks. Maybe today's win is by Linden and Marcell as well as Linden, Marcell, and Carter. This is Lila Adams with Channel Six News. Back to you, Dustin."

"And cut," the cameraman said.

Lila lowered her microphone. "Thank you both, and congratulations."

"Thanks." Tyler shook her hand. The reporter had barely left before Tyler's parents and the Donnellys rushed toward them.

"That was incredible." His mom gave him a hug.

"It really was," his dad agreed.

"I still can't believe we won," Tyler said.

"Winning was always the goal," his dad said.

"True."

"And, Amaliya." His mom took her hand. "Truly, you were stunning out there."

Amaliya's cheeks warmed. "Thank you."

"Only one more round of qualifiers and you two will be looking forward to the U.S. Pairs Final."

"What do you mean 'one more round'?" Amaliya asked.

"We qualified today for the eastern sectionals. If we place in the top five there, we qualify for finals."

"When are sectionals?"

"First weekend in October," Tyler said.

"I guess I have to figure out my double axel by then."

"That would be helpful, but we still have plenty of time," Tyler said. "You'll get it eventually."

Chapter
NINETEEN

AMALIYA WALKED INTO THE RINK on Monday morning with a new optimism. She and Tyler had won gold. Finally, she was a real skater.

The door opened behind her, and Tyler walked in. "Morning." He slung his arm over her shoulder. "How does our newest gold medalist feel today?"

"Like I can do anything."

"Great, because your double lutz is next on our agenda."

Some of her optimism faded. "Is that what Scarlett wants us to work on?"

"I haven't talked to her about it, but I know she wants us to upgrade the difficulty in our routines."

"If Beth lives up to her reputation, that will happen shortly," Amaliya said. "I'm looking forward to doing something fresh."

"Me too. By the way, Carolyn called yesterday. She said to tell you congratulations."

Scarlett walked in while they were stretching, but she passed by without her typical greeting.

Amaliya lowered her voice. "That was odd."

"I think she's annoyed that Marie only placed second."

"Yeah, but Becky got third. That's pretty impressive to have two of the top three spots in the women's event as well as the winner in pairs."

"You would think so, but I think she was trying to bolster Marie's confidence."

Amaliya reached back and took hold of her blade, lifting her leg to stretch out her quad. "Marie doesn't look to me like she has a confidence problem."

"She hides it well, but she's only beaten Olivia Garfield twice, and both times, Olivia was coming back from an injury."

Amaliya switched legs. "I'm sure that isn't easy."

"Like I said, half of this sport is mental," Tyler said. After they warmed up, he led her to where Scarlett stood on the edge of the rink. "What do you want us to work on now?"

Scarlett's eyebrows rose. "Didn't Carolyn give you a workout?"

"Why would Carolyn give us a workout?" Tyler asked. "She lives in California."

Awareness dawned, and Amaliya struggled for the right words to say. She and Tyler hadn't intended to offend Scarlett during their television interview after the competition, but apparently, they had done just that. Opting for simplicity, Amaliya said, "I'm sorry, Scarlett—"

Scarlett pointed across the rink, effectively interrupting her. "Work on your combination spins."

"Okay." Tyler led Amaliya to the far side of the rink. "What was that about?"

"I'm pretty sure she's upset that we talked about Carolyn during our interview but never mentioned our coach."

"You don't really think she's mad about that, do you?"

"I can't think of any other reason she would have brought up your sister."

"That's ridiculous."

"And petty," Amaliya added, "but I'm afraid we didn't gain any brownie points with her this weekend."

"Don't worry about it. I'm sure she'll get over it."

Amaliya glanced at their coach, who met her with a cold stare. "I'm not sure about that."

"Come on. Let's work on spins."

They ran through their various spins, working on timing on their side by sides and on their combined moves.

"I need to check with Hank to see if he needs me to run the Zamboni this morning," Tyler said when their practice time came to an end. "But I can give you a ride either way."

"Thanks. I'll see you in a minute." Amaliya approached the bench where she had left her things.

Marie stood nearby, talking to her mother in French.

"The restaurant opening is only a month away. Are you bringing a date?"

"Of course," Marie said. "I'll have Tyler bring me."

"You haven't been out with him lately. Are you two still dating?" her mother asked.

"Of course. In fact, the way he was talking last time we went out, it wouldn't surprise me if I have a ring on my finger by Christmas."

Amaliya's heart sank. Disappointment and something else swept through her. It was one thing to know Tyler dated Marie, but marriage?

"If you're getting that serious, you need to spend more time together," Marie's mother said.

"I know, but he's had to spend most of his free time trying to teach his new partner." Disdain carried in Marie's voice, and she glanced at Amaliya. "I don't know why he chose her. She isn't nearly as good as Tyler thinks she is."

"That doesn't matter. They aren't competing against you, and you're the one Tyler plans to marry."

"You're right."

Amaliya turned away to hide the fact that she understood every word perfectly, even though Marie and her mother obviously assumed she didn't speak French. She hefted her bag and headed for the locker room. Scarlett stood by the rink entrance and glared.

Great. Her coach was mad at her, and Tyler was talking marriage with Marie. So much for optimism. This was not her day.

Chapter
TWENTY

THE CLASSROOM DOOR OPENED AND closed. A moment later, Madam Martin approached and handed Amaliya a note. "You're needed in the office."

Amaliya read the pass, and concern bloomed when she saw that Miss Thurston wanted to see her. What would her counselor want with her? Were her parents okay? Had something happened to Miles or Linda?

She quickly gathered her things and left the room. When she reached the office, Miss Thurston was waiting for her.

"Is something wrong?" Amaliya asked.

"No, but I'm hoping you will do me a favor."

Amaliya took a moment to let her relief push back her earlier fears. "What kind of favor?"

"Let's talk in the conference room."

Amaliya followed her down the hall to the last room. Miss Thurston closed the door behind her and motioned for Amaliya to sit.

They both settled into chairs across the table from each other.

"Do you know Jeff Pearson?" Miss Thurston asked.

"I think I've heard his name, but I don't know who he is," Amaliya said.

"He's a senior this year and is the captain of the baseball team." Miss Thurston paused before adding, "Jeff's father had a heart attack last week."

"I'm so sorry. Is he going to be okay?"

"I think so, but Jeff's having a difficult time dealing with the uncertainty. You know what it's like to have your parents in the hospital, and you understand the stress that can cause," Miss Thurston said. "I hoped you might be willing to spend some time with him."

"And do what?" Amaliya asked, uneasy. "I don't even know him."

"Sometimes it helps to talk to people who have been through a similar situation when something like this happens. Since you know what it's like to face this kind of stress, I thought he might be able to relate to you."

"Don't you think he would be more comfortable with his family or friends?"

"Let me ask you this." Miss Thurston leaned forward. "Did you talk to your friends after your parents' accident?"

The flash of memory of those first days surfaced, of desperately wanting to talk to her parents and to know what was going on. "All I wanted was to talk to my parents, so I didn't really want to talk to my friends."

"I think Jeff is going through something similar," Miss Thurston said. "Can you please try?"

"I guess so."

"Wait here. Jeff is supposed to meet with me this morning. I'll introduce you as soon as he gets here."

Before Amaliya could reconsider, Miss Thurston stepped out of the room, leaving Amaliya with an abundance of doubt. What was she supposed to say to this guy? He didn't know her. And if he was anything like her, he wouldn't want to talk to her, no matter how much they might share in common.

The door opened, and Miss Thurston escorted a tall guy with sandy-blond hair and deep-blue eyes into the room. Amaliya had noticed him at lunch before. He was the type of guy who was hard to miss, even when he wasn't surrounded by a half dozen girls trying to get his attention.

"Jeff, this is Amaliya Marcell. Amaliya, this is Jeff Pearson."

"Hi," Amaliya said, but Jeff didn't even look at her.

"Jeff, I'd like for you and Amaliya to talk for a bit. No one will need this room until lunchtime." Miss Thurston left them alone.

Amaliya remained in her seat, not sure what she should do or say. Jeff clearly didn't want to be here. She didn't want to be here. Whatever experiment their counselor hoped to accomplish had already aligned itself in the failure column.

"I'm sorry. Miss Thurston means well," Amaliya finally managed to say. "She thought if we talked, it might help."

"Help what?" Jeff turned his gaze on her, his blue eyes flashing with anger. "Are you going to tell me that talking to you will make me feel better?"

"Honestly, I doubt it."

"Then why are you here? And please don't tell me it's because you know what I'm going through." The muscle in Jeff's jaw twitched as though he were fighting for control of his emotions. "You have no idea what it's like to watch your dad collapse right in front of you."

"You're right." A lump formed in her throat, and tears threatened. "I wasn't there when my parents were taken to the hospital."

He looked at her now. "Both of your parents?"

"Yeah. A car accident. I found out when the police showed up at my door."
A tear spilled over. "Maybe this isn't such a good idea. You'll probably be more
comfortable talking to your own friends."

"I'm sorry. I didn't mean to take everything out on you. I'm just so sick of
everyone either pretending everything is normal or wanting to talk about my
dad all the time and how they're sure he'll be fine."

"I'm sure they mean well."

"I guess." Jeff took a step closer. "How long did it take for your friends
to treat you normally again?"

"I didn't have the chance to find out. I moved here a few days after the
accident, and I didn't tell anyone here who I live with," Amaliya said. "You're
the first person, besides some of the faculty, who knows my parents are in the
hospital."

"How long have you lived here?"

"Since early January. My parents have been in the hospital since then."

"That long?"

"Yeah." Amaliya forced herself to confide in this complete stranger. "My
mom broke her back and has been in traction since her last surgery. My dad is
in physical therapy now, trying to learn to walk again."

"Wow. I'm sorry."

The simple sentiment resonated through her. He understood what she was
feeling, at least to some extent. "I'm sorry about your dad too."

"Thanks." Jeff took a step back. "I guess I'd better see if Miss Thurston has
my homework for me. Tomorrow's my first day back at school."

"Good luck."

"Thanks." Jeff took another step back but stopped. "Can I ask you something?"

"Sure."

"How long did it take you to start feeling normal again?"

"I don't know. I'll tell you when I get there."

Chapter
TWENTY-ONE

AMALIYA SETTLED IN AT HER usual corner table in the cafeteria with the muffin and orange juice Tyler had insisted he buy her on his way to drop her off at school. In moments like this morning, she could almost pretend they were dating, but every time he drove away, she was reminded again that they lived in different worlds. She still had another month of high school left. Tyler hadn't dealt with homework for years. Not to mention, he was still dating Marie.

"Is this seat taken?"

Amaliya startled at the familiar voice. Jeff stood beside her, his backpack slung over one shoulder.

"No." She waited for him to slide into the seat across from her before she asked, "Are you ready for your first day back?"

"I doubt it." Jeff glanced across the cafeteria before focusing on her again. "I've already had a dozen people tell me how sorry they are about my dad and ask how he's doing."

"I'm sure they just want you to know they care about you." Memories of how she had avoided those sentiments surfaced. "It's really annoying, isn't it?"

"Very. Maybe I'll go late to all my classes. Then no one can talk to me."

"That would work if you had a place to hide. From what I've seen of this school, you don't have a lot of choices."

"Yeah, you're right. It's not like I want to hide in the bathroom."

"Miss Thurston would let you hide in her office if you wanted," Amaliya suggested.

"And get a lecture on avoidance? I don't think so." The first bell rang. "Can I walk you to class?"

"Using me as a barrier between you and your friends?"

"Maybe. Do you mind?"

"Not at all." Amaliya tucked her book into her bag and stood.

"Which way?"

"Madam Martin's room."

"That's not far from my first class. I'm surprised I haven't seen you before."

Amaliya didn't mention that he'd passed by her nearly every day.

"Hey, Jeff." One of the boys from Amaliya's English class approached.

"Hey, Brad." Jeff put his hand on Amaliya's back and guided her past him before the conversation could continue.

Three more boys and five girls tried to engage him in conversation before they reached Amaliya's classroom.

She stopped a few feet short of the doorway. "Good luck today."

"Thanks. I'll see you later."

Amaliya entered her classroom and slid into her seat. A moment later, Sarah sat beside her.

"Was that you with Jeff Pearson a minute ago?"

"Yeah. Why?"

"I thought you were dating Tyler."

Amaliya shook her head. "Tyler and I are just friends."

"I know you've said that, but I see him drive you to school all the time, so I thought . . ."

"And before you get any ideas, I'm not dating Jeff either."

"Two good-looking guys are hanging around, and they're both just friends." Sarah shook her head. "You need to do something about this."

"There's nothing to do."

"You could flirt a little, let them know you're interested." Sarah leaned forward. "If you could go out with either one of them, who would you choose? Jeff or Tyler?"

"I don't know," Amaliya said, though she wasn't sure she believed her own words. She and Tyler had been skating together for almost four months now, and even though she saw him twice a day, she always looked forward to being with him again.

"Jeff's not dating anyone," Sarah said, breaking into her thoughts.

"Right now, all Jeff wants is to get through the day without talking about his dad all the time."

"Maybe, but he's single, and he's cute."

"Does Kent know you're checking out other guys?" Amaliya asked.

"I'm not looking for me. I'm looking for you."

Amaliya simply shook her head. "You keep telling yourself that."

"Oh, I will."

Tyler landed his double lutz and automatically glanced to his side, where Amaliya remained upright.

Shock and wonder illuminated her face.

Tyler drew her into his arms for a hug. "That was great."

Her hands lifted to his waist, and she squeezed. His stomach lurched, even as she pulled back. "I can't believe I finally landed it."

"Ready to try again?" Tyler asked.

"I don't know. Maybe we should end on a high note. Practice is almost over."

From across the rink, Scarlett called out. "Double lutzes. Again."

"You heard her." Tyler dropped his hands and took one of hers. "Come on. You did it once. You can do it again."

Amaliya took a deep breath and nodded as Tyler started forward. He released her hand and counted off their timing. He launched into the air, made two rotations, and was again greeted by the dual scrapes of blades against ice.

His face broke into a grin. "Five jumps down. One more to go."

"Okay, everyone," Scarlett called out. "That's it for today."

Tyler put his hand on Amaliya's back and guided her forward. "Once you get your double axel, we'll have all the required elements for international competition."

"It's hard to believe how far we've come."

"Yes, it is." Tyler followed Amaliya off the ice and to the bench where she sat down to take off her skates. He started to sit beside her, but Marie grabbed his arm before he had the chance.

"Tyler, I've been meaning to ask if you wanted to come with me to the opening of my father's new restaurant. It's tomorrow night."

"That sounds great, but I don't know if I can make it," Tyler said, both because he was speaking the truth and because he wasn't sure he wanted to give Marie his free time when he could spend it with Amaliya instead. "Amaliya and I usually go over film on Friday nights," he added.

"You know what they say about all work and no play," Marie countered. "Besides, don't you think it's a bit premature for Amaliya to worry about watching film? She doesn't even have the basics yet."

"She landed her double lutz today."

"It only took her four months to get it."

Behind him, Amaliya picked up her bag and headed for the restroom. Tyler glanced over his shoulder as the door closed behind her. "I don't know about you, but it took me a lot longer than a few months to land my first double lutz."

"Yeah, but how old were you? Nine?"

"That's beside the point," Tyler said. "What's your problem with Amaliya?"

"I just think it's a waste of Scarlett's time to have to teach her basics when the rest of us are so much further along than she is."

"She's catching up quickly," Tyler said, pride swelling within him, along with a sense of loyalty. "Not to mention, we won the pairs competition last weekend."

"Yeah, against a bunch of amateurs. There wasn't a single top pair entered in our division."

"Winning at our first competition together was a big deal," Tyler said. "If Amaliya keeps it up, she'll be passing all of us by in no time."

"You can't really believe that." Marie shook her head.

"With the way she moves and her athletic ability, yeah, I do." The phone in the office rang. "I'd better get that." Tyler grabbed his bag and skates and hurried into the office. He snatched up the phone. "Central Skating, how can I help you?"

"Hey, Tyler. It's Miles Donnelly. Is Hank in yet?"

"No, not yet."

The door opened and closed behind him.

"Can you leave him a message to call me? I need to change a couple of my practices for next week."

"Sure. No problem." Tyler said his goodbyes and jotted down the message.

He stored his skates in the corner beside Amaliya's and walked back toward the rink to wait for her.

He noticed a few paper cups the night shift hadn't cleaned up, so he took care of the task himself and glanced at his watch. Where was Amaliya? She should have been ready by now.

He grabbed his jacket and tugged it on. Marie, Becky, and Scarlett were nowhere to be seen. With no one to send into the ladies' room to check on her, Tyler approached the restroom and knocked on the door. "Amaliya? Are you ready?"

No answer.

He waited a minute and tried again. "Amaliya?"

Again, nothing.

He knocked a third time, this time pushing open the bathroom door to find the interior dark. "Amaliya?"

Tyler flipped on the light and walked inside. Empty. If she wasn't in the restroom, where was she?

Tyler went back to the rink to find it also empty. Had she left without him? Irritation surfaced. He crossed to the door, opened it, and looked out. Only his car remained in the parking lot, and Amaliya was nowhere to be seen.

He walked outside and stared down the street. In the distance, Amaliya walked toward the high school. Though tempted to get in his car and go after her, he fought against it. By the time he reached her, she would already be to the school.

What was with her? He had given her a ride to school nearly every day for the past few months. She could have said something if she didn't want one today.

Seeds of disappointment and hurt grew alongside his irritation. He turned back and walked into the rink. Apparently, he didn't need to take a break before work today.

Hurt, anger, frustration. All three emotions overshadowed Amaliya's sense of accomplishment at landing her double lutz. She had worked so hard to learn that single element, and her success had brought with it the reminder of how far behind the others she continued to lag.

Though she had bypassed the diner and her usual stop for breakfast, she claimed a seat at her usual table in the cafeteria. She'd barely sat down when Jeff appeared and sat across from her.

The expression on his face told her everything she needed to know. He was hiding. "It couldn't have been that bad yesterday."

"I must have told a hundred people I didn't want to talk about my dad before the day ended."

"Maybe everyone has the message by now," Amaliya said. "I'm sure today will be better."

"I hope so." He leaned back and stretched out his long legs. "I looked for you at lunch yesterday. I was hoping you would save me from my friends."

"Sorry. My last class is fourth period, so I don't always stay for lunch. Yesterday I went to practice early."

"What kind of practice?"

"Ice skating."

"Do you have to go early today?"

The frustration from this morning flooded her mind. "No. Today, I'll probably stay and eat here."

"Good. Save me a spot, and we'll eat together."

"I'd like that."

The bell rang, and they both stood.

"Come on. I'll walk you to class." Jeff took her hand. Amaliya's stomach filled with butterflies. She looked up at him with confusion and a spurt of attraction. Was it possible to fall for two guys at the same time? And was it time to let her crush on Tyler fade and open herself up to the possibility of a relationship with someone closer to her age?

Several people glanced their direction as they passed, but Amaliya couldn't tell if they were drawing attention because Jeff was back in school after his father's heart attack or because Jeff was holding her hand.

When they met for lunch a few hours later, the spotlight on them intensified.

Amaliya leaned forward. "Do people always stare at you wherever you go?"

"It's worse today." Jeff put his hand on hers and gave it a squeeze. "At least they're staring now because they're trying to figure out if we're dating instead of wanting to talk about if my dad's going to survive."

"I guess I make a good distraction."

"The best," Jeff said. "Any chance you want to keep up the good work this weekend?"

Though she and Tyler had planned to watch film tomorrow night, she wasn't sure that would still happen after Marie's invitation this morning. "What did you have in mind?"

"I have a game tomorrow night. The team usually goes out for pizza afterward. I thought maybe you could come watch and then come with us to dinner."

"That sounds like fun."

"I have to go to the game early. Can you meet me there?" Jeff asked. "If you can get someone to drop you off, I can take you home."

"Yeah. I can do that."

"Great. It's a date."

Tyler's annoyance simmered all day. When Amaliya arrived at the rink, she cast her gaze to the floor, avoiding him.

He waited by the office door so she had no choice but to pass him to get her skates.

"Excuse me." She slid past him and grabbed her practice bag.

"What happened this morning?" Tyler stepped into the doorway, effectively blocking her inside. "You could have told me if you didn't want a ride. I waited for you a good ten minutes before I realized you'd already left."

"You were busy, and it was nice out."

"So rather than wait for me to finish a conversation, you took off without a word?" Tyler asked, his anger rising.

"What do you expect of me?" Amaliya asked, her own voice increasing in volume. "Do you think it's easy for me to sit by and listen to Marie cut me down all the time? I know I have a lot to learn. I don't need the constant reminders."

Tyler saw the hurt now. "I'm sorry she hurt your feelings, but this sport isn't one where you'll make a lot of friends. Unfortunately, competition is the name of the game."

"I'm not competing against Marie, or Becky, for that matter."

"Maybe not directly, but we share a coach," Tyler reminded her. "If Scarlett is working with us, she isn't working with Marie."

"You really think that's all it is?" Amaliya asked. "She doesn't want me around because I'm in the way."

"In the way of what?" Tyler asked. "It doesn't matter who I partnered with; Scarlett would have to divide her time among all of us."

"I'm not talking about skating."

Tyler's eyebrows furrowed. "You think she's jealous of you because of me?"

"From the way she talks, it sounds like you spent a lot more time with her before I got here."

"Well, yeah, but it wasn't anything serious."

"Does she know that?" Amaliya picked up her bag and slipped past him. "By the way, do you mind if we wait until Saturday to watch film? I have plans tomorrow night."

Tyler followed her out of the office, noting Marie and Becky already standing at the edge of the rink. "You have plans?"

"A friend from school invited me to go to a ball game."

An image of Sarah flashed into his mind. "I guess we could do Saturday night."

"Great." She stepped toward the restroom. "I'm going to change."

Marie approached and hooked her hand around his arm. "Did Amaliya just say she has plans tomorrow night?"

"Yeah."

"Great. Then you can come to the restaurant opening with me," Marie said.

Tyler glanced at the restroom door, a sinking feeling in his stomach. Did Amaliya really have plans, or was she deliberately clearing a path for Marie to date him?

He turned his attention back to Marie. "What time should I meet you?"

"Six o'clock." She gave his arm a squeeze. "Come hungry. The food is amazing."

Tyler let her pull him toward the rink, but he couldn't resist glancing behind him again. As much as he tried to ignore it, the sizzle of attraction he had experienced when he first met Amaliya hadn't ever faded. Did she not feel it too? Was the connection between them all in his imagination? Why else would she intentionally set him up to go out with Marie? Or was it possible that Amaliya was interested but didn't want to be part of the imagined competition Marie had created? Either way, maybe it was time they cleared the air.

Butterflies took flight in his stomach as a new thought formed. Maybe it was time to stop waiting and tell her how he felt.

Chapter
TWENTY-TWO

"MILES, YOU CAN'T BE SERIOUS." Amaliya sat in the car beside him and looked out the window at the ball field.

"Sure I can." Miles turned the engine off. "I'm not letting some boy drive you home until I've met him. Which one is he anyway?"

Amaliya scanned the field. When Jeff had asked her to come, she'd been so shocked she hadn't thought to ask him his position. "That's him at second base."

"You know, I played baseball as a kid."

"Yeah?"

"Yeah. I can't throw worth a darn." He climbed out.

"Miles, they're already warming up. I can't exactly pull him off the field to meet you."

"That's okay. I'll stay and watch the game with you, and you can introduce me to him afterward."

"You aren't going to give up on this, are you?"

"Nope."

"Fine, but can you promise not to embarrass me?"

"Where's the fun in that?"

She stepped beside him. "Are you having fun playing the protective father?"

"As a matter of fact, I am."

Amaliya couldn't help but laugh. "I hate to admit it, but I think my dad would approve."

"We should have broken him out of the hospital so he could come too." Mile started forward. "What do you say? Should we sit front and center so I can yell at the umpire?"

"No. That's taking embarrassing me way too far."

"Fine. You can pick our seats."

Amaliya scanned the bleachers and led the way to an open spot at the top. She sat, and Miles settled beside her.

"Could you have gotten any farther away?"

"We'll have a great view from up here."

"You know I'm a hockey coach, and I can be loud."

"I also know where you're hiding those Oreos Aunt Linda doesn't want you eating."

"You are your father's daughter." Miles leaned against the back of the bleachers. "When does this game start anyway?"

"Any minute."

"Our table should be ready any minute," Marie said.

Tyler breathed in the scent of fresh baguettes and took in the elegant restaurant with its candlelit tables and muted lighting. A mural of the Eiffel Tower covered the wall to his left, and tasteful artwork hung opposite it.

Nearly every table was occupied, a low buzz carrying over the Chopin that played in the background.

"Your dad did a great job on this place."

"I thought so too," Marie said. "It's not as big as his restaurant in the city, but now that he's hired a new chef, he's planning to spend more time at this one."

Marie's mother approached and kissed Tyler's cheek. "Tyler, it's so good to have you here."

"I wouldn't miss it." He waved toward the mural. "It feels like we've been transported to Paris."

"Ah, that is the idea," she said with her thick French accent.

The maître d' approached. "Your table is ready now."

"Thank you, Charles," Marie's mom said. "You two enjoy your dinner."

"Thank you, Mrs. Averett."

Charles retrieved two menus from beneath the discrete podium by the entrance and weaved past several tables. He motioned to a table for two in the center of the room.

"Here you are."

Tyler waited for Marie to sit before he lowered himself onto the padded chair.

Charles handed them both a menu and a wine list. "Your waiter will be with you shortly."

Tyler set aside the wine list and picked up the menu. "Any recommendations?"

"The foie gras is amazing."

"Thanks, but goose liver doesn't sound terribly appealing to me."

"If you want boring, you can always try the steak."

Their waiter arrived. "May I start you off with some wine?"

"Yes, I'll have a glass of chardonnay," Marie said.

"Very good. And you, sir?"

"Just water, thanks," Tyler said.

"Tyler, tonight is a celebration. Have a glass of wine with me."

"I don't drink."

"One glass is hardly drinking."

The waiter waited patiently.

"Just water," Tyler repeated. He studied his menu, and a moment later, the waiter reappeared with their drinks and took their order.

"I meant to ask you, What was Beth Williamson doing at our practice last week?"

Tyler's stomach clenched. "How do you know Mrs. Williamson?"

"I saw an article on her in the newspaper when she signed on to choreograph *Swan Lake*," Marie said. "How do you know her?"

"She's an old friend of Amaliya's mom."

"Really?" Marie's eyebrows lifted. "I don't suppose you have her number, do you?"

"No, why?"

"I need fresh programs for worlds next year, and everyone knows Beth Williamson is brilliant."

"Sorry, but she isn't choreographing for skating anymore."

"She's choreographing for you though." Marie reached across the table and put her hand on his. "Surely, it wouldn't be that hard for her to do mine too, especially if she's already coming down here."

"Sorry, Marie. She was very clear that she was only doing this as a favor." Tyler drew his hand away.

"And you could do me a favor by introducing me."

"It isn't that simple," Tyler said. "I wouldn't want to take advantage of her."

"No." Marie's voice turned sharp. "Of course you wouldn't."

"What about the choreographer you worked with last year?"

"I need someone new, someone who can help me get to the next level." She sipped her wine.

A camera flashed, and Tyler turned toward it. An instant later, Marie leaned closer and put her hand on his back as the camera flashed again.

"Why is a photographer here?"

"Like I said, it's the opening for this restaurant." Marie straightened again. "The New York papers are all doing reviews."

Marie finished her wine and signaled for another. The camera flashed again.

The strategic location of their table suddenly made sense. He and Marie were on display for everyone to see.

Tyler took a drink of water. This dinner couldn't end soon enough.

Jeff stepped into the batter's box, and Amaliya clasped her hands together. Two outs, the bottom of the ninth inning, a man on third, and the score was tied.

Jeff took a strike as though it were no big deal being the person who held his team's fate in his hands.

"I don't know how he can be so calm out there. He's only been back at school for two days, and now here he is like everything is normal."

"Everyone has different ways of dealing with a crisis," Miles said.

"I guess." Amaliya held her breath on the next pitch. Ball.

"If this goes to a full count, I don't think I'll be able to watch."

Another pitch, but this time, Jeff swung, and his bat connected. The ball dropped into the outfield, and the runner on third scored. The crowd jumped to their feet. The home dugout emptied. Cheers echoed.

"That was a nice way to end the game."

"A little too stressful for me."

"What are you talking about?" Miles asked. "You used to hope for your dad's games to go into overtime."

"Yeah, but that was so I could stay up later."

The stands cleared out, and Miles nudged her. "Come on. Let's go meet that friend of yours."

Amaliya stood. Knots tangled in her stomach as the opposing team left the field and Amaliya and Miles approached the fence on the home-team side.

Jeff spotted her and left his team's celebration to join her. "Hey, Amaliya. Glad you made it."

"Jeff, this is my Uncle Miles," Amaliya said. "He wanted to meet you."

Apparently not fazed by Miles's presence, Jeff extended his hand. "Good to meet you, sir. Is it okay if Amaliya comes with me for pizza with the team?"

"You have a car?"

"I'm driving my dad's," Jeff said, a little hitch surfacing in his voice.

Miles ignored it. "Drive safe."

"I will."

Miles squeezed Amaliya's shoulder. "Don't be out too late. You have practice in the morning."

"I know."

"Have fun you two." Miles left them alone.

"Sorry about that," Amaliya said. "He's very protective."

"Nothing wrong with that," Jeff said. "I need to shower and change. I hope you don't mind waiting a few minutes."

"No, that's fine."

"Let me grab my stuff." He jogged back to the dugout, collected his glove and duffel bag, and joined her on her side of the fence.

"Great game, by the way."

"Thanks. Nothing like facing the final out to get your blood pumping."

"You sound like you enjoy the pressure."

"I guess." He glanced behind him where his team was straggling along the path that connected the ball field to the school. "It was nice having everyone worrying about the score instead of how I was going to play."

"I have to think they were all pleased with your performance tonight."

"We won. That's what counts." They walked into the school together. "I'll be back in a few minutes."

Jeff disappeared into the locker room, and Amaliya leaned against the wall opposite the door. Several other players followed him inside, a few of their girlfriends waiting out with Amaliya.

Lisa, one of the girls in her English class, approached her. "Amaliya, I thought I saw you in the stands earlier," she said. "Did you come to watch Jeff play?"

"Yeah."

"I didn't realize you two were a thing."

Not sure how to categorize her relationship with Jeff, Amaliya asked, "Are you dating one of the players?"

"My boyfriend is the catcher." Lisa motioned to the pretty blonde next to her. "This is Vicky."

"I don't think I've seen you around before," Vicky said. "Do you go to school here?"

"Yes. I moved here in January," Amaliya said. "I gather you're both going to get pizza with the team."

"It's tradition," Vicky said. "You stick around long enough and you'll get to know all of the players and their girlfriends."

Memories surfaced of Friday nights with her friends in Virginia, Saturday afternoons at the mall or with her dad at the Cap Centre, ice skating on Saturday nights. Was it possible Jeff was giving her the chance to build a circle of friends here in Connecticut?

The locker room door opened, and several of the players walked out.

Jeff approached her. "You ready?"

"Yes."

"Great." He slid his arm around her shoulders. "Let's go."

Chapter
TWENTY-THREE

"Tyler," Scarlett called to him as he approached the ice.

"Yeah?"

"Why didn't you tell me you hired Beth Williamson to do your choreography?"

Here we go again. So much for keeping Beth's involvement a secret. "We kind of hoped to make it a surprise."

"When is she coming back to work with you and Amaliya?"

"I'm not sure. We gave her our music, but we haven't finalized our plans," Tyler said. "Last time she was here, she said she wanted us to master a few more lifts before she puts our long program together."

"I'd like to see if she can choreograph at least one program for Marie," Scarlett said. "It could make all the difference for her in moving onto the medal platform."

"Marie already asked about that, and as I told her, Beth is doing this as a favor to Amaliya. She specifically said she wasn't taking on any new skating clients."

"Well, we can talk to her when she comes to town," Scarlett said. "Go warm up."

Tyler stepped onto the ice, eager to end the conversation. He circled the rink three times before Amaliya joined him. "How was the game last night?"

"Good. We won." She matched her stride to his. "How was dinner?"

"Don't ask."

"What happened?"

"For one thing, Marie wanted me to give her Beth Williamson's phone number."

"She didn't."

"Oh yeah. I thought that was her main reason for inviting me last night until the photographers showed up."

"What photographers?"

"The ones from the newspaper who were covering the restaurant opening. They got enough photos of me and Marie that I was starting to wonder if we would ever get to eat our meal."

"Was the food good, at least?"

"Yeah, it was great, but the company wasn't the best."

"I thought you and Marie have dated quite a bit."

"It hasn't been that much, but after last night, I don't think I can take another date with her."

"Why not?"

"Let's just say Marie and I don't have as much in common as she thinks we do." Tyler took her hand. "Speaking of which, if she tries to corner me into going out with her again, can you run interference?"

"How?"

"I don't know. Maybe say we have plans, or ask me to do something."

"I can do that." She shrugged. "It's not like she can resent me any more than she already does."

Tyler didn't dispute her claim.

"What do you want to work on today? Double axels?"

"I've barely got the double lutz down. Maybe we should make sure I keep that skill before moving on to a new one."

"Maybe you're right, but I did want to work on a new lift today. We need to add a few more to our repertoire before Beth can finalize our choreography."

"Is Scarlett helping us with that?"

"I hope so. Speaking of Scarlett, she also asked about having Beth help Marie."

"You realize that if they start hounding her, we're going to lose our chance to work with her."

"I was thinking about that too." Tyler went over the rink schedule in his mind. "Any chance you'd be able to skip a day of school to work with her between practices?"

"You mean do our choreography when Scarlett and Marie aren't around?" Amaliya asked.

"It's not ideal, but it's better than having Beth back out on us."

"Summer break is in a few weeks. What about waiting until then?"

"That could work."

"That's going to be a lot of skating," Amaliya said, "but I don't know how else to protect Beth from getting hounded."

"We could say one of us is going out of town," Tyler suggested.

"Or we could go out of town," Amaliya said. "Maybe instead of having Beth come to us, we could go to her. Spend a week down there learning the new routine."

"Spend a week in New York?"

"Yeah. We can either take the train in every day, or we can stay in a hotel for a day or two," Amaliya said. "It would also give me the chance to visit my parents more often."

"That's not a bad idea."

"I'll talk to Linda and see what she thinks."

"Let me know." Tyler reversed direction so he was skating backward. "Ready to practice that double lutz?"

"I'm ready if you are."

A flutter of anticipation rose within Amaliya when she walked into the cafeteria Monday morning and found Jeff waiting for her at her usual table. After a rough morning at practice and receiving news that Scarlett didn't think it was worth her time to film Amaliya and Tyler, Amaliya was ready to put skating out of her mind. Whether Jeff meant to or not, he provided a welcome distraction.

He stood. "I was wondering what time you would get here."

"Did you have a good weekend?" She set her bag on the floor and sat down.

"It would have been better had I remembered to get your phone number. I was going to call to see if you wanted to do something Saturday."

"Anxious to get out of the house?" Amaliya asked.

"Something like that, but I also wanted to see you."

A new set of butterflies took flight. She retrieved a notebook and a pen from her bag, wrote down the Donnellys' phone number, and handed it to him.

"Thanks." He motioned to her pen. "Can I borrow that?"

"Sure." She handed it over.

Jeff tore the paper in half and used the blank piece to jot down his number. He handed it to her, along with her pen. "Here you go. Now you have mine too."

"Thanks." She tucked everything back into her bag. The first bell rang, and she glanced at the clock. "I must have been later than I thought today."

"Come on. I'll walk you to class."

As soon as she stood, Jeff took her hand in his. The familiar sensation of being watched surfaced, overshadowing the butterflies still battling in her stomach.

"I have a game Wednesday night. Any chance you can come?"

"What time?"

"Six thirty."

Amaliya did a quick calculation in her head. If she went straight home after practice, she would have time to borrow a car and drive herself to the game. She might be up a little later than her usual, but surely that wouldn't be a big deal this once. "I think I can be there."

"Great." They started down the hall, but Jeff stopped when they reached a poster for the prom. "Do you already have a date to this?"

"No."

"Want to come with me?"

"You want me to go with you to the prom?"

"Yeah. What do you think?" Jeff asked. "I know it's not a lot of time to get a dress, but I thought it would be fun. Besides, it is our senior year."

Go to prom with one of the most popular guys in school. She hadn't seen that coming. Her thoughts went to her original plans with Tyler for Saturday, plans that wouldn't be happening this week since they didn't have film to review. Slowly, she nodded. "I'd love to go with you."

"Great. It's a date."

His words resonated with her. "You realize you just asked me out on two dates in less than five minutes. Is this getting serious?"

"Would you mind if it were?"

Again, Tyler's image surfaced in her mind, but she pushed it aside. "No, I wouldn't mind at all."

Tyler dropped Amaliya off at her house, and she rushed inside to the scent of beef stew and cornbread. She passed through the empty living room and found Linda in the kitchen.

"Linda, I need a huge favor," Amaliya said.

"What's that?"

"I need a prom dress for this weekend."

"You're going to prom?" Linda asked. "Is Tyler taking you?"

"No, actually, I'm going with Jeff."

"The baseball player?"

"That's him."

"I see." Linda stirred something on the stove. "That's awfully short notice. Are you sure you're up for that? We have tickets to the ballet for Friday."

"I'll be fine, but first, I need to find a dress."

"That is an important thing to have for prom," Linda said. "The local dress shops all close at five. Would you be able to take a day off of practice for us to shop?"

"I don't know." Amaliya snitched a piece of cornbread and popped a bite into her mouth. "Scarlett hasn't been thrilled with us lately. I'm not sure that would go over well." Amaliya went over her schedule in her head. Even if she left straight from practice, she still wouldn't get to the nearest dress shop before it closed. "Are you going into the city this week? Maybe you could pick something up for me."

"I may go in tomorrow, but I don't know that I would have time to do any shopping."

"Maybe I'll have to pretend I'm sick one day to get an afternoon off from practice," Amaliya said.

"Are you sure you want to do that? You're already missing Friday afternoon to go to the ballet," Linda said. "You really should talk to Scarlett about skipping Saturday morning too. We'll get home so late, neither you nor Tyler will be capable of practicing anyway."

"Yeah. Tyler mentioned that we might be able to get some ice time before free skate so we can sleep in and do a later practice."

"That's a good idea."

Amaliya ate another bite of cornbread as the door opened behind her. "I still need a dress though."

Miles walked in from outside. "A dress for what?"

"Amaliya has been asked to prom."

"Jeff or Tyler?"

"Jeff," Amaliya said, not sure why both Linda and Miles thought Tyler might have asked her.

"Linda has lots of dresses. Why not borrow one from her?" Miles asked.

"For one thing, I'm two sizes larger than Amaliya. Besides, every girl needs the chance to pick out her own prom dress."

"When is she going to do that?" Miles asked. "She's either at school or practice all day."

"That's true," Linda said. "If we could go into the city, the stores would be open later, but here in Connecticut, the only time you would have open would be on Saturday, and that's cutting it close."

"Or we could go early to the ballet on Friday and do some shopping then," Amaliya suggested.

"You want me and Tyler to go dress shopping with you?" Miles asked, a hint of panic in his voice.

"He's right," Amaliya said. "That would be weird shopping for a prom dress with Tyler there. Besides, I kind of wanted to stop by the hospital and introduce Tyler to Mama and Papa."

Linda stirred the stew and held up the spoon. "I have another idea."

"What?"

"Go get your photo album."

"Okay." When Amaliya returned a minute later, the stew and cornbread were already on the table.

Linda held out a hand and took the album from her. "You're about the same size as your mom, right?"

"Yeah. Why?"

"What about one of these?" Linda held the album out and pointed at a page that featured her parents on various opening nights at the ballet and an awards dinner for her father.

"My mom has a lot of beautiful dresses, but they're still in Virginia. I'm here."

"Maybe Eleanor could ship some up for you," Linda suggested. "I'm sure she would be happy to pack them up and put them on the train for us."

Wear one of her mother's dresses. Amaliya stared at the evidence of happier times.

"What do you think?" Linda asked.

"Do you think my mom would mind?"

"I'm sure she won't. We can call her after dinner. If she's okay with it, I'll call Eleanor and make the arrangements."

"Thanks." Amaliya took another look at her parents' photos before she gently closed the album.

"Now that we have that settled, let's eat."

Chapter
TWENTY-FOUR

KATERINA HELD HER BREATH AND watched her husband. His hand on his cane, Robert took a step forward. Then another. The air whooshed out of Katerina's lungs when Robert made it two more steps before he had to put the cane on the ground to steady himself.

"Robert, that was great," Katerina said.

"It only took me four months to be able to walk without help, and I still can't make it all the way across the room."

Katerina bit back her own frustration that she was still tethered to her hospital bed. "You're getting stronger every day."

"You're right. It won't be long before I'll be cheering you on."

The doctor walked in holding two clipboards. "I really wish you two would speak in English so I would know if you were planning to break out of here or just having a conversation."

Robert switched from French to English. "Doctor, I helped my wife defect from the Soviet Union. If we wanted to break out of here, we would have been gone weeks ago."

"I hadn't thought about that." Dr. Caldwell glanced at Katerina before he turned his attention back to Robert. "As it turns out, I have good news. Robert, we're releasing you. You're ready to move on to your next stage of rehab."

"I'm not going anywhere." Robert shook his head. "I'm not leaving here until my wife can come with me."

"The nurses said you were stubborn." Dr. Caldwell glanced at the top chart he held. "I'll see what I can do to extend your physical therapy here through the hospital. In the meantime, let's see what we can do to help your wife catch up to you."

"What?"

"Today, you get your freedom back." Dr. Caldwell said. "It's time we get you out of bed."

Delight and excitement shimmered through Katerina. "I thought this day was never going to come."

"I'm not going to lie to you. You still have a long road to recovery, but depending on how the next couple weeks go, I hope to be able to transfer you to a rehab facility before the end of the month." Dr. Caldwell glanced at Robert. "Both of you."

Katerina smiled at the doctor. "We'll take that kind of news any day."

Amaliya hurried from the parking lot to the bleachers. An impromptu practice with Tyler after their usual session ended had made her late, but she hadn't wanted to mention to Tyler that she had plans.

In truth, it was her fault Scarlett was being so difficult. If she could land her double axel, their coach would be able to focus on how they should put together the required elements for their new programs instead of trying to teach the skills to her. Regardless of Scarlett's recent behavior, Amaliya had to believe their coach would come around once they reached that point. After all, except for that one element, their short program was ready for the highest level of competition.

When Amaliya reached the seating area, Jeff's team was already on the field, a batter at the plate. Amaliya started up the bleachers toward where she had sat at the last game with Miles.

"Amaliya." Lisa waved. "Come sit with us."

Amaliya changed her path and slid past a couple to join several of the other players' girlfriends. She sat beside Lisa. "What inning is it?"

"Third." She motioned to the scoreboard, where it noted the inning as well as the one–nothing score in Jeff's team's favor.

"Who scored?"

"Jeff. He hit a double, and Eddie singled him in."

"Sorry I missed that."

"Why were you late?" Lisa asked.

"My practice ran over."

"What kind of practice?"

"Ice skating."

"Do you know Marie Averett?" Lisa asked.

"Yes. We have the same coach." Amaliya's eyebrows drew together. "How do you know Marie?"

"I'm dating her brother." Lisa pointed at the catcher.

"I didn't know Marie had a brother."

"Yeah. Their family is so athletic. Marie made it to the world championships in figure skating, and Charles set the school's homerun record last year," she said. "He'll probably break it again this season."

"That's impressive."

Amaliya rolled her shoulders to work out some of the tightness that had settled there, then turned her attention to the game as Jeff fielded a ground ball and threw out the batter. His team jogged off the field, and Jeff glanced at the bleachers, his eyes searching until he found her.

Amaliya waved, and he gave a subtle nod as he continued to the dugout.

"You have good timing. Jeff is up next," Lisa said.

Amaliya leaned forward and gripped her hands together. Jeff swung and missed at the first two pitches and watched a third pass by for a ball. He connected with the next pitch, but the ball flew straight into the shortstop's glove.

The game went back and forth, the away team scoring two runs in the seventh inning only to have Jeff's team tie the score in the eighth. Neither team scored in the ninth or the tenth.

Amaliya fought back a yawn. Two more scoreless innings passed, her energy steadily draining. She checked her watch. Almost ten o'clock.

Marie's brother stepped into the batter's box, and Lisa jumped to her feet to cheer. She wasn't the only one. Most of the crowd rose, and Amaliya followed suit. Even though she didn't know Charles Averett, she wanted nothing more than for this game to end so she could go home and go to bed.

The home run everyone hoped for wasn't to be, replaced instead by a strikeout. The thirteenth inning ended, and a new one began. Amaliya reclaimed her seat, and she blinked several times to remind her eyelids that they were supposed to stay open.

The opposing team scored in the top of the fourteenth inning, and Jeff's team failed to follow suit. Once the game was over, she approached the fence to wait for Jeff. Lisa stepped beside her. "I should probably tell you Jeff isn't the easiest guy to be around when they lose."

"Thanks for the warning."

Several of the other players stopped to chat with their girlfriends, arranging rides home or making plans to talk tomorrow. Jeff remained by his coach for several minutes. Amaliya yawned again and debated whether she could afford to lose any more sleep waiting for him. Finally, Jeff grabbed his mitt and started behind the rest of his teammates. He glanced at her briefly, but instead of diverting to talk to her on his way to the locker room, he walked past without a word.

Was Jeff mad at her for being late? Or was the loss fueling his mood? Anger bubbled inside her. She had lost sleep just to wait for him to ignore her? Too tired to find out why Jeff was acting this way, she turned her back on the field and made her way to her car. Time to go home and get to bed.

Chapter
TWENTY-FIVE

EVERYTHING WAS OFF. TYLER GLANCED at Amaliya as they completed their spins; she was nearly half a rotation behind him. He glanced at Scarlett, expecting her usual rant when their timing didn't match.

When no correction came, Tyler focused on Amaliya, "You look tired today."

"Sorry. I didn't get much sleep last night."

"Maybe we should work on figures," Tyler suggested. "If you're tired, you're too prone to injury."

"What about our lifts?" Amaliya asked. "An extra hour on Saturday isn't going to be enough to get us where we need to be."

"I was thinking about that. Any chance you can get here earlier for practice?" Tyler asked. "I can pick you up at the school if you want."

"That would work if I skip lunch at school," Amaliya said. "I usually pack my lunch anyway, so I can eat here."

"Great. I'll pick you up out front when you get out of class," Tyler said. "That will give you time to eat, and we'll still have a good forty-five minutes before Scarlett shows up."

"How much longer do you think Scarlett will ignore us?"

"I don't know, but this is getting old," Tyler said. "It's time she earns the coaching fees we're paying her."

"I agree."

"Come on." Tyler pushed off and created the path of a figure eight for Amaliya to follow. She fell in behind him, concentrating on following his track precisely. When they completed the simple figure, Tyler walked her through a more complicated variation.

Fifteen minutes later, Scarlett finally addressed them. "Tyler, Amaliya, you're supposed to be working on spins."

"Ready to try again?" Tyler asked.

Amaliya nodded. He counted off their first spin, the same one they had been out of sync on twenty minutes ago. This time they started in unison and ended a half beat off.

Despite her command on what to do, Scarlett again didn't comment.

Tyler glided to Amaliya. "Better."

"Again?"

"Might as well. Either you need to speed up your rotation or I need to slow down."

"I'll try to match you," Amaliya said. "Count it off."

"One. Two. Three."

Amaliya entered the school with a sense of dread. If Jeff hadn't talked to her after the game last night, what should she expect the morning after the loss?

She debated whether to even go to her usual spot in the cafeteria, but she was only a few steps inside when Jeff approached.

"What happened to you last night?" Jeff asked as though he was unaware that he had ignored her after the game.

"What do you mean? I was there. You were the one who didn't talk to me afterward."

"Sorry. I always need some time to myself after a loss." Jeff waved that away like it was a known fact. Maybe it was to everyone else. "I figured you'd wait for me afterward."

Her eyebrows drew together. "You wanted me to wait for you even though you never spoke to me?"

"Well, yeah, especially since you were late to the game," he said. "Why were you late anyway?"

"Sorry. My practice ran over," Amaliya said, instantly annoyed at herself for apologizing. "Look, I know it probably didn't seem like a big deal to you, but it wasn't easy for me to stay out that late and then turn around and get up at four o'clock this morning."

"Yeah, I guess I didn't think about that." Jeff took her hand. "I should have told you that I get moody when we lose. I promise if we lose on Friday, I won't take it out on you."

"Friday?"

"Yeah. We have an away game," Jeff said. "It's only about a twenty-minute drive, but if you don't want to drive yourself, my mom can bring you."

"Sorry, but I can't make it."

"Why not?"

"I'm going to the ballet in New York."

"The ballet?" Skepticism filled his voice. "You like that kind of stuff?"

She stiffened. "One of the last conversations I had with my parents before their accident was trying to convince them to let me move to California to join the San Francisco Ballet, so yeah, I guess you could say I like that stuff."

"I'm sorry. I didn't know." Jeff took a step closer. "Maybe we should start this day over."

"Maybe so."

Jeff took her hand. "Hi, Amaliya. I'm glad you're here. Can I walk you to class?"

The tension that had been building inside her faded. "I'd like that."

"Great." They started down the hall. "Are we still on for Saturday night?"

"I'm looking forward to it." Assuming she could get some sleep between now and then.

They reached her classroom, and Jeff said, "I'll see you at lunch."

"Actually, I can't stay for lunch today," Amaliya said. "Tyler and I need to work on a few things before our regular practice time."

"Who's Tyler?"

"My partner."

"I'm not following. Your partner for what?"

"Skating. I'm a pairs skater."

"I didn't know that."

"You only met me a week and a half ago."

"I guess that's true," Jeff said. "Did you want to do something tonight? Maybe grab some dinner?"

"Thanks, but I'd better pass. This is the only night I'll be able to get any sleep before the ballet tomorrow and the dance on Saturday."

"This skating stuff really cuts into your social life."

"I guess. I never noticed before." She stepped back. "I'll see you tomorrow."

"Yeah. Tomorrow."

After visiting her parents every Sunday for almost four months, Amaliya suspected she could work at the information desk of the hospital. Yet, in all these weeks, this was the first time she was bringing anyone in her new life to meet her parents. This was also the first time she'd had occasion to dress up for her visit.

Amaliya greeted the nurse at the desk and continued to her parents' room with Tyler, Linda, and Miles.

Tyler straightened his tie. "Do you want to make sure your parents are okay to have an extra visitor before I go in?"

"They know you're coming." Amaliya smoothed the skirt of her dress and led the way inside. Her eyes were drawn to her mother's empty bed before she focused on the two wheelchairs by the window. Her father sat in one, a cane leaning against the wall beside him, and her mother sat in the other. "Mama! You're out of bed!" Amaliya automatically spoke in French before repeating her words in English for Tyler's benefit.

Her mom smiled, her eyes bright. "Yes. The doctor said I can finally start learning to walk again."

"I'm so glad." Amaliya motioned to Tyler. "This is Tyler Linden. Tyler, these are my parents, Katerina and Robert Marcell."

"It's nice to meet you both." Tyler stepped forward and shook hands with each of them. As had been the case with the few boys Amaliya had dated in the past, her mother offered a smile and her father glared.

"So, you're my daughter's skating partner." Robert straightened in his seat.

"Yes, sir." Tyler stepped back and positioned himself at Amaliya's side.

"The two of you are spending a lot of time together," Robert said.

Tyler's eyes darted to meet Amaliya's as though not sure how to answer. "We have two practices a day."

Embarrassed by her father's protective behavior, Amaliya moved to her father's side and put her hand on his shoulder. "Papa. Tyler isn't a boyfriend you need to scare away."

Linda stepped forward. "Has the doctor said anything about when you'll be released?"

"They tried to release me a few days ago, but I convinced them to let me stay here with Katerina," Robert said.

"Mama, how much longer will you have to stay here?"

"I'm not sure." Her mother's voice went soft, the way it often did when she was trying to hide her emotions. "The doctor is hoping I'll be out of here sometime in May, but then I'll have another six to nine months in a rehab facility while I learn to walk again."

"I'm so sorry," Amaliya said.

"We're both making progress." Pride and determination filled her father's voice.

"Any idea what rehab facility you'll use?" Miles asked.

"We're leaning toward one in Connecticut so we can be closer to Amaliya," Katerina said.

"That would be great." Amaliya couldn't begin to imagine how life would change once her parents took those next literal steps forward.

"We'll be getting out of here before you know it," Robert said with conviction.

"If for no other reason than for the nurses to get your father to leave." Katerina focused on Tyler. "My husband isn't the best patient."

"I don't think I would be either," Tyler said.

"I understand you're all going to the ballet tonight," Robert said.

"Yes, sir."

"I'm sorry you won't be there with us," Amaliya said. "It won't be the same without you."

"It won't be long before we'll all be going together again." Katerina looked at Miles and Robert. "Well, you, Linda, and I will be going while the men stay home and pretend they have something better to do."

"Darling, if you were the one on stage, you know I would be there every night," Robert said.

"It's true," Katerina conceded. "He would."

"I wish I could have seen you dance," Amaliya said.

"You've watched me dance your whole life." Her mom took Amaliya's hand and squeezed. "Enjoy tonight."

"I'll try."

Backstage at the New York City Ballet. When Beth invited them to attend tonight's production of *Swan Lake*, Tyler hadn't expected a tour through the preshow chaos. Dancers stretched in every possible space, costume designers made last-minute adjustments, and hair and makeup artists took care of the final touches.

The buzz of the crowd already carried through the curtain, even though the show wouldn't start for another twenty minutes. Beside him, Amaliya walked slowly, taking it all in.

Tyler leaned down to be heard over the backstage buzz of conversation. "I had no idea so many dancers were in the show."

Amaliya didn't answer, but Beth must have heard his comment. "It's a demanding production."

"The first time I met Amaliya's mother, it was backstage after she performed in *Swan Lake* in Canada," Linda said. "I'd dragged Amaliya's father along, completely unaware that the two of them had already met."

"This must bring back a lot of memories," Tyler said.

"It does," Linda said. "For all of us."

Tyler noted the moisture forming in Amaliya's eyes and the way she blinked rapidly to fight the tears. He thought the news about her mother's recovery would put her in a good mood, but ever since they'd arrived, she had grown quiet.

"Should we go find our seats?" Tyler asked.

"That's a good idea," Miles said.

"Linda can show you the way." Beth pointed to the right.

"Thanks for the tour and for the tickets," Tyler said.

"Glad to help, but part of my reason for wanting you here tonight is so you and Amaliya can gain inspiration on which movement we should use for your choreography."

"Giving the kids homework already," Linda said. "Why am I not surprised?"

"Because you know me well." Beth waved at someone a short distance away. "I'd better get back to work. You enjoy the show."

"We will." Tyler glanced at Amaliya again in time to see her swipe at a tear trying to fall. Not sure what was causing Amaliya's emotional upheaval, Tyler took her hand and leaned closer. "Are you going to be okay?"

"It's hard knowing my mom used to dance the lead in this production and now she can't even walk across the room."

"She'll get better. Give it time," Tyler said.

Her lips pressed together, but she nodded.

"This way." Linda guided them to a short hallway that connected the stage to the seating area and then to the center of the fifth row.

"Wow." Tyler took in their unobstructed view of center stage. "When Beth gives a gift, she goes all out."

Amaliya sat down, and Tyler claimed the seat beside her. He stretched his arm behind her and gave her shoulder a squeeze. "I know this can't be easy for you."

She sniffled and swallowed hard, then took another moment before she managed to form words. "This is the first time I've been to the ballet since the accident."

"If you need a break, let me know. We can always go into the lobby."

She shook her head. "No. I want to watch." Her teary eyes met his. "I need to."

Amaliya accepted the tissue Linda handed her and wiped at her eyes. She'd known tonight would bring out her emotions in full force, but she hadn't expected her tears to start before the first act. She thought she had come to terms with her decision to walk away from the ballet, but the combination of seeing her mom in a wheelchair and coming to tonight's performance had created a perfect storm to sweep her emotions into uncharted territory.

Tyler's arm around her and an occasional pat on her hand by Linda gave her the reassurance that she wasn't alone, but the moment the curtains opened, the heaviness in her chest returned.

That could have been her on stage. Had her parents' accident not turned their lives upside down, had she not walked away from ballet, she would have already auditioned for a spot with the New York City Ballet. She would have been planning her move into the city or at least been battling with her parents about whether she should be allowed her own apartment as an eighteen-year-old instead of commuting in from Miles and Linda's house in Connecticut.

Ballet might not be part of her life anymore, but dance was, even if it was now in the form of figure skating. She was ready to explore the artistic side of the sport, to bring dance back into her daily routine.

Tyler squeezed her shoulder again and whispered in her ear. "You doing okay?"

She nodded, her attention on the ballerinas on stage. The dancer performing the part of Odette and Odile emerged, and Amaliya tried to imagine her mother going through the same movements.

Twenty minutes later, when the two principal dancers took the stage alone, possibilities flooded Amaliya's mind. With each minute that passed, she could visualize the dance recreated on the ice, with her stepping into her mother's shoes but in a pair of ice skates instead of ballet slippers.

She tilted her chin to look at Tyler. "This is it. This is what we need to use for our program."

A smile spread across Tyler's lips. "Yeah. This is it."

Chapter
TWENTY-SIX

TYLER DIDN'T KNOW IF IT was the chance to sleep in for an extra hour this morning, the good news about her parents, or attending the ballet that had awoken something in her, but Amaliya was a new person.

With the rink currently occupied with skating lessons, Tyler and Amaliya had opted to work on their lifts on the mats in the training room rather than on the ice. With no one to give them feedback, they used the mirrors on the walls to correct their errors.

"What do you think?" Amaliya asked, her hands animated. "Can we create a lift similar to the movement we saw last night?"

"It's really only a variation of what we already do," Tyler said. "If I start my spin a half beat after I lift you, it should be close to the move we saw at the ballet."

"And the transitions should be easy to work with."

"Let's try it." Tyler circled behind her and put his hands on her waist. "We'll start with the basic lift first."

"Tell me when."

Tyler counted to three and lifted Amaliya as she pushed herself into the air. Mimicking the ballerina from last night, she arched her back as though reaching her head and hands toward the ice.

Tyler's balance shifted. "Down." He lowered her to his shoulder and then back to the mat. "Sorry, I need to change my hand position so I don't lose my balance when you lean over."

"Try putting one hand here." She took his hand and guided it to her back.

"Okay. Let's try again."

Four more failed attempts. Four more adjustments. They tried again, and this time, Amaliya arched gracefully, and Tyler could imagine himself being the ballet dancer holding the ballerina.

He lowered her back to the floor. "That's it."

"What do you think? Are you ready to take it to the ice?" Amaliya asked.

"Let's try it a couple more times first."

"Okay."

They ran through the basic lift twice more until Tyler trusted he could re-create the movement on the ice. "Ready to try?"

"Yeah." He glanced at his watch. "The skating lessons should have cleared out by now."

They retrieved their skates and put them on.

Miles walked in as they reached the ice.

"Miles, what are you doing here?" Amaliya asked.

"Linda sent me. She wants Scarlett to get some film of your lifts and turns for Beth to work with." Miles looked around. "Where is Scarlett?"

"She isn't here," Tyler said.

"Why not?"

Tyler glanced at Amaliya. Had she not told Miles and Linda about their difficulties over the past week with their coach?

"Scarlett isn't happy that we wouldn't give her Beth's phone number," Amaliya said. "She wanted us to help convince Beth to do a routine for one of the other skaters."

"That doesn't explain why you're here and she isn't."

Amaliya glanced at Tyler, a silent plea for him to take over the explanation.

"Beth needs us to perfect our lifts before she choreographs our routines," Tyler said. "Scarlett is focused on jumps."

"So you used the ballet as an excuse to skip practice this morning with Scarlett so you could work on lifts on your own," Miles said.

"Something like that."

Miles waved toward the office. "Does Hank have the camera equipment in the office?"

"Yeah. It's in the storage closet."

"Go do your thing. I'll get the camera."

"Thanks, Miles." Amaliya stepped onto the ice.

"You haven't told him about Scarlett's temper tantrum?"

"This week's been so crazy, I hadn't gotten around to it yet."

They circled the rink several times while Miles set up the camera.

"Okay, I'm ready when you are," Miles said.

"Are we starting in motion or from a stand?" Amaliya asked.

"Let's start from a stand." Tyler placed his hands, counted to three, and lifted Amaliya above his head, his arms straight, her body arching artistically as he balanced on two blades.

He lowered her.

"That felt solid," Amaliya said. "Want to put it in motion?"

"Circle once, release, and lift three beats after I grab your waist," Tyler said. "You count it off for me."

"Okay."

They circled the rink, skating backward. Tyler released Amaliya's hand, they both squared their skates so they were skating straight, and he positioned his hands on her back and waist.

"One, two"—Amaliya's legs bent in anticipation—"three."

Tyler lifted her again, concentrating on keeping his ankles straight as he balanced her overhead. He glided the length of the rink before he said, "Down," and lowered her back to the ice.

"Wow." Miles clapped his hands together. "That was something."

"Did we look like the dancers from last night?" Amaliya asked.

"No." He shook his head. "Better. Much better."

"Maybe we can get together tonight and watch the film before we send it to Beth."

"I'd love to, but prom is tonight."

"Oh." Disappointment settled in his stomach. "Do you have a date?"

"Yeah. It's a friend from school. His dad is recovering from a heart attack, and we've been spending some time together."

Tyler's heart sank. "He's the friend you went out with last Friday?"

Amaliya nodded.

"You could come over tomorrow after we get home from church," Miles said, interrupting Tyler's interrogation. "Maybe we can convince Beth to join us for Sunday dinner."

"That would be great," Tyler said. "Thanks."

"If we're seeing Beth tomorrow, maybe we should have Miles film our spins and jumps," Amaliya said.

"Good idea. Sit spins first?"

"Sure."

Unlike when they'd struggled on Friday morning, today they executed the spins in unison. Tyler straightened and came to a stop beside Amaliya. How could they be so in tune on the ice, yet he had missed all the signs that she had started dating someone?

A wave of jealousy washed over him, and he accepted it for what it was. Even though he had kept Amaliya firmly in the friend category, he wanted more. Had he waited too long to share his feelings, or was there still time to convince her that he was the guy for her?

Amaliya descended the stairs, her hand on the railing, her mother's rose-colored, tea-length dress swishing as she walked.

"Oh, Amaliya. You look stunning." Linda grabbed the camera. "I have to take a picture."

Amaliya took her spot in front of the fireplace while Linda snapped a photo.

Miles walked in from the kitchen and stared. "You look just like your mother."

"You think so?" Amaliya asked.

Miles nodded.

The doorbell rang. Amaliya took one step toward the door before Miles brushed by her.

"I'll get it." He pulled the door open and ushered Jeff inside.

Jeff's eyes widened when he saw Amaliya. "Wow. You look beautiful."

"Thank you."

"Here." Jeff lifted a white flower box into view. "This is for you."

"Thank you." She opened it to reveal a corsage created from three white rose buds. "It's beautiful."

Jeff helped her put it on, and she, in turn, helped him with the simple white boutonniere Linda had picked up for her this morning at the florist.

"Come stand over here, and we'll get a picture of you two," Linda said.

After another round of photos, Jeff and Amaliya walked out to Jeff's car. He opened the door for her and waited for her to settle inside before he closed it. When he started the car, he turned the radio on and asked, "How was the ballet last night?"

"It was good. *Swan Lake* is one of my favorites."

"I guess you've been to a lot of performances."

"I have. My mom and I used to go every time a new production opened in DC," Amaliya said. "During the summers, we would come visit Miles and Linda and see some of the New York productions."

A new song came on, and Jeff turned the radio up. "I love this one."

Amaliya hadn't ever heard it. The oddity that she primarily listened to classical music and Jeff clearly preferred contemporary struck her. Tonight would be all about his kind of music.

When they arrived at the school, the gym was already crowded. White lights twinkled overhead, illuminating the dimly lit room. A DJ stood on the stage, changing the music from fast to slow.

"Perfect timing." Jeff took her hand. "Do you want to dance?"

"I'd love to." Amaliya followed him onto the dance floor, and Jeff slipped his hands around her waist. Amaliya settled her hands on Jeff's shoulders as they swayed to the music.

He drew her closer, and his foot landed on hers. "Sorry."

Though her big toe throbbed, she said, "It's okay."

The song ended, and a fast song came on.

Eddie, one of Jeff's teammates approached. "You made it."

"Yeah." Jeff slid his arm around Amaliya. "Where's everyone sitting?"

"Over here." Eddie lowered his voice. "We already have the refreshments going."

Amaliya and Jeff followed him, and Amaliya leaned closer to Jeff. "What's he talking about?"

"It's nothing."

They reached two round tables that had been pushed together, a half dozen baseball players and their dates circling around them.

"Jeff here is ready for a drink," Eddie said.

"Yeah!" one of his teammates cheered. He poured something from a small flask into a cup of punch and handed it to Jeff.

"Is that . . . ?" Amaliya started to ask if it was alcohol, but when Jeff took a sip, she didn't have to finish. She could smell it.

"That's good." Jeff offered his cup to Amaliya. "Try some."

"No, thanks. I don't drink."

"It's just punch," Jeff said.

"With a little fun mixed in," Eddie added.

Another slow song came on. Jeff tipped back his cup and finished the drink. "Come on. Let's dance."

More than happy to leave the spiked punch behind, Amaliya followed him onto the dance floor. The cycle repeated twice more, but by their fourth dance, Amaliya was assaulted by the scent of alcohol on Jeff's breath.

She turned her head and caught sight of Sarah and Kent a short distance away.

Jeff stepped on her foot again, but this time he didn't apologize.

When the song ended, he nudged her toward their table, but Amaliya stepped to the side. "I'm going to say hi to Sarah."

"Who?"

"Sarah Jensen. She's in a couple of my classes."

"Shhure." Jeff slurred the word. "See ya later."

Amaliya crossed the dance floor, searching for Sarah. She found her beside the refreshment table and tapped her shoulder.

Sarah turned, and her eyes brightened. "Amaliya. You look amazing. I love your dress."

"Thanks. Yours is gorgeous too."

Sarah looked past Amaliya. "Where's Jeff?"

"With his team." Amaliya tilted her head in the direction of her date and his friends.

"Uh-oh."

Kent edged forward. "How much has he had to drink?"

"Four that I know of." She glanced at Jeff, who was holding a glass up as though offering a toast. "Make that five."

"You aren't going to let him drive you home, are you?" Sarah asked.

"Actually, as much as I hate to ask, is there any way you could drop me off when you leave?"

Sarah glanced at Kent, who nodded.

"We'll find you before we leave and give you a ride," Kent said. "If Jeff wants to leave before we do, just come hang out with us."

"Thanks. I really appreciate it."

Kent offered Amaliya a glass of punch. "Do you want a drink?"

"No, thanks. I think I'll stick with the water fountain tonight," Amaliya said. Deciding now was as good a time as any to get some fresh air, she said, "I'll see you guys later."

Amaliya went into the hall, where a chaperone stood watch. Amaliya got a drink from the water fountain and checked her watch. Only another two hours to kill. She wondered if Jeff would even notice she was missing.

Amaliya watched the prom king and queen share a dance. She nibbled on a cookie at the refreshment table. She chatted with Sarah and Kent when they took a break from dancing. What she didn't do was return to where Jeff remained with his buddies.

"Are you about ready to go?" Sarah asked, coming off the dance floor a few minutes before the dance was scheduled to end.

"Whenever you are," Amaliya said. "You can stay for the last dance if you want."

"We've had enough," Sarah said. "Does Jeff know you're coming with us?"

"I guess I'd better tell him."

"We'll meet you by the door," Kent said.

Amaliya squared her shoulders and crossed to where she had last seen her date. She was nearly to the table when she finally spotted him slumped over, one arm hooked around the back of his chair, the other arm leaning heavily on the table.

"Jeff?"

He looked up bleary eyed. "Where'd ya go?"

"Sarah and her boyfriend are going to take me home."

"S-stay. We'll dance."

"The dance is almost over, and you shouldn't be driving."

"'M fine." He leaned back in his chair.

"See you later." Amaliya made her way to where Sarah and Kent waited. "Should we tell someone he and his friends shouldn't be driving?"

"Don't be mad, but we already did," Sarah said.

"I'm glad you did. It saves me from being the one to tell on him."

"Come on." Kent slipped his arm around Sarah's shoulders. "Let's go."

Ten minutes later, they pulled up in front of Amaliya's house.

"Thanks again for the ride."

"No problem," Sarah said. "See you Monday."

Amaliya dragged herself up the front walk and let herself in. She was greeted with the sound of skates against ice.

She continued into the living room, where Linda was curled up on the couch, the projector running.

"What are you watching?"

"The tape of you and Tyler."

"Why are you watching that? We're showing it to Beth tomorrow."

"I know, but I wanted to remember what your mother looked like when she could dance," Linda said. "You remind me so much of her when you're skating."

Amaliya sat beside her. "Do I really remind you of her?"

"I've always thought you looked a lot like her, but the way you carry yourself reminds me most of her," Linda said. "I can't wait for her to see all you have accomplished."

"It will be nice to have her able to come to things again." Amaliya settled on the couch beside her. "I wasn't sure about skating to *Swan Lake* at first, but I'm starting to get excited about it."

"You want it to be a tribute to your mother."

"I do. Is that silly to do something for someone who is just an hour away?"

"Not at all. Your mom will love seeing what you and Tyler create," Linda said. "By the way, how was the dance? Did you have fun?"

"The night started out with great promise."

"And then?"

"Jeff spent the whole night hanging out with his buddies from the baseball team."

"Did you talk to him about it?"

"I didn't get much of a chance." Amaliya didn't mention Jeff was too drunk to have a conversation within an hour of their arrival. She stood. "I'd better go to bed."

"Good night, honey."

Amaliya made her way upstairs to her room and changed into pajamas. She flopped down on her bed, the night replaying through her mind. What a disaster. It never occurred to her that Jeff would not only ignore her but that he would also get drunk.

Her gaze landed on her skates. Was she so spoiled being around Tyler that she expected every guy to act like a gentleman?

She suspected Jeff would call and apologize tomorrow, but after the way he had ignored her tonight as well as after his game, she suspected it was time to redefine their friendship into simply that: friendship.

Chapter
TWENTY-SEVEN

TYLER CLIMBED THE STEPS TO Amaliya's house with a sense of anticipation. Even though he had seen her only yesterday morning, he'd missed her. How was that possible?

He knocked on the door, and it swung open a moment later.

Miles waved him inside. "Perfect timing. We were just getting ready to watch film."

Tyler walked into the living room. The curtains were closed, and Beth, Amaliya, and Linda were seated in front of a portable screen. His gaze was drawn to where a corsage box lay on the mantel. He turned away from the reminder that someone else had taken Amaliya to prom. Why hadn't he asked her to go? He remembered what a big deal it was for the girls he went to high school with to attend that particular dance. Amaliya would graduate soon, and she had turned eighteen months ago. Even if the gap in their ages wasn't closing, the possible stigma of him dating someone in high school would soon be behind them.

"Tyler, I'm glad you're here. I understand you and Amaliya have already chosen the passage you want to use for your long program."

"Yes. I know we should probably work on the short program, but we were inspired after watching the ballet on Friday." Tyler claimed the open spot beside Amaliya.

"I think we would do well to focus on the long program first. It plays to your strengths," Beth said. "Let's see what you have for me to work with."

Miles started the projector, and the image of Tyler lifting Amaliya came on the screen. Though Tyler intended to analyze his own movements, his gaze was drawn to Amaliya. When they had practiced in the workout room at the rink, his focus had been on finding the right grip so he could balance her over his head, but now he was captured by her grace and elegance.

"This is perfect," Beth said. "It's precisely what I was hoping for."

"It was Amaliya's idea," Tyler said. "She wanted to try something different."

"Both of you are every bit as graceful as I'd hoped," Beth said.

They watched the rest of the film, stopping a few times and rewinding it when Beth wanted to rewatch and discuss a particular segment.

When the film ended and they were all seated at the dinner table, Beth said, "I've made a few notes of what skills I would like to incorporate into your program. They're preliminary, but after dinner, I'll make a copy so you can pass them on to your coach."

Tyler glanced at Amaliya; his doubt reflected in her gaze.

Beth must have picked up on their concern because she asked, "Is there a problem?"

"Their coach hasn't been cooperating lately," Miles said.

"Explain."

Amaliya didn't answer, and Tyler searched for words. Opting for the truth, he said, "One of the other skaters recognized you when you came to the rink to watch us."

"She wants to hire me."

"Yes. Our coach has been pressuring us to put them in touch with you."

"I have to say I'm impressed."

"With what?" Linda asked. "The fact that you were recognized or that Tyler and Amaliya didn't break their promise to you?"

"Both," Beth said. "Tell me about your coach."

"My sister and I started skating under her eight years ago," Tyler said.

"She's the only coach I've had, except for when Tyler's sister was helping me," Amaliya added.

"How much time does she spend working with you every day?" Beth asked.

"We practice two hours every morning and another two hours in the afternoon."

"That's not what I meant. How much time does she actually spend with you? Correcting technique, introducing new skills, discussing programs, that sort of thing."

"Honestly, not a lot over the past few weeks," Tyler admitted. "She's mostly been focused on Amaliya landing her double axel, but she's teaching through repetition rather than correction."

"Tyler, I love that you recognize the difference," Beth said. "You have the makings of becoming a coach someday."

"Thanks, but for now, I prefer to *be* coached."

"Maybe it's time to shop around," Beth suggested.

"I've been thinking the same thing," Miles said. "We sure aren't getting our money's worth out of Scarlett."

"Find a new coach?" Tyler asked. He could barely remember what it was like to skate for someone else.

"You need someone who is involved in every aspect of your skating career," Beth said. "It didn't take fifteen minutes in the rink with you to know you aren't Scarlett's priority. She's putting all of her money on the little blonde, and she doesn't appear concerned at all if she leaves the two of you behind."

"I think that's largely because of me," Amaliya said. "Once I land my double axel, Scarlett will know I'm capable of competing at the national level."

"That's fine, but I thought you were shooting for the international level." Beth focused on Tyler. "You've already been to the world championships. Are you going to be satisfied with only making it to nationals?"

"I don't think either of us would be," Tyler said. "Amaliya and I are capable of much more than that."

"I agree." Beth took a sip of water. "I still have a lot of contacts in the skating world. Let me see what I can come up with."

"I can already tell you Scarlett is the only world-class coach in the immediate area."

"We'll worry about logistics later," Miles said.

"That's right," Linda agreed. "For now, work with Beth on your routine."

"Should we show Scarlett our new lift?" Amaliya asked.

"She hasn't seen it yet?" Beth asked.

"No. We worked on it yesterday after she left the rink for the day," Amaliya said.

"Keep it to yourself for a while longer," Beth said. "It's deceptively simple, but the judges will recognize the skill it takes to execute, and the crowd will love the novelty of it. You don't want to share something too soon when it's uniquely yours."

"It's like we're navigating our way through a spy movie," Tyler said.

"Give me some time," Beth said. "Everything will fall into place eventually."

Eventually. Tyler really wished that word would stop being part of his future and fade into his past.

Chapter TWENTY-EIGHT

Jeff never called. Amaliya thought for sure he would call yesterday and apologize, but the phone hadn't rung, except when her parents had called to check in and when Beth had called to ask Linda to pick her up from the train station.

Amaliya walked into school, the chatter in the hall buzzing at a higher volume than usual. She walked past a group of girls, the phrases "Did you hear . . . ?" and "He left with . . ." carrying to her.

She doubted she and Jeff were the topic of conversation, but from what she had seen of him and his teammates, she had little doubt they had created enough gossip for the rumor mill to last through the end of this year and reach into the next.

Only ten more school days until graduation. Then freedom.

Amaliya sat in her usual spot in the cafeteria, her mind playing over possible conversations with Jeff. Would he apologize for getting drunk and leaving her bored and neglected at the dance? Or would he assume it was no big deal, as he had when he had ignored her after his team lost?

The bell rang, her questions going unanswered when Jeff never showed up.

She made her way to class and slid into her seat beside Sarah. Sarah leaned closer. "Did you hear what happened?"

"No. What?"

"The entire baseball team got called into the principal's office this morning."

She supposed she shouldn't be surprised. While Kent had technically informed the school of the drinking going on at prom, if he hadn't, she would have.

"Is it because someone told the chaperones they were drinking?" Amaliya asked, careful not to mention it was them in case she was overheard.

"Actually, they already knew," Sarah said. "Rumor has it that Eddie got sick in the bathroom, and a teacher figured out what was going on."

"What do you think will happen?"

"I have no idea. It's not like this doesn't happen every year, but usually, it's someone slipping something into the punch and the teachers changing it out if they notice anything."

The second bell rang, ending their conversation.

For the rest of the day, Amaliya listened for any snippets of conversation that would reveal Jeff's fate, but if anyone knew what punishment had been doled out, they weren't saying. After her last class, she walked outside and found Jeff waiting near the entrance.

"What are you doing out here?" she asked.

"Waiting for you." He stepped toward her. "Did you hear?"

"Someone said your team was called into the principal's office, but that's all I heard."

"Three-day suspension for all of us who were drinking at prom."

"Sorry."

"Hey, three days off school." He shrugged. "It's no big deal."

"No big deal?" Amaliya repeated.

As though she hadn't spoken, he said, "You want to go grab some lunch? The diner down the road isn't bad."

"I need to get to practice."

"You usually eat lunch first."

"Tyler and I have some things to work on before our regular practice session starts."

"How about tonight?" He took her hand. "We could go out and grab a bite to eat."

"I'm confused. You're here acting like you want to take me out, but when we were at prom, you hardly talked to me."

"That was only because you took off with your friend."

"I went to talk to my friend because I didn't want a front-row seat while you and your friends got drunk."

"That's part of going to prom. I thought you knew that."

"Our views of what you do at a dance are very different."

"So we won't go to dances together. That doesn't mean we can't go out."

"Baseball season is almost over. Graduation is less than two weeks away," Amaliya said. "Maybe it's better if we just stay friends."

The absolute shock on his face was instant. Had no one ever turned him down before? He gaped at her for a moment before he found his voice. "Are you serious?"

"I'm afraid so."

A car pulled up, and Amaliya glanced over to see Tyler behind the wheel.

"That's my ride. I'd better get going." Amaliya squeezed his hand before she drew hers away. "If you ever want to talk, you have my number."

"Wow. This has never happened to me before."

"I'm sure if you want a girlfriend, you have plenty of girls who would be interested in hearing your voice on the phone."

Jeff put his hand on her shoulder before she could turn away. "Thanks for being there when I needed you."

"You're welcome." On instinct, she gave him a hug. "Goodbye, Jeff."

He'd waited too long. All of Tyler's plans to ask Amaliya out after she graduated shattered into a million pieces when he saw Amaliya hug the guy beside her.

She waved at her boyfriend and approached the car. Though Tyler didn't know how he would feel to see another guy picking up his girlfriend, he climbed out and opened the car door for Amaliya.

"Thanks." She set her bag on the floor and climbed in.

As soon as he reclaimed his seat, Tyler motioned to the guy still standing on the front steps of the school. He tried to sound casual when he asked, "I guess that's the guy you went to prom with."

"Yeah. Jeff Pearson." Amaliya waved at Jeff again as they pulled away. "Any idea what Scarlett has planned for practice today?"

"I don't know." *Focus on skating.* Tyler repeated the words in his mind three times as he fought against the knots in the pit of his stomach.

"Tyler, are you okay?"

"Yeah." What were they talking about again? He replayed her earlier question and struggled to gather his thoughts. "If Scarlett isn't there when we get to the rink, I'd like to work on our lift again."

"You sure?" Amaliya asked. "Beth was pretty adamant that we not show it to Scarlett yet. There's no way of knowing when she, Marie, or Becky will show up."

"The rink is closed until one. I can lock the exterior doors until fifteen minutes before our practice time."

"Will Hank be okay with that?"

"Only one way to find out." They reached the rink, and Tyler led the way to the door. He pulled on the handle, and it didn't budge. He reached into his pocket for his keys. "Looks like Hank went out to lunch."

"In that case, he can't be mad that we kept the door locked."

"My thoughts exactly." Tyler unlocked and opened the door. "Hurry and change. Who knows when Hank will show up again."

"Be right back." Amaliya headed toward the restroom.

Tyler walked into the office and sat in Hank's chair so he could reach under the desk where he had stored his skates this morning. He pulled his bag out and started to stand, but a note on Hank's desk caught his eye.

Tyler read over the note and read it again. He checked the calendar. Sure enough, the note about extra ice time was penciled in for Saturday.

"Tyler?" Amaliya appeared in the office doorway. "Are you ready?"

"Look at this." Tyler waved her closer.

"What?"

"Scarlett booked extra rink time on Saturday morning before our practice."

"Maybe she wants to work with Marie or Becky on their programs."

"No." Tyler tapped on Hank's note. "These are invoices for ice time for two skaters at the same time."

"Who are they?"

"Local skaters who both did well at juniors."

"You think Scarlett has agreed to coach them?"

"Either that or the extra rink time is a tryout."

"Has she ever coached this many skaters at once?"

"No."

Awareness dawned in Amaliya's eyes. "You think she's going to drop us."

"If she picks these two skaters up, it's only a matter of time."

"Should we talk to her about it?"

"I don't think it's worth it. She's made it pretty clear over the past couple months that Marie is her main focus now." Tyler shook his head, and disappointment seeped through him. It was one thing to consider leaving Scarlett because they wanted someone better, but to find out the choice might not be theirs rocked him to the core. "Eight years I've been with her."

"I'm sorry." Amaliya put her hand on his shoulder. "This is all because of me. Had you chosen a new partner who already had skills comparable to yours, she wouldn't be doing this."

"Who knows what she would have done," Tyler said. "It's not like she helped me search for Carolyn's replacement."

"I didn't realize that. I always assumed she didn't like me because I wasn't her choice," Amaliya said. "That and not mentioning her during our TV interview."

"I don't think it has anything to do with you. Carolyn was the skater Scarlett wanted to coach. I was just the muscle who could make her shine."

"Don't sell yourself short. You're an amazing skater, and as you've said before, it takes two well-matched skaters to compete in pairs." Amaliya grabbed his hand and tugged. "Come on. Let's work on our lift. Our new coach, whoever that is, will want to see a polished version."

Tyler followed her to the bench and wished he could tap into her optimism. Then again, she had only lost a coach today. He had lost a coach *and* something much more precious.

Chapter
TWENTY-NINE

AMALIYA GRIPPED HER HANDS TOGETHER as Miles turned into the rink parking lot on Tuesday morning. Monday afternoon's practice had proven Tyler's suspicions. Scarlett had barely spoken to them. Even when she called out skills she wanted Marie and Becky to perform, she didn't include them. She and Tyler had become invisible.

"What's going on with you?" Miles asked.

"Skating is supposed to be fun," Amaliya said.

"I agree. It is," Miles said. "What's taking the fun out of it? Your coach? Or are you burnt out?"

"My coach," Amaliya answered without hesitation. "When I studied ballet with Mama, she always made me feel like I could do anything. Scarlett makes me feel like I can't do anything right."

"You said Tyler thinks she's going to drop you two anyway. Maybe you should get your own ice time and work without her for a while. It's not like having her there is helping you any."

"You could be right. I'll talk to Tyler."

"You're going to have to go inside to do that." Miles waved toward the rink.

"Okay, okay. I'm going."

"Try to have fun."

"I always try." Amaliya climbed out and walked inside. She had thought things couldn't get worse, but she was only a few steps inside the door when Marie approached Tyler and slipped her arm around his waist.

"We should go out this weekend," Marie said. "My father has a new dessert on his menu that is amazing."

Amaliya waited for Tyler to refuse. He was going to turn her down, wasn't he?

"Yeah, that sounds good. What night do you want to go?"

"Saturday. Say seven o'clock?"

"See you then."

Amaliya's heart cracked a little. She knew Tyler only thought of her as a friend, but she kept hoping that once she graduated from high school, he would see her as an adult instead of a little high schooler.

Tyler noticed Amaliya and turned toward her. "Morning."

"Morning." She put on her skates and walked to the ice.

"Want to work on our death spiral today?" Tyler asked. "That's one I wouldn't want to do without someone else around."

"With the way this week has gone, maybe we should stick with something a little less risky."

"Any suggestions?" Tyler asked.

"If you don't mind coaching me on them, my combination jumps could use some work." Amaliya glanced at where Scarlett now stood beside Marie and Becky. "Unless you think she has something planned for us today."

"That's not likely," Tyler said. "I assume you haven't talked to Beth lately."

"No. I know it's only been a couple days, but I really wish she would call with some ideas for a new coach for us."

"I wish there were another coach in the area," Tyler said. "I was looking through all of the top skaters in the country, and not one of them lives near here."

"There has to be a decent coach in New York City," Amaliya said.

"There are a few, but no one who has put out a world-class skater in the past decade," Tyler said. "Besides, do you want to drive into the city every day at three in the morning?"

"No." Reality warred with her dreams. No matter what happened, it was very possible things were about to go from bad to worse.

Marie skated past them. Then again, maybe they already had.

Katerina cradled the phone against her shoulder, the cord stretched out to reach her hospital bed. She'd had enough of lying around and waiting for life to begin again. Her little girl needed help, and for the first time since the accident, she could do something to help her.

"Are you sure about this?" Robert asked from where he sat in his wheelchair beside her.

"I'm sure. Gordon is one of the best coaches in the country," Katerina said.

"You haven't talked to him more than once or twice since his wife's funeral."

"That's not from lack of trying," Katerina said. "From what I understand, he hardly talks to anyone these days."

"It can't be easy for him. He and his wife were together for a long time, both as skating partners and as a couple. I have a new appreciation for how terrifying it must be to lose the woman you love." Robert rested his hand on her knee. A thrill shot through her for two reasons: the touch was a reminder of their solidarity, and the feeling in her leg proved that she did have a chance at a full recovery.

"If something had happened to me, I wouldn't have wanted you to stop living. Gordon needs a push." Katerina motioned to the phone. "Dial the number for me."

"Okay." Robert punched in the long-distance number.

The phone rang and rang and rang. "He isn't answering."

After six rings, Robert pressed his finger down on the phone base to end the call.

"Try again," Katerina said.

This time, the phone rang eight times before Robert hung up. "He must not be home."

"Try one more time."

"Okay." Robert dialed again.

Once, twice, three times.

This time, someone answered and barked out a hello. Typical Gordon.

"It's about time you answered," Katerina said.

"Who is this?"

"Katerina Marcell."

"Katerina, how are you? I heard you and your husband were in an accident a few months ago."

"Yes, we're both still in the hospital in New York."

"Wow, I'm sorry."

Katerina's gaze met Robert's. "We're both getting better, but I need a favor."

"A favor from me?" Gordon asked.

"Yes. I need your skating expertise."

"Let me guess. You have a skater you want me to look at." The derision in his tone spoke volumes. Obviously, Katerina wasn't the first of his friends to make such a call.

"Gordon, don't even think about hanging up on me."

"I'm taking a break from coaching," Gordon said. "You know that."

"Your break has lasted long enough," Katerina said. "I wouldn't have called if these skaters weren't worth your time."

"Who are they?"

"You've probably heard of one of them: Tyler Linden."

"Yeah. Tyler and Carolyn Linden. I saw them at worlds a couple years ago."

"Carolyn retired, but Tyler partnered with my daughter, Amaliya."

"I thought your daughter was a ballerina."

"She was." Katerina's Russian accent thickened with emotion. "She's a figure skater now."

"Since when?"

"Since my accident."

"A new skater? Katerina, I'm sorry, but I don't work with beginners."

"She isn't a beginner. She's studied ballet her whole life, and she has grown up on the ice," Katerina said.

"You said yourself you've been in the hospital the last few months. Have you even seen them skate?" Gordon asked.

"No, but Beth has. She's doing their choreography, and she said Amaliya and Tyler are incredible together."

"Have they even competed?"

Pride swelled within her. "They won pairs at regionals in Boston last month."

"That's not exactly a high-level division in the pairs category."

"You need to see them," Katerina said.

"I don't need to do anything."

"Gordon, it's been two years. Irene wouldn't want you to sit around and mope for the rest of your life."

"You sound like my daughter."

A seed of hope sprouted. "Smart girl, as I remember."

"I'm telling you I'm not interested."

Refusing to give up, Katerina said, "Fine, but I'm not taking no for an answer until you see them skate."

"You want me to hold a tryout for someone, even knowing I don't plan to coach them?"

"That's right."

"You are persistent."

"I'm going to have Beth Williamson call you tonight to discuss the details," Katerina said. "And, Gordon?"

"Yes?"

"Pick up the phone."

Chapter THIRTY

TYLER WAS ALREADY DREADING SATURDAY night. He had managed to avoid getting cornered by Marie for weeks, but for the past few days, she had been hovering nearby every time he'd sat down to put on his skates or when he'd been waiting for Amaliya so he could take her to school each morning. It was like Marie knew Amaliya had a boyfriend and a path had been cleared for Marie to date Tyler again.

He supposed, in a way, that was exactly what had happened. Had he not been upset about seeing Amaliya with Jeff at school on Monday, he doubted he would have agreed to dinner. At least since he and Amaliya had come to practice early, he wouldn't have to deal with the small talk that usually occurred while they all stretched and got ready for practice.

Focusing on the task at hand, he positioned himself behind Amaliya and put his hands on her waist. He lifted her above him, their timing on their new lift now automatic. After he lowered her back to the ice, he said, "I think we've got it."

The door opened, and Scarlett walked in. She glanced at them on the ice and approached the barrier. "What are you doing? Our time doesn't start for fifteen minutes."

"She finally caught us," Amaliya whispered.

"I'm tired of hiding from her." Tyler released Amaliya and crossed to Scarlett. Amaliya followed.

"Tyler, you know better than this," Scarlett said.

"We talked to Beth Williamson on Sunday. We need to figure out our lifts for our long program."

"I told you we'll work on those when Amaliya is further along on the basics."

"She has the basics," Tyler said. "She has everything except the double axel, and that will come in time."

"Then work on the double axel until she gets it."

Fury bubbled inside him. "For what we're paying you, don't you think you should be helping her figure it out instead of having me coach her?"

"You're the one who chose a ballerina instead of a skater as a partner." Scarlett gripped the edge of the barrier and leaned in. "Don't get mad at me if she's a year or two behind where you want to be."

"Maybe she would learn faster if you actually coached her instead of just shouting out what move to practice next."

"Tyler." Amaliya put her hand on his arm. "Maybe we should—"

"No, it's time Scarlett decides if she's going to coach us or if she's planning to replace us." Tyler crossed his arms. "We know you have extra ice time scheduled for Saturday. Do you really think you can handle taking on new skaters when you barely spend any time with us as it is?"

"If you don't like the way I coach, you're welcome to find someone else." Her haughty tone only served to fuel Tyler's anger further. "If you find another coach capable of taking you beyond nationals anywhere within a hundred miles, I'd love to know about it."

The truth of her statement hung over his head. How could he and his family possibly afford to continue training if he had the extra expense of rent, not to mention the cost of a move?

"We're paid through the end of the month," Amaliya interrupted. "Why don't we take some time to think about this."

"The end of the month is ten days away," Scarlett said. "I suggest you decide quickly before I fill your spots."

"We both know you are already planning to fill our spots," Tyler shot back.

Amaliya took his hand. "Come on, Tyler. Let's go practice."

Tyler fell in step beside her and let Amaliya guide him across the ice.

"Are you okay?" Amaliya asked.

"I still don't understand how things changed so quickly."

"Life changes, Tyler, whether we want it to or not."

Her wistful tone defused his anger, and he focused his attention on Amaliya. "I'm sorry. I shouldn't have gone after her like that. I should have at least talked to you first."

"No, it's fine. I just wish things weren't so unsettled again."

"Again?"

Her shoulder lifted. "I've only lived here four months. I went from ballet to ice skating. We have a coach, but we know we have to make a change, which could lead to another move right as my parents are getting ready to move here."

"And you're about to graduate."

"And I'm about to graduate." She rubbed her lips together.

"Are your parents going to be able to come to graduation?"

"My dad plans on it. He's still struggling to walk without a cane, but he's making progress."

"I assume your mom won't be able to come."

"I doubt it."

"You handle everything so well that sometimes I forget your life changed so drastically not very long ago." Tyler squeezed her hand. "I'm sorry."

"You don't have anything to be sorry about." Amaliya glanced past Tyler, and her tension rose visibly.

He looked behind him at Marie standing beside Scarlett. "Do you think Miles and Linda would mind if I invite myself over for dinner tonight?"

"You're always welcome. Why?"

"We need to talk about options," Tyler said. "And I think we need to tell Beth that we're ready to make a move."

"She said she would call when she knew something."

"I know, but since we're going to be coachless in less than two weeks, maybe she can give us a list of people to call so we don't have to wait on her."

"It's worth a try." Amaliya drew a deep breath and let it out. "What do you think? Should we try my double axel?"

"No. Today, let's work on our figures and our double lutz-double toe loop combination," Tyler said. "We'll let our new coach teach you how to do a double axel."

"Okay. Lead the way."

Amaliya assumed Linda and Miles would be okay with her inviting Tyler to dinner. She hoped they would be. She led him inside and called out, "Linda?"

Miles appeared a moment later. "Oh, good. You're both here."

"I hope you don't mind, but I invited Tyler to eat dinner with us."

"Didn't you get my message?" Miles asked.

She shook her head. "What message?"

"I asked Hank to tell you I needed to talk to Tyler."

"We never went into the office after practice today," Tyler said.

Linda came down the stairs. "Did someone call me?"

"Yeah, I wanted to make sure it was okay for Tyler to have dinner with us."

"Well, that's convenient," Miles said.

"I'm confused." Amaliya looked from Linda to Miles. "What's going on?"

"Have a seat." Miles motioned to the couch. Everyone sat down. "We received a few phone calls today."

A seed of hope sprouted inside Amaliya. "Was one of them from Beth?"

"Actually, it was your mom who called. She and your dad helped arrange a tryout for you this Saturday."

"That's great." Tyler leaned forward and rested his elbows on his knees. "We talked to Scarlett today. Things did not go well."

"If this tryout goes the way we hope, you'll have a new coach as soon as Amaliya graduates."

"That timing would be perfect," Amaliya said.

"Who is this coach?" Tyler asked. "Is it someone who has world-level experience?"

"He's coached three pairs of Olympians, including two former national champions."

"Seriously?" Amaliya's hopes rose with her excitement. "I thought there weren't any good coaches around here besides Scarlett."

"That's the catch," Miles said. "He isn't around here."

"Where is he?"

"Northern Virginia."

"I'd be moving home?" Amaliya asked.

"Yes," Miles said. "Will Rowbury already moved back to New Jersey, so your house is available."

"I hate to put a damper on our plans, but I can't afford to pay for rent and training fees, especially if I give up my job," Tyler said.

"I'm sure Amaliya's parents would let you live at their house," Miles said.

"I appreciate the offer, but that would give the wrong impression," Tyler said. "Kids look up to Olympic athletes. If they found out Amaliya and I were living in the same place . . ."

"It wouldn't be like that," Miles interrupted. "You can have the guest house."

"What about Eleanor?" Amaliya asked.

"Who's Eleanor?" Tyler asked.

"Our housekeeper."

"Your parents want her to live in the main house so you aren't there alone," Linda said.

"Have you talked to my parents about this already?" Amaliya asked.

"Not about Tyler staying in the guest house, but I'll give them a call tonight to make sure they're okay with it," Linda said.

"I'm not just talking about that," Amaliya said. "Mama and Papa were planning to move into a rehab facility here in Connecticut."

"That's actually happening on Friday. It's bad timing if you do move back to Virginia, but the rehab facility here specializes in the kind of care your mom needs, so it's probably better for her to stay up here for the first few months," Linda said. "Depending on her recovery, she should be able to move home sometime this fall."

"So it will just be me and Eleanor in the main house," Amaliya said.

"Not exactly," Miles said. "If Gordon agrees to coach you, it would make sense to offer him the downstairs guest suite to offset some of the coaching fees."

"Wait. Are you talking about Gordon Alexander?" Tyler asked.

"Yes, we are."

"That would be amazing," Tyler said. "He's incredible."

"How do you know Gordon Alexander?" Amaliya asked.

"He's one of the top coaches in the country. He's a pioneer in the skating world."

Tyler's excitement enhanced her own. "And he has room to take us on?"

"He hasn't been coaching for the last couple years," Miles said.

"Why not?" Amaliya asked.

"His wife died of cancer during the last Olympics," Tyler said.

"That's right," Miles said. "He skipped the games to be with her, and the pair he was training moved on to work with a new coach. Gordon hasn't come back to the sport yet, but when your mom talked to him about the two of you, he said he would give you a tryout."

"Where is this tryout going to happen?" Tyler asked.

"New Jersey," Miles said. "A friend of mine got me some ice time there."

"Tyler, I know this would be a big adjustment for you," Linda said. "We wanted to make sure you're interested before we move forward."

Amaliya put her hand on his. "What do you think? Would you be willing to move?"

"If Gordon Alexander agrees to coach us, I'll do whatever it takes to make it happen."

"Great." Miles stood. "I'll make the call to Gordon."

"And I'll call Katerina and Beth. I told Beth about the tryouts, and she wants to come, too, so she can go through some of the choreography for your long program with you."

"That would be great," Tyler said. "What time do we need to leave on Saturday?"

"Not until eight thirty. Your tryout isn't until eleven."

"Eleven on a Saturday?" Tyler asked. "How did you get rink time at that time of day?"

"We're going to a private rink. Princeton."

"Princeton University is letting us practice on their ice?" Tyler asked.

"Like I said, a friend owed me a favor."

Awareness surfaced. "Will pulled some strings, didn't he?" Amaliya asked.

"Maybe a few."

Seeing Tyler's confusion, Amaliya said, "Will Rowbury was an assistant coach at Princeton before he took over as head coach for my dad. We let him rent my house for the rest of the Capitals' season."

"And now he's returning the favor?" Tyler said.

"He would have done it for Amaliya anyway. He was one of many players for the Washington Capitals who watched her grow up," Miles said.

"Thank him for us," Tyler said.

"I will."

Linda stood. "I'd better get dinner started. Tyler, are you staying?"

"Actually, can I take a rain check? I should get home and talk to my parents about all this."

"Of course."

"Maybe we can all go out to dinner after we meet with Gordon," Miles suggested. "With any luck, we'll have a lot to celebrate."

"I think Tyler—" Amaliya began, remembering his date with Marie.

"That would be great," Tyler interrupted. He stood. "I'd better get going."

Amaliya rose as well. "I'll walk you to your car."

Chapter
THIRTY-ONE

TYLER LED THE WAY OUTSIDE. "This is incredible. To even get an audition with Gordon Alexander is huge."

"Let's hope we can get past the audition stage," Amaliya said. The door closed behind her. "I still can't do a double axel."

Tyler stopped at the bottom of the front porch steps and waited for her. "He's going to take one look at the way you move and jump at the chance to coach us."

"There's that positive thinking again," Amaliya said. "We haven't had a lot of that lately."

"I guess we haven't," Tyler said. "Scarlett has slowly sucked the joy out of skating over the past few months."

"Yeah." Amaliya glanced at her house. "Are you sure about Saturday night? I know you had a date with Marie."

"I've been looking for an excuse to cancel all week."

Something flashed in Amaliya's expression. Was that hope? "Why do you want to cancel?"

"I'm not interested in her that way, and quite honestly, I don't really enjoy going out with her."

"But I thought . . ." Amaliya began. "She said . . ."

"She said what?" Tyler's eyebrows drew together. "I told you a while ago I didn't want to go out with her."

"I know, but before that, I overheard her talking to her mom. The way she described things between you, it sounded like things were serious," Amaliya said. "When you made plans to go out with her again, I thought you'd gotten back together."

"No." He shook his head. "If she hadn't caught me in a weak moment, I never would have said yes to Saturday night."

"A weak moment?"

His emotions somersaulted, and he let the truth spill out. "I'd just seen you with your boyfriend. I figured if you were going out with someone else, I might as well too. I should have been more selective."

"Jeff isn't my boyfriend."

"But I saw you hug him, and I assumed . . ."

"I was breaking things off with him." Amaliya's eyes lifted to meet his. "The whole time I was at prom, I kept thinking about how you would never treat me that way."

"What way?"

"He spent the entire night ignoring me while he got drunk with his friends."

"I'm so sorry. No guy should ever treat a woman like that."

"I agree. And you never would."

"No, I wouldn't." The tender feelings that had bloomed and grown over the past few months took root. "If you don't have a boyfriend and I'm not dating Marie, does that mean we're both single?"

"Yes." Her eyes met his, uncertainty reflected there. "Does it matter if we are?"

Tyler let out the breath he hadn't realized he was holding. "The only reason I agreed to go out with Marie was because I was jealous."

"You were jealous of Jeff?"

"Yeah." Tyler stepped closer so there was only a foot between them. "I wanted to ask you out the first time I met you, but when I found out you were in high school, I knew I should wait until after you graduated."

"I graduate next week."

"Yeah, you do." Tyler's hands found hers. "Would it be okay if I took you out on a proper date on Friday night?"

"I'd like that, but what happened to waiting until I graduate?"

"I'm tired of waiting." As though his emotions had a mind of their own, he leaned forward. He hesitated when his lips were a mere inch from hers. Her breath caught, and his heartbeat quickened. His body trembled in sweet anticipation, building in that fraction of a second before he closed the distance between them and kissed her. His stomach, already unsteady, bounced into his throat. A shiver ran through him, and he couldn't resist deepening the kiss.

Amaliya's fingers tightened on his, and her eyes were wide when he drew away.

"I've dreamed about doing that for a long time," Tyler said.

A blush rose on her cheeks, and a smile formed on her lips. "Me too."

Like a kaleidoscope shifting position, the pieces of his life jumbled and reassembled into a new, brighter reality.

"So what do you want to do Friday night?" Tyler asked. "Dinner? A movie?"

"How about watching film at your house? We can order pizza."

"That's what we do every Friday night."

"Yeah, but it might be smart to do what we always do. I'm not sure it's a good idea to announce we're . . . that things are different between us before we get our coaching situation sorted out," Amaliya said. "I doubt Miles and Linda will be eager to send us off to Virginia together if they knew . . ." Her blush deepened.

"I've waited months to be able to call you my girlfriend. It's hard to imagine being with you like this and trying to hide my feelings from the people who matter most to you." The moment Tyler said the word *girlfriend*, Amaliya's eyes darted up to meet his. The uncertainty reflected there pushed him to continue. "I don't want to date anyone else, and I hate the idea of you going out with another guy. Are you okay with that?"

Delight replaced the uncertainty. "Yeah, I am."

"But you want to hide our relationship."

"I just want to keep it between us for a little while," Amaliya said.

Though he wanted nothing more than to announce his newfound joy to the world, he couldn't dispute her logic. "You really think we can fool them?" Tyler asked. "They're going to notice if things are different between us."

"They've suspected I've had a crush on you since we started skating together."

"And have you?"

"Tyler, you're every girl's dream. Who wouldn't have a crush on you?"

His own cheeks heated. "Now you're exaggerating."

Amaliya's smile bloomed fully. She reached up and pinched his cheek. "You're so cute when you're embarrassed."

"Okay, that's enough." He took her hand and pulled it to his side. Unable to resist, he leaned down for another kiss. "I'll see you tomorrow."

"Let me know how things go with your parents."

"I will. I'll call you later."

She smiled. "I'd like that."

Tyler climbed into his car. Amaliya walked back to the porch before turning and waving goodbye. He waved back. Was he dreaming? Had this really happened?

In less than an hour, he had a new girlfriend, the prospect of a new coach, and the possibility of a move to another state. He gripped the steering wheel.

After so many months of feeling like he'd been standing still, it was like the floodgates had opened and the water was rushing him toward a new future.

He glanced back at Amaliya, and excitement bubbled inside him. He couldn't wait to see what this new future held.

Katerina sat by the phone and willed it to ring. She had already spoken with Eleanor about moving back into the main house so Amaliya wouldn't be alone if she moved back to Virginia, but Katerina had yet to hear if Miles had ever reached Gordon. Would Gordon follow through with the tryout? And if so, would he be able to get past his grief and reenter the skating world?

Robert set his newspaper aside. "Staring at the phone isn't going to make it ring."

"I know, but I hate not knowing what's going on." Katerina rubbed her hands restlessly over the arms of her wheelchair. "For all I know, Gordon is still ignoring his phone."

"We can only do so much from in here."

Katerina's gaze lifted to meet her husband's. "You sound like you don't care if she gets this tryout."

"Of course I care." Robert dismissed her concern with a wave of his hand.

Katerina's eyes narrowed. She wasn't buying Robert's laissez-faire attitude. "What's bothering you?"

"Nothing's bothering me." Robert kept his eyes on hers for a second before he wavered. "Okay, so maybe I'm not thrilled with her spending so much time with a man who is three years older than her."

"You're three years older than me."

"That's beside the point."

The phone rang, and Katerina snatched it up. "Hello?"

"It's all set." Linda's excitement vibrated over the line. "Amaliya and Tyler have a tryout with Gordon on Saturday."

"Did you already talk to Tyler? Is he willing to move?" Katerina asked.

"He was pretty excited about the chance to skate for Gordon, but he was worried about the cost of renting an apartment," Linda said. "I hope I didn't overstep, but Miles and I thought he could live in the apartment over your garage."

"That's a great idea." Katerina visualized the possibilities as Linda mentioned Miles's suggestion about having Gordon move into their house too. Lower fees and an extra chaperone. Katerina approved.

"Will Robert be okay with this?" Linda asked.

Katerina cringed inwardly. Her husband wasn't going to like this, but she had to believe he would support their daughter's dreams. "Tell Tyler the apartment will be ready for him if Gordon takes them on."

Robert straightened. "What apartment?"

Katerina held up a hand so he would let her finish her conversation.

"Gordon had better take them on," Linda said. "They are incredible. I can't wait for you to see them."

Katerina fought back a sigh. "I'm looking forward to the day when that can happen."

"I know. We all are," Linda said. "I'll call you after the tryout and let you know how it goes."

"Thanks." Katerina said goodbye and hung up the phone.

"What did you do?" Robert wheeled his chair so he was facing her more fully. "You didn't say that boy could live at our house, did you?"

"No." Katerina waited until his posture relaxed before she added, "I said he could live in the apartment."

"What?" His voice rose.

"Don't shout. We don't want the nurses to come running in here again. They already want to kick you out of here." Katerina kept her gaze steady on Robert's. "Tyler needs a place to stay. It only makes sense to have him in the apartment, especially since we'll have Eleanor and Gordon living there too."

"Gordon?"

"Miles thought we could have him live downstairs in the main house as part of his salary."

"Gordon hasn't said yes," Robert said.

"Not yet, but as soon as he agrees to coach Amaliya and Tyler, you can call him," Katerina said.

"Why me?"

"Because you can appeal to him as one overprotective father to another."

"I'm not overprotective. I just want to make sure no one takes advantage of my little girl."

"Our little girl is an adult."

"Doesn't matter." Robert pointed a finger. "That boy had better stay on his side of the garage."

Katerina smiled. "On that point, we can both agree."

Amaliya dried the last dish and put it into the cabinet. How was Tyler supposed to call if Miles and Linda wouldn't get off the phone?

Miles said his goodbyes and hung up. Finally.

"Okay, we're all set." Miles opened the freezer and pulled out the ice cream. "Gordon will meet us at eleven on Saturday, and Beth should arrive by eleven thirty."

"What do you think the chances are that he'll agree to coach us?" Amaliya asked.

"It's hard to say. According to your mom, several other skaters have tried to hire him, but this is the first time he's even agreed to a tryout."

"I wonder why he agreed, especially since he has to drive all the way to New Jersey to meet us."

"He said he remembered Tyler from the world championships," Miles said. "A couple of his former skaters also took ballet from your mom."

"Really? Small world."

"It is."

The phone rang. "That's probably Tyler."

"Let him know we'll pick him up at eight thirty on Saturday."

"I will." Amaliya snatched the phone off the cradle as Miles left the kitchen. "Hey, Amaliya," Tyler said. "Sorry I didn't call sooner."

"That's okay." The mere fact that he'd called when he said he would drove home how different Tyler was from Jeff. "We only finished dinner a few minutes ago."

"It's almost seven. I thought you were eating a little while after I left."

"We were going to, but Miles and Linda were busy making phone calls, getting things confirmed for Saturday."

"Yeah, that's why I was so late in calling. I wanted to break my date with Marie before I called you."

"How did that go?"

"She was annoyed, but that isn't anything new," Tyler said.

"She isn't usually annoyed at you though," Amaliya said. "It's me she can't stand."

"Only another week and a half and you won't have to deal with her anymore."

Amaliya let that truth seep through her. "Did you talk to your parents about everything?"

"Yeah. They were way more supportive than I expected."

"Really?"

"The only thing that worried them was the idea of me living at your house," Tyler said. "They want to talk to Miles and Linda about the living arrangements."

"I'm sure they'd be happy to talk to your folks. And you can tell them the guest house has a separate entrance. It's not even part of the main house. That might make them feel better."

"I'll let them know, but don't be surprised if they call right after we hang up."

"I won't." Amaliya tried to visualize life in Virginia with Tyler living so close. "It's hard to believe everything is changing so quickly."

"I was thinking that when I left your house today," Tyler said. "Are you ready for all this? You've barely had time to settle here in Connecticut."

"Actually, I'm not sure how I feel," she said. "I'm excited about going home, but I also don't know what it will be like living there without my parents."

"I'm sure it will take some getting used to, but it won't be for long."

"That's true. Of course, this is all assuming Gordon will take us," Amaliya said.

"He'll take us."

"How can you be so certain?"

"Positive thinking."

"Right. How could I forget?"

Chapter
THIRTY-TWO

AMALIYA COULDN'T REMEMBER BEING THIS excited about practice in weeks. She awoke early and stretched while listening to her tape of *Swan Lake*, her mind replaying her time with Tyler yesterday.

Her fingers lifted to her lips when she thought of the kisses they had shared. It was hard to believe that only a week ago, she had looked forward to spending time with Jeff, and now everything had changed so completely.

She supposed if she were honest with herself, her feelings for Jeff had had more to do with finding acceptance at school and sharing a common struggle. Beyond the surface, nothing had remained.

With Tyler, her admiration and respect had deepened with every passing day. Her parents liked him enough to agree to let him live at their house. That realization brought with it a sense of wonder. Did they trust Tyler to live so close to her because of everything they had heard about him from her and the Donnellys or because of their impression of him after their one brief meeting? Regardless, next week, she would graduate, and if all went well, a move back to Virginia would soon follow.

"Amaliya? Are you ready?" Miles called.

She checked the clock, surprised that she had dawdled her extra time away. "Coming."

She grabbed her bag and hurried down the stairs. "Sorry. I lost track of the time."

"You sure you aren't avoiding Scarlett?"

"Maybe that too."

"Another week or two. You can last that long."

"I hope so." She followed him out to the car.

"Do you want me to film you this morning?" Miles asked.

"That would be great, if you don't mind."

"I'd rather do it now than this afternoon."

They arrived at the rink as Tyler was getting out of his car. The familiar butterflies in Amaliya's stomach started a new set of flips and turns.

Tyler waited by the door for them to join him. "Morning."

They all walked in together, new voices carrying to them. As soon as they passed the office, the newcomers came into view, two girls, both of whom went to high school with Amaliya.

Tyler leaned over and whispered, "Looks like Scarlett picked up some new skaters."

"Our replacements," Amaliya whispered back.

"I'll get the camera," Miles said.

"Thanks." Tyler put his hand on Amaliya's back to guide her toward the office rather than the benches beside where Scarlett stood.

"We can put our skates on in here," Tyler said. "Let's get warmed up and work on our throws this morning. The ice is going to get crowded quickly with the extra skaters out there."

Miles retrieved the camera equipment.

Amaliya sat and traded shoes for skates. "I'm ready when you are."

"Come on." Tyler led her onto the ice five minutes before their official start time. They circled the rink. "What do you think? Double lutz?"

"Yeah. It would be nice to be able to consistently land that one."

"You can do it." Tyler put his hands on her waist. A moment later, Amaliya was flying through the air, rotating twice before her skate connected with the ice. She stumbled with her second foot but remained upright.

"Not bad," Tyler said.

"Not great," Amaliya countered.

"Let's do it one more time, and then we'll move on to something else." He lowered his voice to a whisper. "We want to have plenty to watch for our date on Friday."

A smile instantly formed, and she tried to visualize their plans together. "Are your parents going to join us?"

"I hope not," Tyler said. "Maybe we should go out to dinner and a movie in the traditional sense."

Amaliya noted Miles aiming the camera at them. "For now, we'd better stick with the plan."

Tyler followed her gaze. "You're probably right."

Tyler threaded the film into the projector, nerves humming through him. He didn't know how he was supposed to act. For the past three days, he and Amaliya had rarely had a moment alone, and tonight would be their first official date, a date that needed to look like any other Friday night.

He didn't like the idea of misleading their parents or Miles and Linda, but Amaliya was right. If the parental figures in their lives knew his interest in Amaliya went beyond skating, they wouldn't be so quick to encourage them to live in close proximity.

The doorbell rang, and Tyler opened the door. Amaliya stood on the doorstep, her dark hair cascading over her shoulders. The mere sight of her sent his heart racing.

Remembering himself, he waved at Miles in the driveway and stepped back. "Come on in."

"Miles needed his car tonight. I told him you could probably bring me home."

He grinned and whispered, "The chance to take my date home? I'd like that."

She smiled and continued into the living room. "Did you already order the pizza?"

"Dad's picking it up now."

"Do you want to start watching while we wait?" Amaliya asked.

"Sure, but I have something to show you first." He picked up a newspaper clipping he'd saved from the last national championship Gordon had coached. He handed it to her.

She sat on the couch. "What's this?"

"That's a picture of Gordon Alexander and the two skaters he was coaching for the last Olympics."

"Why do you have this?"

"It was in the articles I saved from nationals that year. I was studying my competition."

Amaliya read the caption. "Are Nicole Walker and Andrew McCallister still skating?"

"They are. They're the reigning national champions."

"So if Gordon Alexander agrees to coach us, he would be preparing us to compete against his former athletes."

"Yes."

"Wow. That's a lot of pressure." She set the article on the coffee table.

Tyler turned out the lights, started the projector, and sat beside her. His fingers brushed over hers, and Amaliya turned her hand over, lacing her fingers through his. His stomach jumped, and he looked down at her instead of at the screen. Amaliya angled her face toward his, and Tyler leaned in.

The front door swung open.

Tyler straightened. Amaliya withdrew her hand.

"Pizza's here," his dad announced as he entered the living room. "You two are already starting?"

"Yeah. I wasn't sure how long you would be," Tyler said.

"Are you going to eat with me and your mom, or do you two want to eat in here?" he asked.

Tyler glanced at Amaliya. She shrugged.

"I think we'll eat in here if that's okay," Tyler said. "We have a lot of film to go over."

"That's fine. Come fix your plates when you're ready."

Tyler paused the projector. "Want to get some now?"

"Might as well." Amaliya followed Tyler's dad into the kitchen. Five minutes later, they were back on the couch with their pizza in front of them on the coffee table.

Tyler started the projector again. His eyes were drawn to the screen now, to the graceful movements of Amaliya's arms. "This lift is looking amazing."

"I love the feel of it, but we probably need to make it more difficult if we want to use it in competition."

"We could have you cartwheel down from it."

"With my head already behind you, it would make more sense for me to do a back flip."

"I don't know. You'd be landing right in my path," Tyler said. "We could do a position change to give us a better transition for you to either flip or cartwheel back to the ice."

Amaliya fell silent as they watched their images going through their lift again. They discussed several possible changes to enhance the element.

"It's hard to believe that after tomorrow, we could have a coach to brainstorm these ideas with instead of trying to do it all on our own," Tyler said.

"It'll be different, that's for sure." She shifted to face him more fully. "How do you really feel about moving to Virginia? Are you having any second thoughts?"

"Not really." Tyler couldn't deny he'd miss the familiar, but getting out on his own, making his own way, fed into his sense of adventure. "I've dreamed about the Olympics since I was big enough to lift my sister over my head. If moving can help us get closer to Leningrad, then I'm all for it."

"Leningrad?" Amaliya repeated.

"Yeah. That's where the next winter Olympics are being held."

"I didn't realize that," Amaliya said. "That's where my mom is from."

"You're kidding."

"*Nyet.*"

"I forgot you speak Russian," Tyler said. "This is great. We won't even need a translator when we get there."

"I love how you talk like we've already made the Olympic team."

"We will make the Olympic team," Tyler said. "We still have over a year and a half to get ready for the trials."

"That seems like such a long time and, at the same time, not nearly long enough."

"You worry too much." Tyler slid his arm around her shoulders and pulled her close.

"It's hard not to worry when we aren't even qualified to try out for nationals."

"After we get through sectionals in October, we'll be qualified."

"That's only five months away. I'm still missing a required element."

"Let's worry about getting a coach before you start stressing over your double axel."

"That jump has become my new nemesis."

"You'll conquer it just like you did your double lutz." One of their intricate spins came on the screen. The beauty they created together swamped over him and left him reeling. His hand on her waist, Amaliya's eyes on his.

"Sometimes it's hard to believe that's us," Amaliya said.

"I was thinking the same thing." Unable to resist, Tyler leaned down and pressed his lips to hers. "You're stunning on and off the ice."

In the wash of light from the projector, Tyler could see her cheeks redden.

Footsteps approached, and Tyler pulled his arm back to his side.

Tyler's mom appeared in the doorway. "How's it going in here?"

"Fine."

His dad walked up behind her. "Mind if we join you? I want to see this new lift of yours."

"Sure." *Come crash my date.* Tyler fought back his impatience and said, "Grab a seat."

Tyler's dad plopped down in his favorite chair. "Don't mind if I do."

Chapter
THIRTY-THREE

IT WAS LIKE COMING HOME. Even though this was Amaliya's first time in the Hobey Baker Memorial Arena at Princeton, the safety glass encircling the entire rink, the rows of seating, the lingering scents of sweat, popcorn, and hamburger grease were all too familiar.

She approached the ice but stopped as memories seeped through her, pure and sweet. She couldn't count the number of times she had sat in the bleachers and waited impatiently for her dad's practice to end so she could get on the ice to play.

Tyler touched her back, a reminder that they were supposed to be moving forward, not living in the past.

Amaliya looked around. "I don't see anyone else here."

"We have a few minutes," Tyler said.

"Time to stretch?" Amaliya asked.

"I guess so." Together they followed their usual stretching routine and put their skates on. Still no sign of anyone in the facility.

Tyler turned to where Miles and Linda sat behind them. "Do you think it would be okay for us to warm up?"

"The ice is ours until one," Miles said.

"In that case, let's take advantage of it," Tyler said.

Amaliya nodded as the sense of familiarity rushed through her again. She took a deep breath. Today was the day. One way or another, she and Tyler were going to find their way forward. She hoped Gordon Alexander was willing and able to help them navigate in the right direction.

Amaliya spun around to skate in front of Tyler, and pure joy washed over her. "Can you believe this?"

"What?"

Amaliya spread out her arms and twirled. "We can do anything we want, and no one will care. We don't have to worry about Scarlett walking in or Marie being . . . well, Marie."

The tension she had sensed in Tyler during the ride to New Jersey faded. "It is pretty amazing."

Amaliya took his hand. "We should try our lift."

"If you're up for it." Tyler took her hand, and they circled the rink. "Ready?"

"Ready." Amaliya let go of his hand and let herself glide in front of him. His hands gripped her waist, he counted to three, and she pushed herself into the air. In that instant, she might as well have been on a stage instead of the ice. She floated above Tyler as though weightless, the magic of the ballet piercing through her.

She closed her eyes and arched her back as she envisioned how the music from *Swan Lake* would sound in time to her movements.

Tyler's voice broke through the illusion. "Down." He lowered her to the ice, her hand finding his. They circled once more.

"Double toe loops?"

"Sure." She followed his lead, timing her takeoff and rotation in her head to match his. Magic struck again, their blades connecting with the ice in unison.

"Do it again." A man's voice carried to them.

Amaliya did a half turn so she could see who had spoken. Gordon Alexander. He was older now than in the picture Tyler had shown her, his dark hair peppered with gray.

"Again," he repeated.

Tyler looked down at her, and his shoulders lifted in silent communication. He took her hand, and they circled halfway around the rink before he released her. They performed their jumps a second time.

"Now show me a double flip," Gordon said.

Amaliya fell in step with Tyler. They'd barely completed their jumps before Gordon barked out the next order.

"Double lutz."

One by one, they performed each jump without error.

The dreaded moment came when he commanded, "Double axels."

Amaliya looked at Tyler, not sure whether to admit she couldn't do one.

"Want to try?" he whispered.

Though she wanted to say no, she nodded. At least Gordon would be able to see Tyler had the skill even if she didn't. Tyler gave her hand a squeeze before releasing it as they lined up for their jumps. As expected, Tyler landed his. Amaliya fell.

Tyler circled beside her and offered his hand.

Gordon walked onto the ice. "You can't do a double axel."

Even though he didn't phrase it as a question, Amaliya shook her head. "Not yet. I'm sorry. I think I need more time with that one."

"No, you need to correct your posture when you transfer from your back foot to your front before your takeoff," he said. "Your balance is all wrong."

"I never noticed that," Tyler said.

"You're a skater, not a coach."

"We've had a coach. She never said anything about it," Amaliya said.

"Never mind that. This is easy to fix." Gordon waved dismissively. "Let me see your spins. Side-by-side camels."

After they completed the next skill, Gordon said, "Amaliya, lift your leg another inch. Tyler, straighten your back."

Amaliya followed his instructions, oddly comforted by having a specific area to improve upon.

They finished their spins nearly in unison. Beth's voice carried to them. "Oh, I can work with this."

"Take a break," Gordon said. "Go get some water."

Amaliya and Tyler headed for the water fountain.

"What do you think?" Amaliya asked.

"He's given us more correction in an hour than Scarlett has given us in the past month."

"That isn't saying much." Amaliya took a drink of water before turning back to where Gordon now stood with Beth. "Can you imagine yourself being in the rink every day with him?"

"From what I've seen, he would be demanding and push us hard," Tyler said. "He's exactly what we need."

"The question is, Will he agree to coach us?"

"We'll find out soon enough." Tyler took a drink. "Come on. Let's see what else he has planned for us today."

Choreography, jumps, spins, throws, new variations of old skills. Gordon packed more into two hours of practice than most coaches managed to work through in an entire week.

"Tyler, your left hand on Amaliya's waist."

Tyler took position behind Amaliya and slipped his arm around her, his left hand on her stomach. The familiar sizzle of attraction shot through him, and he fought it back. This wasn't the time to notice the raspberry scent of Amaliya's shampoo or the graceful line of her neck.

"Chins up."

Tyler lifted his head slightly.

"Good. Now push off with your right foot. Circle the rink for me."

They pushed off together and circled, their steps in sync. When they reached Gordon again, they slid to a stop.

"We're done for today." Gordon walked off the ice and stopped beside Beth. "How long will it take you to finish the short program?"

"With what we accomplished today, another few days or so."

"Good." Gordon nodded his approval. "And the long?"

"I need the timing on the technical skills to make the last adjustments, but it's basically done," Beth said.

Tyler and Amaliya joined them as Miles and Linda approached.

"What do you think?" Miles asked.

Gordon ignored Miles and addressed Tyler and Amaliya. "How far do you want your skating to take you?"

"We want to go to the Olympics," Tyler said without hesitation.

"Do you want to go to the Olympics, or do you want to win?" Gordon asked.

Taken aback by the question, Tyler said, "Everyone wants to win an Olympic gold medal. That's the dream."

"Do you believe in working hard enough to make the dream a reality?"

Hope took flight in Tyler's chest. An Olympic gold medal. He had barely dared dream of the possibilities, yet here he was being asked if he could take that leap of faith, if he could believe in the impossible. "Yes." Tyler's hand found Amaliya's. "We'll do whatever it takes."

Gordon turned back to Miles. "How soon can you get them to Virginia?"

"Amaliya graduates next week. We could feasibly drive down on Saturday."

"I'll look into rink time when I get home," Gordon said. "Amaliya, where's the closest rink to your house?"

"It's the one near Mount Vernon."

"Does this mean you'll coach us?" Tyler asked.

Gordon gave a single nod. "We'll meet a week from Sunday at Amaliya's house in Virginia to go over a few things. If all goes well, we'll start practice a week from Monday."

"What should we work on this week at practice?" Tyler asked.

"Not Amaliya's double axel."

"I like skating for you already," Amaliya said.

"Let's sit down, and I'll give you some practices to get you through the next few days."

Tyler and Amaliya followed him to the first row of bleachers, and Tyler let the events of the past few minutes sink in. He and Amaliya had a new coach, and he was moving to Virginia.

Chapter
THIRTY-FOUR

TYLER AND AMALIYA WALKED INTO the skating rink, Amaliya's hand in his. A wave of nostalgia washed over him, and he stopped by the edge of the rink. Scarlett stood in the center, her hand on Marie's arm as she demonstrated the position she wanted Marie to achieve. How many times had he received similar instruction from the coach with whom he had spent the better part of a decade?

He pushed aside the negativity of the past few months with Scarlett and focused on the many fond memories he had made here. For so many years, this rink had been the center of his skating life. He had learned to skate here. This was where he and his sister had moved through the various levels until they'd reached world-class status. His relationship with Amaliya had been born within these walls. Yet, after Friday, this would only be a place to visit.

He had arranged a later ice time with Hank so he and Amaliya wouldn't have to deal with sharing the ice with Scarlett and her skaters. He looked forward to having drama-free practices for a change.

Amaliya squeezed his hand. "I can't believe we only have one more week of practices here."

"Me neither."

Together they put their skates on and went through their stretching routine. When Scarlett ended her practice, she and Marie were the last two to leave the ice.

Scarlett shot Tyler a condescending look. "You missed practice. Where were you this morning?"

Tyler stiffened. "You weren't interested in coaching us, so we found a new coach."

"Who?" Scarlett demanded.

"It can't be anyone worthwhile if you're still skating here," Marie added.

"Actually, we're moving." Amaliya put her hand on Tyler's arm as though aligning herself with him.

"That's right." Though part of him wanted to prove himself to Scarlett by letting her see them place in sectionals in October, he couldn't resist sharing their good fortune. "Our new coach is Gordon Alexander."

Surprise and disbelief surfaced on both Scarlett's and Marie's faces.

"The Olympic coach?" Marie asked. "The former Olympian?"

"One and the same," Tyler said.

"Gordon Alexander isn't coaching anymore," Scarlett said.

"He *wasn't* coaching anymore," Amaliya corrected.

Tyler couldn't keep the smugness out of his voice. "Gordon gave us a tryout, and now he's going to be working exclusively with us."

"You don't really think he's going to get you to the Olympics," Scarlett said, a childish sneer in her voice. "He didn't have the best track record at the last one."

"He's ready for a fresh start, and so are we," Tyler said. "Gordon believes we can get to the Olympics, so we're going to believe it too."

Amaliya stepped past them and glided onto the ice. "Maybe we'll see you in Leningrad."

"Best of luck to you." Tyler moved to the ice and took Amaliya's hand. Leaving Marie and Scarlett behind, they pushed off together and started around the rink.

When they reached the far side, Amaliya lowered her voice. "Is it bad that I want to make it to the Olympics as much to prove to Scarlett she was wrong about us as to try to win a medal?"

"I had the same thought." He reversed direction and grinned at her. "It doesn't matter though. After this week, we don't have to worry about what Scarlett thinks."

"Or Marie," Amaliya added.

"True." Tyler changed direction again and slipped his arm around Amaliya's waist. "Come on. Let's enjoy our last practices here. By next week, we'll be with a real coach."

"I'm looking forward to that."

Amaliya unhooked her mother's ballet slippers from the bedpost, tucked them into her purse, and took another look around. So much had happened since she'd moved into this bedroom. The grief over the loss of her old life and the uncertainty that had consumed her when she'd first arrived had faded, replaced by hope for the future.

Miles and Linda had helped her find a sense of normalcy despite the many changes and her earlier fear that her parents wouldn't fully recover. They still had a long way to go, but seeing her father at her graduation had gone a long way in making her believe they would all find their way back to their old life.

Both of her parents had transferred to the rehab facility twenty minutes from the Donnellys' house. If the doctors were correct, her father would be there for only a few weeks. After that, he would continue his recovery at the Donnellys' house so he would be close to her mom until they could both come home together.

They were making steps forward, and so was she. Today, she was starting on a new journey.

With a rush of excitement, she lifted her suitcase and carried it downstairs. She walked onto the front porch, where Linda stood watching Miles and Tyler load Tyler's car.

"All set?" Miles asked.

"I think so."

Tyler approached and took her suitcase. "I'll put that in the car for you."

"Thanks." Her fingers brushed Tyler's, and a tingle shot up her arm. She fought to keep her face expressionless.

"Are you sure you don't want us to drive down with you?" Linda asked.

"We'll be fine." Amaliya gave her a hug. "It's only a five-hour drive, and you said yourself that you have to be in New York on Monday."

"I know, but we could drive back tomorrow."

"We'll be fine," Amaliya said again. "And I promise to call as soon as we get there."

"Make sure you do." Miles gave her a hug in turn.

Amaliya dug her fingers into his shirt, an unexpected wave of homesickness washing over her, but this time, not for her home in Virginia but for the home she had made here in Connecticut.

As though reading her thoughts, Miles said, "You know you're welcome back here anytime."

"Thanks." She fought the rise of emotions. "Thank you for everything."

"We'll be down in a few weeks to check on you."

"Maybe by then, we'll have our new routine to show you."

"We look forward to seeing it," Linda said. "When you stop to see your parents, tell them I'll come by to visit tomorrow."

"I will."

Tyler slammed the trunk closed. "I think we're ready."

After another round of goodbyes, Tyler opened the passenger-side door for Amaliya, and she slid into his car. A minute later, he put the key in the ignition.

"Ready?" he asked.

"I think so." She put her hand on his. "What about you? Are you ready?"

"Ready for the drive, yes. Ready for everything else—ask me in a week."

"Why a week?" Amaliya asked.

He put the car in gear and backed out of the driveway. "Because by then, we'll know what skating for Gordon Alexander is really like."

Tyler didn't know why he was nervous about visiting Amaliya's parents. It wasn't like he hadn't already met them, but as he followed Amaliya into the rehabilitation center, his palms dampened.

"Is something wrong?" Amaliya asked.

"I feel like I'm meeting your parents for the first time."

"You are."

"What?" Tyler glanced down at her. "I met them the night we went to *Swan Lake*."

"Yes, but we weren't dating then."

"If you tell your parents we're dating right before I move into your guest house, this move is doomed before we even leave Connecticut, remember?"

"Don't worry. I wasn't planning on announcing the change of our relationship status."

A little seed of guilt sprouted. He hated feeling like he wasn't being completely honest.

Amaliya led the way into her parents' new room. Though it looked similar to the hospital room they had shared, the walls were painted a soft blue rather than stark white, and two dressers lined the near wall.

Amaliya rattled off a greeting in French. At least, Tyler was pretty sure it was a simple greeting. The way Robert glared at him, Tyler decided Amaliya might as well have announced she was being abducted by aliens and he was the one driving the spaceship.

Katerina gave him a welcoming smile and spoke in English. "Are you all packed up?"

"I don't think we can fit anything else in my car," Tyler said.

"Speaking of which"—Amaliya opened her purse and produced a pair of worn ballet slippers. She held them out to her mom—"I thought you might want these. They can be your motivation to get through all the therapy you have in the next few months."

Katerina took them from her and ran a finger along the pink satin. "Where did you find these?"

"In your closet. I hope you don't mind, but I hung them up in my room here in Connecticut to remind me of home."

"Are those the same ones . . . ?" Robert began.

"They're the ballet shoes I wore the night I defected." Katerina clutched them to her chest. "Thank you."

"You're welcome," Amaliya said. After she and Tyler talked to her parents for a few minutes, Amaliya leaned down and hugged her mom. "I'm going to miss you."

"We'll miss you too," Katerina said. "We'll talk every Sunday."

Amaliya nodded and turned to hug her father.

When she pulled back, Robert shifted his attention to Tyler. "My house rules are pretty straightforward. Number one is you'll stay out of each other's living areas."

"Yes, sir," Tyler said.

Robert gave him a curt nod before he spoke to Amaliya again. "Eleanor is in charge."

"Yes, Papa," Amaliya said obediently. "Love you."

"Love you too." Robert gave her a fierce hug. When he released her, he looked at Tyler. "Drive safe."

"I will." Tyler stepped forward and shook Robert's hand.

"Call us when you get there," Katerina added.

"I'll talk to you tonight." Amaliya kissed her mother's cheek.

"I hope we see you in Virginia soon," Tyler said.

Katerina offered a wistful smile. "Me too."

Tyler couldn't get enough of this view. The Potomac River flowed alongside the George Washington Parkway, and huge homes rose up on the opposite side of the road as though lording over the incredible scenery.

"Where to next?" he asked.

"Turn left up here."

"Where? I don't see a street sign."

"Into that driveway between the brick pillars."

Tyler signaled and made the turn. He slowed as he got his first look at the massive house that had moments ago been obscured by the trees lining the driveway. Two stories, brick-fronted, and sprawling the width of his house twice over, the mansion dominated the bluff overlooking the river.

"This is your house?" he asked.

"Yeah." She waved at the oversized garage. "Park on the left side. Once we go inside, we can open the garage door and bring our stuff in that way."

Tyler took the spot she indicated and turned off the engine. "This is your house," he repeated.

Amaliya opened her own door and climbed out. "Come on. I'll show you around." She retrieved her purse but didn't bother with anything else in the car.

Tyler followed her, not sure what to think. He knew Amaliya's dad had been a professional hockey player for a lot of years and had ultimately become a coach, but Tyler had never considered that Robert would have amassed this kind of wealth.

"How long have you lived here?" Tyler asked.

"My whole life."

"Wow." Tyler stopped on the front walk and stared out over the parkway. "You grew up with this view right outside your window?"

"Yeah." Amaliya pointed. "That's my room up there."

She took his hand and tugged to put him back in motion. When she reached the front door, she pulled on the handle, but it didn't open. She drew out her housekey and slid it into the lock. She'd barely pushed the door open when a woman appeared in the entryway.

"Amaliya! You're home." The slightly rounded woman with silver hair enfolded Amaliya in a hug.

"Eleanor, I missed you."

"And I missed you." Eleanor glanced at Tyler. "You must be Tyler." She released Amaliya and reached for his hand. "Come. Come. Let me show you your apartment."

"Linda said you were going to move into the main house," Amaliya said. "I hope that was okay."

"It's more than okay. Living back in the main house reminds me of when you were little and I used to babysit you when your mama was teaching."

Eleanor led the way through the two-story entryway and into an expansive living room. Tall windows on one wall framed the view of the Potomac, and a fireplace was situated along the adjoining wall.

They continued past a formal dining room and into an oversized kitchen. Four stools were spaced along a high countertop that separated the main kitchen from the eating area. A table and six chairs occupied the space beside a window that looked out over the grassy backyard that abutted the woods.

Amaliya set her purse on the counter and continued to a door on the far side of the kitchen. "Tyler, your apartment is this way."

"Are you two hungry?" Eleanor asked. "I have a casserole I can put in the oven."

"I'm not hungry now, but that would be great for dinner," Amaliya said.

"Let me know when you're ready to eat."

"We will. Thanks." Amaliya opened the door beside her. "We'll be right back."

Tyler followed Amaliya into a four-car garage, three of the spaces already occupied. She crossed the garage to the far side. He expected her to go through the door opposite where they had walked in from the kitchen, but she headed for a flight of stairs.

"What's in there?" Tyler pointed to the door next to where a blue sedan was parked.

"The weight room."

"You have your own weight room?" Tyler asked.

"Take a look." She waved at the door.

Tyler pushed it open, found the light switch, and flipped it on. Mirrors covered the walls of the windowless room. An exercise bike occupied one corner, and a set of weights lined the opposite wall beside a weight bench. Barbells, more weights, several mats stacked in the corner. Everything he would need to stay in shape.

"You can work out here anytime you want." Amaliya motioned for him to follow her. She reached the top of the stairs and pushed open the door. She stepped aside and let Tyler enter first. "This is yours."

He walked inside, immediately drawn to the window. Like Amaliya, he, too, had a view of the river and the front lawn. To his left, he could also see the driveway and the woods beyond.

The modest living room boasted a loveseat, a chair, and a coffee table. To his right, a small kitchen nook contained a full-sized refrigerator, a sink, a hotplate, and a microwave.

"There isn't a stove or oven up here, but you can use the kitchen anytime you want," Amaliya said. "Eleanor only cooked up here on her day off, when she didn't want to bother coming downstairs."

He noted the doorway opposite the kitchenette. "Is that the bedroom through there?"

"Yes."

Tyler opened the door. The room was similar in size to his own back home, the furnishings simple yet adequate.

"You have a private phone line. Eleanor can give you the number," Amaliya said.

"This is great," Tyler said.

"Want to unload our stuff first, or do you want the grand tour?"

"We're on a roll. Let's finish the tour."

"Okay." Amaliya led him back into the house. They reached the entryway, but this time, she continued into the hall opposite where the living room was.

"That's my dad's office in there." She opened the door. A desk sat in one corner, but the other half of the room was adorned with three leather chairs facing a screen. A sheet hung over what could only be a projector.

Tyler walked inside and peeked under the sheet. He was right. "You already have a projector set up?"

"Dad used it all the time when he was coaching."

"This will be great." He let the dust cover fall back into place.

"This is my dad's domain; let me show you my mom's." Amaliya continued down the hall to the next set of doors. This time, she hesitated before she pushed the double doors open.

Tyler stepped forward and walked into Amaliya's past. He knew it the moment he entered. This wasn't just Amaliya's mother's space. It was hers too.

The home dance studio exuded elegance and class. Wooden floors, a barre stretched along one wall, a framed photograph of a ballerina in the middle of an elegant jump.

Tyler took another step inside. Amaliya remained in the doorway. He took a closer look at the oversized image.

"She looks like you."

"My mom was the most amazing dancer I've ever seen," she said wistfully. "My dad said she was even better when she was younger."

"You must have inherited your grace from her."

"I guess." The subdued tone was one he hadn't heard in months. He crossed to her and pulled her into his arms.

"I'm sorry they aren't here with us now."

"Me too." She took a deep breath. "At least they're out of the hospital."

"We were supposed to call them."

"We'd better do that now, or they'll send Miles and Linda to look for us." Her hand still around his waist, Amaliya tipped her chin up. "I'm really glad you're here."

Tyler leaned down and kissed her. "Me too."

❦

Amaliya carried her suitcase up the stairs, Eleanor and Tyler trailing behind her. The moment she reached the upstairs landing, her gaze found the double doors leading to her parents' room.

"Which room is yours?" Tyler asked.

"Over here." Amaliya reached her doorway and stepped through, a rush of emotions washing over her. Home.

The chair in the corner was where her mother had rocked her when she was little. Her father had helped her paint these walls multiple times, changing them from pink to yellow to blue and finally to their current antique white.

Amaliya stepped to the side to make way for Tyler and Eleanor.

"Where do you want this?" Tyler asked.

"By the bookshelf."

Tyler set down the box he carried where she'd indicated and stopped to look out the window. "I was right. You do have a great view."

"Yeah. It's better than any painting I could put on a wall."

"I agree." Tyler relieved Eleanor of the box she held and set it on top of his. "Maybe we should take a break after we finish unloading the car and go for a run along the river. It's gorgeous outside."

"I'd like that."

"What time do you want dinner?" Eleanor asked.

"It's almost three now. What do you think, Tyler?"

"How about six?" Tyler suggested.

"Six it is." Eleanor led the way back into the hall.

Twenty minutes later, the last of Tyler's and Amaliya's belongings were in their respective rooms. Amaliya changed into shorts and a T-shirt and walked outside, where Tyler waited.

"Ready?" he asked.

"Yeah." Amaliya walked down the driveway. She stopped when she reached the end, looking and listening for oncoming traffic. When the road cleared, she and Tyler jogged across the street and made their way to the paved path runners and bicyclists alike shared.

"Which way?"

"This way." She took a step to her left. "Too many tourists if we go the other direction."

"What's the attraction?"

"Mount Vernon," she said. "George Washington's home."

"Maybe if we have some time off, you can show it to me."

"I can do that." She started at an easy jog, and Tyler fell into step beside her.

"How are you doing being back here?" Tyler asked.

"It's great being here where all my memories live . . ."

"But it's hard at the same time." Tyler finished for her.

"I think the right word for it would be *bittersweet*," Amaliya said. "It's hard being here knowing my parents still have so much therapy in their future."

"A few months from now, they'll be back, and everything will be back to normal."

"I'm not sure what normal even looks like." Her ponytail swinging behind her, she glanced at Tyler. "What about you? How are you feeling about moving five hours away from your parents?"

"Honestly, it's kind of nice. As much as I love my folks, sometimes they forget I'm an adult. Even my sister calls every couple weeks to make sure I'm not getting sidetracked from my training," Tyler said. "I think twenty-one is old enough to not need a curfew."

"Enjoy your one night without one," Amaliya said. "If Gordon is anything like my mom was when I was studying ballet, we'll have a curfew."

"You're probably right. Maybe we should go out on a real date tonight while we have the chance."

"What did you have in mind?"

"Want to go to a movie? I bet there's one that starts at seven or seven thirty."

"I'd like that."

"Great." They ran in silence for a minute. "Eleanor isn't going to expect us to invite her along, is she?"

"I doubt it, although we should probably do some unpacking when we get back or she may do it for us. It drives her nuts when things are left out."

"This is going to take some getting used to."

"What?"

"Having a housekeeper."

"Trust me. It isn't much different than having your parents around," Amaliya said. "Eleanor keeps the house in order, but she'll make us pick up after ourselves."

"Good to know."

Tyler stretched his arm across the back of Amaliya's seat and rested his hand on her shoulder.

A dark theater, the light from the movie screen washing over them, a bucket of popcorn between them. He couldn't remember the last time he had been on such a carefree date.

With Marie, it had always been about going places to see and be seen. Sitting still and simply being together had never been her thing. He shook that thought away. Amaliya was nothing like Marie, and his feelings for Marie had never deepened beyond basic friendship and a desire for companionship.

Amaliya nestled closer. Her hair was down the way he liked it tonight, and a faint dusting of makeup enhanced her fair skin. Had he ever seen anyone more beautiful? Warmth rushed through him.

His hold on her shoulder tightened, and he leaned down to kiss her temple. Her eyes flashed up to meet his briefly, and he couldn't resist lowering his lips to hers.

His free hand lifted to caress the softness of her cheek before he drew away and straightened. He didn't miss the slight flush of color in her cheeks before she turned her attention back to the movie.

Enamored by her reaction, he settled back in his seat, reveling in the simplicity of being together without an audience. Or, at least, without an audience they knew.

His own cheeks heated when he glanced around the crowded movie theater. Maybe they should try for someplace more private for their next date.

He took a bite of popcorn and pondered how long Amaliya would want to hide their relationship from everyone. They were in Virginia now. Did that mean they could open up to those close to them? He couldn't imagine Gordon would have any issues with him and Amaliya dating. After all, Gordon had married his skating partner when he had been in competition.

He reached for another handful of popcorn, and his fingers brushed Amaliya's. He was worrying too much. Tomorrow they would meet with their new coach. This week, he would look for a new job. By this fall, he and Amaliya would take their next step toward elite competition.

He ran his fingers along Amaliya's arm. One thing at a time.

Chapter
THIRTY-FIVE

AMALIYA LEANED BACK IN ONE of the leather chairs in her father's office, Tyler beside her and the film of them skating displayed on the screen on the far side of the room. Just like when she'd received her offer from the San Francisco Ballet, excitement stirred within her. She couldn't wait to see what she and Tyler could accomplish with their new coach.

"I think with a little more height, we can turn that throw double salchow into a triple," Tyler said.

"Maybe, but don't you think we should wait for me to get the basics down first?" Amaliya said. "I'll feel a lot better once I can land a double axel."

"You heard Gordon. He'll help you get it." When knuckles rapped against the doorframe, Tyler glanced up and stood. "Mr. Alexander. I'm sorry. I didn't realize you were here."

"You had it right the first time. Call me Gordon." He stepped farther into the room. "We're going to be spending a lot of time together. No reason for formalities." He took a good look around. "This is a nice setup here."

"Thanks." Amaliya started to stand, but Gordon motioned for her to stay put.

"Rewind that. Let me see this throw double salchow." Gordon took the empty chair while Tyler complied.

Gordon leaned forward as the image of Tyler throwing Amaliya into the air played before them. Nerves fluttered in Amaliya's stomach. Even though she had yet to get used to seeing herself skating, she braced for the criticism that had become so familiar since switching to the sport.

"Rewind it again," Gordon said.

Tyler did so.

When he played it a second time, Gordon nodded. "I agree with Tyler. With some work, we can make that a triple."

Gordon located the light switch beside him and flipped it on. "Since we're already in work mode, I have your schedule for tomorrow."

He slipped two papers out of his attaché case and handed one to each of them. "Ice time will start at seven, but I want you there fifteen minutes early to stretch."

Tyler and Amaliya scanned over the information.

"We'll get to sleep in," Tyler said. "That will be nice."

"I spoke with the rink manager. Tyler, you have a job interview with him after our morning session," Gordon said. "Keep in mind, though, that I don't want you working any late shifts, even on weekends. Your bodies need to follow the routine I laid out for you regardless of what day it is."

"Are you expecting us to practice seven days a week?" Amaliya asked.

"No, we'll do six. Monday through Friday, ice time will be from seven to ten and from twelve to three. For Saturdays, I was only able to get one session from five to eight," Gordon said. "On Sundays, you rest."

Amaliya's head was spinning. Gordon's schedule included not only ice time but every other aspect of their lives as well. Meals, sleep, weight and strength training, dance classes. Even specific times for them to carry part-time jobs.

"You mentioned Tyler might be able to work at the rink. Is there a chance I might be able to get a job there too?"

"After talking to Beth and Linda, I thought it might work better for you to try to get a job teaching ballet."

"I haven't studied ballet since—" Amaliya stopped herself and started again. "It's been a while."

"I'm interviewing a dance instructor tomorrow. We can see if her studio is hiring when we meet," Gordon said.

Amaliya tried to visualize studying dance under someone other than her mother and couldn't.

Gordon continued. "I'm still looking into local gyms for you to do your weight training."

"I don't think that will be necessary," Tyler said.

"Weight training is essential, especially for you, Tyler."

"That's not what I meant." Tyler glanced at Amaliya. "Maybe we should show Gordon around."

"That's a good idea." Amaliya led the way into the hall. She fought against the hollow feeling inside her and forced herself to turn toward what had once been her favorite room in the house. "Let's start with the studio." Her footsteps slow, she made her way down the hall and opened one of the two double doors.

Gordon walked inside and turned in a circle. "This is nice. If the dance instructor is agreeable, we can have her come to you."

"That would be great," Tyler said.

Eager to move on, Amaliya said, "Let me show you the rooms that will be yours if you decide you want to move in."

She continued down the hall to what was, in essence, a second master bedroom suite located at the end of the hall. "This would be yours."

Gordon walked into the outer room, which included a couch, television, and round table that could be used as a workspace or a dining area.

"The bedroom is through that door." Amaliya waved at the bedroom entrance. "There's a private bath as well as a separate entrance that leads to the backyard."

Gordon walked into the bedroom and let out a low whistle. "Nice. Very nice."

"Are you moving in, Gordon?" Tyler asked.

"I still have a few weeks left on my lease, but I'll move a few things over and stay here during the week so I don't have to fight traffic," he said. "At least until I have time to get everything over here."

"Come on," Tyler said. "Let us show you the weight room."

Amaliya noted Tyler's excitement and let him take the lead. She hadn't ever thought to tell him about the various amenities she had grown up with. They had always been there, advantages she had previously taken for granted.

They entered the garage, and Tyler opened the weight room door.

Again, Gordon walked inside and took a look around. "This will work nicely." Gordon turned back to Amaliya. "If you had your own ice rink, we'd be set."

The fact that her father had tried to build one brought a smile to her face. "I'm afraid my dad wasn't ever able to talk my mom into that one."

"Let's go back inside and chat with your housekeeper."

"Why?" Amaliya asked.

"Because we need to have a nice discussion about nutrition."

"We both eat pretty well," Tyler said.

"Pretty well isn't going to cut it," Gordon said. "Your body only works as well as the fuel you put into it."

Amaliya smiled. "My dad always says the same thing."

"Smart man."

The sweet memory rose within her. "Well, except for when Eleanor made chocolate chip cookies."

"A mostly smart man," Gordon said.

"Sounds to me like he had his priorities straight," Tyler said.

"Maybe he did," Gordon said, "but I'm the only one around here who's going to be eating cookies."

Amaliya grinned. "Yes, Coach."

Chapter
THIRTY-SIX

TYLER ROLLED HIS SHOULDERS AND circled the rink again. Only an hour into practice and he was exhausted. When they'd arrived at the rink near Amaliya's house, six other skaters had already been on the ice. And he'd thought it was bad sharing with only two others before.

Amaliya fell into place beside him.

"Let me see that combined spin again," Gordon said. "Amaliya, I want your wrists to be more fluid when you reach above your head."

Amaliya nodded.

They took their starting positions opposite one another, circled, and met in the center of the ice. Tyler's hand gripped Amaliya's waist as they started their spin in unison. Two position changes, multiple rotations, and they transitioned out of the spin.

"Better. We'll work on that some more this afternoon in your studio."

An unidentified emotion flashed on Amaliya's face. Tyler lowered his voice. "You okay with that?"

"I'm going to have to be." She drew a breath and blew it out before speaking to Gordon. "What's next?"

"Figures."

"That's something I can do," Amaliya said.

"You can do it all," Gordon countered.

"Except a double axel."

"You won't be saying that by the end of the week." Gordon skated a pattern for them to trace. "Tyler, start us off."

He pushed off and followed the track Gordon had left. It wasn't until he'd completed the figure that he realized he was alone on the ice with Amaliya and Gordon.

"Where did everyone else go?"

"The ice is ours alone from nine to ten every Monday and Wednesday."

"Nice."

"Amaliya, your turn."

Amaliya performed the task. When she finished, Gordon said, "You're right. You can do this."

He gave them each a few pointers before they repeated the skill again, this time creating their own figures rather than following Gordon's tracks. When Gordon finally called them to the side of the rink, Tyler glanced at the clock on the wall to see their practice time was over.

"I can't remember the last time I spent a full hour on figures."

"It's 30 percent of your total score. Don't lose sight of that."

"I doubt you'll let us," Tyler said.

"You've got that right." Gordon waved across the rink. "Tyler, you'd better get to your interview. Bruce, the rink manager, should be in his office."

"Good luck, Tyler," Amaliya said.

"Thanks."

Amaliya pushed off to follow Tyler, but Gordon stopped her.

"Sorry, Amaliya, but you aren't done yet."

"I thought our ice time ended at ten."

"I asked Bruce for some extra time for you today," Gordon said. "It's time we work on your double axel."

The familiar sense of anxiety and failure rose within her. "Wouldn't it be better if we did that at the beginning of a practice when I'm not so tired?"

"We're just getting ready for this afternoon," Gordon said. "Show me your single axel."

"Okay." Amaliya started forward and executed the jump that a few months ago had seemed so difficult.

Gordon had her repeat it twice more.

"Let me see it again, but this time, I want more bend in your right leg when you push off."

"Still a single?"

"Yes."

Amaliya performed the jump again, but when she landed, she over rotated and struggled to keep her balance when her skate hit the ice.

Gordon approached her. "Better."

"I almost fell."

"You almost fell because you didn't know what to do with the extra height."

The memory of a similar conversation with Tyler flashed through her head. "Tyler said the same thing when he was teaching me my first double toe loop."

"That's enough for now," Gordon said. "I'd like to work on this in your dance studio after lunch. I think if you can get comfortable on land first, you'll have this down."

"I can't tell you how nice it would be to land a double axel without falling."

"I remember those days."

Amaliya cast him a wry look. "How old were you when you learned it?"

"Learned it? Ten. Mastered it? Fourteen." Gordon motioned her to the opening at the side of the rink and fell in beside her. "You have to remember, most skaters don't even start learning a double axel until they've been taking lessons for at least five years. From what Beth told me, you've covered a lot of ground in a very short period of time."

"I'm trying."

"Keep trying."

"When are we going to learn our short program?"

"We'll work on it this afternoon."

They reached the benches, and both sat to change out of their skates.

Tyler emerged from a doorway a short distance away, followed by a man in his early fifties.

"Well?" Gordon asked.

"I got the job," Tyler said. "Bruce, this is Amaliya."

Amaliya stood and shook Bruce's outstretched hand. "Good to meet you."

"You too." Bruce glanced at Gordon. "Are you going to let me hire her too?"

Surprise surfaced. Was Bruce serious?

"You have another opening?" Gordon asked.

"I had to let two of my skating instructors go yesterday," Bruce said.

"Two?" Suspicion colored Gordon's voice.

"They were helping themselves to the till."

"That's never good," Gordon said. "What would their hours be?"

"Classes start right after your afternoon practices. I can have them both teach from four to six every day, with another class or two on Saturdays."

Amaliya tried to picture it, being the teacher instead of the student.

"What do you two think?" Gordon asked. "Amaliya, would you rather teach ice skating or ballet?"

Her stress over walking back into the world of dance melted away. "Ice skating. This would be so convenient for both of us to have the same work schedule."

"True. I doubt you'll find any job that will work better with your schedules than this."

"I agree," Tyler said. "Amaliya, what do you think?"

Another new beginning. Amaliya stepped into it. "When do we start?"

"A week from today."

"Great. That'll give us time for Amaliya to land her double axel before she joins the workforce."

"I've been working on it for four months. Do you really think you can teach it to me in one week?"

"I guarantee it."

Tyler knocked on the door leading from the garage to the kitchen of the main house. After their afternoon practice, he'd gone upstairs to shower and change. Now he was in search of food. He sincerely hoped dinner would be provided tonight because he didn't think he had the energy to stand long enough to fix something for himself. He couldn't remember the last time he had worked so hard in practice.

When no one answered, he knocked again.

"Come in," Eleanor called from inside.

He entered to the scent of beef stroganoff and bread baking.

"Tyler, you don't have to knock. You live here," Eleanor said. "Are you hungry?"

"Starving." He inhaled deeply. "It smells like I have perfect timing."

Eleanor waved a hand toward a cabinet beside the refrigerator. "The glasses are in there. Get yourself something to drink. Dinner will be ready in five minutes."

"Eleanor, you're a saint."

"Remember you said that when I put you and Amaliya on dish duty."

Amaliya entered from the living room. "Eleanor, did you make beef stroganoff?"

"I did. It was on Gordon's approved lists of food."

"I'm relieved to hear that," Amaliya said.

"Me too," Eleanor said. "Amaliya, can you set the table?"

"Sure."

Tyler filled his water glass and asked, "What does everyone want to drink?"

"Milk for me," Eleanor said.

"I'll stick with water." Amaliya set three plates on the table.

Within minutes, they were all seated and ready to eat.

The stroganoff was even better than Tyler had expected, and he finished two servings by the time Eleanor pushed back from the table.

"I'm going to watch some TV in my room. Can you two put away the food and finish the dishes?" she asked.

"We can do that," Amaliya said.

"Thank you for dinner." Tyler plucked another roll from the bread basket. "It was amazing."

"Glad you liked it." Eleanor rinsed her dishes and put them in the dishwasher before disappearing into the living room.

"Is she going to cook for us every night?"

"Pretty much. She usually takes the weekends off, but during the week, we'll be spoiled."

"That works out great for us. Saturdays are a lighter day, and we don't practice on Sundays."

Amaliya finished the last bite of her roll and leaned back in her chair. "I don't know about you, but I'm exhausted."

"I'm with you." Tyler spooned some more stroganoff onto his plate. "Do you want to watch a movie in the living room tonight, or did you want to go to bed early?"

"It's only six thirty. I think I can make it a couple more hours before I collapse," Amaliya said. "My parents have a bunch of movies."

"Want to go pick one out while I do the dishes?"

"I can help with the dishes first." Amaliya rose from the table and rinsed her plate.

Tyler finished his dinner and joined her by the sink. "Why don't you let me load the dishwasher and you can put the leftovers away."

"Sounds good." Amaliya opened a cabinet and retrieved some Tupperware containers.

As soon as they were done cleaning the kitchen, they picked out a movie and settled on the couch together.

Tyler stretched his arm out and pulled Amaliya closer. "If Gordon really does move in here, it's going to be an interesting challenge trying to find privacy."

"It won't be any worse than when my parents move back home, but that is going to be weird, living with our coach."

"It'll be a first for me." Tyler leaned down until his lips were a whisper from hers. "I'd better take advantage of our alone time while I can."

"You think so?" Amaliya asked, amusement lighting her eyes.

"Oh yeah."

Chapter
THIRTY-SEVEN

Amaliya circled the rink with Tyler at her side, a half dozen other skaters practicing with their various coaches.

For four days, Gordon had worked with her on her double axel. It wasn't like what she had experienced with Scarlett. Instead, with each practice session, Gordon gave her a new point to focus on, both on the ice and in her studio. Each day between practice sessions, he had joined her and Tyler for lunch and worked with Amaliya on her form in the studio while Tyler lifted weights.

Now here she was, ready to try again.

"Remember, not too much knee bend," Gordon said. "You have the strength. Use it."

Amaliya nodded.

"You can do this." Tyler moved to stand beside Gordon.

"Let me see it," Gordon said.

Amaliya straightened her shoulders and pushed off. Skating backward, she circled once, checked the other skaters to make sure she was clear, and then let the many lessons of the week flow through her mind. As she had so many times before, she reversed direction, bent her knee, and launched herself into the air. One rotation. Two. Two and a half. Her right foot connected with the ice. Her free leg extended.

Surprise shot through her, followed by exhilaration. "I did it!"

Gordon clapped his hands, and Tyler joined in.

"You did it!" The excitement on Tyler's face mirrored her own.

Amaliya spun around to face him. "I can't believe I didn't fall."

"I told you I'd have you doing a double axel before the week was out," Gordon said. "Now, do it again. Remember, not too much knee bend. Let your speed and strength carry you through the jump."

The oddity that he would repeat the instruction after a success struck her. Gordon wasn't checking off boxes for the skills she needed to learn. He was making sure she mastered them.

"Should I have Tyler do it with me?"

"Not today. You need to worry about you for a bit longer before we add Tyler into the mix."

Five more attempts, three of which she landed.

"I guess I still have to work on consistency."

"It'll come," Gordon said. "I'll film you tomorrow so we can review film tomorrow night."

"Sounds good," Amaliya said.

"When are you interviewing the dance instructor?" Tyler asked. "I thought that was supposed to happen Monday."

"Today. I asked to meet her at your house," Gordon said. "I'm going to move a few more things into my room."

"I think he's afraid if he doesn't finish moving in soon, we'll convince Eleanor to bake cookies for us."

"No, but I may get her to make me some," Gordon said. "You two go cool down. We meet the dance instructor in half an hour."

Tyler took Amaliya's hand and led her around the rink. "Looks like we're having company for dinner."

"With Eleanor and Gordon both living at the house, it's almost like having parents watching over us."

Tyler lowered his voice. "Are you sure Miles and Linda and your parents don't know we're dating?"

"Yeah. Why?"

"Just wondering if they offered to let Gordon stay at your house to give us an extra chaperone."

"I wouldn't put it past any of them. They may not know we're dating, but they aren't stupid," Amaliya said. "They have a good idea how I feel about you."

"How do you feel about me?"

Amaliya looked up, surprised by the raw vulnerability visible on his face. "You're the best thing that's ever happened to me."

Tyler's expression changed, softened somehow. "I feel the same way about you."

Amaliya's throat clogged with her rising emotions. They circled the rink once in silence.

Gordon left the ice, and Tyler spoke again. "I really think we need to come clean with everyone, especially our parents and the Donnellys."

"I don't know . . ."

"What are you afraid of?" Tyler asked. "We're both adults, and we aren't doing anything wrong. Don't you want to share what we have with the people who are important to us?"

"Everything has changed so fast," Amaliya said, grasping for how to explain her hesitation. "We're finally in a good situation. I don't want to do anything to upset the balance."

"Are you embarrassed to tell people we're dating?"

"Of course not. I . . ." Love you? Amaliya couldn't believe those words had almost spilled out of her. It couldn't be true. She was only eighteen. "Of course not," she repeated.

"Then help me understand why," Tyler said. "I hate not being honest with my folks."

"I don't like hiding things either, but the Donnellys aren't going to keep anything from my parents. And my parents have a lot going on right now. What if they object to us living here by ourselves?"

"We have live-in chaperones, remember?"

Amaliya tried to visualize the conversation with her parents. They liked Tyler, but did they trust him to live so close, especially since they'd only met him twice?

"Wouldn't you rather they find out from us than hear about our relationship from Eleanor or Gordon?" Tyler asked.

"I guess so."

"When did the Donnellys say they're coming to visit?"

"They haven't said anything about a date, but I have to think it'll be in the next couple weeks," Amaliya said. "I still haven't heard if my dad is going to come down with them or not."

"I doubt we'll see my parents until we compete next, but I plan to talk to them every weekend, and Carolyn calls me at least every week or two." Tyler reversed direction and stopped in front of her. He took both of her hands. "Please, Amaliya. I don't want to keep secrets, not from our families and not from each other."

Amaliya tried to imagine the worst-case scenario of telling Linda and Miles and her parents the truth, but when she weighed it against hiding it from them, the scales tipped in Tyler's favor.

"This is important to me," Tyler said.

"Maybe it's time we both make some calls."

"Yeah?"

Amaliya tugged his hand to bring him closer. She reached up and kissed him. "Yeah."

Tyler answered the door. A petite woman in her early forties stood on the doorstep, her blonde hair pulled back in a tight bun, her posture perfect.

"I'm looking for Mr. Alexander," she said in a thick French accent.

"You must be Mrs. Solis." Tyler offered his hand. "I'm Tyler Linden."

"Madam Solis," she corrected.

"Please, come in." Tyler escorted her inside and started down the hall. "Gordon is in the dance studio."

"Let's see this studio of yours."

Tyler led the way and made the introductions. "Amaliya, Gordon, this is Madam Solis."

"I appreciate your coming to meet with us here." Gordon offered his hand.

"Of course." She shook it but turned away before Amaliya could offer a similar greeting.

"My skaters have very tight schedules, so we hoped you would be able to teach them here once or twice a week."

Madam Solis turned around, taking in the details of the space. Her gaze landed on the framed photograph of Amaliya's mom. "This is nice. We might be able to work something out, but I would have to charge for my travel time. My studio is fifteen minutes away, twice that if I'm traveling during rush hour."

"We would prefer to have you work with them between their practice sessions. Twelve thirty on Tuesdays and Thursdays would be the ideal," Gordon said.

Madam Solis's gaze again landed on the photo on the wall. She glanced back at Amaliya. "This must be your studio."

"Yes."

"Katerina Petrova. That's an interesting choice." A hint of disdain accompanied the words.

"Why is that?"

"I danced with her many years ago," Madam Solis said. "I always thought she was overrated."

Amaliya stiffened, and Tyler's hand instinctively went to Amaliya's back. Clearly, Gordon hadn't mentioned Amaliya's heritage.

"If you'll excuse me." Amaliya took a step back. "It was nice to meet you, Madam Solis."

"Is she always this temperamental?" Madam Solis asked as soon as Amaliya left the room.

"Well, thank you for coming out to meet with us." Gordon took Madam Solis by the arm and guided her out of the studio.

Tyler followed.

The dance instructor held up a piece of paper. "Don't you want my fee schedule?"

"That won't be necessary." He escorted her down the hall and opened the door.

"I don't understand." She straightened and lifted her chin. "You asked me to help you."

"I did, but I didn't expect you to insult my skater's mother while standing in her studio."

"Her mother?"

"That's right. This house belongs to Katerina Marcell, also known as Katerina Petrova."

"I . . ."

Gordon nudged her out the door. "Have a nice day."

Chapter
THIRTY-EIGHT

"Amaliya." Tyler caught up to her in the living room. "I'm sorry."

She shook her head. "It's okay. Everyone is entitled to their opinion."

"Yes, but most people would have the good sense to not share it about someone while standing in that person's home."

"True, but she obviously didn't know Katerina Petrova is my mother."

Gordon walked in. "Well, we won't be using her for dance lessons."

"I'm sorry, Gordon," Amaliya said. "I shouldn't have just walked out like that."

"Why not? I would have." Gordon sat on the couch and motioned for them to join him. "I'm not sure you two would have wanted to pay her fees anyway."

Tyler was all for anything they could do to keep their costs down. He and Amaliya sat on the loveseat across from Gordon.

"What do we do now?" Tyler asked. "How important is it for us to have a dance instructor?"

"It can help with your artistic scores if you incorporate dance with the rest of your training," Gordon said.

"What if we work on our own?" Amaliya asked. "We have the studio with mirrors. If you really want, we could use my dad's video camera to film ourselves."

"I don't think we need film for anything off the ice," Gordon said. "Amaliya, can you handle working here?"

Amaliya tensed, and Tyler instinctively put his hand on hers.

"I don't know what it is about the studio that is hard for you," Gordon said.

"I stopped dancing after my mom's accident. It's hard being in there without her," Amaliya said.

"From what I understand, she'll be back here again in a few months. Until then, would you prefer to work somewhere else?"

Amaliya shook her head. "No, I'd rather work here."

"Okay. I want you to start with the dance elements for your short program. We'll put the rest of the pieces together tomorrow night when we watch film." He pointed at their joined hands. "This isn't going to cause problems with you two down the road, is it?"

"What?"

"You two. Together."

"No," Tyler said.

"Good. I've seen too many pairs teams break up because a relationship failed." Gordon stood. "You have to stay in tune for success. That's true both on and off the ice."

"Speaking from experience?" Tyler asked.

A flash of grief appeared on Gordon's face. "I certainly am."

Amaliya picked up the phone beside her bed and dialed the Donnellys' number. A clash of emotions swirled within her. Excitement to share her latest news about today's practice, fear that they would disapprove of her living situation when they learned of her feelings for Tyler, hurt and anger after the incident with the dance instructor.

The phone rang twice before Linda's voice came on the line.

"Aunt Linda, it's Amaliya."

"So good to hear from you. How was your first week with Gordon?"

"It isn't over yet, but it feels like we've put in three weeks' worth of work over the past few days."

"You knew he would work you hard."

"We did, and it's already paying off." A grin spread across her face. "I landed my double axel today."

"You did? That's fantastic!" Her voice faded as she spoke again. "Miles, Amaliya did a double axel."

Within seconds, a click came over the line, followed by Miles's voice. "Congratulations!"

"Thanks. I can't believe Gordon taught me to do it in four days."

"That's the difference a good coach can make," Miles said.

"You're right. Skating for Gordon is so different from when we were with Scarlett." Amaliya twirled the phone cord around her finger. "He's already taught me so much."

"How is Tyler doing?" Linda asked.

"He's doing well, but he's actually one of the reasons I'm calling." She freed her finger from the cord only to twist it up again. "I hope you're okay with this, but Tyler and I started dating."

"I was afraid of that," Miles said.

"I have to say, I thought this might happen," Linda added.

Amaliya's stomach clenched. "I hope you can be happy for us. I really care about him."

"It's not that we aren't happy for you, but it is a bit unsettling that the two of you are living in the same house," Linda said.

Amaliya suspected Linda's concerns would mirror her parents'. "We might be at the same address, but it's hardly the same house."

"Close enough," Miles said. "I have to run and help a neighbor with his car. I'll let you girls chat, but you tell Tyler he'd better stay on his side of the house."

"I will."

As soon as Miles hung up, Linda said, "Is everything else going okay?"

"Mostly. Tyler loves using Dad's gym, and Gordon and I did some work in the dance studio when I was working on my double axel."

"It's hard being back there without your mom, isn't it?" Linda asked.

"Yeah." The word escaped on a sigh. "Gordon interviewed a dance instructor today, Madam Solis."

"Claudette Solis?"

"I don't know. We didn't get that far. She saw the picture of Mama on the wall and said she thought Katerina Petrova was overrated."

"That was jealousy talking."

"Why would she be jealous of Mama?"

"Because when your parents first moved to DC, your mom joined the Washington Ballet for a couple years," Linda said. "She beat Claudette out for the lead in several productions."

"That explains a lot."

"You should ask your mom if she has any suggestions for another instructor."

"I don't know. Gordon said if I'm willing to work here at home, we might be able to do without one, but it's hard imagining dancing again no matter where I am."

"Talk to your mom. She's been part of your dancing career your whole life. Don't shut her out just because she can't dance right now."

"You're right. Thanks, Aunt Linda."

As soon as they said goodbye, Amaliya called her parents. Her mom answered.

"*Privyet*, Mama." Amaliya said, automatically greeting her mother in Russian.

"How are you?" Katerina asked, also speaking in her native tongue. "How is your new coach?"

"Good. Tough." Amaliya smiled. "He reminds me a little of you."

"Ah, demanding."

"Something like that. How are you doing?"

"I made it a few yards with my walker today."

The enthusiasm in her mother's voice contrasted with the stark reality. Katerina Petrova had once been the envy of other dancers. Now she was celebrating taking a few steps. Amaliya tried to focus on the positive. At least her mother could walk, kind of. "I'm glad you're making progress."

"One step at a time," she said. "Tell me how things are in Virginia. Is Tyler all settled into the apartment?"

"Yes, but he's one of the reasons I'm calling." Amaliya gathered her courage. "I know I should have said something before we moved down here, but Tyler and I started dating a couple weeks ago."

The harsh consonants of Russian were instantly replaced with her mother's accented French, a sure sign she wanted to share the information with her father. "You and Tyler are dating?"

"Yes, we . . ." That was as far as she got before her father's voice came over the line.

"What is this about you dating your partner?" Robert demanded. Unlike her conversation with Miles and Linda, his tone carried accusation rather than understanding. "He's too old for you."

"He's only three years older than me."

"You're barely out of high school."

"Yes, and Tyler didn't even ask me out until the week of graduation." Amaliya twisted the phone cord around her finger again. "How is your therapy going?"

"Did Miles know about this?"

So much for changing the subject. "I just told him and Linda about it a few minutes ago. They like Tyler."

"They're not your parents."

She tugged her finger free of the phone cord. "Papa, give him a chance. He's a good man."

"I don't like this. I don't like this at all."

Unaccustomed to hearing disapproval in her father's voice, especially when addressing her, she gathered her courage. "Papa, you need to trust me. Besides, before you know it, you'll be back home and you'll see for yourself what a great guy Tyler is."

"Yes, but until then—"

"Until then, Tyler will be a perfect gentleman, just like he always has been."

"Has Gordon already moved in?"

"He's brought a few things over."

"Good. The sooner he moves in, the better."

Some of the tension in Amaliya's shoulders eased. She chatted with her dad for a minute about his progress and his upcoming release date from the rehab center. Though neither of her parents was thrilled with her relationship with Tyler, at least they calmed down before she hung up.

Restless, she crossed to her closet and opened it wide. Her fingers brushed against the numerous ballet skirts that hung inside.

She glanced at the clock. Nine o'clock. Tyler had already gone to his apartment with the intent of calling his parents, and surely, Eleanor and Gordon would already be in their rooms.

Amaliya stood on the edge of the possibilities for a full minute before she retrieved a leotard and skirt from her closet and changed her clothes.

Moving quietly, she padded downstairs. The studio doors hung open, and she looked up at the young version of her mother.

With some effort, Amaliya forced herself to walk inside. She could do this. She sat on the floor and laced up her ballet slippers. Then she stood and stretched.

Another glance at her mother's photo pushed her to select *Swan Lake* from the collection of music in the corner. She set the record on the record player and put the needle in place. Then she closed her eyes and imagined her mother was beside her as she had been before the accident. She let the music sweep over her, and her body began to move.

Tyler made it only as far as the living room before he heard the music. *Swan Lake.*

He followed the sound, slowing when he reached the open doors of the studio. Inside, a vision of elegance and beauty danced to the music.

Tyler's heart stumbled. He had recognized Amaliya's background in dance from the first time he'd seen her, but this . . . He hadn't expected this.

She leapt into the air, landing on one foot as though the movement had taken no effort. A pirouette, followed by another. Her arms extended, and she spun again, but this time her gaze met his. She stopped abruptly.

"I'm sorry. I didn't mean to interrupt. I heard the music and . . ." Tyler stepped forward. "Wow. I had no idea you were this incredible."

"It's been a long time."

Tyler read between the lines. "Dance is part of who you are. I'm sure your mom doesn't want you to lose it, even if she can't join you right now."

"The last conversation we had before the accident was about me moving to San Francisco to join the San Francisco Ballet."

"You were moving to California?"

"I wanted to. I had the offer, but since I wasn't quite eighteen yet, I couldn't take it without my parents' permission." Amaliya crossed to the record player and lifted the needle. "My mom wanted me to wait until after I graduated, and my dad agreed with my mom."

"You could have gone anyway. You must have been close to your eighteenth birthday."

"I was, but I didn't want to disobey them." Amaliya turned back to face him, her churning emotions evident in her expression. "After the accident, they offered to let me go since we couldn't be together."

"But you didn't."

"No, I didn't," she said softly.

"What changed now?"

"I don't know. I guess it was a lot of things. Our talk with Gordon, my talk with Linda, my talk with my mom." Amaliya shrugged. "I was dreading studying ballet under someone new. If I can learn to dance again here at home, maybe I won't have to."

"I think you already have the learning part down. In a few months, maybe your mom can be our dance instructor."

"That would be the best possible scenario."

Tyler took her hand. "How did your talk go with the Donnellys and your parents?"

"Miles and Linda were concerned, but I think they know you well enough to trust us."

"How about your parents?"

"I think they need time to get to know you better."

"I had a feeling that might be the case," Tyler said, though he couldn't deny his disappointment. "Your dad strikes me as the protective type."

"He is. What did your parents say?"

"I think they were a mix between your parents and the Donnellys. They were pretty excited about Gordon moving in with us."

"So were my parents. Maybe they did invite him to live here to keep an eye on us."

Gordon appeared in the doorway. "You'd better believe it."

"Gordon." Tyler dropped Amaliya's hand and turned. "I didn't realize you were still up."

"I had some unpacking to do," he said.

"We don't start our jobs until next week. Let us know if you need any help moving stuff in this weekend."

"I may take you up on that." Gordon checked his watch. "What are you two doing in here this time of night?"

"I was talking to my new dance instructor," Tyler said.

"Is that so?" Gordon folded his arms. "Let me see what you've got."

Tyler moved to the record player. "Go on. Show him what I saw a minute ago."

"I was just messing around."

"Please?" Tyler said.

"Okay. Put on the music." Amaliya closed her eyes and waited for the music to start. Then she pushed onto her toes and began.

Tyler backed up to give her room, again amazed by her elegance. She danced for only a few minutes, but each movement flowed beautifully into the next and demonstrated potential beyond what Tyler had imagined.

When she stopped, she looked from Tyler to Gordon.

"Wow. You are good," Gordon said.

"Thanks."

"And I agree with you, Tyler. Amaliya will make a fine dance instructor for you."

"So you aren't going to look for someone else?" Amaliya asked.

"No reason to," Gordon said. "Beth is planning to come down next week to work with you on your long program. She'll want to see what you can do before she finishes it."

"I'd like the chance to help her," Amaliya said.

"I'll give her a call and let her know what she has to work with." Gordon pointed at the doorway. "As for you two, it's time for bed."

"I guess turning eighteen didn't get me out of my curfew," Amaliya said.

Gordon shook his head. "Not at all."

Chapter THIRTY-NINE

AMALIYA NIBBLED ON A CELERY stick Eleanor had packed for her snack. "I really miss when Eleanor sent cookies as my dessert." Amaliya held up the celery. "This just isn't the same."

"Hey, at least she sent us food. I don't think I'd be able to last until dinner after that practice."

"What do you want to bet Gordon views all of the film he took today by the time we get home?"

"I'm not taking that bet." Tyler finished off his banana. "Are you ready to go to work?"

"I think so."

"Come on." Tyler gathered their trash and threw it away before heading to the skating office.

Amaliya's stomach jumped with nerves. Their first day of teaching classes. She didn't have a clue what she was supposed to do.

Bruce looked up. "Oh good. You're here. I was about to come looking for you."

"We're here," Tyler said. "What do you need us to do?"

"You'll each have two classes. Our advanced classes will be first." He handed each of them a student roster and a skills sheet. "Tyler, I have you with the top group, and, Amaliya, you'll work with the intermediate-level kids. The objective is to teach the kids all of the skills on that list so they can advance to the next level."

"What about the second hour?" Tyler asked.

"Those are both beginner classes. One is for beginning figure skating. Amaliya, you'll have that one." Bruce sorted through some papers on his desk and came up with two more class rosters. "This one is yours."

"And for me?" Tyler asked.

"You'll have the beginning hockey skaters." He offered Tyler the other roster.

"Um, maybe Amaliya and I should switch those second classes," Tyler said. "I've never played hockey before."

"I doubt Amaliya has either. Besides, these kids and their parents will expect to see a male teacher for hockey," Bruce said. "This is teaching them how to skate, not how to play the game."

"Yeah, but I've never even worn a pair of hockey skates," Tyler said.

"And Amaliya has?"

"Actually, yes," Amaliya said. "My dad was a hockey player, so I've done my fair share of time on the ice with a hockey stick."

"Okay, if you're sure want to take this on."

"I'm sure," Amaliya said. "Do you mind if I borrow your phone though? It will be easier to teach them if I can have someone bring me my hockey skates from home."

"You have your own hockey skates?"

"I do."

"Okay. Sounds like you're the right person for the job," Bruce said. "Fair warning though. You may get some parent complaints the first day."

"I can handle it if you can."

Bruce lifted the phone off the cradle and handed it to her.

"Thanks." Amaliya dialed her home number. Eleanor picked up a moment later. "Eleanor, it's Amaliya. Can you do me a big favor?"

"Of course. What do you need?"

"Could you please bring me my hockey skates? They're on the floor in my closet."

"What do you need your hockey skates for?"

"I'll explain later. Oh, and can you grab me one of my dad's jerseys while you're at it?"

"I can do that. How soon do you need them?"

"In about forty-five minutes."

"Okay. I'll take care of it."

"Thanks." Amaliya hung up the phone. "I'm all set."

"Good luck, you two." Bruce pointed at the benches a short distance away. "The classes will meet over there. Go on over now so you can meet your students."

"Okay." Amaliya and Tyler approached the group of kids and parents clustered together.

"Who's here for skating lessons?" Tyler asked.

Several hands shot into the air.

"When I call your name, line up over here." Tyler called out his students' names, and they joined him by the entrance to the rink.

Amaliya followed suit. Seven girls ranging in age from six to ten.

"Let's go warm up, and then we'll get started." Amaliya led them around the rink, moving to the middle so she could evaluate their skill level. When they reached their starting point, she moved them to an open space on the ice, and they began working on spins.

The forty-five minutes flew by, and before she knew it, she was saying goodbye to her new friends as she relinquished them back to their parents.

Tyler skated to her. "How was your group?"

"Good. They are so eager to learn," Amaliya said. "How about yours?"

"I have four future Olympians in my class."

"Wow. That's promising." Her eyes narrowed. "You had five kids in your class."

"Yeah, and the funny thing is, the only one who didn't declare herself a future Olympian is the most talented of the bunch."

"Sounds like you're going to have fun."

"Speaking of fun." Tyler pointed at the side where Eleanor stood holding Amaliya's hockey skates, hockey stick, and jersey.

"I'd better change my skates." Amaliya crossed to Eleanor. "Thank you so much for bringing these for me."

"You're welcome. I didn't know if you needed your stick, but I grabbed it just in case."

"This is great. Thank you."

Eleanor handed the hockey gear to Amaliya. "You looked good out there."

"Thanks. It was fun."

"That's what your mom used to say when she was teaching." Eleanor gave Amaliya's arm a squeeze. "I'll see you at home."

Amaliya found an empty bench and changed her skates. After she stored her figure skates in the office, she slipped her dad's jersey over her head and walked over to where Tyler stood calling out names.

When he finished, Amaliya stepped forward. "Okay, I'm going to be teaching our future hockey players." Amaliya called out the first name but was interrupted before she got any further.

"You're teaching the hockey kids?" one of the kids asked. "You're a girl."

"I am a girl, but I'm also really good at hockey." Amaliya called out the next three names.

A dad interrupted this time. "We didn't sign Timmy up to learn how to skate from a girl."

"I promise you by the time he's done with these classes, he'll be ready for one of these." Amaliya held up her stick. She quickly read out the last two names. "Okay, boys. Let's hit the ice."

She led the way, these students much more reluctant to follow her. Two grabbed onto the wall as they slipped and tried to keep themselves upright.

Amaliya gathered them in the corner of the rink where she was away from the parents but also close to the wall so the kids could hold on to it.

"How many of you have skated before?"

Three hands went up.

"Do you really know how to play hockey?" one boy asked.

"I do." Amaliya moved closer and lowered her voice. "Want to know a secret?"

Everyone nodded.

"My dad was a great hockey player." She tugged on her shirt. "This was one of his jerseys when he played for the Washington Capitals."

"Your dad played for the Capitals?" a boy of about seven asked.

"He did, and then when he retired, he became the coach," Amaliya said. "So even though I might not look like a hockey player, I know a lot about hockey. Now, let's get started. Everyone keep your ankles straight." Amaliya gave them basic instructions, guiding them through the most rudimentary skills. When they finished, she said, "Okay, I'll see you all on Wednesday."

The boys stumbled their way off the ice, and Amaliya followed. She bit back a grin when several of the boys started raving about how her dad played for the Capitals.

She waited for Tyler to finish with his class before she joined him on his side of the rink.

"How did it go?" Tyler asked.

"I used my dad's fame shamelessly with the kids, and now I'm a hero."

"Good job."

"Thanks." Amaliya took his hand. "Ready to go home?"

"Yes. More than ready."

Chapter
FORTY

Amaliya opened the door, and her smile was instant. "Aunt Linda, Uncle Miles. What are you doing here?" She hugged each of them in turn. "I thought you were Beth."

"She's getting something out of the car," Linda said. "We thought we would come down and surprise you."

"Well, it worked. Is Papa here too?"

"I'm afraid not. He had a little setback in physical therapy this week, and the doctor said a long drive wouldn't be good for him."

"That's too bad." Amaliya waved them inside as Beth approached carrying a portfolio case. "Beth, thank you so much for coming."

"It's my pleasure." She lifted her case. "Gordon called and asked for some changes, but I think you'll like what I have planned."

"I'm sure it will be wonderful," Amaliya said. "Tyler and I love our new short program."

"I can't wait to see it." Beth followed Amaliya inside.

Tyler approached and greeted everyone. "This is an unexpected surprise."

"Linda and I didn't have anything going on for the next week. We thought we would come down and take care of a few things here at the house for Amaliya's folks."

"Will you be able to come back down for our competition?" Amaliya asked.

"That's the plan," Miles said. "Your dad should be able to travel by then too."

"That would be great." Amaliya's gaze fell on the luggage Miles and Linda had carried in, and realization dawned. With Eleanor and Gordon now living in the main house, they only had one guest room remaining.

"Beth, let me show you to your room," Amaliya said.

"I can show her," Miles said.

"It's the second door on the right," Amaliya said. "Eleanor took the first guest suite."

Miles started up the stairs with Beth behind him. Linda laid her hand on Amaliya's arm. "I hope you don't mind it if Miles and I stay in your parents' room."

"That's fine. I have no idea what condition it's in. I haven't been in there since I've been back."

"Why not?"

"I don't know. It's just weird with them not being here."

"I can understand that, but I'm sure they don't want you living any differently now than when they were here."

"You're right."

Tyler picked up the remaining suitcases. "Upstairs?"

"Upstairs." Amaliya led the way to the double doors that had remained closed since before she'd left home. She opened them wide and stepped inside. It looked the same. The white comforter and blue throw pillows on the king-sized bed, the trunk at the foot of the bed, a blue-and-white afghan lying across it. The typical pile of clothes on the chair by her dad's side was missing, as was the usual clutter on her mom's bedside table.

The room smelled different, the scents that were uniquely her parents' now faded. Instead, the scent of lemon furniture polish lingered, a sign that Eleanor regularly cleaned in here.

"It looks like it always did when we came back from vacation," Amaliya said to no one in particular.

"What do you mean?" Tyler asked.

"Eleanor always came into our rooms when we traveled and cleaned up the clutter."

Tyler set the suitcases down and put one hand on Amaliya's back, a silent show of understanding.

Amaliya's gaze landed on the framed photographs on her parents' bedside tables. Even after more than twenty years of marriage, they kept each other's pictures by their side of the bed.

Amaliya picked up her father's photo. "I've always loved this picture."

"Why don't you take these into your room?" Linda held up the photo of her mom. "You should keep them until your parents move back home."

Though part of her didn't want to change anything, Amaliya nodded.

Tyler gave Amaliya's shoulder a squeeze.

Emotions rose within her. "I'd better get some lunch before we have to leave." Amaliya took the photo from Linda and clutched both pictures to her chest. "I'll let you settle in."

Amaliya left her parents' room and walked into her own. She set the two pictures on her own bedside table, a new wave of emotions crashing over her.

Her parents were going to be okay, but would they fully recover? Would things ever be the same as they had been before?

Knuckles sounded against her door. She looked up at where Tyler stood outside her room.

"Are you okay?" he asked.

Amaliya didn't think. She crossed the room and threw her arms around him, tears welling up in her eyes.

"Hey, what's wrong?" Tyler pulled her close, and his hand stroked up and down her back.

She swallowed the wave of emotions. "I'm sorry. I don't know what came over me."

"It can't be easy being away from your parents for so long."

"That's part of it." She leaned back and lifted her eyes to meet his. "I can't help but wonder what they'll be like when they come home. Will Papa be able to coach? Will Mama be able to dance? Will we have to move if Papa has to retire early?"

"Trust that everything will work out." He kissed her forehead. "I'm here for you whenever you need me."

"I know. That's one of the things I love about you."

Surprise and an unexpected intensity flashed in his eyes. As though taking an emotional step back, he nodded toward the stairs. "We should get ready for practice."

"Yeah, we should."

The surprise Tyler had experienced when he'd seen Amaliya dance the first time paled in comparison to witnessing her work on their choreography with Beth. For the past three days, they had worked at practice, on the ice, even at the dinner table to create their long program. It would undoubtedly undergo some changes as he and Amaliya increased the level of difficulty they were capable of, but he couldn't have asked for something more suited to who he and Amaliya had become as skaters and as a couple.

Amaliya looked up from their notes that were currently spread out on the table. "Do you think we have enough difficulty in this routine to qualify for nationals?"

"I think so." Tyler took a bite of an apple and leaned against the kitchen counter. "Other than increasing the difficulty of our jumps, the skills aren't much different from the program Carolyn and I did when we competed in the world championships."

"No offense to your sister, but I think you and Amaliya have a stronger artistic element," Gordon said.

"I would hope so with all the hours we've put into this," Beth said.

Tyler let that truth seep in. The choreography was stronger than what he had created with his sister, but had Amaliya caught up to Carolyn in skill level?

"You and Carolyn were a beautiful pair," Gordon said, "but you and Amaliya have a spark that is going to captivate."

Tyler stepped behind Amaliya and put his hand on her shoulder. The simple connection sent that spark Gordon had mentioned coursing through him. "Carolyn said when God closes a door, He opens a window. Never in a million years did I think things could be better than they were before."

"You and Carolyn had a real shot at winning nationals last year," Gordon said. "You and Amaliya are every bit as capable."

"Assuming we can qualify to compete."

"You'll qualify," Gordon said. "Between now and October, we'll focus on your routines and your figures. You'll go through your programs every day until you can do them in your sleep."

"You'll certainly have the choreography down if you practice it that often," Beth said.

"That's not going to be easy when we're sharing the ice with so many skaters," Tyler said.

"That's another thing."

"What?"

"Your ice time is now going to be from seven until eleven thirty every morning and one to three thirty every afternoon."

"Seven hours of ice time every day?"

"If you want to be the best, we have to put in the time," Gordon said. "We'll alternate working in the studio and the weight room on Mondays, Wednesdays, and Fridays."

"That's a lot of hours, especially with us working."

"Do you want to be the best?" Gordon asked.

Tyler stiffened. "You know I do."

"Good. I already talked to Bruce about changing your hours so you'll only work Tuesdays, Thursdays, and Saturdays."

"He was okay with that?" Amaliya asked.

"Turns out you two are his most requested teachers," Gordon said. "He's adding another class for each of you on Tuesdays and Thursdays, but you'll only have five minutes in between classes instead of fifteen."

"So we're really only staying an extra half hour each day," Tyler said.

"Exactly."

"And on Saturdays?" Amaliya asked.

"Same thing. You'll both teach three classes instead of two," Gordon said. "He's agreed to pay by the class instead of by the hour, so you won't take much of a pay cut."

"Okay," Tyler said. "You're the boss."

"I love it when you see things my way." Gordon turned his attention back to choreography. "Now, about the first lift. I want to start out with your best move to get the crowd involved."

"Which one did you have in mind?" Tyler asked.

"The one you created together."

Chapter
FORTY-ONE

TYLER CARRIED A PLATE OF banana bread from the kitchen toward the office. How Eleanor had time to keep up with the house and make sure everyone had everything they needed was beyond him, but he loved having her constant support as well as her baked goods.

He knocked on the office door to get Gordon's attention. "Gordon?"

Gordon looked up from the desk. "Do you need something?"

"Eleanor thought you might want a snack."

"That woman thinks of everything." Gordon stood and took the offering. "Come in and close the door. I wanted to talk to you."

Uneasy, Tyler did as he'd asked. "Is something wrong?"

"Not wrong. Unexpected." Gordon handed Tyler a piece of paper. "Here's the list of skaters coming to sectionals."

Tyler scanned the list. His heart sank when he reached the third entry. "Kimball and Park. They're always tough to beat."

"Keep reading."

Tyler kept reading. Four more lines down, he identified the source of Gordon's concern. "Nicole Walker and Andrew McCallister." Tyler lowered the paper. Gordon's former skaters, the top duo in pairs figure skating in the country. "I thought they had moved to Minnesota."

"Apparently not. Or if they did, they registered for competition in this region."

"When was the last time you saw them?" Tyler asked.

"Right after the Olympics."

Tyler's eyes widened. "You haven't seen them at all since then?"

"Haven't seen, haven't communicated." Gordon waved his hand as though he could brush away the past with a flick of the wrist. "This isn't about me. It's about you and Amaliya. I didn't expect the field to be so deep at this one."

"We'll have to compete against them eventually," Tyler said.

"Yes, but this will be Amaliya's first time on the big stage," Gordon said. "With Nicole and Andrew competing in your sectionals, we have six teams in the competition who have advanced to finals before."

"Which means we have to beat at least two of them to move forward."

"I'm afraid so."

"I never thought it would be easy . . ." Tyler trailed off, his eyes on the schedule. "I didn't realize the women's competition would be right before pairs."

"Why does that matter?" Gordon asked. "You aren't worried about seeing your old coach, are you?"

"No, but I know Amaliya won't be thrilled to see the people we used to train with. Seeing them is more likely to throw her off than seeing the other pairs," Tyler said.

"You were successful the last time you competed. How did you help her manage her nerves?"

"We didn't watch any of our competition so we could stay focused on our routines and what we had to do."

"I've often used a similar approach," Gordon said. "Do you and Amaliya have Walkmans with headphones?"

"Yeah. Why?"

"Bring them. That will help you block out the noise of the crowd while you wait."

"That's a good idea." Tyler handed the information sheet back to Gordon. "Should we tell Amaliya about all of this?"

"I'll leave that up to you. Singles will be completed before we get there, so we might not see your old training partners at the arena."

"If there is media coverage, Marie will be around," Tyler said. "She likes to be seen."

"Is there some sort of history with Marie that I should know about?"

"Not really. I dated her for a while before I started dating Amaliya."

"I'll bet that didn't go over well."

"Actually, Marie doesn't know Amaliya and I are together," Tyler said. "We only started dating right before we moved down here, and we kept it pretty low-key."

"Do Marie and Amaliya get along?"

"Marie thinks Amaliya is an amateur and not worthy of my time."

"Well, if she comes to the pairs event, she'll find out how wrong she is."

"As long as Amaliya knows what she's capable of, it doesn't matter what Marie thinks."

"Very true."

"I'd better go talk to her." Tyler reached for the doorknob. "Are you going to be okay seeing your old skaters again?"

"I'll be fine." Gordon looked down at the names again. "Nicole and Andrew aren't my skaters anymore. They're the competition."

Amaliya curled up on the couch and leaned her head back against the cushions. Saturday night and she didn't have any place to be. Miles and Linda had driven back to Connecticut a few days ago after a week-long visit. Beth had accompanied them, her work on Tyler and Amaliya's choreography done for the moment. She had agreed to work with them again next year when they were ready to create something new for the Olympic trials and the Olympics.

Amaliya wasn't sure what to think about everyone's unwavering confidence that she and Tyler would compete in the Olympics, but she wanted to believe they were right.

Within a few months, she and Tyler would compete in the U.S. Pairs Final and attempt to qualify for nationals, a feat she still didn't understand the full magnitude of. Her weekly calls to her parents gave her hope that her father would be able to attend the competition, but her heart ached a bit at the thought that her mother's slow recovery would likely keep her in Connecticut through October.

At least her parents had mellowed a bit about their concerns over Tyler's living in the apartment over the garage. She looked forward to the time when they would get to know him in person.

Tyler walked into the living room. "You look comfortable."

"It's so nice to sit down and know I don't have to be anywhere for hours and hours."

Tyler stepped behind the couch and massaged her shoulders. Amaliya tipped her head forward. "That feels so good."

"It's supposed to." He rubbed her shoulders for a moment longer before he circled the couch and sat beside her.

"Did you want to watch a movie?" Amaliya asked.

"Sure, but I wanted to talk to you first."

"Is something wrong?"

"Not wrong, just something I thought you should know." Tyler put his hand on her knee. "The schedule came out for sectionals. Marie and Becky will be competing in the session before us."

"Great." Amaliya let her head fall back. "I was really looking forward to competing without having them around."

"I know. We might not even see them, but I didn't want you to go in unprepared."

"I appreciate it." Amaliya put her hand on his. "At least this time, I don't have to worry about Marie competing with me for your attention."

Tyler's eyebrows drew together. "You know, I never really thought about it before, but it kind of makes sense that she never warmed up to you."

"It was pretty obvious that I was invading her territory in one way or another."

"I think she knew I was interested in you from the first time she met you."

"I don't know how," Amaliya said. "The two of you went out a lot in those first few weeks that we were skating together."

"Yeah, probably more than we ever had before."

"She was staking out her territory."

Tyler stretched his arm out and drew her closer. "I don't think it worked out the way she planned."

"Hopefully, she won't come to the pairs competition," Amaliya said.

"Oh, one more thing. Gordon wants us to bring our Walkmans to the competition."

"Why?"

"We'll use them to block out what's going on while we wait to compete."

"This is the strangest sport. You go to compete against a bunch of people, but you deliberately don't watch your competition," Amaliya said. "Why is that?"

"It's so you stay focused on what you can control. We can't do anything about how well someone else does or if they're going to make a mistake," Tyler said. "By blocking them all out, we don't psych ourselves out by thinking we don't have a chance or that we've already won."

"I'm so new to this. I'll trust you and Gordon to guide me through this maze."

"A couple more months and we'll be on our way."

The familiar doubts surfaced. "What if we don't make it?"

"Then we'll try again next year. Every competition is another chance to improve, and with these new routines, we're going to be serious competitors in any competition, no matter who else is in the rink."

The way he said it raised a red flag. "Who else is going to be in the rink?"

"What do you mean?"

"Is there something else you aren't telling me?"

He glanced away as though debating how much to say.

"Tyler? Who else is going to be there?"

"Nicole Walker and Andrew McCallister."

Amaliya straightened and turned to face him. "Gordon's former skaters?"

"Yes."

"This can't be easy on him." Amaliya snuggled against Tyler again.

"It's not. He said he hasn't spoken to them since right after the Olympics."

"Why not?"

"I don't know, but I've heard rumors that they blamed their loss at the Olympics on Gordon not being there."

A wave of loyalty rose within her. "We should beat them just for talking about him like that."

Tyler grinned.

"What?"

"You were just sitting here worried about whether we would qualify for finals, but as soon as it's about someone else, your competitive streak kicks in."

"I guess I want to prove to everyone that you and Gordon made good decisions when you took a chance on me."

"Taking a chance on you was one of the best decisions ever." Tyler leaned forward and pressed his lips to hers.

Her stomach flipflopped, and her voice grew husky. "I can't begin to imagine what life would be like right now if I hadn't met you."

"I feel the same way."

Chapter
FORTY-TWO

KATERINA STARED OUT THE WINDOW and longed for the view from her home in Virginia. Somehow, the parking lot of the rehab facility simply didn't give her the same peaceful feeling that she had every time she looked out over the Potomac River.

"Do you think we'll ever get out of here?" she asked.

"A few more months," Robert said. "We can make it that long."

"If we don't get home until October or November, you'll miss the first month or two of games."

"I already talked to Capitals management. Miles has agreed to step in if we can't get back to Virginia before the season starts."

"He would do that? What about Linda? Would she stay in Connecticut?"

"Yes, but it would only be for a little while," Robert said. "If all goes well, we'll be back by the season opener."

"Or you could go home without me." Katerina said the words even though she couldn't imagine going through her physical therapy without Robert's encouragement. "You're getting released in a few days."

"I'm getting released, but I'm not going anywhere." Robert took her hand. "My job will still be there when we get home. For now, my only job is being here for you."

"But if you're here with me, you aren't in Virginia for Amaliya."

"She's in good hands," Robert said. "Besides, I don't want anyone at home to have to help me with my therapy. If I stay here, we can both keep getting better together."

"I really do love you."

"That's good because you're stuck with me forever." Robert pointed at the phone. "For now though, it's time to call and check on the kids."

"Who are we calling tonight? Gordon or Eleanor?"

"Gordon. He's got his finger on the pulse of what's going on."

"I'm sure he does."

Katerina reached for the phone. It rang as her fingers brushed against the receiver. She answered it. "Hello?"

"Mrs. Marcell, this is Tyler Linden. Is your husband available?"

"Yes, he is." Though curious about why Tyler would be calling Robert, she held out the phone. "It's for you."

Summer in Virginia. It was hot and humid and busy, but Tyler loved it. Runs and walks along the Potomac, an occasional Saturday afternoon visiting the sites in DC, movie nights at home, and date nights in Old Town Alexandria. And practice. Lots and lots of practice. At the center of it all was Amaliya.

Tyler hadn't known what to expect when he and Amaliya had started dating, but every day, his feelings for her deepened until he couldn't imagine life without her in it. She belonged in every aspect of his life, but oddly enough, she didn't dominate it the way Marie and previous girlfriends had.

If Tyler wanted a night to relax on his own, she was content to curl up with a book. If she wanted to go out with old friends, he always had the choice of whether to join her without any of the commonplace pressure of past relationships. And he loved the way Amaliya welcomed anyone and everyone who wanted to see their home.

His parents had already come to visit once, Gordon's daughter twice, and Linda and Miles three times. Amaliya's dad had tried to come down with the Donnellys, undoubtedly to check up on them, but the doctor had insisted he remain in Connecticut.

Their newest houseguests had arrived a week ago, this time in the form of his sister and brother-in-law. Carolyn had shadowed them for several days, joining in on their daily routines, but today, she and Dan had agreed to do the legwork for a gift Tyler had been planning for weeks. With practice and work behind him, Tyler showered and went in search of his family to make this intended present a reality.

He passed through the empty kitchen, the scent of pot roast hanging in the air. When he discovered the living room was also unoccupied, he continued into the hall. Voices carried from the dance studio.

Tyler walked inside, where Amaliya and Carolyn both stretched at the barre. "Looks like Carolyn does miss this."

"Maybe a little." Carolyn turned in a circle. "I still can't believe the setup you have here. This house is incredible."

"I've been very blessed," Amaliya said.

"Amaliya?" Eleanor called from down the hall.

"Yes?" Amaliya poked her head out the door.

"Can you set the table?"

"Coming."

"I can do it," Tyler offered.

"That's okay." Amaliya pushed up onto her toes and kissed his cheek. "Enjoy spending time with your sister while you can."

As soon as Amaliya disappeared, Carolyn lowered her voice and asked, "What would you have done if she'd taken you up on your offer?"

"I knew she'd tell me to stay with you." Tyler glanced behind him. "Where's Dan? Did he get everything?"

"Yeah. He's out front."

"I'll go help him bring the stuff in. Can you make sure Amaliya doesn't come back into the studio?"

"I can do that."

Tyler opened the front door. Dan stood outside beside two large packages wrapped in brown paper.

"Grab one of them," Dan said. "I'll get the other."

They carried the packages into the studio, and Tyler retrieved the hammer, nails, and step stool he had stashed in the office.

Five minutes later, Carolyn rushed back in. "She's coming."

"We're ready." Tyler adjusted one of the newly hung photographs on the wall and folded up the step stool. He stepped back and took a good look at their handiwork. On either side of the photograph of Amaliya's mother hung two similarly sized photographs. One was a photo of the great Robert Marcell on the ice, a hockey stick in his hand. The other was a photo his mom had taken of him and Amaliya at their first competition, Tyler's hands on Amaliya's waist and her arms lifted above her head as though she were a ballerina who had been transported onto the ice.

"Dinner's ready," Amaliya called out.

His heartbeat quickened, and eagerness rose within him. He opened his mouth to call her into the studio, but she appeared in the doorway before he could form the words.

"Didn't you hear me? I said—" Her eyes lifted to the wall, and tears welled in her eyes.

All his excitement drained from him. "I'm sorry. I thought . . ."

Amaliya took two steps forward, her gaze still locked on the new photographs.

Tyler crossed to her. "I can change it back."

"No, don't do that." She gave him a watery smile.

Tears of joy, not tears of pain. Relief poured through him.

"How did you . . . ?" Amaliya began. "When did you . . . ?"

"Dan and Carolyn helped me. This room is so special to you, I thought you'd like it if we had a picture of us in here." Tyler motioned to the photo of her father. "I didn't want to leave your dad out, so I called your parents to make sure they were okay with my plans. Your dad had the Capitals print a photo for us, and Dan picked it up for me."

"This is perfect. Thank you." Amaliya hugged him before turning to Dan and Carolyn. "Thank you all."

"We were happy to help," Dan said.

Carolyn took her husband's hand. "We'll see you in the kitchen."

As soon as they left, Amaliya studied the photos again. A tear spilled over.

"I was hoping you would like this, but I didn't expect tears," Tyler said.

Amaliya sniffled. "The day before my parents' accident, my mom told me that someday my photo would hang next to hers."

"I had no idea," Tyler said, his own throat clogging with emotion.

"I know." She clasped her hands around his waist. "No gift has ever been more perfect."

Tyler pulled her closer and pressed a kiss to the top of her head. His heart opened, and a warmth rushed in. Could he and Amaliya really be so in sync that they could understand each other's needs and wants without them being spoken? He couldn't deny he was still falling for her, and he hoped this connection between them would never end.

Amaliya fell. Again. Even though she had finally landed her double axel four months ago, she still couldn't seem to find any consistency. She had fallen four times already today and hadn't landed the jump once.

Tyler offered her a hand, and she let him pull her to a stand.

"What did I do that time?" Amaliya asked Gordon. "We compete in two days. What if I fall?"

"You're overthinking this," Gordon said. "You can do it, but you're doubting yourself. Chin up, blade even with the ice."

"Don't think about falling," Tyler added. "If it happens, it happens."

"And if I can't do the required elements, we can't qualify for nationals, even if we nail everything else."

"We still have a full year before we have to qualify for the nationals competition that counts."

"Yeah. Like that won't be any pressure."

"Positive thinking, remember?"

"That's right." Gordon moved back. "Let's go through that segment again. Start with the approach into the double axels."

Amaliya reached for Tyler's hand. She waited until they rounded the far side of the rink before she said, "I don't want to mess this up for you."

"What if I fall?" Tyler asked.

"You hardly ever fall."

"But I could." He stopped and waited for her to face him. "We're a team. Win or lose, perfect program or not, we're in this together."

Love, warm and sweet, seeped through her. She opened her mouth, the words aching to be spoken.

"Come on, you two," Gordon called. "Let's see it again."

"You ready?" Tyler asked.

Ready? With her heart lodged in her throat and three little words burning on her tongue? She loved him, but she had never dared tell him. She had come so close that day he had hung the photos of them and her dad in the studio, but she had been so emotional, she'd barely been able to speak.

"Amaliya?"

She swallowed hard.

"Remember, we're in this together." Tyler took the lead, and they fell into step together.

Amaliya concentrated on the many steps Gordon had taken her through when teaching her the jump. Ankle straight, knee bent, push off, rotation, blade even with the ice. She reversed her direction from backward to forward, launched herself into the air, and made the two and a half rotations. Her toe pick caught the ice as she landed. She stepped out of the jump, but she didn't fall.

"I'm sorry."

"Don't apologize." Tyler came to a stop. "You managed to stay up on that one."

"One more time," Gordon said. "A little more height and you'll have it."

Tyler took her hand and gave it a squeeze. The simple gesture sent a new wave of love through her, love and support. She could do this. The desire to succeed for herself faded, replaced by the need to do this for Tyler.

They executed the jumps again, this time both landing cleanly.

"You got it." Tyler grinned. "See. Positive thinking."

"Okay, let's go through the whole short program. We only have two more days left."

Two more days until they would try to qualify. Two more days until her father would see her skate in competition for the first time. Two more days and she had landed her double axel only one out of five times. Not exactly great odds for success.

Chapter
FORTY-THREE

TYLER TOOK ONLY A FEW steps inside the arena before the nerves surfaced. He was back. This competition would define whether he and Amaliya were part of the top echelon of pairs figure skating in the United States or whether they were wannabes.

"Wow." Amaliya turned toward the stands. "There are a lot of people here."

"The session before ours must have gone over." Gordon pointed at the hallway to their left. "The locker rooms are that way. Go change. I'll check you in."

"Okay." Tyler fell into step beside Amaliya. They reached the women's locker room. "I'll see you in a few minutes."

Amaliya nodded and disappeared inside. Tyler continued down the hall. He found a spot in the crowded locker room to change, then reemerged into the hall and leaned against the wall to wait for Amaliya. His gaze was still focused on the locker room door when his name was called.

"Tyler!" Marie repeated and hurried toward him. "I didn't realize you would be here."

"Hey, Marie. Did you just compete?"

"Yes." She beamed at him. "I'm in second place after the compulsories."

"Congrats. That's great."

"Thanks." Marie reached out and gave him a hug. "I've missed you."

Tyler returned the hug, but when she didn't let go, he took a step to the side to create distance. "It's good to see you."

He glanced across the hall where Amaliya now stood, her face pale. Great. The one thing he hadn't wanted was for Amaliya to have to deal with Marie, and here they were, only a few minutes inside the building, and it had already happened.

"Excuse me, Marie, but Amaliya and I need to find our coach."

Marie latched onto his arm, her bright red nails digging into his sleeve. "Wait. Before you go, let me get the phone number of where you're staying. We should go out."

"Sorry, but I already have plans with my girlfriend."

"Girlfriend?" Marie's eyebrows lifted.

Tyler stepped around Marie and slipped his arm around Amaliya.

Marie's jaw dropped. "Wait. You're going out with her?"

"That's right."

"Why?" Marie asked with her typical arrogance.

Because I love her. Tyler swallowed his knee-jerk response, as surprised by it as he was by Marie's question. He looked at Amaliya as love, admiration, and hope rose within him. Warmed by the connection between them, he spoke to Marie once more. "I don't have enough time to list the reasons. We do have to skate at some point today."

Amaliya's gaze flashed to Marie's for a brief moment before she looked up at him and asked, "Are you ready?"

"I am. Let's go find Gordon." Tyler took a step down the hall. "Congratulations again, Marie."

They reached the spot where they had last seen Gordon. Tyler pulled Amaliya to the side of the entrance so they were away from the stream of people coming and going.

"Sorry about that," Tyler said.

"I have to admit, it wasn't easy walking out of the locker room and seeing you hug Marie."

"She hugged me, not the other way around, and you don't have anything to worry about." The words he'd thought earlier burned on his tongue. He knew it wasn't the right time or the right place, but he couldn't stop them from coming out. "You're the one I'm in love with, not her."

Amaliya's breath hitched, and her eyes widened.

"Sorry, I guess I don't have the best timing." Tyler leaned down and pressed his lips to hers for a brief kiss. "I do love you though."

Amaliya's lips rose into a smile, and her hands found his. "I love you too."

Tyler's heart squeezed in his chest. Disbelief surfaced before hope overshadowed it. "Yeah?"

"Yeah."

"Amaliya, Tyler," Gordon called to them. "This way. You're in the first warm-ups."

"I guess it's time to get to work." Tyler slipped his arm around her shoulders again.

"Time to make our dreams come true?" Amaliya asked.

"My dreams are already coming true."

Amaliya reached up and kissed him. "So are mine."

They were in fourth place. Tyler had hoped he and Amaliya would score higher in the compulsory figures, but he supposed he should be grateful they had done as well as they had since they had been placed in the first group with the other unranked skaters. Judges were notorious for scoring the early groups lower to make sure there was room to push the advanced groups to the top of the rankings.

Amaliya emerged from the locker room, a vision in blue. Her dark hair was swept up in a bun, her makeup enhancing her beauty.

"Ready?" he asked.

Amaliya pressed a hand to her stomach, undoubtedly trying to settle the nerves they were both experiencing. "I think so."

"Come on." Tyler took her hand and headed for where Gordon waited. The outer door opened, and Nicole Walker and Andrew McCallister walked in with Bob Phillips.

Tyler slowed his pace when Gordon's former skaters spotted their former coach.

Nicole offered a slight nod of acknowledgment to Gordon before she spoke to her current coach. "Bob, I'm going to change."

Bob closed the distance between him and Gordon. He extended his hand. "Gordon, it's good to see you."

"Thanks, Bob." Gordon shook hands with him before addressing his former skater. "Andrew."

"Gordon. I didn't know you were coaching again."

"It was time."

"Good luck to your skaters," Andrew said. "It's been a while since you've been part of this world. I hope they know what they got themselves into."

"They are well aware," Gordon said.

Tyler led Amaliya past the crowd of coaches and skaters near the check-in table.

"Andrew, I thought that was you." Tyler shook Andrew's hand. "Good luck today."

"Thanks." Andrew's gaze took in Amaliya. "Who's this?"

"Amaliya Marcell." Tyler put his hand on Amaliya's back. "Amaliya, this is Andrew McCallister."

"Good to meet you." Amaliya offered her hand, but Andrew didn't take it.

"So, this is your new project." Andrew crossed his arms over his chest. "Tyler, I heard you were skating with an amateur."

Amaliya's hand dropped to her side, and Tyler's anger surfaced.

Before he could respond, Gordon said, "Andrew, trash talk doesn't suit you. It never has."

"You aren't my coach anymore. You aren't in a position to give me advice."

"You're right." Gordon glanced at Bob. "Good luck today. Tyler, Amaliya, time to warm up."

Tyler and Amaliya followed Gordon to the staging area, where they could wait for their turn to compete.

"Has Andrew always been that cocky?" Tyler asked.

"Come to think of it, yes," Gordon said.

"Maybe we should thank him for letting you go," Amaliya added. "I probably still wouldn't be able to do a double axel if you weren't our coach."

"Let's not worry about the competition today." Gordon extended his hand and took both of their skate guards. "Go get loose. Keep everything simple during your warm-up. I don't want you doing much with all the traffic out there on the ice."

"You got it." They took their place beside the doorway leading to the ice and waited for the signal that it was their turn to warm up.

As soon as the ice cleared, Tyler put his hand on Amaliya's shoulder, a silent gesture of support. He positioned himself behind her to protect her from the rush of people walking past them. Amaliya leaned against him, and his love swelled inside him.

Nicole and Andrew approached with Bob, but Tyler looked away. He didn't need to know what the competition had planned today. His goals hinged on the woman beside him and what they could accomplish together.

The signal came for warm-ups to begin. Tyler took Amaliya's hand, and they moved onto the ice. He glanced back at their coach as Gordon smiled. The unexpected satisfaction on their coach's face sent a new ripple of excitement through Tyler.

He squeezed Amaliya's hand. They had something special both on and off the ice, and he couldn't wait to see how far it would take them.

Chapter
FORTY-FOUR

AMALIYA KEPT THE HEADPHONES IN place and her back to the rink. Her heart pounded, and she clasped and unclasped her hands while she and Tyler waited their turn to compete. The first pair was already on the ice. They would compete second in the final group tonight, with the three teams ahead of them going last.

Amaliya closed her eyes and visualized the routine she and Tyler had practiced so many times over the past month. Mentally, she paused when she reached the moment of truth—her double axel. Would she fall?

She shook that thought away. If she second-guessed herself, she might as well plan on falling. She began the mental exercise again, this time allowing herself to see her own success with each movement.

Tyler's lips pressed against her forehead and broke her out of her trance. She looked up as he removed her headphones.

"It's time."

"Remember," Gordon said. "Just like you practiced."

Amaliya drew a deep breath and straightened her shoulders. Then her hand was in Tyler's, and they were on the ice. She closed her eyes for a moment to block out the crowd and the lukewarm reception to their appearance.

The music started, and her gaze met Tyler's. They moved together, mirroring each other until they came together for a combination spin. A simple lift, a dance sequence, followed by a double lutz–double toe loop combination.

The crowd applauded with intent now, but Amaliya's focus was on the movements she had memorized so completely.

A pair's camel spin. A throw double salchow. Side-by-side sit spins. One element after another, she and Tyler moved with deceptive ease. Her body tensed when she looked forward to the next skill, the one she dreaded. Her mental preparations reminded her to relax.

Side by side, she and Tyler reversed their direction and launched themselves into the air. Two and a half rotations, her arms crossed tightly over her chest. Their blades landed in sync, and the crowd cheered. Relief flowed through her, and her smile was instant.

Before she knew it, Tyler pulled her into his arms for their final pose, and the music ended. Out of breath, she straightened, and the applause increased. Relief, amazement, joy, excitement. All four emotions swirled within her and were reflected on Tyler's face.

Tyler pulled her into his arms for a hug before he took her hand and they bowed to the crowd.

"That was incredible." Tyler scooped up flowers and handed them to her.

They started across the ice, and she glanced into the stands. Her eyes searched for her father and the Donnellys. She saw Tyler's parents first. When her gaze shifted to the couple in front of them, her jaw dropped. Not her dad and the Donnellys but both of her parents and the Donnellys.

Amaliya's grin widened, and she waved.

"Are those your parents sitting in front of mine?" Tyler asked.

"Yes." She glided across the ice with Tyler to where Gordon waited. "Did you know both my parents were going to be here?"

"Yes," Gordon said. "They wanted it to be a surprise."

"It was a good one," Amaliya said.

"You did a good job surprising the crowd out there. Well done." Gordon handed both of them their skate guards. "Come on. Let's see what the scores say."

The three of them moved to the small platform that had been set up with a bench where the skaters could wait for their scores. Amaliya sat down, and Tyler and Gordon sat on either side of her. The moment Tyler was beside her, he took her hand in his.

The technical scores posted first. Five-fours and five-fives.

"Is that what you were hoping for?" Amaliya asked, uncertain of how they fared.

"Those are decent scores," Tyler said.

Gordon patted Amaliya's back. "Your next set will be higher."

The artistic scores popped up a moment after. Five-sevens and five-eights, with a five-nine thrown in.

"Wow." Tyler hugged Amaliya, his face alive with excitement.

"Those are good, right?"

Tyler chuckled. "Those are great scores."

"Come on." Gordon nudged them to the nearby seating area. "Let's see how your competition fares against you."

A new wave of excitement rose within her. "I get to watch other people skate?"

"Tonight, you get to watch," Gordon said. "Tomorrow, we'll see."

"Why wouldn't you want us to watch tomorrow?" Amaliya asked.

"Because we may be in first place if our scores hold," Tyler said before Gordon could respond.

"We're in first place?"

"For now," Gordon said. "As long as you're in the top three by the end of tonight, you have a chance to win."

"And to qualify for the next level, we have to be in the top five overall, right?" Amaliya asked.

"That's right," Gordon said. "One more night and you'll be on your way."

"One more night, one more program." Nerves fluttered in Amaliya's stomach. "I hope I can survive that long."

"You won't just survive," Gordon said. "You'll thrive."

Tyler made his way into the kitchen for a quick snack before bed, the whirlwind of events from the day swirling through his mind. Amaliya loved him. And they were in third place, but barely. He would have liked to have had more padding between themselves and the pairs behind them, but they could still win. More importantly, they could still qualify for finals.

Unlike at their previous competition, this time they had the advantage of sleeping in their own beds between their short and long programs. Though Gordon had considered staying in a hotel closer to the arena, the hour drive to the venue seemed a small price to pay for them to have the comforts of home and to avoid any unnecessary distractions before tomorrow.

Tyler's parents, Amaliya's parents, and the Donnellys had all agreed to stay in hotels to make sure their presence didn't disrupt Amaliya and Tyler's daily routine. Amaliya had wanted to talk to her parents after the competition, but the Marcells had left right after Amaliya and Tyler's performance to make sure Amaliya's mom could escape the crowd and avoid a potential setback in her recovery.

Eleanor walked into the kitchen from the living room at the same time Tyler entered from the garage. "What are you still doing up? I thought you would be in bed by now," she said.

"I'm heading there, but I wanted something to eat first."

"There are carrot sticks in the fridge."

"Thanks." Tyler opened the refrigerator and retrieved a handful. He bit into one.

"Do you know if Gordon is still awake?" Eleanor asked.

"Probably. Knowing him, he's looking at film from today," Tyler said. "Why?"

"I need to know what time to fix breakfast tomorrow."

"I'll ask him." Tyler ate another carrot and headed down the hall. The first notes of *Für Elise* carried toward him from Gordon's room.

Tyler knocked, and a moment later, Gordon called out, "Come in."

He pushed the door open. "Do you have a minute?"

"Yes. Come on in."

"Eleanor wants to know what time you want us to have breakfast tomorrow."

"The usual time. We need to keep your routine as close to normal as possible." Tyler glanced at the TV, where two skaters performed on screen. It took only a moment to identify who they were. "Is that Walker and McCallister's program for this year?"

"No. It's from the Olympics." Gordon motioned to the chair beside him.

Tyler sat. "How did you get a copy of this?"

"My daughter and a friend from the Olympic Committee arranged for me to see it."

"Why? I know you didn't go to the Olympics because of your wife, but I thought you would have watched it on TV."

"I was watching it." Gordon cleared his throat. "My wife died as Nicole and Andrew's program started. I didn't see it live."

"Gordon, I'm so sorry." Tyler leaned forward and rested his elbows on his knees. "I guess we both have demons to get past when it comes to the long program."

"We do. I forgot you had to skip yours the last time you were at nationals." Gordon's eyebrows drew together. "It was an injury, right?"

"Yeah. My sister had a freak accident and sprained her ankle."

Gordon leaned back in his chair. "How are you and Amaliya holding up? Are you worried about tomorrow?"

"It's hard not to worry about something going wrong," Tyler said. "Amaliya's mostly stressed about landing her double axel again. She's convinced that she only hits it 50 percent of the time, so she's afraid tomorrow she'll be on the wrong side of that number."

"Normally, I would consider taking it out, but I'm afraid messing with your routine at this point would be counterproductive," Gordon said.

"Is the difficulty in our routine enough for us to qualify?"

Gordon glanced at the television screen. Tyler followed his gaze as Andrew sent Nicole flying through the air on their throw triple salchow.

"It depends," Gordon said.

"On?"

"If you both skate cleanly, you have a great shot at keeping your position or even moving up in the standings."

"And if we don't, we're out."

Gordon nodded. "The only place we could increase your difficulty at this point without undermining the work we've already done would be to triple your throw double lutz, but I don't know if that would be too much to throw at Amaliya last minute."

"I know. This is only her second competition, and last time, I kept her away from the scores and the rest of the skaters."

"She has to learn to deal with that side of the sport too," Gordon said. "You can't expect to handle the pressure of the Olympics if you don't both learn how to help each other through the lower levels of competition."

"I know."

"I have ice time reserved in the morning so you can practice in your home rink instead of with the crowd of competitors," Gordon said. "Maybe it's time to see how the triple throw times with the rest of your routine."

"It's an option worth exploring."

Gordon waved toward his door. "Go get some sleep. You have a big day tomorrow."

"We all do."

Fifty percent. That was how often Amaliya landed her double axel. The throw triple lutz was only half that.

The hour-long practice session had given her and Tyler time to work out the nerves about their long program, but it hadn't done much for her confidence where her jumps were concerned. She also couldn't miss the extra tension in Tyler this morning. Something was wrong. She hoped it didn't have to do with her.

"What do you think?" Tyler asked Gordon. "Do we make the change?"

"I think it's too risky," Gordon said. "Concentrate on skating a clean program, and you'll be fine."

"I hate that everything rides on today," Amaliya said.

"Yes, at least for this year," Tyler said.

"Talk about pressure." She blew out a breath. "Does it seem crazy to you that we've been training for months and our success will be decided during the five minutes we compete on the ice?"

"You'll be fine. You are both beautiful skaters, and the long program is your strength," Gordon said. "Don't second-guess yourselves. I want you to go out there today with the intent of winning, not just qualifying."

"Gordon, you aren't helping," Amaliya said.

"Trust yourself." Gordon put one hand on her arm and his other on Tyler's. "And trust your partner. You can do this."

"We can do this." Amaliya let out a sigh. "Okay. When do we leave for the arena?"

"We're in the last group, so we have time to go home and eat a good lunch before we leave."

"Should we try the throw triple lutz one more time?"

Gordon shook his head. "There's no need for that. You're ready."

A new kaleidoscope of butterflies took flight in her stomach. "I hope you're right."

Chapter FORTY-FIVE

THEY WERE GOING LAST. UNDER normal circumstances, Tyler would have celebrated when the random draw had given them the concluding spot in the
competition, but with all they had riding on tonight, he would have preferred
a less stressful finale. This was their shot. If they wanted any chance for international competition before the Olympic season, they had to place in the top
five tonight.

He made the mistake of taking his earphones off as Nicole and Andrew
finished their program. Then again, with as loud as the crowd was cheering, he
probably would have heard the applause over his music anyway.

Beside him, Amaliya took off her earphones. "Someone did well."

"We only have to place in the top five," Tyler reminded her. He turned to
Gordon. "How is it looking?"

"A clean program should do it."

Tyler read between the lines. Any mistakes, and they wouldn't make it. Great.

Amaliya slipped her hand into his. "Positive thinking, remember?"

"You're reading my mind again, aren't you?" Tyler asked.

A smile lit her face. "Part of my charm."

"I really do love you, you know." The words spilled out before he considered
that he was standing beside Gordon and that other people were nearby.

Gordon didn't seem the least surprised by Tyler's declaration. "This is what
I want to see on the ice."

"What do you mean?" Amaliya asked.

"The two of you are a unit. You're a couple in love. Let the audience feel
the magic of what you create together."

Nicole and Andrew exited the ice and walked past them, their faces alight
with victory.

Ignoring Gordon's former skaters, Tyler lifted Amaliya's hand to his lips. "Come dance with me?"

Her smile was instant. "I thought you'd never ask."

Amaliya spotted their personal cheering section as they circled the ice. Her parents, Miles and Linda, Tyler's parents, Gordon's daughter, Eleanor, Beth. A wave of love and appreciation swept through her as she considered that they were all here to show their support. Her father's power and her mother's grace. That was what Beth had said when she'd seen Amaliya skate. Amaliya would need them both today.

She came to a stop beside Tyler.

He squeezed her hand. "I love you. No matter what, we're a team."

"No matter what," Amaliya agreed. "You ready?"

Tyler nodded, and they took their starting pose.

The music began, and Amaliya let herself get swept into the dance. Her love for Tyler added to her emotions as they moved from one skill to another. Their combination jumps, side-by-side spins.

Excitement rose within her as Tyler took position behind her for the lift they had created. It was all part of the dance, and Amaliya was as captivated by the music as if she had been on stage. She mentally counted the beats and pushed herself into the air. Then she was floating, the music barely audible above the cheers of the crowd.

She cartwheeled down, and her skate aligned with Tyler's once more. His hand took hers, and the connection between them sparked. The look on his face told her everything she needed to know. He loved her. Nothing mattered more than that.

Katerina's heart swelled in her chest. Never had her daughter been more beautiful. Never had Katerina been more proud. Whatever doubts she'd had about Amaliya sacrificing her ballet career dissolved. Amaliya had taken the best of everything she and Robert had to give and had created something wonderful, something beautiful.

Robert's hand clasped hers, the connection between them every bit as strong as the first time they had met. She could see that spark in the young couple on the ice. Whether she was ready for it or not, Amaliya no longer belonged to her and Robert alone. Tyler had won her heart, and everyone in the arena could see it.

Robert leaned closer. "He's in love with her."

"Yes. And she is in love with him."

"She's too young."

"You can't choose when magic will strike." Katerina turned her hand over and laced her fingers through her husband's. "We know that better than anyone."

"I'm not ready for this."

"It doesn't matter if we're ready." Katerina nodded at their daughter as the dance on ice continued. "It matters if they are."

They were magic. Tyler had competed countless times, but never had he experienced anything like this. Every move, every step. It was as though he and Amaliya were a single unit, their bodies in perfect harmony.

He held his breath on the double axels. Two blades landed as one. Perfect. Gordon's shout of approval carried over the crowd.

Halfway through. They were halfway there. They segued into a dance sequence, the vibrance of their love reflected in every move, in every touch.

Two more minutes. That was all Tyler and Amaliya needed before they would not only qualify but win.

Side-by-side double salchows came next. Tyler released Amaliya's hand. They entered their jumps. Tyler sensed the error the moment he lifted into the air. Too much excitement. Too much height.

Amaliya came down cleanly, but Tyler over rotated and stumbled. His hand touched the ice to keep himself from falling completely, but the magic bubble burst. The deduction would be mandatory for such an error and could very likely drop them out of the top five despite the brilliance of the rest of their program.

He used his hand to push himself back up, and he recovered quickly, matching his steps once more to Amaliya's. They couldn't win now with their program as scripted, but could they still qualify?

Play it safe or take a risk? They skated past Gordon, and Tyler saw the signal. Three fingers. They needed the triple.

Amaliya's pulse still hadn't steadied since Tyler's error. She knew a mistake could occur, but she had assumed it would be her who made it.

Could they still qualify?

Tyler pulled her close as they prepared to move into a lift. "We need a triple."

He pressed her into the air above his head, and she held her pose to the delight of the crowd. She flipped forward, her skates meeting the ice. Had she heard him right?

They came together again for a pairs spin.

"Throw triple?" she asked.

"We need it to place." Tyler's hand gripped her waist, and they spun together, changing positions twice. "Are you up for it?"

Before she could answer, they moved apart and began the series of crossovers that would lead them to their final move, the skill that had originally been planned as a throw double lutz.

Tyler's gaze met hers, the question in his eyes. Pressure built up within her. She understood what was at stake. If they gambled, they could still place. If they didn't, they could fall too low to qualify. She nodded at Tyler. All or nothing.

He pulled her closer, and his hands gripped her waist.

"You've got this," he said.

Amaliya counted off the beats of the music. She planted her foot, bent her leg, and combined her power with Tyler's. She crossed her arms over her chest, rotating quickly as she moved through the air. One, two, three. Her foot came down. Her skate connected. Her leg extended. And the crowd went wild.

They reached their final pose as the music faded. She curtsied to the crowd, and then she was in Tyler's arms. "Do you think we qualified?"

"I have no doubt. You were amazing."

She couldn't help but smile. "We were amazing."

With Tyler's arm firmly around her waist, she searched the crowd until she found her parents. Both of them stood clapping amidst the cheering crowd. At the side of the rink, Gordon gave them a thumbs-up and a huge grin.

Reality crashed over her. They had done it. Her parents were coming home. And she and Tyler were on the road to the Olympics and to their future together.

from best-selling author

TRACI HUNTER ABRAMSON

Olympic DREAMS

of the DREAM'S EDGE series

COMING FEBRUARY 2022

Amaliya wrapped her fingers around the silver medal hanging from her neck. Excitement and disbelief rose within her along with a sense of accomplishment. Before she met Tyler at the skating rink nine months ago, she had never considered competing in figure skating. Yet tonight, they had taken second place in the Eastern Sectionals in the pairs competition. More importantly, they had qualified for nationals.

From her father's spot beside her in the back seat of her coach's car, he leaned closer. "Let me get a better look at that medal."

Amaliya couldn't keep her grin from forming. Tyler glanced at her from the passenger seat, his own smile mirroring hers. Amaliya leaned closer to her dad and held up her medal.

"That is something," her dad said. "You were incredible tonight."

"You did teach me how to skate."

"Yes, but on hockey skates. We both know your grace comes from your mama."

"On stage, maybe, but not on the ice," her mom said, her Russian accent still noticeable even after more than twenty years of living in the United States.

Amaliya ignored her mother's modesty. "I wouldn't have been able to get this far if it hadn't been for you."

"That's sweet of you to say—"

"Sweet and true," Amaliya said.

Until her parents' unfortunate car accident last January, an accident that had required months of rehab, Amaliya had studied ballet under her mother nearly every day for as long as she could remember. Her mother's experience as a professional dancer had greatly helped smooth Amaliya's transition from ballerina to figure skater.

Gordon turned onto the George Washington Parkway and headed down the road that separated a row of mansions from the Potomac River. Moonlight shimmered off the water.

Her mother gazed out the window. "I've missed this view."

"You'll get to see it every day from now on." Her father reached across Amaliya and patted her mother's hand. "We're almost home."

In the front seat, Tyler turned around again. "It couldn't have been easy, being away for so long. The view really is incredible."

Her mom's voice turned wistful. "Yes, it is."

A new wave of excitement washed over Amaliya. Though her mother's doctor had wanted her to stay another week in a rehab facility in Connecticut, her parents had arranged for her to be released early so they could both be at sectionals tonight. Now, for the first time since January, Amaliya's family would be living together again. She didn't know what she was more excited about, her medal or her parents coming home.

"Are the Donnellys bringing your luggage to the house?" Amaliya asked, referring to their family friends from Connecticut, the same friends Amaliya had lived with during the last semester of her senior year of high school. They had driven down for the weekend and brought her parents with them to the competition.

"Miles and Linda had to drive home tonight," her dad said. "When you and Tyler were changing, we put everything in Gordon's trunk."

Gordon slowed and turned into their driveway. The mansion that had been Amaliya's home since birth claimed a sizeable portion of the wide lawn and tidy landscape. With its brick front and wide columns, it could have been plucked right off a Southern plantation, but to her, it was simply the house where her memories lived. At least, most of her memories.

The Donnellys' house in Connecticut certainly held a good share now too.

As soon as Gordon parked in the garage, he turned off the engine and swiveled in his seat. "Amaliya and Tyler, you have fifteen minutes to help Robert and Katerina bring in their luggage and get to your rooms to stretch. After that, you'd better be in bed."

"Yes, Coach," Amaliya said.

"Katerina was right," her dad said. "You do run a tight ship, Gordon."

"I do my best." Gordon climbed out of the car and opened the door for Katerina.

They all got out of the car, Papa using his cane to steady himself. While Tyler and Gordon collected the luggage, Amaliya opened the door leading from the garage to the kitchen and held it for her mother.

"Spasibo." The simple thanks offered in her mother's native Russian brought with it a sense of home Amaliya had missed for so many months.

Amaliya responded with the Russian equivalent of you're welcome. "Ne za shto."

Her father walked in next, followed by Tyler and Gordon.

"I assume these are going up to your room?" Tyler asked.

"I need a few more weeks before I tackle the stairs," her dad said, his tone cooling considerably. "We'll stay in the downstairs guest room for now."

"Yes, sir." Tyler led the way into the living room and headed toward her parents' temporary bedroom. Gordon followed.

Amaliya's stomach clutched at the contrast of her family's reality before and after the accident. Her life had moved forward as though the world outside the ice rink didn't exist, while her parents' lives had essentially stood still. Once so active and capable, they still needed time to heal.

They would heal.

She hoped.

Amaliya stopped by the fireplace. She pasted on a smile and slid her arm around her papa's waist. "Welcome home."

"Thank you, sweetie." Papa kissed her forehead. "We'll see you in the morning."

Her mom hugged her before following Papa to her new bedroom.

Now alone in the living room, Amaliya slipped off her medal and studied the image of a pair of ice skates etched in the center. Anticipation leapt in her chest. She and Tyler had qualified for nationals. If they performed well there, they might even advance to worlds. Of course, next year's Olympics were the ultimate goal. She prayed they could make it that far.

Footsteps approached a moment before Tyler's voice broke into her thoughts. "You really were incredible tonight."

"We were incredible." She glanced toward the hall to make sure she and Tyler were alone before she reached up and gave him a kiss good night. Her stomach fluttered the moment her lips touched his, another reminder of her good fortune. "I'll see you in the morning."

Tyler took her hand and leaned closer for another kiss. "I love you."

Warmth and contentment flowed through her. "I love you too."

About THE AUTHOR

TRACI HUNTER ABRAMSON WAS BORN in Arizona, where she lived until moving to Venezuela for a study-abroad program. After graduating from Brigham Young University, she worked for the Central Intelligence Agency, eventually resigning in order to raise her family. She credits the CIA with giving her a wealth of ideas as well as the skills needed to survive her children's teenage years. She loves to travel and enjoys coaching her local high school swim team. She has written more than thirty best-selling novels and is a seven-time Whitney Award winner, including 2017 and 2019 Best Novel of the Year.

She also loves hearing from her readers. If you would like to contact her, she can be reached through the following:

www.traciabramson.com

Facebook group: Traci's Friends

bookbub.com/authors/traci-hunter-abramson

@traciabramson

facebook.com/tracihabramson

instagram.com/traciabramson.com